MW00416927

Sold to
the Highest Bidder!

The black doorman bowed low and called
for Felipe's carriage. Felipe helped Caroline
into it, and then climbed to the seat beside
her. A stiffness had come into her, and she did
not know why she was just a bit afraid again.
Certainly Felipe was to be her lover; that was
why he had spent three thousand in gold
pieces for her.

But it seemed as though taking a man should
be different, should be her own choice. She had
been overwhelmed by Felipe at first sight;
still, she would have liked to have had the
opportunity to say no. *White women's ideas,*
she thought; she would have to get them out
of her head. . . . Please Felipe de Alcantari she
would, whatever his tastes. She must bind him
to her with flesh and spirit, with invisible
chains as strong as the slavery which held
her. . . .

If he loved her, he would set her and her
mother free.

His hand was warm upon her own; Caroline
felt his breath stir against her cheek. "I—I will
be all that you wish, m'sieu."

Felipe laughed again. "I do not doubt that,
my sweet. There is a wild animal within your
lovely body, and tonight I will unleash it."

Books by Con Sellers

Marilee
Sweet Caroline

Published by POCKET BOOKS

Sweet Caroline

Con Sellers

PUBLISHED BY POCKET BOOKS NEW YORK

Another *Original* publication of POCKET BOOKS

POCKET BOOKS, a Simon & Schuster division of
GULF & WESTERN CORPORATION
1230 Avenue of the Americas, New York, N.Y. 10020

Copyright © 1979 by Con Sellers

All rights reserved, including the right to reproduce
this book or portions thereof in any form whatsoever.
For information address Pocket Books, 1230 Avenue
of the Americas, New York, N.Y. 10020

ISBN: 0-671-81750-7

First Pocket Books printing July, 1979

10 9 8 7 6 5 4 3 2 1

Trademarks registered in the United States and other countries.

Printed in the U.S.A.

This one is for Muley,
or La Bella Maria,
depending upon her mood.

Chapter 1

Gratefully, happy for the budding greenness of a spring day, Caroline moved lithely down the dusty street, so glad to be beyond the stifling confines of the little house and its imprisoning yard. Her daddy's dinner bucket was light in her hand as she looked quickly right and left, trying to absorb everything at once.

There really wasn't much to see in Marion, Illinois, only Main Street and dirt alleys entering it from off angles, but she was enthralled by shops filled with glittering, exciting things, and by a bakery that smelled heavenly. Stopping to peer in store windows, she turned often to smile at passersby, so filled with gaiety and the freshness of a special day that almost invariably they smiled back. Only a grand and beribboned lady in an ornate carriage sniffed and quickly looked away, but her black driver gave Caroline a barely perceptible nod of greeting.

Barefoot, she was conscious of her scrubbed-thin cotton dress a bit too small for the new fullness of her body, of its careful patches. But it was clean as the air itself, and this was a holiday because she was allowed to bring M'Nele's dinner bucket to the smithy. Wind ruffled through the cascading richness of Caroline's midnight hair, bound loosely with a faded ribbon, and touched her throat with caresses. She just managed to keep herself from skipping, remembering that she was now seventeen and a woman grown.

A pudgy man doffed his tall hat to her, and Caroline

dimpled at him, passing quickly by a knot of staring loafers gathered on the board walk in front of the feed store. The smithy was only a little farther on, and she would have lingered at the horse trough, drawing out this rare adventure a little longer, but she knew that might upset M'Nele. He didn't like her ever to come to the shop. Horses were tethered outside, and she could hear the steady ring of his big hammer, smell the crisp scent of charcoal blending with that of white-hot iron.

Caroline went around back, past the heap of rusted shoes that would someday be salvaged, past the cocoon oven of clay where her daddy made his own charcoal, to stand waiting in the open door of the smithy until he noticed her.

M'Nele was stripped to the waist, leather apron about his hips, powerful black body glistening with sweat, arm muscles coiling as he pumped the giant bellows and wisps of acrid smoke blew around him.

Beyond the forge, a white man sat upon a barrel, shiny boots thrust out, head back against a post. His horse stamped impatiently as M'Nele turned from the coals with a glowing shoe clamped in his tongs. It sizzled when he plunged the iron into a bucket of water, and Caroline watched how deftly he spaced nails in his mouth, how powerfully he lifted the reluctant mare's hoof and clamped it between his knees. M'Nele hammered the nails home with quick precision, and dropped the foot to step back.

"Pretty girl standing in the back door," the white man said, and Caroline's face went warm. "See to the lady, Manuel."

Frowning, M'Nele turned, and Caroline took a step forward, extending the dinner bucket. "Mama's feeling poorly, so she sent me."

Roughly, he took the bucket from her, set it aside. "Best I missed dinner," he said. "Get on home now."

"What's this?" the white man said, getting to his feet. "What's this—her mama sent *you* dinner?"

M'Nele jerked his head at Caroline, signaling her to be gone. "This here's my gal, Mister Williamson."

2

"Your gal, and so—well; seems to me I did hear something about you having a light-colored daughter, Manuel, but I never figured she could be so white. Well, and beautiful, to boot. You going to introduce us?"

"What you standin' there for, gal?" M'Nele said. "Get on home."

Caroline saw the white man's face tighten, a not unhandsome face, but somewhat pouty—pale blue eyes, a yellowish moustache, the mouth a bit too full, the jaw a shade weak. He said sharply, "Manuel! You deaf, or maybe you think her too good for a Williamson, bigod?"

"Mister Williamson," M'Nele said slowly, "I don't want no trouble, but this here child—"

"Child? Why damn, she's more woman than any I've seen in this town, or up in the capital, either." He strode around the horse and past M'Nele to stand looking down into Caroline's uncertain eyes. "Since black Manuel won't mind his manners, I'll introduce myself—Tucker Williamson, at your service, ma'am. And your name?"

"Caroline," she murmured, "Caroline Monteleone. I—I'll have to be going now."

"Mighty fancy name for a mighty fancy baggage," Williamson said. "Might I escort you, Caroline Monteleone?"

"No!" M'Nele said.

Williamson whirled on him, face going tight and mean. "You forget yourself! Escaped slaves are safe in Illinois, but freedom doesn't put them on a footing with their betters. Even if I wasn't Senator Williamson's son, I'm white and you're still *black*. Mind your place, smith, or be taught where you stand."

Stubbornly, M'Nele said, "Man's got the right to guard his child, black or white. Carrie, I ain't tellin' you again—get for home."

Blocking the doorway, Williamson's eyes slid arrogantly over Caroline's body, somehow making her feel undressed. "Black or white," he said, "that's interesting."

3

She swallowed and touched her lips with the tip of her tongue, her voice small: "P-please, sir; I'd obey my father and return home."

"I wonder if you know your father," he said, then made a mock bow and swept off his hat. "But of course, Miss Caroline, you may pass. We will meet again, and very soon, I promise you."

Caroline dropped her eyes and slid past the man, her skirt brushing his knee. Her heart was racing, and she felt the heavy weight of M'Nele's disapproval, the tension that hung sharply in the heated air of the smithy. Hurrying now, she went around to the street and strode quickly down it, looking back over her shoulder just once to see Tucker Williamson staring after her.

The holiday feeling was gone, and she didn't smile at anybody now. Her small feet lifted puffs in the dust as Caroline made for the house, and she kept her eyes straight ahead, paying no attention when some man called after her.

She didn't like Tucker Williamson; she could easily hate the man for trying to shame M'Nele in his own smithy, for waving his white color like a conquering banner. M'Nele was a free man, a man strong and proud of his true name and tribe; he did not accept whites as inherently superior to blacks, and no other man had a right to challenge him so.

For the first time in years, Caroline felt a twinge of guilt. Long ago, when she was a child, she'd asked her mama why she was so pale, why she wasn't a nice, dark color. Solah passed over that with the explanation that people were made like they were, with no sayso in the matter. And when Caroline wanted to know more, her mama had pressed on into the language lessons, changing to swift, clicking Ashanti.

Pausing before the fenced yard, Caroline looked behind her, but no man followed on a prancing horse. The town basked sleepily in the welcome warmth of spring, knowing nothing of the ugliness between Tucker Williamson and M'Nele. *I wonder if you know your father,* Williamson had said. She pinched her lower lip between her teeth; that remark had cut deeply into M'Nele, hurting him where he could not be salved.

Caroline had realized some years ago that M'Nele was probably not her father. He had always known it. That was why he was remote, never putting out his hand to her, never holding her in those powerfully bulging arms. Possibly, it was the reason she was kept a virtual prisoner, his shame hidden from the prying eyes of the world. M'Nele was not cruel to her; there was just no tenderness in him for the child of another man—a white man.

Beside the house, an apple tree flowered pink and white, and a lark trilled from its branches. Caroline opened the gate and closed it behind her. Her mama Solah—whom the whites called Sarah—was soft and gentle as those apple blossoms, with more melody to her than the song of the lark. If she had been taken by some slave master in the South, it was not her fault, and knowing that, M'Nele was caring to Solah. He was distant only to the living proof of his wife's degradation, and Caroline knew she could not change him in that, no more than she could trade her own pale skin for a rich, dark one.

She went quietly to the kitchen and looked through the door, seeing the curve of Solah's cheek touched by a shaft of sunlight, all dark gold, not black. Caroline frowned; color was too much on her mind. She said, "I'm back, mama. You ought to be resting, not stirring around the kitchen."

Solah looked up from her chair. "Just a spell of the miseries. How your daddy?"

"He's all right," Caroline said. "He—I guess he's mad at me. There was a white man in the smithy wanted to walk me home."

"Oh lord," Solah said, "oh lord. Should of toted that bucket myself. He didn't—M'Nele didn't do nothin' rash?"

Taking a sip of water from the dipper, Caroline said, "There were words between them, mama, but I don't think it was serious. It wasn't daddy's fault."

"Always a nigger's fault," Solah said, rocking in her

5

chair with hands clasped against her stomach. "Your daddy right; nothin' but trouble, do they get to sniffin' after you."

"Sniffin' after me?"

Solah aimed a workworn finger. "How many times I tell you, child—don't talk like me, like no field hand; talk like the school man tells you. Sniffin' after is what dogs does when the bitch comes in heat; come from miles around, fightin' and carryin' on to see which gets hooked up with her."

Caroline put down the dipper. "Am I in heat?"

"Women don't come in—but that ain't all the truth, neither. Women comes prime, and seems like menfolks can tell it right off, 'special with a pretty child like you. Reckon I got to talk to you about that; always meant to, but kept puttin' it off; tryin' to keep you my baby, I 'spect."

"I'll always be your baby, mama."

Putting out her hand, Solah said, "Prays to God that's true, even if I knows better. And now it's started, and I just don't know what to do about it. Had the cash money, could send you off somewheres, but times been a mite hard, and—"

Caroline went to her mother, kneeled beside the chair and took Solah's hand. "I don't want to leave you, ever."

"Bird got to fly off sometime, build its own nest. Lord knows I tried to keep you safe, but—" Solah changed into the Ashanti language, as she often did when the family was alone, or when she was under stress. "Daughter, something must be done, and I am not wise enough to know what. Your father must decide."

In the same tongue, Caroline said quickly, "I will not go into the town again. I will stay here behind the fence."

"Even the strongest thorn fence cannot hold back a hungry lion."

Caroline clung harder to Solah's hand. "But where will I go?"

6

"I do not know, daughter. May all the old gods help me, I do not know."

The sense of guilt was heavier upon her when she left her mother chanting to the Ashanti gods, the dark ones of Africa. She went into the back yard, thickly screened by bushes and fruit trees, to the small garden plot where succulent green shoots were beginning to appear. Why should she bring such trouble to her parents? Was there some curse upon her?

No, she told herself sternly; Solah would not hear of *juju* curses in this land. Solah was also of this land, and urged her daughter to accept the good things of both Africa and America, to reject the bad. There was no *juju* here. Caroline kneeled beside the garden, head bent as her fingers sought the few weeds and pulled them. She knew that years of toil had paid for her tutors, washing brought home, houses scrubbed on hands and knees, white women's dresses sewn with tiny stitches, far into the night.

Because Solah was determined her daughter be educated, that she know things about the world and not forget one of the languages she had been born to. And because Caroline was pale-skinned, she could not go to school with other children, and the French teacher and the reading master must come to the little house. So much slave's work by a loving mother, so the daughter might grow up to be—what?

M'Nele had never complained; there were times when Caroline thought she saw a flash of pride in him at her accomplishments, especially when she recited one of the ancient legends in flawless Ashanti. He worked himself to the bone, six days in the smithy, the seventh as a brick mason, for he did not revere Christian Sundays.

Sitting back upon her heels, Caroline grimaced. If those who used her parents' sweat were Christians, she was glad M'Nele remained true to his own gods. He had come late from Africa, not like Solah, and slave traders and overseers had not broken him. Tilting her face to the sun, she closed her eyes, remembering the

7

story, dredging through her own hazy memories of the escape.

She had been so small, and all she could truly remember were days of lying hidden in fear, nights spent traveling off the roads, and once, a warm cabin where a kind woman gave her milk. But Caroline knew the story well, how M'Nele had taken them away from the plantation and its chains, how his fierce strength and need to be free brought them through wilderness and slave catchers and dogs to this place in Illinois. Here he worked for others until he became his own man; here he built this tidy house brick by slow brick; here he had secreted a girl child too white to be his own.

"Carrie," he said behind her, and she jumped.

"Yes, father?"

In his own tongue, he said, "It was not your fault, girl. Perhaps it will be all right. Your mother knows?"

"I told her, father."

M'Nele sighed, and looked older than she had ever noticed. "The teachers, women calling for their dresses; we could not hide you from all these, and you grow toward the sun, as you should. I go to speak with Solah; stay here until I call for you."

She nodded obediently and watched his strong back move into the house. Never had M'Nele come home in the afternoon before; he was a fine smith and there were always jobs waiting to be done, always the need for coppers or a bit of silver. But he had been forgiving of her.

She pulled weeds diligently and waited to be called. When the garden was done and no shout had come, Caroline stood up and brushed her hands. A horse snorted from beyond the fence, and she turned to stare up at the man in rich clothing, the man with light blue eyes and yellowish moustache.

"Miss Caroline," he said mockingly. "We meet again."

Glancing over her shoulder at the house, then back at Tucker Williamson, she said, "Please—my father is a good man. Do not—"

He laughed and the big horse pawed the earth.

"That black never sired a piece sassy as you, but I tell you what—you slip out and meet me by the river tonight, and I'll see he doesn't come to trouble."

"But he hasn't *done* anything, so what kind of trouble—"

"Oh," Williamson smirked, "like his smithy burning down, or finding him with a horseshoe stomped into his head; trouble like that."

Caroline looked quickly at the house again. "Oh please, I—I—don't let him see you. After dark, then; by the—the river."

He grinned, thumbed his moustache and spurred the horse hard, so that it raced away, but no faster than her heart was pounding.

Chapter 2

The faded mirror reflected candlelight and the trembling of her hand as Caroline brushed her hair. Her tiny room seemed to close in upon her, and warmth flooded her face as she caught sight of the image of her own body.

After M'Nele returned to the smithy, Solah had sat her down to tell her the puzzling yet somehow wondrous workings of a woman's body. Speaking always in Ashanti, her mama explained carefully and in shocking detail what men and women did with each other. After a while, Caroline had gotten over the embarrassment, because Solah also imparted the Ashanti woman's sense of pride in being female.

The whites do not think as we do, Solah said; their women are not supposed to enjoy making love, not their wives, anyway. Among the Ashanti, any woman who does not give herself fully and happily to the act will be scorned by all; any man who does not make his woman groan upon the mats is laughed from the tribe. So I have been told.

Running the brush steadily down the thick cascade of her ravenwing hair, Caroline looked into the mirror at the swelling of her high breasts, their protruding nipples, and turned warm again. Solah had been instructed by her mama, who was pure Ashanti, a strong woman much sought after by her white master and one who gave him many yard children. In turn, Solah passed along the secrets of fulfillment to her own daughter, but she did not come out and name Caroline's father.

To the mirror, Caroline said: "M'Nele is my father, no matter what white mounted my mother in a slave cabin. In all ways, M'Nele is my father."

And now she must disobey him for the first time. She must sneak from the house to meet Tucker Williamson beside the river, to keep M'Nele's smithy from being burned, to protect her daddy from harm. Surely the man would listen and see the wrong he was doing. He was son of the state senator and educated, and Caroline could make him understand that she didn't love him and so could not, would not, sleep with him.

So many pictures kept flashing through her head, strangely disturbing scenes perforce hazy because she had never felt or even dreamed them—a man's naked body covering a woman, the deep penetration, the rapture Solah said such coupling would bring. There would be hurt, her mama warned, but a welcome pain soon over if the man was deft. And there would be babies. So many unthought ideas, unheard terms, that Solah's black English would never have conveyed them all, but the Ashanti language made them clear and less frightening.

Putting down the hairbrush, Caroline slipped her only cloak about her shoulders and glanced down at her second best pair of shoes. They were worn and would not creak when she moved across the kitchen. She wished she didn't feel so guilty.

"You have been blessed with beauty," Solah had said, "such white skin and long black hair, the black eyes of the Ashanti and a strong, slim body; many men will pant after you, and you must choose carefully among them, for many will also lie and scheme to possess you."

And Caroline had answered, "I would rather have skin like yours, like M'Nele's; I would rather be pure Ashanti."

"No!" Solah said, "no! Look about you, child. Here the blacks are free, but not free; where we came from, they are in chains. Only whites are truly free, and if

11

someday you must deny your—if you must pretend—
oh, child, child—what have we done to you?"

That much still puzzled Caroline, her mama's sudden
agony and the way she had stopped talking. For a moment, Caroline wanted to tell her not to worry, that
she meant to fix it so M'Nele would be safe, but something warned her not to. Now she waited impatiently
for them to fall asleep, so she could do what she had
to do.

Easing from her room, she padded across the kitchen
and stopped in panic when she heard their voices
through the other bedroom door.

"She got to know sometime," M'Nele said. "Just
bad luck that man at the smithy today."

"Reckon he keep sniffin' after her?" Solah asked.

The cornshuck mattress rustled and Caroline could
picture her daddy's big body turning restlessly on the
bed. "Reckon we best see to the lawyer man and get
them papers."

"M'Nele—our house, your shop—"

"If'n things get bad, pays to be ready."

Caroline pulled her cloak tightly about her and
moved on, pushed by the soft sound of what might
have been her mama crying. Cautiously, she slid
through the door and into the night. A lawyer, mysterious papers—oh, if only she hadn't gone to the smithy,
if only Solah hadn't been ill. How could just carrying
a dinner bucket bring on so much trouble?

Across the back yard and around the house, Caroline paused to look toward the town, bathed in the
golden shine of oil lamps. This was all she had known,
beyond memories that flickered at the very edge of
consciousness—a glimmer of a big white house, green
fields stretching off into forever, and at night, a marvelous perfume drifting on a warm breeze. Had she
crouched in the door of a slave cabin and stared off
at a plantation mansion, a little yard child stealing the
scent of Cape Jasmine?

The air placed cool fingers upon her face now as
Caroline made her way across the wagon road and
down a grassy slope toward the river. Stars winked at

each other high in a clear sky, and brush strokes of silver hinted at the new moon about to rise beyond a hilltop. A concert of crickets fell silent while she passed, then picked up the melody. She heard the river talking quietly to itself, and stopped, her hands drawing her cloak close.

He was upon her almost before she knew it. Warned by a footstep, Caroline turned as the moon came up, a pulse throbbing in her throat and her flesh going tight all over.

"You're prompt, missy," he said, towering above her. "Did black Manuel send you out to make amends?"

"I—I came on my own," she answered, seeing the planes of his harsh face in the wan moonlight.

"Then you're smarter than he is," Williamson said. "Don't just stand there, wench; spread your cloak and lie down."

Hands going to her throat, she said, "N-no; I came only to ask you to listen to reason, to beg you not to harm my father."

His laugh was brittle. "No nigger sired you, girl. But there's just enough of the tarbrush in you to excite a white man. Oh, I've had my share of tavern wenches and the like, but never have I bedded a black. Don't know as I could stomach diddling a full African; the smell of them and all. But *you*, now——"

Taking a step back, Caroline said quickly, "Mister Williamson, you're educated, and your father is a public figure. Surely you wouldn't force yourself upon a woman?"

"Not upon a white woman," he said, long arm snaking out to fasten a hand upon her cloak. "Niggers don't count, and they do say all of you hope to have a white man someday."

"Please, please! Don't—oh, don't—"

But his arms were around her, his body forcing against her own. Caroline tried to turn her head, but his mouth found hers roughly, crushing her lips until she opened them in pain. Then she shivered at the thrusting of his tongue, the grating of their teeth. She

13

tried to cry out, but her breath only mingled with the man's, and as his grip tightened, she felt her knees go weak.

On her knees, Caroline fought to tear herself away from him, but he tangled a hand in her hair and jerked her to the ground. A terrified sob broke from her then, as Williamson ripped at her dress. She gasped when his fingers discovered a tender breast. Somehow, he had forced a knee between her thighs and spread them while she writhed in shock.

This was ugly and hurtful, with none of the beauty Solah talked of. This was only dirty and shaming, and Caroline suddenly arched her back, twisted and drove a bent knee upward. His mouth sucked noisy air. "You —you black bitch! Do that to a man, would you!"

The brutal slap of his open hand flashed a thousand bright candles behind her eyes and Caroline's body sagged. His hands were everywhere, grasping and squeezing, probing, paining, reaching into her secret places. She tasted blood in her mouth and shuddered.

"Spread those legs, damn you!"

"No," she hissed fiercely, "damn *you!*" And clawed at his face. When he flinched back, she kicked up and this time landed. He grunted and held himself while Caroline rolled from beneath him. Her hand fell upon a stone, and when he pawed for her legs, she hammered him with it, striking again and again until the stone flew from her fingers.

She was up and running then, her shoes gone, cloak torn away and air blowing through the rips in her dress. But she was only halfway up the slope when she heard Williamson's choked curses and the sledging of his boots behind her. Blindly, she ran on, crossing the road, skirting the fence of her own home, fumbling for the gate latch as every nerve in her outraged body shrieked *hurry, hurry!*

There was only time for a single scream when his hands closed upon her neck from behind. Caroline fought desperately for breath when his hand clamped harder, as his fist axed the side of her head. Eyes gone dark, she had lost, and was falling, falling. . . .

14

Dimly, through a roaring in her ears, she heard Williamson bellow, and the pressure left her throat. On hands and knees, she saw feet scuffling and tasted rising dust. Instinctively, she rolled aside and came up against the opened gate, staring at swaying figures interlocked in the moonlight.

"Black bastard! You'd attack me, *me?*"

Caroline saw him fall then, heard the echo of the powerful blow that drove Williamson to his knees.

"Crawl on off," M'Nele said above him, "while you can. Come on, girl."

Williamson came up wobbling, and the moon glinted on the pistol in his hand. Caroline screamed warning, but M'Nele was already leaping into the other man. The pistol skidded at Caroline's feet, and another hand snatched it up.

Beside her, tugging, Solah hissed, "Stay out'n the way. He hurt M'Nele, I gon kill him."

With Solah's arm about her waist, Caroline wavered back through the gate, where Solah propped her erect. M'Nele was rolling on the ground with Williamson, and the sounds they made were terrible. It was suddenly quiet then, and one man rose to stare down at the still form of the other.

Solah moved to him. "He dead?"

" 'Spect so," M'Nele panted.

"Lord god, what we gon do?"

Still pulling hard for air, M'Nele turned to Caroline. "How come you triflin' with him?"

"He said—said he'd burn your smithy, hurt you, if I didn't meet him by the river." Caroline massaged her throat, sickened and weak.

M'Nele said, "You done that for me?"

"You're my father," Caroline said simply.

"Tote him down and drop him in," M'Nele said. "Turn the horse loose; give us some time."

Caroline said, "But you were only protecting me, and he tried to kill you with a pistol—"

"He *white,*" Solah said.

M'Nele stooped and grunted, came up with the limp body over his shoulder. "Wuss'n that; he Senator Williamson's boy. Might be they think horse throwed him, broke his neck, if'n folks didn't see him after Carrie today, didn't hear him jawin' at me. And ol' Senator, he don't hear nothin' but what he wants. You all get in the house; I be back in a minute."

Inside, Caroline sat shaking while her mama hid the pistol in a sack of flour. She said, "I th-thought I could reason with him, tell him I didn't love him, and he would let daddy alone."

"You played the fool," Solah said. "Love got nothin' to do with it."

"But you said—"

Solah's mouth was sad. "Said love was best, but all that man craved was your flesh, girl. Most mountin' got no love to it, and 'cause you carry black blood—"

M'Nele came in the back door and barred it. "Do I be careful, lawyer man will wake up without no racket, and I gets them papers, puts my mark to sell the shop and house. Takes my cash money and gets us gone afore daylight."

"Horse and wagon," Solah said.

"At the smithy. You bring 'em back quiet, and girl —just clothes and beddin' and vittles."

Caroline put a hand to her mouth. "You mean, pack up, leave everything you've both worked so hard for? Must we?"

"Got to," M'Nele said. "That horse gets home totin' a empty saddle, ol' Senator goes huntin' his boy, and by 'n by, they find him. Pretty soon, they come for me."

"But where will we go?" Caroline asked. M'Nele was already at the door, already hurrying into the night. She looked at Solah, who was putting on a ragged coat. "Mama, where will we go?"

"M'Nele worried this out a long spell back, child. Us hoped to send you off somewheres afore anything bad happened, but that never come off, so we got other plans. Roll up some beddin' and put victuals in a sack and tie up what clothes you can. I got to go for the wagon now."

Alone, Caroline stared at the candle flame for long

moments before she could force herself to move. All the years of struggle, the slavery in all but name, about to be destroyed because of one white man and his lusts. The schooling they'd worked so hard to give her, a peaceful life together—all gone now. If she could run away, if that would somehow protect them, Caroline wouldn't hesitate. But Tucker Williamson was dead, and nothing any of them could do would bring him back to life; nothing would stave off the senator's vengeance. It wasn't fair, and it wasn't right.

She packed food and made bundles of blankets and quilts; she collected their meager store of clothing and piled everything in the kitchen. Her throat ached, and the breast Williamson had bruised ached, but the greatest pain was in Caroline's heart. As Solah said, she had played the fool by going out to meet the man. She had brought this catastrophe upon her family, a tragedy that wouldn't have happened if they were white.

She heard the wagon creak up behind the house, and opened the door for her mama. Grim-faced, Solah helped her load their things, and spared hardly a glance for the treasured belongings they were leaving behind. "Sulphur matches," she said, "and that bag of flour with the pistol in it; they got to go, too."

"Mama—"

"Never mind, child. Had to happen sometime, I reckon. You too pretty to keep hid out, and M'Nele— he never was no man to let hisself get handled by nobody. Never could be a slave, nor be *owned* by nobody, and if it hadn't been for me, I 'spect he mighta got hisself all the way back to Africa, somehow. Hand me them quilts."

"But he's losing all of it—the smithy, our house—"

"Keepin' our *lives*," Solah said. "Yonder he comes. Best us blows out the candles now."

"Lamps still on in town," M'Nele said. "Don't seem like they heard nothin'. Lawyer man was some surprised, but he's a good man, and it's all took care of."

"Our papers," Solah asked, "the 'mission papers?"

"Them, special. Well—"

17

"No sense lookin' back," Solah said. "Child, climb up in the wagon."

Seated in the wagon bed, surrounded by what little they could haul with them, Caroline said, "Where are we going?"

"One place they might not think to look first," M'Nele answered. "Place no nigger in his right mind'd run *to*." He clucked to the horse and moved it through the yard. "Down south."

Chapter 3

Once beyond the last straggling houses, M'Nele had put the horse into a trot, and the wagon jounced along through the night, hurrying out of Williamson County and into Johnson County. They kept on, resting the horse when they had to, until dawn lightened trees along the road. Then M'Nele pulled the wagon off into the woods and stiffly climbed down to brush out its tracks with a leafy limb.

"Best eat cold," he said. "I stakes out the horse to graze over yonder."

Chilled by the long night ride and aching a little from being jolted, Caroline lifted bedding from the wagon. Making pallets beneath the down-swinging limbs of a pine, she watched her mother do something with cornmeal and water, saw her cutting smoked meat.

"Make do," Solah said as they squatted together to eat. "Cold mush and meat'll carry us a spell. Reckon we can build us a fire afore dark and cook a proper meal."

Chewing on dry beef, M'Nele said, "Made do with less'n this, hidin' from the paterollers." He seemed easier now that Williamson County was behind them.

Caroline was very sleepy, and when the sun rose high enough to poke some warmth through the thick forest, she caught herself nodding off.

" 'Spect we in Massac yet?" Solah asked.

"Close; be there tonight. Then we got to circle

around Paducah, just in case. Lord, lord; never figured to be headin' back thisaway."

Caroline was drowsing again, but roused to hear her mother say, "Maybe they ain't after us yet; maybe they ain't found him."

"Hope so," M'Nele said. "Time they do, ol' Senator gon be on his horse, with a heap others at his back. Take him a spell to study out where we gone, but he be lookin'. We gets into Tennessee, got us a good start."

Solah said quietly, "Looziana agin; 'spect it's the only way."

"Right smart mixed up down yonder, I hears. Talkin' about Britisher folks acomin' in to fight. Be good time for us to slip in without nobody payin' never mind."

Even softer, Solah said, "M'Nele—you think it's forgot?"

"Can't say, woman; been a mighty long time."

Unable to keep her eyes open any longer, Caroline crawled into her quilts and breathed deeply of dewy morning air. A small bird twittered close by, and she heard the horse pulling grass. Only yesterday, she thought, she had been so happy with springtime. Now there seemed to be a curse on it, a *juju*.

She slept restlessly and dreamed of hands upon her writhing body, of a hot, moist tongue playing inside her mouth, the dizzying sensation of pressure between her thighs. But there was no tenderness, no gentleness, and there must be that; there must be.

Waking to small, bothersome sounds, Caroline struggled up and walked into the bushes. When she came out, she tried to do something with her hair, then collected more dry twigs to feed the almost smokeless fire. Stew simmered in the old iron pot, and somehow, her mother had managed to cook cornbread on a flat rock. It tasted wonderful; she was wolfishly hungry.

M'Nele finished first and went to see to the horse, to creep out to the road and look for trouble. Caroline washed tin plates in a little spring, and scoured them with sand. "Mama," she said, "what was it like down there, before you ran away?"

20

Rolling the quilts, Solah lifted them to the wagon. "Bad, child. You don't recall nothin'?"

"Just little bits and pieces—a big white house, some cabins; a lady giving me milk, sleeping in the woods, hiding; that's about all."

Solah's eyes were serious. "Sometimes I wonder if'n us did right—never mind. Gets down south, you gon pass, hear me?"

"Pass as white? But I'm not ashamed of—"

"Don't sass me, gal. You think it's bad in Illinois, with the likes of that Williamson. It ain't *nothin'* next to Looziana, where they still owns folks, and you can't pick your man, or who you gon bed with, can't even keep your chillun, if'n they wants to sell 'em off. Your daddy ain't give up all he had just to see you turned into a white man's whore."

Bowing her head, Caroline murmured, "All right, mama. But I'm *not* ashamed of being part Ashanti, and I'll never forget the language."

Solah ran a work-roughened hand over Caroline's head. "You a good child, Carrie. Now kick dirt on them coals and help hitch up. We a long way from bein' clear."

Tucked between their belongings in the wagon bed, Caroline watched the passing scene, ducking from sight whenever they passed other travelers or came to a settlement. M'Nele's back was stiff and straight, as if he was always tense, but he drove in thoughtful silence, swaying with the wagon, and her heart went out to him. "Not her fault," he'd said, but because of her he was a hunted man once more. Because she was the wrong color, M'Nele, son of an Ashanti chief, was putting himself back into the lion's den of the South.

It was too late for her to run away and lift this impossible burden from her parents. If she left now, just slipped over the tailgate and took to the woods, M'Nele and Solah would still be hunted by vengeful Senator Williamson and his hired bullies. Caroline thought it through, and was determined to stay with them to the end, no matter what that might be.

21

Miles down the road, Solah said, "Ain't nobody lookin' hard."

"Ain't nobody heard," M'Nele said, "but pretty soon, ol' Senator gon hear from somebody passed us by. Ain't many niggers travelin' by theyselfs and headin' for Kentucky. Can't study 'bout it, though; just keep goin'."

In Massac County that night, they drove a good distance from the main road and hid the wagon in brush beside a stream. Caroline was thankful for the chance to bathe in chilly water, to rinse out her long hair and bind it up in a *chignon*. Feeling clean in a fresh calico dress, she fed the horse from their store of corn, and staked him out to graze.

At the campfire screened from the road by the bole of a gigantic beech, Caroline helped with the stew that was to be their fare until they were out of danger. It was quick and easy to cook, and it was filling. After they ate, M'Nele said he'd try to catch a few perch they could boil up for dinner on the road, and took a line to the creek.

Caroline said, as she scoured the pot, "If I'm to pass as white, how do I do it, and what about you?"

Solah said in Ashanti, "We thought this out long ago. There was a time, at first, when M'Nele would not think on it, but as the seasons passed, he understood we must."

Looking up, Caroline asked, "He did not love me because you—because a white man—"

"He loves you now," Solah continued. "You are his child, as much as if he sired you himself. So he thought of the time we might have to flee, and he prepared for it. We carry papers that say we are free persons of color, and it has been so long that none will know the difference, or that these papers are forged."

Solah added dry sticks to the small fire and crickets chirruped beyond the little circle of dancing light; a gentle wind moved trees above them. "Before we get where we are going," Solah said, "you will be put on a stagecoach, so you may enter the town as a white stranger. Together, we will think up a story to explain

22

why you left the North, and perhaps you can teach school. There is always need for teachers."

Caroline said, "And you, mama—M'Nele?"

"Close by; another smithy if the gods wish it, perhaps another small house. But we must be careful, all of us. You will be white, and we remain black. You must never visit us, but I can pick up your laundry—"

"Oh, mama, no!"

Lifting her head, Solah said, "Understand this, child: our lives are changed forever. This *must* be, and anything you do foolishly will endanger us all."

Chastened, Caroline fell silent. Stars were coming out in a low and cloudless sky and the night was mildly cool. Teach school, she thought, and rarely see her parents, pretend not to know them, place herself above them because they were black. They were such terrible thoughts she couldn't voice them, and she went to her pallet beside the glowing coals to curl into quilts and pillow her head upon her arm. It was a long time before sleep came.

When they moved on, Caroline tried to do everything, hitch the horse, cook the meals, spread bedding, until she got in Solah's way and was told to do only her share. She became used to hiding in the wagon bed, so no passing stranger would look at her and wonder, and she was always glad when they were off the road at night, when they could get back some small part of being a family.

Bypassing Paducah on twisting back roads hardly more than cowpaths, they moved down across Kentucky and into what M'Nele said was the very tip of Tennessee. M'Nele could chuckle then, and Solah brightened, for it seemed they had left immediate danger far behind.

The countryside changed, turning more hilly and rough. The wagon roads were rutted and in disrepair, but the air was winey, and a profusion of spring flowers stunned Caroline's eye with color. The land was wild, away from villages, and three times she caught sight of Indians sliding through the forest. When M'Nele had to go into some trading post to replenish

23

their supplies, she waited in the woods with Solah, and they fretted until he returned, worried that some official might not believe his freedom papers.

When he was gone, Caroline asked Solah questions about the South, what life was like before M'Nele escaped and brought them to Illinois. And in time, Solah began to tell of it, the bad times and the good. There had been joy—at jumping the broomstick, which meant a couple was married, the untroubled birth of a child, holidays when the field work was behind them, visits to other plantations, a new bolt of bright cloth.

The bad—and not all masters were bad, Solah pointed out—was not being your own person, being owned like a mule or cow. There were sometimes whips, and sometimes manacles; dogs and slave patrollers set after runaways; cruelty, determined or unconscious. For slave women, everything was worse, because they were always fair game for white boys and men; they were hospitably offered to visiting planters as casually as a glass of wine. And they were bred like animals, mates chosen for them by their owners.

"It was the selling," Solah murmured in Ashanti, "that was the worst. Children raised up so far, then snatched away to go in a slave cavvy, so their mothers never saw them again. White men crossing themselves on black women because light-colored girls brought better prices and mulatto boys made good house servants. They said mulattoes and octoroons were smarter because they had *human* blood. And they wanted no slave, man or woman, standing up to them about anything; niggers were always wrong."

Caroline put her back against the base of a sweetgum tree. "Did you and M'Nele jump the broomstick?"

Nodding, Solah said, "Yes. Master figured we would make strong babies, good field hands. But we never had sons."

"Only me," Caroline said. "Did that bother the—master?"

Again Solah nodded, a faraway look in her eyes. "And you were not— Keep trying, he ordered, and when nothing happened, he picked new mates for us.

24

That is when M'Nele said we must escape, so we planned carefully and ran away in the night. A long trip, my daughter, long and full of dangers, but we reached freedom."

Caroline put a hand to her head. "And left it for me."

"We do what we must," Solah said, and lifted her head to listen. "M'Nele is coming back."

When he broke through the brush that surrounded them, the horse was laboring, blowing through distended nostrils. M'Nele slid off him with the provision sacks, his face set and hard.

"They have found us," Solah said.

He shook his head. "Not yet, but they lookin'. Storekeeper asked me did I see a wagon and some women on the road, one of 'em most white. Told him I come up from Mis'ippi and ain't seen nobody like that."

M'Nele dropped the sacks and took a long drink from the water gourd. "Man run off at the mouth right smart; said a de-tective from the North was nosin' around, and had him some helpers. I was just a dumb nigger buyin' vittles for my master, gruntin' and shufflin'; got out'n there and to the horse. Three men trailed me out'n town, one with a bad eye. Lost 'em four, five miles back when I took to the woods. Ol' Senator's men, I 'spect."

"They wasn't certain it was you," Solah said, "else they pick you up."

"Else they want us all," M'Nele grunted. "Can't use the roads no more; they be watchin'."

A shadow of pain crossed Solah's face. "We got to leave the wagon?"

"No more'n us and the horse can tote," he said. "Woods and rivers, looks like. Mis'ippi ain't far."

"They won't stop," Solah said.

"Paterollers didn't neither, woman; us made it anyhow. Better off this time. Got us gold and silver, vittles and a horse."

And an extra mouth, Caroline thought, another woman to worry over. But she would do her very best

25

not to slow them down. She said, "Daddy, shall we pack up now?"

M'Nele looked at her. "Can't get used to you talkin' like gentry, 'cept when I close my eyes and hear this Ashanti woman, black as midnight. Open 'em and see white gentry. Yeah, child—best us moves right out. Make up bedrolls to tote crost shoulders and load vittles on the horse, clothes, too. Solah, just the stewpot and cups; leave the plates."

"Lord," she said. "Get to livin' like folks a spell, then back to animals. That Williamson scutter—hope he knowed death was acomin' for him. Cause of all this, that 'un."

"Hadn't been him, been somebody else, and come down to it, I reckon it felt right good to act the man myself, stand up to 'em for oncet."

Solah glanced sharply at her husband. "You ain't fixin' to stand to them hunters?"

"If'n it comes to it," M'Nele said.

The woods were shadowy and difficult to penetrate; bushes clung to Caroline's skirt and unseen branches snatched off the kerchief that bound back her hair. She stumbled over roots and almost cried out when a startled rabbit broke from underfoot. Without hesitation, at home in the forest as any wild beast, M'Nele pointed their way, leading the laden horse while they followed.

They were leaving a trail that the hunters could follow, if they should stumble across the abandoned wagon. That could happen, even though they had covered it with branches and moss. How far would the men follow them? How long would they stay on a trail they only suspected?

A bluejay cursed them raucously from the top of a pine, and a scarlet cardinal flitted through the undergrowth. A bramble scratched Caroline's arm and she ducked low to avoid a patch of moss like a curly, greygreen beard. Locusts whirred off to the right, brilliant, jeweled gold and deep green; some hidden wildflower spread rich fragrance upon warm, humid air that caressed her skin. If it hadn't been for the sense of urgency, Caroline might have enjoyed this forest.

They stopped beside a clear spring so the horse could drink, and Caroline sank gratefully to earth. M'Nele said, "Go till near sundown afore we eats; put miles twixt us and them."

"Daddy," Caroline said, "will they find where the wagon turned off the road?"

"Find anything," he answered, "they looks hard enough. Just hope they got no dogs."

As if in answer, they heard it far off upon the wind— the eager belling of hounds upon a scent.

Chapter 4

By dead reckoning and Andy Jackson's luck, Jubal
Blaze figured they were somewhere in the territory
of Alabama. Kicking a foot free of the stirrup, he
curled one long leg over the pommel of his saddle,
resting his buttocks in the new position. Behind him
straggled a hundred Tennessee volunteers, and ahead
as many more infantrymen pushing south and west.
They were a long way from home and had a far piece
to go; could be, they'd traipse all over these chill and
brooding woods and never see hide nor hair of an
Indian. Jubal would just as soon be back in Charleston
where it would be lively, the crops all in and all those
sweet little girls with so much time on their pretty little
hands.

Pushing back his cocked hat, he sighed; somebody
had to ride out with Andy when word came about the
massacre at Fort Mims. So Jubal joined up with the
Tennessee folks who weren't the sort to take kindly
to redskins lifting hair without catching what-for. Indian wars were too close to home, and hardly a family
back yonder hadn't lost somebody to tomahawk or
scalping knife or silent arrow.

A man tugged at his stirrup and Jubal looked down
into the freckled, upturned face of Barton Roberts,
who owned a piece of land down the road from the
Blazes in Carolina. "Hey now, cap'n," Roberts said,
"reckon Ol' Hickory goin' to let us rest our bones to-

28

day? Plumb wore us to a nub yesterday, and we ain't got over it yet."

"Hell," Jubal said, "you trot that far chasin' wild turkey. Just 'cause Colonel Coffee wasn't in a bind like the messenger said, that don't mean we can dawdle. Them Creeks ain't about to wait on us."

"Wisht to God I *was* stalkin' turkeys," Roberts said. "Been so long since I et, my belly figures my neck's tied shut or froze tight."

"Andy'll find vittles," Jubal promised. "I hear tell he's got some of them peaceable Choctaws bringin' in corn and deer meat."

Roberts brushed back his coonskin hat and spat. "Ain't no peaceable Injuns, less'n their toes is turned up, and I aim to turn up many as I can."

"The gen'l is havin' the tame ones wear white feathers," Jubal said, "and tie white deer tails to their belts. Draw down on one of 'em, and Andy is liable to be a mite riled, since there'll be a heap of flat bellies without 'em."

Grinning, Roberts said, "Don't want him raisin' his hackles at *me;* that ornery ol' bastard kin out-holler, out-stomp, and for certain out-cuss any man in Carolina. Washington, too, I expect."

"That's howcome he didn't get on so good with them lace shirt senators and such," Jubal said. "Pass word about them feathers and deer tails, Barton. I'll mosey up yonder and see can I find out when we make camp."

Dropping his leg, he squeezed his gelding forward, swinging out alongside the lead company and nodding howdy to Captain Houston as he passed. Jubal hoped the tame Indians toted in plenty to eat. The men had run out of rations almost two days past, and if they didn't get fed soon, many would be slipping off to hunt for themselves. Some might not get back to the marching column, because the Creeks would pick them off; some wouldn't return out of pure cussedness.

Couldn't hardly blame them, Jubal thought. It had been a long march and when they didn't find Indians right off, the mountain men took to grumbling; man came to fight, there ought to be somebody to tangle with, else he'd just as soon go on home.

Around a bend in the track, he saw a big field and men sprawling on the ground, a little creek where some dipped water gourds and a few splashed their faces, a few soaked tired feet. At the base of a big oak, Jackson sat with his bony knees drawn up, cradling his left arm in a grimy sling, gnarled and weathered as the tree itself. Beyond him were piled deer carcasses and hides filled with corn. Jubal drew up his horse and stepped down.

"Howdy, cap'n," Jackson said, his craggy face not betraying the constant pain from the wound that had damned near killed him, and might yet. "Your boys comin' along smart?"

"About froze and hungry as whelpin' wolves," Jubal said. "Proud to see them rations."

"After they've et, you might toll off half a dozen for pickets; rest of the companies doin' the same."

Jubal thought he might say something about how restless the men were getting, but just then a big man in buckskins came trotting up, coonskin hat flapping its tail behind. Jubal backed off and shook his head at how easy Davy Crockett ran, how slick he could scout the woods. Jubal was never much for walking, if he could ride a horse.

He watched Crockett hunker down and talk to the general, and felt a lift of excitement. They must be getting close to an engagement with the Creeks, and he wanted to wait and find out, but he had his company to see to. Jackson would call in officers if the scout's news was important.

Tying off his horse, Jubal paced out an area in the field for his men and started gathering fallen limbs for their fires. Again he thought he should have brought at least one of the house servants along to do this kind of work, but there was always the chance a nigger might run off and join the Creeks. There was word of its happening before, and even though the Blaze niggers were content, a frivolous one might be lured

30

off by Indians. Niggers cost too much to be wasted like that.

When meat and corn were divided up, Jubal ate with Barton Roberts and some other boys from around home, roasting acorns in the coals after, because the rations were scanty. Seeing to his horse then, staking him out after a rubdown and a handful of corn, Jubal chose the night pickets and sent them out, then wandered over to the fire where Jackson's blankets were spread.

"Set a spell, cap'n," the general said. "Naught to drink but acorn coffee. Just about to send for you."

The leaders were gathered around the fire—Sam Houston; Colonel John Coffee, a far piece from his cavalry; Major Tom Benton, who had more than his share of gall to stay with the expedition, in light of what his kin did to Jackson; Willy Lessman; and Davy Crockett, squatting on his haunches like Indians did. If those buckskins got any blacker, Jubal thought, Davy would have to take to wearing a white deer tail, too.

"Well now," Jackson said, "Mister Crockett brought news. The Creeks are gatherin' at a loop in the river folks call Horseshoe Bend, and buildin' a fort acrost a narrow neck of land. Most all the Alabama tribes are there and Red Eagle struttin' amongst 'em."

Jubal tightened a big fist. Red Eagle had led the raid on Fort Mims, presided over the bloodletting there that left near five hundred whites dead, women and children among them. A renegade, a war chief who was only one-eighth Creek and the rest white, his real name, and one he scorned, was William Weatherford. General Jackson wanted the man real bad, almost as much as he wanted to run the Spanish out of the Floridas.

"That breed has the devil's own luck," Jackson went on. "Got away from Colonel Coffee here by jumpin' his horse off a bluff into the river. I don't want him gettin' away from us. We march on the morrow, quick time."

When the meeting broke up, Jubal paid his respects

to the general and made his way back to his own company. Word spread rapidly around the camp that a fight was in the offing, and a ripple of excitement ran through the men. They whispered and stirred around long after they normally would have fallen asleep.

When the fire died to red coals, Jubal put his feet to it and turned in his blankets, pillowing his head upon his saddle to blink drowsily up at cold stars. A mockingbird saluted the rising of an icy moon, and the smell of frosty pine lay heavily upon the field. The ghostly whistle of a screech owl echoed far back in the trees as Jubal snugged his cheek against worn saddle leather and his eyelids fell.

His saddle was not smooth like the curve of Dulcie Fitzgerald's cheek, nor fragrant like her golden hair. He could still taste the ripeness of her full mouth and the darting of her mischievous tongue, and feel the tossings of her amazingly supple body as her tender flesh devoured him. Ah, had ever a man such a farewell? It had topped the offerings of Eva Marks and Georgiana Oldfield, both lusty lasses doing their bounden duty to the country and Tennessee by bidding fond goodbye to a dashing captain of volunteers. But Eva and Georgiana had not the wide and willing experience of Mistress Fitzgerald, whose merchant husband had taught her some amazing tricks.

Jubal smiled in his sleep and allowed that other planters could sport with nigger wenches to their heart's content, and hold their own ladies in pristine reverence. What those befuddled gentlemen didn't know would not force them into calling for pistols at dawn. Wenches had never been Jubal's failing; somehow he couldn't bring himself to soil the whiteness of his bed linens with a black and sweaty hide. They had a musk about them he could not abide. Niggers were stock, and to be handled as such. A man didn't mistreat his horse, didn't starve down his cows nor manacle his hogs, and no more ought he to beat on his slaves. But he didn't accept them as humans, either.

Dreaming more of Dulcie Fitzgerald and the times her husband was traveling to Georgia, Jubal slept the night away in contentment, and only frowned when he shivered awake at noises about the camp. Giving his last handful of corn and a lick of salt to his gelding, he hunkered at the rejuvenated fire to get his share of leftover venison.

"Cap'n," Barton Roberts said with a wink at the others, "we was speculatin' on them Injun squaws. Reckon they can burn off a man's pizzle, or be their hides a mite too dark for you?"

Grinning with them, Jubal said, "You boys get to diddle ary squaw, best you watch yourselves real close. Hear tell they tote sharp knives up inside, just waitin' to geld the first white stud that mounts 'em."

Mason McGee's unshaven jaw fell. "Shore nuff, cap'n?"

Barton Roberts roared with laughter. "You ijiot! How you expect them knives to tell the difference twixt a white and red pizzle?"

Seriously, Jubal said, "The squaws know, and they got these special muscles—"

"You funnin' us, cap'n," Mason McGee grinned. "Account of you never diddled a black wench. You'd flat out think *they* had special muscles up in there, the way they wiggle and carry on. Shore missin' somethin'."

"Oh," Roberts said, "Cap'n Blaze don't hurt none for nooky, but one of these times a daddy's goin' to come callin' and totin' a shotgun, and yonder stands Jubal Blaze afore a preacher. Ain't no fear of that, with a nigger wench. I do swear, though, can't understand what them gals see in our cap'n, big and ugly as he be."

They laughed again, and James Greer said, "If'n ol' Andy sashays on acrost to the Floridas, or down to N'Awlins, maybe Cap'n Blaze kin find him a pure white lady. He don't, it's certain sure for wet blankets time he gets home again."

Jubal shook his head and chuckled with them, then rose and stretched. "The gen'l is ridin' out, so I reckon we best follow. Quick time, Andy said, so save your breath. I'm purely sorry to have to ride whilst you boys go shank's mare."

They groaned behind him as he saddled his horse. In the saddle, he checked pistols and the long gun he slung over his back. Back in Charleston, he'd been presented with a sword, but left it in favor of a skinning knife.

Everybody in Tennessee knew Andy Jackson's feelings about taking the Floridas for the United States, and how put out he was that British men-of-war were impressing American seamen. The Creek uprising was a good reason to raise volunteers, and already the column was picking up Alabama folks eager to avenge Fort Mims. Could be the general had it in mind to fight two or three wars all at once if need be, and when these riflemen tasted blood and booty, they'd follow Old Hickory to the gates of Hell and kick off its redhot hinges.

Major Thomas Benton rode by just then, and Jubal put his back to the man. The general might be forgiving, but it was foolishness between Benton's brother Jesse and Major Micah Carrol that near killed Jackson, through no fault of his own. Better they'd shot each other in the damned fool duel they'd planned, than get Andy mixed up in their spat.

All the talk and threats, and naturally Andy put a pistol on Tom Benton when he saw a hand go for the pocket. But he only backed the major into the tavern at gunpoint, when here came Jesse Benton to fire a coward's load up close at the general—two balls and bits of chain. It was a wonder the general was alive, and Colonel Coffee said it was only the smell of battle that brought the old warhorse out of his sickbed.

Jubal rode at the head of his company in early morning shade of interlaced pines, glad for pale sunlight. At this pace, the boys were sweating and grunting; come noon, they'd be stiff and footsore, but never a man among them would quit. They'd come to kill Creeks for Andy Jackson, and be damned to the skulker who turned tail now that action lay before them.

These Tennesseans were good men all, Jubal

thought, and he was proud to fight alongside them. Few owned more than one or two slaves, and they all farmed their own land. Most had fought Indians before, and their fathers had gone against the Redcoats; they were the best riflemen in the world, and would do themselves proud in the upcoming fight.

Hours down the trail and half dozing in the saddle, Jubal felt guilt creeping up on him again. Pa was getting on in years and had a chest misery; as the elder son, Jubal by rights ought to be home in Carolina tending the plantation. But he told himself, as he had when he signed on with Andy, that he'd be back in time for spring planting, and his brother Abel could see to the land meanwhile. This might be Jubal's last chance to hooraw off adventuring, for his pa didn't take to fighting wars unless they came close to home.

Pa wanted him married and settled, too, wanted grandchildren at his knee. "Boy," his father would say, "first you know, you'll be past prime and naught to show for wasted years. Every lad in these hills your age is wed and siring younguns, and I ain't been given to stay on earth forever."

And Jubal always answered: "Plenty of time, Pa. Besides, you'll outlive us all, and you got grandchildren aplenty from my sisters."

"Ain't the same," Pa said, chewing on the pipestem, "ain't the same, because they don't carry the name. Bigod, *Blazes* cleared this land and whupped Indians and growed the crops, and when I'm put to ground I won't rest easy less'n *Blazes* set my tombstone."

"Now, Pa," Jubal said, "there's more Indians to be whipped down to Alabama Territory. If the uprising ain't stopped there, next one's liable to be here, and Andy Jackson says—"

"Jackson!" the old man snorted and near bit his pipestem in two. "Jackson's got one eye cocked on the Floridas and the other aimed clear back to Washington."

"That wouldn't be tolerable hard to take," Jubal said. "Be a change from nothin' but Virginians settin' all gentlemen and uppity in the president's chair."

35

There had been more talk, but Pa knew Jubal was set on going, and when the time came, he gave his blessing as they both knew he would.

Straightening in the saddle, Jubal peered ahead, thinking he'd heard a rattle of musket fire far off, but it was only a horse moving over dry branches. If the Creeks didn't know they were coming, they were all stone deaf. He had the feeling they'd been watched all the way by black marble eyes.

Barton Roberts pulled on his stirrup. "You gettin' tired settin' on that horse, I'd be proud to let you stretch them long legs down here."

Jubal pulled the corncob stopper from his water gourd and took a long swallow. "Can't hardly do that, Barton, what with all these here heavy wet blankets I got to pack. 'Sides, it wouldn't look right for one of Andy's officers to be stompin' down the road with a pack of field hands."

"Shit," Roberts said. "When we hit them Injuns, let's see how long you make yourself a big ol' target up yonder."

"Well now," Jubal said, "I reckon that's another story."

The column hurried on into the chill shadows of afternoon.

Chapter 5

"Lead that horse in the creek," M'Nele hissed, "whilst I try to fool them dogs."

Solah put out a hand. "Don't—oh M'Nele, don't let them—"

"Hurry, woman," he commanded. "Right on down the middle now. I be with you in a minute."

Caroline paused at the bank to look back at her daddy climbing a tree after rubbing himself all around its bole.

"Come *on,* girl!" Solah snapped. "M'Nele know what he up to."

The water was cold, reaching her knees, her waist, and Caroline caught her breath, but it rose no higher. Feet slipping on hidden stones, she followed her mama downstream. At a curve in the creek, she looked back again at the big tree and saw M'Nele crouching far out on a bending limb, saw him suddenly hurl his big body into the air, straining so that he landed in the water with a mighty splash. Water flew and M'Nele disappeared in a rainbow spray, only to rise immediately and cup his hands to scatter water along the creek bank, throwing it far as he could.

"*Girl!*" Solah insisted, and Caroline waded after her mama, bedding held atop her head, slipping and reeling as the creek bed became more uneven underfoot. The horse staggered and snorted, almost falling as Solah pulled on his lead.

M'Nele caught up with them then, panting a bit, to

take some of their loads upon himself and lead the way, feeling with callused bare feet for deep holes that might engulf them without warning.

Gasping, Caroline followed, her arms aching, the cold water biting into her flesh, into her very bones so that her teeth chattered. Finally M'Nele climbed out upon a grassy bank and helped them from the water. Caroline put down her load, sank to her knees and began to wring out her skirt.

"That coon-treein' trick won't hold 'em long," M'Nele said, "but maybe time they get to our camp, water'll be dry on our scent and they won't know 'zackly where we took to the creek."

"They gon know, though," Solah said.

"Brace up, woman," M'Nele said. "We whupped 'em afore. Catch your breath now. If'n them ain't right smart dogs, they gon bell that tree just like I was up it, and it take them hunters a spell to see I ain't."

Now Caroline understood that he'd climbed to fool the dogs and buy them precious time to escape. M'Nele gave them only a little while to rest before they were on their feet once more, hurrying through the woods. Hours later, they crossed the creek three different times, circling back once in their own tracks. When Caroline caught sight of her mama's face, she saw the pace, the strain beginning to show. But M'Nele was relentless, driving them on with the whiplash of his voice, jerking the horse when the beast faltered.

"Got to put miles atwixt us," he grunted during an infrequent rest stop. "Keep goin' far as we can git. Wipin' out tracks fools men, not hounds. Next time we gets out'n the creek, we stays out, puts vinegar and red pepper on our feet. Might throw off them dogs."

"Might not," Solah muttered.

M'Nele frowned at her. "What you want me to do, woman?"

"Nothin', I reckon; does the best we can and prays."

In Ashanti, M'Nele said, "To the old gods, the true gods, not the white man's."

"To all of them," Solah answered, "to anything that can help."

"Best we help ourselves," he said, and rose to drag the pack from the horse. He removed the halter and slapped the horse on the rump. Surprised, it wheeled and trotted off through the woods. "Keep 'em guessin'," M'Nele said. "Horse goes one way, we goes t'other."

Heavily laden, M'Nele led them on, plodding slowly now under the added weight, shirt torn and great black muscles bulging and sweating through the rent. Shadows lengthened in the forest, and twisted vines took on the shape of serpents. When a rabbit burst frightened from beneath her feet, Caroline barely choked back a scream.

Legs aching, pulling hard for air, she sighed when M'Nele at last stopped in a little clearing. "Creek's gettin' bigger," he said wearily. "Might be, us can float it. See in the mornin'. Mush and salt meat, woman; no fire."

Solah began making the cold meal. "Ain't heard no dogs."

"Could of throwed 'em off," M'Nele agreed, "but might be, they took them hounds on a big loop."

Caroline ate silently, dipping her fingers into the common pot of raw cornmeal mush, chewing salted pork while every muscle in her body ached and her eyelids grew heavy. Why couldn't they be left alone? They were out of the state, far away from where her daddy killed a man to protect her honor, and in self-defense. Why couldn't Senator Williamson call off his hunters and dogs, and let them go their way in peace?

Chopping sounds filtered dimly through her consciousness, and Caroline came awake to discover grey dawn. Guiltily, she hurried out of her blanket to help Solah prepare breakfast over coals that sent no telltale finger of smoke up through interlaced tree limbs. M'Nele was hard at work putting together a raft, axing off short, dry logs and binding them with grapevines, but even his great strength wasn't enough to slide the raft into the water. After they ate, Caroline and Solah helped him, grunting and straining until one end of the raft floated.

"Got poles yonder," M'Nele said, "but y'all use

39

your'n just to fend off the bank, less'n I say different. I be steerin' on the back. Pile everything in the middle and hunker down."

"M'Nele," Solah said, "where this river go?"

"South," he answered. "Away from here, that's all I knows."

They heard the dogs then, the eager yelping that hounds make when they've struck a hot trail, and hurried to get their possessions on the logs.

"Hold on," M'Nele said, and pushed off from the bank.

Out into the rushing waters, the raft moved clumsily, swinging its front this way and that as M'Nele poled frantically, trying to get the hang of steering it straight. Caroline pushed the end of her pole against the bank and ducked under a curtain of weeping willow branches. A thick-bodied moccasin slid soundlessly into the creek, its ugly triangular head lifted, and farther on, a loggerhead turtle plopped from a dark snag into the water.

Around a bend, the sound of the dogs fading behind them, they drifted in quiet water close to the bank where grey moss swung like old men's beards from cypress trees. There were quicker currents ahead.

"Log yonder!" Solah cried, and M'Nele fought to angle the plunging raft away from it. Caroline felt a sharp bump and struggled to keep her balance, to hang onto bedrolls that threatened to slip into the river. Then they were past the obstruction and flying through bubbled water, past a white sand beach where a grey crane rose awkwardly, disturbed at its fishing.

"Stumps!" Solah yelled, and M'Nele poled furiously while Caroline watched the jagged black teeth coming fast and water washed over her feet. Somehow, miraculously, past the barricade then, the raft rocked and pitched until the river grew wider and smoothed itself out. The water was a muddy brown now, stained by dark earth and dyed by ancient oak leaves paving its soft bottom. There were many more snakes, one that Solah struck at as it fell from an overhanging cypress limb. Impossibly bright little dragonflies hovered over quiet backwaters, a red fox squirrel ran chattering up a water oak, and his grey brother sounded alarms from a green-budded magnolia tree.

Caroline was wet through, but exhilarated, because they could hear no baying hounds. Surely the hunters must be left far behind by now. Shaking back her damp hair, she balanced the pole across her knees and watched the banks, high dirt cliffs festooned with trailing vines.

Suddenly the raft changed direction, and Caroline looked around to see M'Nele poling it quickly toward the opposite bank, where it went aground on a little strip of muddy sand. "Y'all climb off and pull it up," he said, "much as you kin."

When they had it fast, M'Nele came ashore, jamming the end of his pole deep into soft ground to keep the raft from drifting. Long-armed, he reached for the sodden bedrolls, then the sacks of food.

"Reckon we come far enough?" Solah asked, and M'Nele shook his head.

"Just as soon ride it far's it reaches, but they's a man fishin' up yonder, white man. Settlement close by, I 'spect. Won't do for 'em to see two niggers and a white gal floatin' past."

"I'm not white," Caroline said.

Her daddy stared at her. "You flat *better* be, gal. Don't forget it no more. You white down here. It's your only chance."

"But I don't want to be like—like *them*," Caroline said. "Chasing us with dogs, hunting us like animals."

"That what we is," M'Nele said. "Animals; nothin' but stock, worth more'n cows but less'n a good blooded horse." He looked away from her. "I make us a li'l fire under the bank yonder whilst you women spreads the quilts to dry back in the trees. Reckon the meal's wet, too."

"I'll spread it on a blanket," Solah said, "but the salt is most washed away." She stared back upriver. "Comin' on dark, and us can't ride that thing at night nohow."

"Don't mean to," M'Nele said. "Sun goes down, I

41

cuts the vines and shoves them logs back in the river. Somebody finds 'em, they'll reckon the raft busted on a stump and us drowned. We eats and lays a wide track around the settlement, afoot. Gets past it, might be we free."

"In slave country," Solah said.

Wincing at the pain and hopelessness in her mother's voice, Caroline worked hard, opening the bedrolls to dry, gathering dry twigs for the supper fire. Heedlessly, the river chuckled past their little beach, and to the right, the sun settled slowly behind towering longleaf pines. Although their fire was dug into a hillside, its flames shielded by a blanket changed often, their bedclothes never completely dried out, and Caroline spent most of the night shivering, never fully asleep.

Next morning they ate quickly, redistributed the bundles they had to carry so that M'Nele bore most of the weight. Then Solah said, "No sign of 'em, thank the lord."

"Thank daddy," Caroline said, remembering the tricks he'd used to throw off their pursuers. She was rewarded by one of M'Nele's swift, rare smiles, and happily she shouldered her load.

It was a long and wearying walk, staying off trails, darting across the occasional wagon road and back into covering woods that were impassable in places. They didn't stop until afternoon, and by then, ropes had worn a tender, hurting path across Caroline's shoulders and she was sticky with sweat.

Head on her pack, face grey with fatigue, Solah said, "Reckon howcome we ain't seen no Indians?"

"Hopes not to," M'Nele said, dipping spring water into the stewpot. "Heard tell they been warrin' down thisaway; them and the British folks, but not agin each other. Talk back in Marion was Britishers put the Indians up to it."

Solah closed her eyes. "Makes no never mind who wins. Them British cap'ns runs slave ships, too."

M'Nele stirred cornmeal into the water, cut off slivers of smoked beef and added tuber roots he'd gathered during the trek. "Agin the law for slavers to bring in any more. Means black meat agoin' to be worth more afore long."

" 'Special the light ones that smells sweet," Solah said, and M'Nele's jovial mood vanished. He said, "Don't run your mouth like that, woman."

Rousing herself, Solah said, "Might's well let the child know what's waitin' her, do we get caught or our papers don't hold up."

"Learn soon enough," M'Nele said, and put the kettle on a tiny fire. "Got to buy us some salt some-wheres."

"Mama," Caroline said, going to her mother. "You're sick."

Putting a hand to her cheek, Solah said, "Just wore to the bone, child."

"I can carry some more."

Solah's smile was weak. "No, you can't; you already totin' enough for a mule."

Defensively, M'Nele said, "Needs every speck of it; no tellin' how long we got to stay in the brush. Near 'bout to Mis'ippi, I reckon. Might be, ol' Senator slacks off."

A spasm passed across Solah's face; Caroline dipped a rag in the spring and held it to her mother's fore-head. Softly, Solah whispered, "Do they catch us, don't fight 'em, baby. You fights, they hurt you real bad, maybe kill you. Let 'em have their way and act like you like it, even. That way, you stays alive. That's what tallies up—stayin' alive."

"You and daddy didn't think so," Caroline mur-mured back. "If you did, you wouldn't have run away."

Solah's hand tightened on hers. "You the good thing come out of it, Carrie. We still got you, and pray God we keeps you."

The stewpot was empty and Caroline was scrub-bing it out with sand when she heard the horses. M'Nele's head jerked up and Solah put both hands to her breasts. Then the baying of dogs reached them, from the other direction.

M'Nele stood up. "Comin' slow and easy in front;

43

hounds ahint us. Ol' Senator ain't quit; son of a bitch is a pure-D bulldog."

Caroline snatched up her pack, but M'Nele said, "Too late. Take your mama in the river; she don't swim so good, but you does."

"Daddy—"

"Here," he said, facing toward the muffled sound of hooves. "Take this here sack and tie it round your belly. Gold pieces and silver in it."

"M'Nele," Solah said in rapid Ashanti, "you cannot stand to them. They are many."

Bringing Tucker Williamson's pistol from his belt, he said, "There will be fewer of them when it begins. You have been a good woman, Solah."

"No," she said. "M'Nele—no."

"There is no time," he said impatiently. "Only enough for a warrior to die bravely. Like a man, like an Ashanti. Take the child and go."

"Father," Caroline said in the same language, "do not order us to leave you."

He put a work-hardened hand on her cheek and looked into her eyes. "And you have been a good daughter. I claim you for my own. Be Ashanti now—go!"

Slumping, Solah stared at the ground while M'Nele picked up the big knife and sat his back against the trunk of a pine. Caroline caught a deep breath and took her mother by the wrist. The money purse was knotted safely about her waist when she pulled the older woman to the riverbank and waded in. Cold water closed about her legs, rose to her hips, and Caroline shifted her grip from her mother's wrist to her braided hair.

"Lie quietly in the water, mama. I will pull you along."

"No use," Solah muttered. "Nothing is of any use. M'Nele will die and they will catch us, torture us."

Glancing back to where her father stood braced against the tree, his knife and pistol ready, Caroline spoke sharply: "Do as M'Nele commands! He is the warrior; we are only women."

44

She drew Solah deeper into the river and the slow current caught them, moved them downstream. Caroline tugged her mother limply behind, and only their heads were showing when the first horses burst from the trees, when the first bearded, gaunt-faced riders sent up a shout of discovery.

M'Nele's pistol rang out, and a man tumbled from his saddle. Caroline saw her father fling the empty weapon and follow it with a full-throated, savage roar of rage. She saw his great knife rise and fall, and heard the agonized yelps of lesser men, the squeal of horses, the smashing of gunfire.

Still M'Nele fought; still he tore men from their saddles and hacked at them, his war chant, his death chant, rising high and pure above the melee. There was primitive glory in the sound, a ringing defiance that was a triumph in itself.

Caroline and her mother drifted around the bend as the chant was abruptly cut off. M'Nele, son of warrior chieftains, had fallen.

Chapter 6

Solah was a heavy weight in the water. She did not want to help herself, and Caroline strained to keep her mother's head above the lapping river, riding with the slow current when she could, stroking them out of trouble when threatening stumps and log jams loomed. Her arms ached, and the taste of river mud was bitter in her mouth, but she wouldn't give up. She couldn't, not after M'Nele had given himself so they might escape the vengeance of Senator Williamson's hunters.

Something cold brushed her leg beneath the surface, and Caroline gasped. A fish splashed ahead of them, and her heart fluttered. Then there was another bend, where the river widened and gentled itself against low, sloping banks. Battling with one arm, she drew them slowly from the middle of the river into slack back-waters, sighing with relief when her bare feet touched a sanded mud bottom.

Helping Solah to her feet, she guided her to shore. Solah fell to her knees. Head down, soaked and muddy, Solah seemed to have surrendered, the life force drained from her by M'Nele's death.

Caroline dragged her farther up the bank. "You call yourself Ashanti," she scolded.

Solah's emptied face lifted. "I am Ashanti."

"Then be proud of the way he died, in battle. It was his right, the destiny chosen for M'Nele by the old

46

gods. Be proud he took enemies with him, as a warrior should."

Beginning to rock from side to side, Solah said, "But I cannot mourn him properly. I have no ashes, and who will scar my face? Who will sing the death song for him?"

"In our hearts," Caroline said, "it is done. He will understand. M'Nele died that his wife and daughter might live, so now we must begin, we must live. By your own words, staying alive is the important thing."

A light flickered in Solah's sunken eyes. "Sometimes you are more Ashanti than I; sometimes you are the mother, and I am the child. M'Nele was proud of you; M'Nele loved you."

"And you," Caroline said. "Let us not shame him."

Sliding from musical, clicking Ashanti, Solah said, "But child—we out here in nowhere, got nothin' to eat, nowhere to go; got *nothin'*."

Touching the deerskin bag at her waist, Caroline said, "He left us this—money. I will find us food and blankets, flint and steel, weapons if need be. I do not know the forest, but the hunters caught my father, and they will not be behind us anymore. We will go in the direction he wanted, to this Louisiana where I may pose as a French schoolmistress, and you as my body servant. We will live, if not for ourselves, for the brave M'Nele."

"*Aiee,*" Solah said. "Perhaps you should have been his son."

"Perhaps I shall have to be," Caroline answered. "Can you walk? We should leave the river and dry our dresses. You still carry the papers in the oilskin bag?"

Solah's thin hand touched her own waist. "Yes. And child, there be other papers at the lawyer man's—"

"Later," Caroline said impatiently. "Come on, now."

Up from the bank they climbed, and into a copse of wild spring huckleberries. Caroline gathered handfuls in her dripping skirt, and they ate them as they walked. When they came upon a wagon road, she had a story ready in her mind. They were travelers from the North,

47

and had lost their horses, their wagon and all their possessions trying to cross the river. Why had they plunged heedlessly into unknown waters? A band of Indians, sir—red savages to chill the hearts of two frightened and helpless women. Luckily, she managed to save a few coins with which to purchase necessities. Surely any Southern gentleman would appreciate her predicament.

Surely they would—if she secreted the bulk of her hoard and carried only pieces of silver. But she didn't quite know how she would cope with a slave-holding Southerner, one of those who kept her people in bondage. Would she be able to hide her repulsion? She must, Caroline decided; she must treat Solah as stock, "worth more than cattle but less than good blooded horses," as M'Nele had said. Should she have manacles and a blacksnake whip?

"Are you very tired, mama?"

"Tolerable, child. I smells smoke."

Stopping in the middle of the road, Caroline peered ahead. "I see a house. Look, this log by the stubby oak tree—I'll bury our gold beneath it. Remember to act as if I'm your mistress."

"Had me plenty of practice," Solah mumbled. "Yes'm; sure did."

Caroline took her hand. "It'll be all right; you'll see."

With Solah a pace behind, she marched up the road and turned off at the log house, ignoring a pack of yapping dogs, walking with her head high.

A man came out onto the sagging porch carrying a long gun, a ratty-looking man gone to seed before his time. Out at the elbows and grimy, he didn't touch a finger to the brim of his slouch hat, but simply stared at them with bloodshot eyes.

"Who be you, girl?"

"Mrs. Monteleone," Caroline said, stressing the *Mrs*. "We are victims of an unfortunate mishap, sir—my servant and I." She ran through her tale, embellishing it here and there while looking for a woman, or for the black faces of slaves. She didn't see either.

"Wal now," the man said. "You a far piece from town, and I'd be proud to help, only—"

"Oh, we can pay," Caroline said. "I saved a little money from the accident."

Now he pushed back his hat, revealing lank brown hair, and set aside the flintlock. "That so? Just a pore dirt farmer myself, but might be I kin scratch together a few vittles and such."

"Blankets," Caroline said promptly, "flint and steel, such food as we may carry, a cookpot. I don't suppose you have a horse?"

"None a few coppers'd buy," the man grunted. "Injuns run off some and et 'em; need the two I got for plowin'. Got two quilts I kin spare, jug of sorghum, dab of cornmeal, salted deer meat, a ol' pot. That suit you?"

"That'll be fine," Caroline said. "We can walk to town then and see about obtaining further assistance."

"Damned if'n you don't talk fancy," he said. "Just you two women, eh?"

"My—my husband and his brother are two days behind," Caroline lied. "They'll be able to trail us."

He frowned, still running his eyes over the wet dress plastered against the ripe curves of her body. "Heared tell there be soljers comin'. Your man amongst 'em?"

"An officer," Caroline said. "One of the best shots in the army."

He scratched a stubbled cheek. "That's well as may be, but I ain't seen the color of your money yet."

Reaching into the flattened purse. Caroline brought out a handful of silver. "This should do."

As the man's muddy eyes widened, Solah said abruptly, "More'n do, missy. That there is cash money, and he don't see that much in a year."

The man straightened and glared at Solah. To Caroline he said, "You got a smartmouth nigger yonder; best you see to her manners."

"Sarah!" Caroline said sharply, and turning back: "Sir, I will not be cheated, but I did not think a gentleman such as you would try."

Swelling visibly, he mumbled, "Quality is as qual-

49

ity does, I reckon. Set yourself on the porch whilst I gets your plunder."

When he was out of sight, Caroline whispered, "I'm sorry, mama, using your slave name."

"Done right," Solah whispered back. "But close watch this peckerwood; he white trash."

Later, as they walked away with food rolled in quilts and the wherewithal to make a fire, the cookpot on a string thumping her leg, Caroline could still feel the sly probing of his eyes upon her. Solah murmured, "He watchin' us go the wrong way; be figurin' us got somethin' hid out and waitin' for us to come back by."

"No fear," Caroline said. "We'll cut through the woods and make for the town he mentioned."

When the gold was recovered and they were well into the trees, Solah said, "Make for town after I rests a spell."

"Soon, mama," Caroline said, "soon as I can find a place where he won't see smoke."

"You learned from your daddy, child; that you did."

"Just a little more—oh yes; there's a big tree over a dip in the ground. We can build our fire down there. Do you think I should have tried to buy a weapon from him?"

Sinking to earth, Solah said, "Didn't have more'n that rusty ol' gun. 'Sides, you got a fine-shootin' officer right ahint you, and that razorback woulda been suspicious."

"Meat and mush," Caroline said. "Someday, mama, I'm going to take you into a fancy restaurant and buy you the very best meal in the whole world, all the things I've read about."

As Caroline struck flint to steel and blew on wood chips, Solah said quietly, "We was right to see to your book learnin', to keep up French talk that you come natural by, and make you talk like gentry. I don't know about Ashanti; someday you slips and gets yourself in a peck of trouble with that nigger language."

When the cornmeal was cooked, Caroline said, "Mama, please try to eat more. You need your strength."

"Keeps thinkin' on M'Nele," Solah said, "and ain't got the stomach for eatin'." Her mournful eyes watched the unfeeling trees, and off in the brush a bird plaintively echoed their sorrow.

They walked awhile and rested awhile, the stops coming more often as Solah tired. The scrawny man hadn't come after them, and for that Caroline was grateful. Her skin crawled at the idea of his hands touching her.

"Town shouldn't be far off," Caroline said, shouldering the pack again. "We've been moving parallel to the road, and I hear horses on it. We can buy another horse and cart, and set our direction straight."

Tired and dispirited, Solah plodded behind, but when Caroline stepped through bushes onto the roadside, her head came up to tilt listening. "No, child!" she said then. "Get back, quick!"

Turning, Caroline said, "What's the matter? I can see the men riding up front and they aren't Indians. There's a lot of dust, though; men marching—"

"*Listen;* don't you hear it?"

Caroline frowned. "I hear only—" and the sounds reached her then, the slow, muffled clanking of chains.

"Slave cavvy," Solah hissed. "Get back—hide—"

But it was too late. The lead rider had already seen them and spurred his horse into a gallop. Pushing her mother ahead, Caroline forced her way through the brush, but the snorting horse was upon them, the man turning it to block them. A long, black whip dangled from his hand. "Looky here now," he said. "Come upon somethin' way out here in the wilds."

Caroline might have brazened it through, but Solah panicked and tried to run. The long whip flicked out and wrapped around one ankle, bringing her down with a crash as Caroline cried out: "Mama!"

He swung down from the saddle, lips peeled back in a wolfish grin. "Mammy, is it? Ain't this a caution? White gal callin' a nigger mammy. Means you ain't white, don't it?"

Solah got to her knees, her face venomous now.

51

"Whiter'n you, slaver. Calls me mammy account I took care her most her life."

Casually, the man jerked his whip handle, and Solah was tumbled over again. "Don't do that!" Caroline snapped. "She's a freed woman with papers to prove it."

"Just can't abide a sassy nigger," he said, "even them light enough to pass for white." His eyes were a washed-out blue, set close beside a crooked nose in a long-jawed face stubbled with a yellowish beard. There was a white scar at the corner of his mouth and a tooth missing when he lifted a thin lip. "Free nigger, you say, and out here in the woods lookin' like you both been dragged ahint a wagon; no man about. I don't see no freed nigger travelin' with her mistress. I see *two* niggers, one of 'em high yeller and t'other a mustee. Runaways up to no good, I say, and it's my bounden duty to round 'em up afore they do harm to decent folks."

From the ground Solah hissed, "No! You can't— my papers—"

Two long strides and he crouched over Solah, jerking at the thong around her waist. The oilskin pouch came loose in his hand, and he slammed hard knuckles against the side of Solah's head. "Told you 'bout sassy niggers."

Without realizing what she was doing, Caroline picked up a broken limb from the ground, and hurled herself at the man, swinging with all her strength. He was quick and strong, blocking her wrist and snatching her to one side. She fell sprawling, her tattered skirt sliding far up her thighs. Furiously, she rolled over and came at him once more, clawing with her fingers. When he slapped her, redwhite stars burst behind her eyes and Caroline staggered. He slapped her again and drove her to one knee.

Through sharp and sudden pain she heard other horses crash through the bushes, other men calling out. Shaking her head to clear it, she focused on the first man, hating him with all her soul.

"What you cotched here, Kleppner?"

52

"Hellfire; one of 'em's white."

Kleppner tore the pouch apart, ripped its papers into bits and scattered them. "No she ain't; just a prime mustee. What you totin', gal—more freedom papers?"

One of the other men whistled when he saw the gold spilled into Kleppner's palm. "Mustee packin' that much cash money?"

"Stole it," Kleppner said, flipping a gold piece to each of his riders, "but we ain't studyin' on findin' who she robbed it from."

They laughed, and one horse jiggled anxiously. Kleppner said, "Get on back to the cavvy. I'll drive this pair to it."

Staring, Caroline said, "What—what are you going to do with us?"

He put the butt of his whip beneath her chin and tilted her face upward. "Uh-huh; mighty prime piece. Why, missy, I'm puttin' your mammy back in irons with the other niggers; looks some used-up, but she can fill in for a wench died of fever on the road. Now *you*—"

That's when Solah tried for him, jerking the whiplash from her ankle and coming off the ground like a tigress whose cub is threatened. Kleppner struck her in the temple with the whip butt, and Caroline screamed. Solah lay with eyes closed, one foot twitching.

"Cavvy'll get by 'thout me for a spell," Kleppner said. "Ain't had nothin' but black meat so long, it'll purely pleasure me to mount a wench near white as you."

A chill gathered in the pit of Caroline's stomach as the man unbuckled his belt to hang it with its pistols over the branch of a pine. "Won't do no good to try for 'em, missy. Cut you near 'bout in two with my whip, if'n you do. And your mammy ain't about to wiggle; wasn't a nigger, her head'd be broke for sure."

Don't fight them, her mother had warned. *If you fight, they'll hurt you bad, maybe kill you.*

Kleppner didn't remove his greasy shirt, just let his buckskin trousers drop and stepped out of them, the whip ready in one clenched fist. Caroline caught her

53

breath; he was hairy down his belly and more so across his crotch, and the thing pointing rigidly swollen from that yellowed nest terrified her.

"Hung good as ary buck nigger, ain't I?"

She turned her face away, but his hand twisted into her hair as he pushed Caroline onto her back. As he felt roughly, cruelly over her cringing flesh, she closed her eyes but could not shut out the reptilian crawl of his probing fingers.

Don't fight them, Solah had said, but already she felt hurt and shame and wanted to crawl off and hide. Caroline was glad her mother was unconscious, that Solah could not be forced to watch this degradation.

Wincing at the crush of his hands upon her tender breasts, Caroline tried to force her mind from what was happening to her, but the rough fondling of her secret, personal places kept bringing her back to ugly reality. Kleppner's breath smelled of chewing tobacco and rot, and his mouth was avid, bruising her lips.

Against her teeth he said, "Purtiest li'l bitch I ever see, skin fine as Chinaman silk—ahh, ahh—all soft and warm—"

He was at her belly then, and she gasped into his mouth, tried to pull back from his reaching tongue, but his heavy body pinned her down. She felt the stabbing of him, the forcing of him between her thighs, in and up—in and up—and a massive shudder wracked her flesh.

There was pain, a quickhot darting of sharp agony that seemed to climb through her stomach and into her very heart. Kleppner nuzzled into her heaving breasts, his teeth cutting, while the thickness of his manhood penetrated deeper into her convulsing body. Then he was buried full length inside her, *inside* her, moving and thrusting and grinding as Caroline's scream built in her constricted throat.

This was what Tucker Williamson had tried to do to her, and there was no tenderness to it, no softness, only this pounding and shaking that was tearing her apart.

Don't fight them, child, her mama had said.

Comes a time you'll be proud of your body, her mama had said.

Caroline knew only shame, a sense of being soiled, somehow owned. She hated it, hated it—but her hips began a slow, sensuous roll, and her back arched. The scream in her throat turned into a moan, and when she clawed at the man's sweaty back, she was not trying to push him away, but to bring him ever deeper.

Something burst wildly within her and her mind reeled even as her body spasmed. Teeth grating, head thrown back and haunches drumming the earth, Caroline whirled madly through a blazing darkness that knew no time and had no limits. Its quivering maw was wet and velvet black and sucking, drawing all strength from limbs gone suddenly limp. Lost in that strange void, Caroline Monteleone was turned over and over until at last she stopped drifting and crashed heavily to earth.

She was conscious first of a wavering face above her, its dim lines slowly taking on shape, sharpening and hardening into Kleppner's leer. Then Caroline felt the stickiness and small aches and the blood rushed to her face. She hid in her hands when the man lifted himself from her despoiled flesh.

"Damn if'n you ain't the goodest piece ever snapped down on a man's pizzle," Kleppner grunted. "Cherry, you was, and would of brung a high price down to N'Awlins. But damn if that wasn't worth the loss, and you and me, we got us a long way to go together."

Stunned, Caroline rolled over and tugged down her torn dress, her eyes searching for her mother. Solah still lay quietly, breathing heavily, but her eyelids were fluttering now. Crawling to her, Caroline stroked her face.

"On your hind legs," Kleppner ordered. "Tote that pack and stay ahead of my horse. Anybody tries to run gets their ass chewed off by this here whip."

Caroline helped Solah to rise, propped her with an arm about the waist. And the moment Solah's eyes cleared and met her own, Caroline realized her mama knew what had happened. It must be branded forever upon her face, she thought. But maybe Solah couldn't see the blacker shame, would never know how Caroline had reacted to being raped.

Chapter 7

In the supply wagon, Caroline looked back at the cavvy tramping along in the dust with a slow rhythmic rattle of the long chain that passed through each set of shackles. Twenty men and five women, now that Solah was locked among them. Caroline gnawed her lip, searching for her mother's face in the choking swirl of fine red dust. Proud Solah, who had lived so long in the sweetness of freedom, was once again in bondage.

All because of me, Caroline thought bitterly; everything lost, brave M'Nele dead, Solah in slavery, and the daughter they'd sought to protect made harlot to a slave trader. She looked ahead again, where Kleppner and the man called Delkin rode point with rifles across their saddles. In back, Ned Barker watched to make sure no prisoner slipped his chains. She glanced at the dusty face of the black driver, an older man who sat hunched, mule reins slack in gnarled hands. This one wasn't chained.

She spoke to him in Ashanti: "Do they not fear you will run away?"

Swiveling his head, he blinked at her. "Reckon that's Africky talk, but I ain't no Africky nigger."

Caroline said, "You're not locked up."

"Uh-uh; Marse Kleppner knows ol' Bobo ain't got no runnin' blood. Cooks for this bunch, too. Howcome a most white gal talks Africky?"

"Why don't you get away?" Caroline asked.

Bobo clucked to listless mules. "Marse Kleppner skin me alive, and nowheres to go, nohow. Howcome you don't run? Ain't no chains on you, neither."

"My mother's back there. I can't leave her."

"Marse get you, if'n you did, or Injuns. That your mammy you got cotched with? Never knowed my own mammy; got sold off young."

Caroline held to the rocking wagon seat. "Where is he taking the cavvy?"

Bobo blinked at her again. "Carryin' you, too, missy. 'Spects you ends up in N'Awlins; gets him a good price for you down yonder. Rest of them niggers— some goes on the block there, best field hands; rest gets swapped around on the way. Marse Kleppner, he always makin' swaps, do we stop by a big farm."

Human beings traded like horses, bargained over, their virtues extolled, their flaws hidden. Caroline trembled. There had to be some way to free her mother, for both of them to get away, even if it meant hiding forever in the woods and living off the land. Maybe they could join an Indian tribe.

Sun beat down upon the shuffling column, and somebody groaned. Reaching for a water gourd behind the wagon seat, Caroline dropped to the road and hurried back along the cavvy, looking for Solah. She found her at the very end of the bedraggled column, head hung down and face crusted where dirt gathered upon sweat.

Giving her mama water, Caroline walked beside her, trying to find something to say, trying to offer some hope. "We'll get out of this, mama. I swear I'll get us out somehow."

Swallowing more water, Solah said nothing, her eyes dull. The man ahead jerked on his chain to keep her from lagging, and Caroline said, "Don't!"

He was big and blueblack, bare-chested and barefoot, a ragged pair of pants tied about his narrow waist with a piece of rope. Glaring around at her, he said, "She draggin' on me."

In rapid Ashanti, Caroline said, "My mother is tired and ill. You are young and strong."

57

This one responded in the same language, but awkwardly. "I am not Ashanti, but Mandingo."

"Care for my mother," Caroline said, "and I will try to help you, also."

The horse came up behind and nudged Caroline up the road. From its back Ned Barker said, "Git your ass back to the wagon, mustee. Kleppner never said you was to trifle with the niggers. Now git!"

At the wagon, Bobo didn't reach down a hand to help her up. Climbing to the seat, Caroline started to return the water gourd to its place, but the driver said, "Best not. Marse find out niggers been drinkin' from that, he whup ass good."

When she stared at him in disbelief, he mumbled, "White man diddle a wench, that be one thing, but he don't drink after one, nor eat out'n the same bowl. Where you been, gal—you don't *know* how to act?"

"Free," Caroline said. "I've been free, and will be again."

"Got you a heap to learn," Bobo said. "Lucky you mustee and diddlin' Marse, else you be chained up, too. No sense talkin' about free, account of Marse beat that out'n you right fast. You just like all us niggers now; you a slave, and does like they tells you."

The wagon jounced and Caroline felt blood rush to her face. "He raped me," she said.

"Just what I means," Bobo said. "Us got no choosin', and quicker you learns it, more trouble you saves."

Settling back, Caroline tried to think the problem through. If she could get Solah loose in the night, they might lose themselves in the forest, but now there were no papers, no money; even their food and bedding had been taken. Without some way to catch fish, make fire and trap game, they would perish. Still, there had to be a way, and Caroline was determined to find it.

Just before sundown, Kleppner stopped in a grassy field beside a creek, swinging his hat as a signal for the cavvy to camp there. Caroline sat stiffly in the wagon as Bobo scurried around to collect wood for the cookfire. The cavvy sagged to earth, chains rattling.

There was a lock at each end, she saw, big iron locks that seemed impossible to break. Kleppner would carry the keys.

He came riding up and put those eyes on her, eyes so like a snake's. "Help Bobo cook," he said, "and clean up after. Wash yourself in the creek, 'cause I don't cotton to nigger musk."

Swinging down from his horse, Delkin said, "You ain't goin' to share her none?"

"Not this'n," Kleppner grinned. "You boys make do with them wenches, try out the high yeller, but keep distance from this here mustee. I don't want no bite marks on her tits nor gouges in her pretty rump. Spoil the price when I go to sell her."

Delkin rubbed a sleeve across his red and sweaty face. "She humps anywhere near good as she looks, damned if I wouldn't hold onto her."

"Humps like a bitch dog in full heat," Kleppner chuckled. "Can't get enough pizzle to suit her. But pussy grows every day, and cash money sure as hell don't. Time I get her to N'Awlins, she'll know every trick ever was."

They were talking around her, through her, as if she weren't there or couldn't understand the language. Jaws tight and face flushed, she moved quickly to help Bobo prepare a huge iron pot of mush, then passed among the chained slaves handing out gourd bowls of the gruel. She smelled meat frying, but that was for the whites.

Bobo whispered, "All we gets, cornmeal with a speck of lard to it, but Marse'll stop a spell and fatten up the cavvy afore he sells. Sometimes they leaves me scraps, and I picks some greens."

"But how can they walk all day, on food like this?"

Bobo wrinkled his forehead at her. "You ain't listened what I told you. Nobody got a choosin'; nigger falls, ol' Barker pops him with the whip. Nigger cotches swamp fever, gits cut out'n the cavvy and left ahint for buzzards to fight over."

"Mustee," Kleppner bellowed then. "Come on over here!"

When she stood next to the fire, he tossed a greasy bone to her. "Suck on that, missy; give you strength and good practice."

The other men laughed, and Caroline let the bone fall to the ground. "I'm not a dog."

Kleppner's scarred mouth curled. "You whatever I say. And I say shuck out'n that dress so the boys kin see what they missin'. All that sweet meat'll make 'em get it up fast, and every one of them wenches kin be sold guaranteed to be carryin' pickaninnies in they bellies, whelps with human blood in 'em."

Trembling, Caroline said, "You—you can't mean for me to stand nude before these—"

"Damn," Kleppner chortled, "don't she talk plumb fancy? But I reckon she don't hear too good, or maybe needs some help." He stood up, blacksnake whip in his hand, and before Caroline could move, the tip of the lash ripped her thin dress halfway down the front.

She tried to cover her exposed breasts, and Kleppner stroked the whip again, two lightning slashes that peeled away the remainder of her clothing.

"You sompin' else with that there whip," Ned Barker said. "Lookee yonder—never raised a mark on her hide."

"Ain't lookin' at her hide," Delkin said huskily. "Just at them high nipples and that shiny young quim."

Kleppner recoiled his whip. "Git on to the creek and wash."

Numbly, glad to cover her nakedness even momentarily, Caroline hurried into the water and crouched there.

Ned Barker said, "Believe you *did* tetch her with the lash, on the left cheek of her rump. Seen a mark there."

"She come with it. Damn if it don't look like some red bug crawlin' on her," Kleppner answered. "Onliest flaw on her skin; seen it when I put it to her back in the woods and popped her cherry. Never raised a mark with this blacksnake I didn't mean to raise."

"Pass on them keys," Delkin said. "Lookin' at the

60

mustee is raisin' this here pole atwixt my legs. Got tc grease it with a wench."

"You goin' to try the high yeller?" Ned Barker asked.

"Don't look pert to me, and she's some long in the tooth."

"Still and all," Barker mused, "she's lighter'n them others. Scrub her down good, might be worth diddlin'. 'Sides, I done stuck the rest of 'em."

Shuddering in the water, Caroline closed her eyes against the horror of it. They were talking about Solah, and one of them would rape her tonight, force himself upon a woman whose husband had so recently been killed by their kind. Before, Caroline had only been puzzled by the color of her skin; now she hated to identify herself with animals like these.

But they didn't consider her white. A single droplet of black blood, and their vaunted racial purity was swept away. Could black blood be so powerful, then, or did they simply fear it so much?

She had nothing to wear, no shred of clothing to hide her naked body. Wringing her hair with both hands and weaving it into loose, damp braids down her back, Caroline stepped from the creek with her head high, determined to show no shame, to give them nothing to jeer at. Bobo looked away as she approached the wagon, but her eyes caught movement where the cavvy lay in its chains. The big Mandingo was sitting erect, staring at her. Somehow that made it worse, and she hurried into the back of the wagon, glad for the hoop of canvas that sheltered her.

Stretched upon blankets, Kleppner cradled an earthenware jug of whiskey. She didn't see the pistols, but the whip was close at hand. He said, "You be a sight for a man's eyes. Wasn't wenches to hand for my riders, I'da never showed you off to 'em. Woulda had to kill 'em, they couldn't dip their wicks after seein' you stripped down."

She felt cold. "Do you mean for me to ride the wagon tomorrow like this?"

"Hell, no. There be wench dresses in the pack

yonder; pick you out two or three. Crawl on over here and have a drink."

Caroline wished she could get away from his eyes. She might as well wish to be free. She said, "I never tasted that."

"Time you did."

The look of him, the set of that long-jawed face told her she'd better obey quickly. Steeling herself, she kneeled beside him, one bare thigh touching his hip, and accepted the tin cup. Kleppner drew a finger-tip lingeringly over her haunch. "How you get that scar?"

"It's—it's a birthmark," she answered, nostrils flaring at the pungent odor of raw whiskey.

"Looks kinda' like a scorpion with his stinger raised up." He laughed. "Only *I* got the stinger. Lookee here at my stinger, missy."

She drank hastily, and felt as if she were strangling when the bite of the stuff jolted her stomach and cut off her breath. She coughed and panted for air as Kleppner snickered.

"Don't know how your black mammy kept you hid out all them years," he said, drinking from the mouth of the jug, "but I'm beholden for it. Now I get all kinds of cherry out'n you—first time you had a man atween them fine legs, first time you take a drink, and pretty soon, I got some more first times for you."

She felt the whiskey warmth spreading in her belly, and forced herself not to draw away when he ran one hand up and down her thigh, when he propped himself on an elbow to take a nipple between his teeth. Would it happen again? Could she be so abandoned, so shameless? Caroline hoped not, and as he caressed her, she tried not to think of what was ahead, tried not to think of what was happening to Solah.

Kleppner kicked off his boots and dropped back to remove his trousers. She said, "May I have some—some more whiskey?"

"Git it yourself. Damned if'n you don't learn quick as a cat. Man gets his pizzle in you and you give him a ride like you been well broke. Take a sup of corn,

62

and you go after it like a bar whore. Just remember, I ain't one to feed likker to niggers as a rule; makes 'em flat out crazy. But as you special to me, I treat you middlin' good."

This time she didn't cough as much and it wasn't as difficult catching her breath. When he told her to straddle him, to climb on top of his furry body. Caroline's head was spinning and her flesh was gently numbed; whiskey had its uses.

There was no pain, only the strong, quick entrance. His fingernails digging into her soft buttocks forced her to wriggle, and his teeth worried at her breasts so that she winced and struggled. That seemed to delight him, but inside her head she kept repeating that she would not let go all reason, that she would hold herself and be her own woman.

But when his breath quickened, so did hers. When he pounded up at her, Caroline's traitor hips pushed back violently; then she was trying to destroy him, to grind off his thing, to batter his pelvis and hurt him, hurt him.

"Mustee bitch!" Kleppner grated. "Take it, take it —*uhh!*"

The same madness unleashed itself within her, its wild edges cutting into her soul and ripping apart her self-respect. Moaning low in her throat, she collapsed in a shuddering heap atop him.

Rolling her off, Kleppner reached for the jug. "Niggers is better'n any white woman for diddlin'. Here, gal—take you a swallow and I'll show you somethin' else."

If she had thought him cruel before, Caroline learned what true torture was that night. She did not fight him; she accepted and obeyed, though every nerve in her body cried outrage. And when he had done all the things to her, when she had performed like the animal he considered her to be, Kleppner was finally, blessedly drained, and lay snoring upon the tumbled blankets.

Carefully, Caroline moved away from him and put her head over the tailgate to be quietly sick. Then she lay beside him and listened to the dying crackle of the cookfire, the subdued clank of chains when a slave turned uneasily. The candles guttered out, and still she lay with open eyes, staring up at nothing. This, she repeated again and again, was what lay ahead of her, night after night until she could escape.

Solah—she dared not think of her mama, so she pressed both hands to her aching breasts and concentrated on hating Kleppner. If her mother hadn't been chained out there like a beast, Caroline might have found a way to kill the thing that slumbered beside her.

Chapter 8

In the dawn, Jubal Blaze led his silent band of woodsmen through the brush, not yet believing their luck. If it was true that Red Eagle was fool enough to quit slipping around and fighting like an Indian, if he'd forted up with his back to the river, the renegade chief and his Creeks were trapped.

Using his rifle barrel to part frosted pine saplings, Jubal sank to one knee and peered ahead. Sure enough, there was the fort Crockett had reported, no more than a mound of logs and mud across the narrow neck of the peninsula. Horseshoe Bend, white men called this spit of land formed by a curious bend in the Tallapoosa River. To Jubal's mind, it was about a hundred acres of nothing, though the Creeks claimed it to be holy land, earth so sacred no white man could set foot on it and live.

Jubal saw movement on the low parapet ahead. He wagered far more redskins than whites would fall this day, for all that divine protection of savage gods. Andy Jackson had troops yonder behind the Indian town, ready for those who tried to get away in the canoes lined snug under the riverbank.

At his ear, Willy Barton whispered, "Cap'n, there's a heap of 'em stirrin' yonder."

"And a rifle ball for every one," Jubal murmured. "Slide on back, Willy, and wait for the signal."

According to Crockett and his scouts, there were about eight hundred warriors behind those breastworks, with near half as many squaws and younguns; a goodly nest of Indians, truth to tell. But Jackson had picked up a passel of Alabama Territory volunteers with a score to settle, lean, hard-eyed farmers who looked as good as Tennessee riflemen.

A musket ball for every Creek, Jubal thought, and hoped it was so, but the shortage of good flints fretted him more. Andy Jackson, fevered and light in the head from his tavern wound, had left Tennessee too quickly to be careful about supplies, and Jubal suspected how low provisions were. If the Creeks weren't smashed here, they could chase Indians through these cold, dark woods for months, and might even have to go back without getting the job done. Old Andy would be some put out, not able to go on to New Orleans for a set-to with the Redcoats, or mayhap to clear the Spanish out of the Floridas.

Rattling through the trees, a war whoop broke shrill around Jubal, and a rifle ball cut leaves from an overhead limb. "Well now," he said, and laid his sights on a bobbing feathered head. Musket fire thundered all around him, and a rolling cloud of gunsmoke wafted through the trees. The Creeks had been surprised, Jubal thought, as he poured powder, patched and tamped the ball, dusted the pan with more powder and cocked the flint. But they were coming just the same, mad as a nest of stirred-up yellowjackets and just as ornery.

Getting off a shot that whipped a big brave around with a hole in his chest, Jubal rose to meet the charge of another, clubbing with his musket butt. That one went down with a broken head, and things got all mixed up, what with the whooping and hollering, the smoke and the firing. He was at the breastworks with his skinning knife bloody in one big fist when Sam Houston limped to the top, an arrow sticking out of his hip. He had a dragoon pistol in each hand and he was yelling for everybody to come on, come on.

When Jubal climbed up, bullets and arrows flicking all around, he saw Sam Houston take a ball, and another, but the man staggered on until he toppled over, still hollering.

Belly to belly with a greasy warrior, Jubal didn't have time to look around anymore. Rolling on the ground, he got a knee into the redskin's crotch and made the slippery bastard turn loose long enough to cut his throat. Panting hard, Jubal reloaded on one bent knee, fired and reloaded, over and over again, while the Creeks were driven back from their shabby fort and toward the river.

Somebody bellowed in Jubal's ear, but the man's face was so black with powdersmoke Jubal didn't know who the hell it was. It didn't matter much, anyhow; they moved together across a field and into the trees, more Tennesseans at their backs. There was more hard times amongst the loblolly pines, with Creeks apopping out from ahint every sapling, but pretty soon the Indians faded back some more, and Jubal's men got to rest a spell.

Willy Barton got laid out, somebody said, and a few more, but they quit thinking about their dead when guns sounded beyond the line of woods.

"Reckon Andy's shootin' up them canoes," Jubal said.

"More fools, them," a strange young man said, "boxin' theirselfs up thisaway. Goin' to be a turkey shoot now."

Wiping at his face and taking a drink from his water gourd, Jubal said, "You Alabama?"

The boy nodded. "From over to West Bend; my paw just got kilt back yonder." Then he got up and walked toward the firing, musket at the ready and a dripping knife in his belt.

Jubal stretched his big frame. "Won't be many Creeks left, time Alabama younguns like that 'un gets in their licks."

"Be none atall," somebody else said. "They ain't forgot Fort Mims by a damn sight."

Climbing up, they went to join the slaughter, for that's what the battle had become, like hog killing time —so much blood and entrails, Creeks being knocked in the head, getting strung up by their heels, gutted like so many fat shoats, only there was no use for this meat.

A few warriors tried to fight, but were swarmed over; most slid into the river like muskrats, where their bobbing heads made good targets for the riflemen gathered on both shores.

The Indian town was burning, the air heavy and clotted with the stench of burning fur and charred flesh. Jubal could hear younguns snuffling, and moved around to see a few squaws and children huddled in a tight and mournful bunch. Some of the men were picking at them, jabbing them with gun muzzles.

As Jubal approached, the Alabama boy said, "Ain't no call for that," and one of the Tennessee volunteers answered, "Pop the nits and they don't hatch into lice."

"We ain't Injuns," the boy said. "Some of us acts like white men."

The mountain man glared. "What you mean by that, boy?"

Putting one hand to his gory skinning knife, the boy said, "Any goddamn thing you want it to mean."

Jubal came between them. "The boy's right. It ain't fitten to war on women. Smith. Youngblood—stand guard around this passel till Andy says what to do with 'em."

One woman caught his attention because she stood straight and slim, her chin up and unafraid. Snapping black eyes stared back at him, and he noticed no papoose clung to her. In soft deerskins, she was young and comely, and more than one man licked his lips over the sight of her.

Jubal found Colonel Coffee first, who told him Jackson was across the river, madder than a bull hornet because Red Eagle hadn't been killed or even found. The squaws and younguns?

"Keep them safe," the colonel said. "Andy's always been a mite particular about womenfolks, be they red or white."

"Saw Sam Houston fall," Jubal said.

"Tougher'n whang leather," Coffee said. "Got them holes plugged up and hollerin' for action. Lost us some other good men, though."

68

"I know," Jubal said and turned away. He hadn't realized he was so bone weary; his knees were shaky, and he had a chunk out of his left arm and a cut across his right cheek. He could taste the leftover tang of burned powder, and other things better off not fired. He rinsed his mouth and spat to clear it, but the stink stayed in his nostrils.

Down by his company, he came across the Alabama boy again, straddling a fine horse that jiggled and blew at the dead man hung across its withers. "Takin' Pa home," the boy said. "We're done here."

Jubal rubbed his chin. "You wouldn't want to come on down to N'Awlins with us?"

"Fit this here war 'cause we had to," the boy said. "Warn't no quiltin' bee, neither. I figure my next war got to come *to* me; I sure as billy hell ain't goin' alookin' for it."

"Reckon you're right," Jubal said, and watched the horse sidestep away. There rode a stubborn lad carryin' a heavy load, toting his daddy's corpse halfway across Alabama Territory, instead of burying him here with the other fallen. But Jubal understood; the dead man was going home, and it was right a man be laid to rest in his own ground, not beholden to anybody else for his grave.

Easing off his ripped buckskin shirt, Jubal squatted by a clay pot and used its water to cleanse his wounds, to wash his face and upper body. When he looked up, the Creek woman was watching him, those black eyes burning into his bare hide. The other prisoners crouched together, touching each other in silent, miserable support. But the woman stood full height, which wasn't all that much, and just as proud as if her tribe had won the fight, instead of being wiped out.

She had a special kind of face, Jubal thought, high at the cheekbones, full in the mouth and a flare to fine nostrils; her eyes kind of tilted up at the corners, and the hair falling down her straight back was dark and shiny as a crow's wing.

One of the boys brought Jubal a smear of cobwebs to rub into the arm a tomahawk had nicked and the thin knife slash across his cheek, and Jubal thanked him kindly. The woman kept watching. like he was the only man around, and Jubal thought her own man must be lying dead somewhere close by.

Nobody would bury the Creek warriors; they'd be stripped of any valuables and left for the buzzards. At least, Jubal thought, *we're* not lopping off scalps nor sawing away privates and stuffing them into dead mouths. Was the shoe on the other foot, those red younguns and squaws would be mutilating corpses, laughing and carrying on all the while. And the slim girl would be right amongst them, those pretty rounded arms stained clear to the elbows.

When Jubal got his shirt back on, Major Benton was close by, looking a mite too clean to have been in the thick of the fight, and pointing his narrow chin toward the captives. "Was I Jackson, every one'd be strung up to tall pines."

"Ain't but one Andy Jackson," Jubal said. "Only one he-coon; nobody else."

"Oh," Benton said, "he's in command, all right; no denying that. But going up against the King's trained soldiers will be some different from running over a bunch of ignorant savages."

Jubal didn't give a damn for Major Benton and never had, even before that sneaky mess at the tavern where Jackson got hurt. Benton and his ilk were too much like the Tories Jubal's grandpa helped run out of the country in another war—fancy planters too uppity for them as didn't have so much land and education.

"We done all right afore," he said.

Benton flicked dust from the toe of his boot with the feathered end of a riding crop. "With more luck than was our due, and never forgiven by the British. They would like this country back in the fold."

Moving away from the major. Jubal said, "What some folks won't understand is we ain't sheep, nor shoats to be herded, but free men."

"Some free men," Benton said as he strode off,

"but more are a dependent rabble, ready to desert if anything doesn't suit them."

Jubal's walk brought him close to the Creek captives. Trying not to stare back at the woman there, he said to Micah Youngblood, "Anybody give 'em water?"

Youngblood shook his head and spat. "Nor a fancy tea, neither. One's right pert-lookin', but little doubt a-crawlin' with fleas and lice, too. They do say Injun lice makes a white man sick."

Passing on, Jubal felt the eyes on him like black augers boring deep under his skin. He found a water gourd and brought it back, his feet somehow reluctant.

"Cap'n or no," Youngblood grunted, "if you aim to mollycoddle this bunch, best you stand guard, too." And he stomped off while Jubal grinned after him. "One of the rabble," Major Benton would claim, a hill man who didn't take to yessirs and shiny boots and such. But Micah Youngblood could knock the head off a running squirrel at twenty paces, even if he couldn't scratch out his name, and when powder got burned, Jubal would a heap rather have Micah at his side.

Across the squatting group, Jamison Smith said, "You ever hear that tale afore, cap'n—about Injun lice?"

Jubal held out the water gourd to a shriveled old woman. "Can't say as I have."

Smith laughed. "Me, neither; told it to Micah so's he wouldn't lay hand to yon saucy wench and oblige me to knock him in the head."

The old woman snatched the gourd and drank greedily. She'd have kept the water to herself if Jubal didn't take it back. The young, arrogant one was close, so near he could almost feel the savage heat of her. He offered the bottle, locking eyes with her, noting the lift of hard young breasts beneath the soft deerskin jacket marked by bright beads and hung with blunted quills.

"No," she said, jolting him to the marrow by her use of English. "Give it to the little ones."

Hurriedly, he passed on the gourd and backed off a few paces. There was a curious singing quality to her voice, and never a trace of fear; what was it then—a challenge? Jubal dug about in his pouch and found tobacco and his small clay pipe. Turned awkward, his fingers fumbled with flint and steel, but finally got the pipe going.

What was he thinking of? This was no white woman, though her skin was no darker than some he had uncovered beneath a bodice. She was a Creek, a savage closer in kind to the nappy-headed slaves on his own plantation, and he'd never had the stomach to bed even a light-colored wench there.

But she spoke English.

Sucking on his pipestem, he hid his face behind smoke and put his errant mind to wondering when Jackson would send rations, and what was to be done with these prisoners. Like as not, old Andy would toll off a man or two—them most anxious to get home— and march the Indians off somewhere, maybe clear on back to Tennessee, as proof of his victory.

Was it legal to sell Indians into slavery? Jubal didn't know, but it was said they made poor workers and ran off at first chance. Niggers took to the yoke, but Indians didn't. Jubal wished to hell the girl would find somewheres else to put her eyes. What did she want from him, to be turned loose in the forest? He couldn't rightly do that, even if he had a mind to.

He said, "Your chief, Red Eagle, hid himself real good."

The small nostrils flared more; her mouth was damp and shiny. "He was not here, or the battle would have gone another way."

She talked like a tiny mockingbird was caught in her smooth throat, he thought, accenting words a touch wrong, a mite foreign, but a man missed most of that, trying to put a name to the tune she made.

"He was a fool," Jubal said, "to let his white blood rule, and fort up here."

Surprisingly, she said, "Yes, he was a fool."

Jamison Smith said, "Now ain't that a pure wonder, Injun squaw talkin' good as arv city lady?"

"She ain't," Jubal said shortly, and turned his back

to her. The others were stunned by defeat, bewildered at the failure of their holy ground. This one wasn't. Why didn't she run for it, take to the trees? Could be, he thought, none of them had anywhere to go. Their town was burned, and the Creek nation broken with the bodies of all its young men.

His arm pained some, and he made a poultice of chewed tobacco and patted it on the slash; good, honest rum would be better, but if he had some, he'd treat the inside of him with it.

Jackson was busy elsewhere, but Crockett's scouts rounded up victuals from Indian stores, smoked meat and fish that went down right good, corn and winter squash the men gobbled hungrily. Jubal saw to it the captives were fed, too, and this time the woman accepted, sitting erect on her knees instead of squatting like the others. He tried to keep from watching her, but his eyes drifted back time and again.

Busying himself at campfires, and seeing that the wounded of his company were tended, Jubal stayed away from her as long as he could. When night fell and there was no sign of troops being moved, he rounded up skins and blankets for the Creeks, so they wouldn't freeze solid before daylight. Jubal found a well-tanned pair of bearhides for himself, too, and snugged down into their hairy comfort. Taking their job seriously, Tennessee men guarded the Indians, but Jubal figured the long, wearying march and the fight had taken a lot out of his men and they'd be hard put to prop open their eyes.

His own lids were heavy and gritty, but no matter how often he changed positions, he couldn't sleep. The fire danced eerie lights; overhead the stars blinked mysteriously in a clear sky. Dream, Jubal commanded himself; dream of the Carolinas and cotton spreading snowy bolls, of good friends and neighbors, and certain neighborly wives with soft and yielding flesh. . . .

There was hardly a stir when she slipped into his bearskins, only a feathersoft movement, a warm touching that was dreamlike. Jubal wasn't certain he was awake, but when he turned to find the sleek,

73

naked body pressing against him, he came alert in every inch of his big, startled body.

Against the shell of a tiny ear, he whispered, "How did you—the guards—"

"They sleep," the answer came leafstir soft. "But I could not. I am Chela."

"Hell—" he said, and her hot mouth covered his own, its honeysweet tongue darting like a feeding minnow. Her hands were bold on his body, more demanding than caressing. and Jubal wasn't used to that. The women back home didn't reach out for a man's rod and hold it so fiercely. but this beautiful savage went at it greedily, and he was caught up in the raging wildfire of her.

Stiffly vibrant nipples dug into his chest, and her legs wound around him, supple and strong and tapered. Jubal cupped her, fingered over the wondrous shapings of her firm flesh and drank the spiced hotness of her gasping breath. Furiously then. she guided him into her, made him her captive, bound him with enchanted claspings of silken wet velvets, and he gladly surrendered.

She was the rushing summertime river, drawing him into swirling unknown depths. tumbling him, rolling him so that he had to cling desperately to her. But he was also powerful, and began to meet every twisting lunge with a penetrating strength of his own, until he found the whitehot, bubbling core of her. It devoured him. touched him off like gunpowder, and left him stunned in the mighty explosion.

Drained, he lay quietly. arms around a slim waist, hands filled with small melon haunches. Against his throat she murmured, "You are a great warrior. You met him chest to chest."

"Him?" Jubal muttered drowsily.

Chela's magic body wriggled against him, her hands stroking his upper arms. "Deer Runner; you brought him down in the dust. As I watched. you cut his throat."

"Cut more'n one throat during the fight." he said, reveling in the inner texture of her flesh. "Didn't get proper introduced to any of 'em."

Her breasts were lifted to his cheek as she straddled him, and Jubal knew a moment of great sadness when his manhood left the narrow cave of her. "This one you will remember," Chela promised, "as I will remember him. Deer Runner was my man."

Only a sudden movement warned him, and Jubal rolled aside and tried to throw her off him. Cold steel hissed into the bearskin an inch from his throat. Blindly, he caught at her wrist, and gasped at the shock of her knee jerked up into his privates. Heaving, he threw her away in a tangle of robes. and she came spitting to hands and knees in the dull glow of a dying campfire.

"My own goddamn skinnin' knife," he said. "Meant to open me up with it."

A guard shifted and raised his head. Chela sprang to her feet, and with a final. venomous glare, wheeled to dart naked into the forest. Jubal's rifle was at his shoulder, but he lowered it and shook his head.

The guard shook himself awake. "S'matter, cap'n?"

"Nothin'," Jubal said. "Got bedded down with a catamount, I reckon."

The man stared. "Panther in here? I never—"

"I never, either," Jubal said, "and damned if I ever will again."

Chapter 9

Caroline ran a slow, teasing finger down Kleppner's hairy chest. He grinned up at her. "Never get you a better teacher, gal. Learned you real fast, didn't I?"

There was a bitter truth to that, which she didn't want to think about, so she said, "My mother, Solah. Do you have to keep her chained up with the others? I'm sure she won't run away, as long as I'm here."

He pinched her bare nipple. "And *you* ain't about to scoot long as she's safe locked up. Anyhow, the boys wouldn't take to me lettin' their newest pussy get away from 'em. From what they say, though, she just ain't all that much. Light skin helps, and bein' as how she ain't so musky, but your ma don't do it like you do."

"I—I could take her some more stew," Caroline said. "She's really not well. She can have part of my ration." She forced herself not to flinch as his fingers tightened around her breast. "You know I can be very good to you."

He grunted and came up on one elbow to reach for a bottle. "If'n you mean to bargain, you got nothin' to trade. You ain't good to me, I take the whip to your ass, but not hard enough to mark you up permanent. But we got plenty of rations, and if that Solah wench is ailin', I'd as soon not lose her. Go tend her, but lookee here now—them boys of mine, they put a hand to you, squall loud and I'll come arunnin'. Mustee wench like you, you're plumb valuable, and I don't mean to see you boggered up none."

76

Kleppner's hand was almost gentle upon her thigh as she slid away from him, and Caroline wondered if there was more to his warning, something beyond having his property marred. But no, he meant to sell her in New Orleans for a good price. There was no good, no love in him. God, how she hated the man, but no more than she hated herself for responding to his insatiable lusts.

Stopping at the cookpot, she filled a gourd with rich stew and took another stoppered gourd of water, a bit of rag. The guards watched her like so many waiting wolves as she passed along the chained cavvy. There the big Mandingo flashed sullen eyes up at her and turned away with a rattle of chains.

"Mother," she said in Ashanti, "I am here. Sit up, so I may feed and clean you."

Dully, Solah blinked at her. "I have prayed to black gods and to the white one, but I am still alive."

Spooning hearty soup into her mother's lax mouth, Caroline said, "Stay alive for me. I cannot do without you."

Solah swallowed and mumbled; there was an odd cast to her face. She said, "As I cannot do without M'Nele."

Feigning anger, Caroline said, "My father gave his life so you and I might live. Will you throw that great gift into the face of his spirit? M'Nele meant us to *live*."

Solah took more food, and slowly straightened her back. "You are right, my daughter. I will survive, then, and when I am stronger, there is a thing you must know."

"In time, my mother," Caroline said, sponging road dust from her mother's face and arms, "in good time. Eat well and strengthen your spirit. I will speak to the slave trader again, and perhaps we may stay together."

"A cruel man," Solah said. "He has hurt you."

"A little," Caroline admitted, "but nothing to an Ashanti. Someday I will spit upon him and his cruelty."

77

Solah managed a tired smile. "My true little Ashanti; I am shamed to have forgotten my own blood."

"You only slept," Caroline said. "Now you are awake again."

Taking the damp cloth, Solah wiped her face. "I cannot eat more."

"Tomorrow, then." Caroline leaned to kiss her mother's cheek. "Sleep well and dream of freedom."

When she rose with the remaining food and water, the Mandingo buck rolled over again, muffling the noise of his shackles in wide hands. "Freedom," he said in his halting Ashanti, "is only for sluts with white blood."

Angered, she hissed at him: "Fool! I am more bound than you. If I am a slut, *your* mother lay with an ape." Without realizing why, she thrust the rest of the stew at him. "Close your mouth with this, Mandingo."

His hand trembled up, then drew back. "I take no gift from whites."

"My heart is Ashanti," she said. "*I* am Ashanti. If you would be free, eat for strength, or die as a weakling; I care not."

A white guard laughed near the fire; the Mandingo took the gourd and gobbled quickly. "Tchaka thanks you, woman."

"Hey," a voice called from too close by, "you lollygaggin' around with them niggers. Don't ol' Kleppner give you enough every night?"

Caroline turned quickly and marched toward Ned Barker, thinking how strange it was that they all looked alike, all lean and rangy men with flat, pale eyes and scraggly beards. "He said I could care for my mother."

She started past him, but Barker's hand closed upon her arm. "He didn't say for you to play up to no buck. Ain't Kleppner hung big enough for you?"

"Let me go," Caroline said.

Barker held her arm, his fingers digging into her flesh. His other hand suddenly cupped her breast, and his breath was warm upon her face. "Damn, but you one fine piece of meat," he muttered. "It just ain't right, him keepin' you all to hisself, when you got plenty for everybody."

Catching her breath, Caroline said, "Please—"

The hand roamed over her hip, her belly, and darted suddenly, painfully, between her thighs. A stubbled mouth sought her own, stifling the cry that rose in her throat. She struggled, conscious of black eyes watching, of the man called Delkin rising from his place beside the campfire and trotting toward them.

" 'Bout time," Delkin grunted. "Throw her down and put it to her, Ned. I'll take my turn soon's you done. Kleppner's sleepin', and if this bitch so much as hollers, I'll twist her head off."

Her skirt was flung up, and Caroline shivered, her throat pulsing against the grimy hand that clutched it threateningly. Dewy grass was chill against her bared flesh as she writhed helplessly upon the ground, every fiber of her being crying out mutely against this added degradation, against being taken while the chained blacks watched, her mother among them.

Barker was between her legs, grunting, forcing himself into her. Delkin held her flat, his hand clamped about her neck. Caroline closed her eyes, shocked and sick and hating.

A full-throated roar broke around them, a bellowing, animal cry. The shriek of savage outrage echoed through the field, across the fire and into the wagon.

Barker's head jerked up. "What the hell—"

"Goddamn nigger squallin'," Delkin grated. "Beat his ass to a pulp."

"Shit," Barker said, rolling away from Caroline and dragging up his pants, "that's certain sure to wake Kleppner."

" 'Bout time we braced him then," Delkin said, fumbling at his belt. "Keepin' all this saucy tail for hisself. 'Share and share alike,' he said. till this wench come along." He brought out a pistol and cocked it.

"Ain't got my gun," Barker panted. "Yonder by the fire." He scuttled to the ring of light.

Rolling away from Delkin. Caroline pulled down her dress, her heart racing. She saw Kleppner leap from the wagon, saw the lightning flick of the bullwhip that coiled about Barker's neck and jerked the running man from his feet.

Delkin leveled his pistol and fired, but the ball passed harmlessly through the canvas wagon top, and Kleppner ducked away before the second barrel could be aimed at him. Barker kicked upon the ground, hands tearing at the whip that was choking life from him. At last, ripping the lash free, he sat up and pawed his throat, head wagging from side to side. A shot rang out, and Ned Barker jumped, then turned slowly upon his knees and tried to get up. When he fell over, his head was almost in the fire.

"Jesus," Delkin breathed, and began to back away, pistol muzzle wavering here and there. "Wench, c'mere —*here,* damn you!" Jerking Caroline to her feet, he used her body as a shield. "Kleppner! You better hear me, Kleppner! I got your prime wench, and I'll for sure blow a hole in her if'n you don't back off."

There was no answer from Kleppner, no sight of him around the wagon, and Caroline felt Delkin's arm tighten about her waist. He backed a step, then another. "Kleppner—the wench teased us, begged us to diddle her. You already got poor Ned, so call it even. Damnit, you need help gettin' this cavvy to market— Kleppner?"

Hissing, he said to Caroline, "He's circlin' us; thinks I won't knock you in the head, but one nigger's the same as t'other to me, white-lookin' or no." Raising his voice, he called out, "Last chance, Kleppner! If'n you don't show yourself, she's dog meat."

Caroline's ears caught the muffled rattle of chains behind them, and she clutched Delkin's gun arm as he swung around. The looming shadow struck quickly, silently, and Delkin dropped away from her. Caroline had his pistol then, held it uncertainly in a trembling hand. She stared at the big Mandingo as he settled back to earth, becoming again only another frightened and faceless animal.

"Damn if'n you didn't drop him your own self," Kleppner said at her shoulder, and reached to snatch the pistol from her hand. "You wasn't a mustee, I'd tell you go ahead and kill him and be done with it. But lowdown as Delkin is, he's a white man."

Kleppner kicked the fallen man in the side. "Git up, you bastard. You got a grave to dig."

Stunned, Delkin wobbled to one knee and held his head in both hands. "What—what you aim to do to me?"

"Like you said," Kleppner grunted, "I need help with the cavvy, but I reckon you kin work as good chained up on your horse."

Rubbing the side of his bruised face, Delkin said, "Chained up like a nigger?"

"That," Kleppner said, "or dig a hole for your own self next to Barker."

Wobbling to his feet, Delkin tried to focus on Caroline. "N-never saw what she hit me with. Hell; you don't have to fret none over me and her no more. I'd sooner diddle a cottonmouth moccasin."

Kleppner pushed the man ahead with his pistol muzzle, jerked his head to Caroline to follow. "Won't fret atall, with you locked safe."

Caroline hesitated, tried to find the Mandingo's eyes in the dark, and realized she should not endanger him by showing her gratitude. She was certain it had been Tchaka's cry that wakened Kleppner and saved her body, certain the swift blow that probably saved her life had been his. She owed him, owed more than a gourd of stew or thankful words, but now she must follow the man who called himself their master.

She glanced once at the corpse beside the fire, the ugly, twisted stillness of it. Shuddering, Caroline could hardly believe that Ned Barker had been between her spread legs but moments before, alive and lusting. He deserved to die, she told herself; any slaver did, but she could not gloat over the body. When Delkin dragged it away by the heels, Kleppner close by with his whip in one hand and a pistol in the other, she climbed up into the wagon and wrapped her arms about her knees. It took a while for the shaking to stop.

From the front seat beyond the canvas where the old driver often slept, Bobo said softly, "Lawd gawd; he gon call me for to chain up Mist' Delkin. Can't say no, but when Mist' Delkin get loose, he kill me for sure."

"Shut up," Caroline said. "Try to be a man."

"Ain't no Africky nigger," Bobo mumbled, "ain't chained up like one neither."

Finding the earthen jug, Caroline took a cautious sip of raw whiskey to clear her head. True, Bobo wasn't manacled, and neither was she. Now only one other man walked without chains—Kleppner himself. Only Kleppner was armed. She took another taste of corn liquor and put the stopper back into the jug as excitement raced through her.

There would be no better time; Kleppner could not stay awake day and night, and when he nodded off— freedom for Solah and herself, for Tchaka and Mandingo, for all the chained blacks. Squeezing her damp hands together, she tried to remember where Kleppner hid the keys to the great padlocks, wondering what she might have to do to get them.

She had to get hold of Kleppner's pistols, his whip, too. And if he came awake suddenly—Caroline took a deep breath—could she shoot him? Her lips tightened. She could and would, if it meant not being owned, not being used as a whore.

Bobo and some of the spiritless ones would have no idea where to go, or what to do with their freedom, but Tchaka might. He was young and strong; he could make his way north to a new way of life. Caroline moved carefully upon her knees, feeling beneath quilts and peeping into boxes as she searched for the keys.

The gold coins; she would get them back. With money, she could do almost anything—pretend to be Solah's white mistress, get them passage to a safe place. Their papers had been destroyed, but that could be overcome. The keys; she *had* to know where Kleppner kept them.

She heard him call to Bobo, heard the old driver clamber down to hammer manacles around Delkin's wrists, and scooted back to sit upon the tailgate of the wagon.

"Them niggers hates you much as me," Kleppner said, "so I'm keepin' you apart from 'em. Locked to that singletree, you ain't apt to creep up on me, neither. Do your ownself good, was you to keep an eye out."

Delkin whined, "How kin I ride thisaway? And do we run up on Injuns, me without no gun—"

"You're lookout," Kleppner said shortly. "You'da kilt me over a mustee wench, so I'll tell you—best chance for you to stay alive is keep me alive. I go down, and them nigger bucks'll jerk out your pizzle and stuff it down your throat."

When he came around the wagon, whip coiled in his hand, Caroline tried to smile at him. He swung up into the bed and ordered her to take off his boots. After swigging whiskey, Kleppner put his pistols under his head and lay back. "Howcome you never squalled out when they messed with you, like I said?"

"I—it was so quick; they grabbed me and held my mouth."

"Which of them bucks hollered out?"

Caroline looked down at her knotted hands. "I d-don't know."

"Funny any of 'em would, you bein' damned near white and all." He tapped the whiskey jug again. "What'd you hit Delkin with? Got him a head swole up here to yonder."

She looked right into his eyes and lied: "A stick. He was about to shoot you, so I hit him and grabbed his pistol."

Kleppner's stubbled grin was sardonic. "Account of you just can't do 'thout me?"

"Because I was more frightened of them."

"That's better," he said. "No sense lyin' to me, gal. Comes to hard cash or soft ass, you just natural lose. Somethin' else—I'd purely hate to scar your hide, 'cause whip marks on a nigger brings down the price,

83

but I'll flat tear you up, do I catch you atryin' to set your mammy loose."

Caroline lowered her eyes. "I understand."

"Barker and Delkin was fools," Kleppner went on, "goin' off their heads over a juicy wench. You be a bigger fool, do you go after my keys or guns, but just in case, ol' Bobo's goin' to shackle you to this wagon. We ain't all that far from N'Awlins, and I kin do 'thout diddlin' for a spell."

Outside in the night, an owl hooted, its lonely cry echoing in the hopelessness of Caroline's soul.

Chapter 10

Chained in the wagon bed, Caroline peered from canvas at the outskirts of New Orleans, seeing a clapboard shack here, a bolder brick house there. As the wagon rattled and jounced through road ruts, her ears picked up musical phrases in French, and a more liquid, tinkling language that must be Spanish.

Behind the wagon, the slave cavvy trudged, clanking and dusty. At the far end of the line Solah walked, stronger now, the big Mandingo a pace ahead. Behind them rode Delkin, unchained now but subdued and uneasy.

An aroma of spicy cooking wafted toward them, and a breath of exotic flowers; there were other odors not so pleasant—black mud and swamp gases, miasmal rot. The air was thick, its heat rising by the hour, and Caroline's thin dress clung to her body.

At Kleppner's shout, Bobo turned the wagon into a high-fenced and grassless yard, and the cavvy came shuffling after, worn down and hungry and dispirited, not caring about the curious who were gathering to stare.

"Take 'em on inside the shed," Kleppner called. "Herd 'em along, Delkin. Bobo—swing them mules around like you got good sense; you done it afore. Damn! Got to tell a nigger ever damn time."

A gate slammed shut, and the wagon slowed to a stop. Caroline waited to be released, but Kleppner seemed to have forgotten her in the business of getting the cavvy under cover. She stared at the fence, tall iron pickets with wicked spear-like tops. Faces peered through the palings, faces black and white and myriad shades of brown.

Swinging down from his horse, Kleppner popped his whip and called, "They be ready for inspection in a few days, folks. Guaranteed prime stock to be sold off in Congo Square."

Only a few small boys remained giggling at the fence after the announcement, and when the shed doors closed, they also left. There was nothing more to see. Still, Caroline waited, wondering at the blacks and mixed bloods walking the street beyond, not manacled and seemingly happy. Why didn't they flee when they had the chance?

Kleppner ducked into the wagon and produced a big key. "Chunk that blanket over you, hide your face comin' out. Don't want nobody to get a look at you till you all spruced up and ready to show."

Bundled up and moving stiffly. she started into the shed, but Kleppner caught her elbow and steered her toward a tired shack whose porch sagged, whose dark interior stank. "In yonder, and git to cookin'. You got hollerin' in your head, nobody pays mind to it here. You thinkin' on runnin', time them dogs is turned loose, you be glad to stay penned up. And don't forget your mammy."

He left her in the kitchen, before a cold and rusted stove. She looked around at the empty whiskey bottles cobwebbed and forgotten, at skillets blackened with grease, a crusted floor and a wobbly table. Kleppner was a pig, but a wily one; how could she forget that her mother was chained in that windowless shed?

Caroline went to work sweeping out the kitchen, building a fire in the stove and heating water to scrub tin plates and utensils. It was better to keep busy, not to think about the grinning, curious faces that had stared at the cavvy as if the hapless blacks were so many wild animals on display.

Stooped and sweating, Bobo carried in supplies from the wagon. "You need water, git it now. Mist' Kleppner, he turn them mean dogs out afore long, and ain't *nobody* travels the yard."

"Help me then," she said. "I have to clean up this pig sty, cook and bathe, and I'm sure he'll want bathwater, too."

"Got my own cookin' to git at," Bobo grumbled. "Got to put fat on them niggers quick, so they bring top dollar."

Catching up a pair of wooden buckets, Caroline marched out past the old man. At the well, she told him, "You're an outcast. You've let them tame and train you to hold your own kind in captivity, an animal turned zookeeper."

Bobo blinked at her. "What you mean?"

"You wouldn't understand," she said. "Bring more water."

Following her into the house, he said, "My daddy said his daddy was a big ol' Africky nigger got cotched by other niggers and sold off to white folks."

Caroline poured water into an iron pot. "You can't mean that—blacks selling other blacks?"

The old man shrugged. "Means I ain't dumb as you thinks, and you ain't smart as *you* thinks. You damn whistlin' niggers sells niggers, and buys 'em, too. Animal, you calls me—well, now, what do that make *you?* Onliest thing is, some us animals wears chains and some don't, and I reckon you kin tell me which the worse off."

"Bobo," Caroline said, "I'm sorry; I didn't mean— oh, there's so much I have to learn about slavery, about the South and—and people like us."

He picked up empty buckets. "You ain't no different, gal. Right now, you buyin' and sellin'—buyin' life by sellin' yo' pretty ass. All I got to swap for my black hide is yassuh and thankee suh."

She lifted a hand, reached out to him, but he shuffled through the door and Caroline turned back to her cleaning and cooking. There was nothing she could say to him anyhow. It was better if she did more listening and watching, and less talking. One thing she would never do, she thought, was accept and submit without hope.

Working steadily, Caroline managed to put a meal of sorts on the back of the stove and get the floor scrubbed, bathwater waiting. Slipping from her shapeless dress, she sat in a rusty tin tub and lathered her body with lye soap so strong it made her skin sting. She would have enjoyed soaking in the water, but she scrubbed quickly, rinsed and wrinkled her nose at the dress she had to put back on. Maybe now that Kleppner was home, he'd give her something decent to wear. How she longed for crisp, clean dresses, but at least her body was clean. She felt guilty when she remembered Solah, imprisoned in the big shed.

Kleppner stamped upon the porch, and she saw the pair of huge, feral hounds pacing the fenced yard behind him. They were great, rangy beasts with bared fangs and a look of terrible eagerness about them. Caroline pressed her hands together and shivered; there'd be no chance of getting to her mother tonight, not with those fierce monsters roaming about.

Grinning, Kleppner said, "You right handy, gal. Keep supper warm whilst I climb in that tub."

She looked away as he stripped, only too familiar with every hard line of his hairy body, but still shamed by its nakedness. Stirring gravy in a skillet, she said, "What happens now?"

Kleppner blew and snorted in the water. "Right now, or when you and the cavvy ready to show?"

"You know what I mean."

"Yeah." He splashed water on the floor as he stepped from the tub. "All them niggers gets lard put on 'em, their woolly heads clipped, scars took care of good's I can. Then they get took out to Congo Square and stood on the block, one by one."

Her hand was steady as she filled his plate. "My mother, too?"

He didn't even wrap a towel about his middle, but sat bare and dripping at the table. "Hell yes."

"Couldn't you—maybe keep her?"

Kleppner cocked his head at her. "Keep you, too,

I reckon?" He shoveled food into his mouth and chewed noisily.

"Please," she said. "We can keep house for you, cook and clean and—and anything else."

Sopping cornbread into gravy, he said, "Told you afore, gal. You got nothin' to swap. Your mammy's perked up some, and I might unload her for more'n I figured. Now you—" Kleppner ran his eyes up and down Caroline's body. "You somethin' special. Mean to fix you up from your pate to your toenails, dress you right fine, and show you off where you'll bring top dollar. Ain't puttin' *you* on no auction block. It's the Quadroon Ball for you, missy. Course, I'll have to come right out and admit you ain't no virgin, but that's all right. I kin make up for that lost maidenhead by testifyin' you the wiggliest, hottest piece of high yeller ass from here to the Carolinas and back."

Caroline winced and forced herself to eat for strength, although the food was heavy and tasteless in her mouth. Outside, one of the hounds growled. Heat from the stove threatened to singe Caroline's back and she moved uneasily in her chair. "There's no way to—to stay with you?"

"You like my diddlin' that much, do you? Lookee here, wench—you bound to like it just as much from other men. You so hot, you can't *keep* from screwin', and law, won't them fine Creole genmun go crazy about that? As for me hangin' onto you, well now; good diddlin' is one thing, and hard cash another."

"But you took our gold," Caroline said. "That should be enough."

Kleppner showed stained teeth at her. "Now what would niggers be adoin' with gold, less'n they stole it? That there pouch was just a bonus like. Pour me some more coffee, gal."

She obeyed, not flinching when he reached up to pinch her nipple. "Mean to catch up on all that good screwin' afore you go to the Ball," he said. "Ought to be right happy you so prime, missy; ain't many as gets the chance to strut around there and hook some fancy, stuckup Creole. Why, them gals been raised all they lives for the Ball, and after they git bought, they live better'n most white women."

"How's that?" Caroline asked.

Kleppner got up, casual in his nakedness, and found his pipe. When he had it going, he sat down again and said, "Ever one gits 'em a little house on the Ramparts, 'cause their man don't rightly *live* with 'em, just visits, like. Some of them quadroons got slaves of their own, and gits treated like they was sure enough *somebody*." He laughed. "The things some fools won't do, over a piece of nooky."

"Never you," she murmured.

"You right as rain," Kleppner answered. "Never this here ol' boy." Stretching, he said. "Time you clear up, I be waitin'. Got to be certain sure you trained proper for them *genmun*. Got to see you remember everything you been showed, to make up for havin' your maidenhead busted. Somethin' else I never could figure out— howcome them lace shirt Creoles set so much store on virgins. Me now, I cotton more to ridin' a mare been well broke, 'stead of a wall-eyed filly don't know which end works."

That's what I am to him, she thought, a mare, a piece of stock to be used and worked and sold for profit. My mother and I aren't human to Kleppner and his kind. Were we any more in Illinois, no matter what their mouths say? Her hand clenched her coffee cup, and she had an almost overpowering desire to hurl the hot liquid into Kleppner's leering face. But we are human, just as much as you, more than you.

"Git with it," Kleppner commanded. "I'm raisin' me a good hard."

He was a predator, feeding upon the miseries of others. Caroline hefted the iron skillet and wondered briefly if she could crush his head with it, if she could get his pistols and kill the watchdogs, free the cavvy and take her mother away. But while her back was to him, she felt the whiplash curl around her ankle, and knew her wild imaginings could not work out. He was too wary.

"Clean up after while," he said from the rumpled bed. "I don't aim to waste this good thing."

Removing her dress, she went to him, determined to hold her dark lusts in check, not to surrender to them this time. She hated the man and everything he stood for, his cruelty, his avarice, his whiteness. Why, how could she respond to him?

Dutifully, Caroline went through the bag of tricks he had taught her, steeling herself against feeling, concentrating not upon the sensations of her own body, but upon her hate for this awful man, this greedy, brutal slaver. Eyes closed, her nostrils filled with the strong scent of him, she performed the contortions and gyrations as if she were somehow standing outside her body and watching the actions in a bad dream. Hating Kleppner so, despising him with all her heart, in the end she was triumphant. She did not reach the searing, foaming crest of that dark wave, and as she lay sweating with the supine man, Caroline savored the honeyed taste of her victory. If she could do it once, she could do it again.

Leaving him half-asleep, but still watchful, she rose from the bed and retrieved her shabby dress. Then she began to clear away dishes, to stoke the stove and heat water again. Kleppner wasn't going to budge; he meant to sell her and Solah, each to different masters. She would have to discover where her mother went and keep close track of her. If, as Kleppner said, a sale at the Quadroon Ball would give her some measure of freedom, Caroline would find a way to stay in contact with Solah, perhaps even wheedle her new owner into buying her mother so they could be together. Kleppner said some of the girls on the Ramparts had slaves of their own.

Her lips twisted; unconsciously, she was using *their* words: slaves, masters, owners, selling and buying. *Stay alive,* her mother had advised. *Don't let them hurt you and stay alive.* Well, she was doing that, playing the white game because there was no choice, but someday—she glanced over one shoulder at Kleppner. The cunning bastard slept lightly as a cat, one hand upon his coiled whip, pistols beneath his head. And if she threw boiling water over him, battered him with something while he writhed in pain, how could she get past those prowling hounds in the yard?

There was the other white man, too. She had forgotten about Delkin. Sullen but obviously relieved to be alive, hopeful he might still get his share of the cavvy sale, Delkin was in the shed. She was certain he was unarmed, except for a big knife, but Delkin was even worse than Kleppner.

Fretting at the washpot, she cleaned dishes and pans, rattling one loudly every now and then to see if Kleppner stirred. He always roused, nervous and cunning as a snake, and every whit as poisonous. She would have to wait until a better opportunity came along, until she was purchased like a side of beef at the Quadroon Ball.

Suppose nobody bought her? Opening the door to dump soapy water, Caroline wondered about that, and jumped back in sudden alarm as one of the dogs made a rumbling, threatening move toward the porch. Her legs a bit weak, she poured rinse water in the pot and hoped she could hold her own with the other girls. If not, Kleppner would sell her as a house servant, or place her in a house of prostitution, and she might never see her mother again.

When she stacked dishes, he was sitting up, smoking his pipe and watching her with beady, unwinking eyes. Caroline said, "The Ball—will I be dressed as well as the others?"

"Damn right; got me an investment to protect. You be wearin' the fanciest gown in N'Awlins, your hair all put up in doodads and such. You talk real good already, so that won't be no bother."

"Will you take me to the shops, so I can choose my own dress?"

Kleppner grinned. "Might's well. Some of them young bloods catch sight of you on Rue Royale, they be sniffin' after and real eager. Wouldn't hurt none was you to give 'em a peek at a leg and a sashay of that fine tail. Might be, you gettin' anxious to be rid of ol' Kleppner? A while back, you was beggin' to stay."

"As you said," she murmured, "I have nothing to bargain with, so I hope to better myself, to do the best I can."

"Now you gittin' smart," he said, coming nude to the stove to rake out a coal for his pipe. "You shine like a star at the Ball, and if'n the right man buys you, damn if'n you ain't got the world by the tail on a down-hilt pull."

"I'll do all I can to tease them," Caroline said, "if you'll let me know who my mother is sold to, and where she will be."

He patted her haunch and blew out a cloud of blue smoke. "Sure will, missy. Most niggers, they don't travel far from the city. Some goes to the cane fields, but them's mostly strong bucks, 'cause niggers don't last long in the cane. Your mammy, now, I'd say she'll git picked up by some planter runnin' short on house niggers, or some shirttail farmer needs a yeller wench to warm his bed. Never can tell, but I'll show you the bill of sale, can you make it out."

"I can read," Caroline said, and Kleppner's grin widened.

"Damn if'n you ain't just full of surprises. A nigger readin'—fancy that!"

She said, "Can *you* read?"

He slapped her hard, so that she staggered, and said, "So's you don't forget your place, mustee."

balanced upon her glossy head. She was tall and
willowy and ... ... a ... question of ...

"As she walks she argued, "I know that a
person with sufficient money to ... to ... be so ...

...
...

Chapter 11

It was the biggest, busiest town Jubal had ever seen,
with so many people going every which way, tall ships
stacked creaking in the great, muddy river, and fancy
carriages rattling over streets of cypress blocks fitted
tightly together. When they first came along the road
and saw the sprawling city, Jubal pulled up his horse
and just sat there looking, like any country yokel.

He'd been to Charleston and Nashville, but they
couldn't hold a light to this place. It had such a foreign feel, foreign smells, and the look of rich age,
like it had been there forever. And the farther the column marched into the outskirts, the more Jubal realized it had another look, another feel—that of bawdy
old tarts plying their trade happily while nobody else
much gave a damn.

Not that the girls who gathered to watch Jackson's
men were old or tattered; far from it. They were
dressed bright as birds and twittered the same, coy
behind spread and fluttering fans while their dark eyes
flashed boldly. Even the slaves seemed happy, Jubal
thought, the men of many hues cavorting beside the
column and joking; the mixed-blood women rolling
their hips and smiling. Jubal shook his head; Andy
Jackson would be hard put to keep the men in camp,
and probably wouldn't try, unless the Redcoats were
closer than anybody figured.

Jubal watched a particularly sensuous woman who
walked straight-backed with a basket of exotic fruits

balanced upon her glossy head. She was tall and willowy and graceful, and every motion of her finely shaped body announced the pride she had in her golden flesh. Through coal-black lashes, she stared back at Jubal, and redripe lips smiled a damp invitation.

Quickly, he glanced away and moved his horse into a jog. The last time, the only time, he'd had anything to do with a woman like that, he'd come within an inch of getting his fool throat cut, and no better for him. The incident had greatly strengthened his normal distaste for dark skin. Ruefully, he smiled; that Creek woman had been an armful of boiling fury, though; thighs smooth and strong, breasts full and firm, and the hungry way she went at a man's privates—

Just to put a blade in him. Good thing she aimed for the neck, or she might have turned Jubal Blaze into a gelding. Still, he couldn't bring himself to put a pistol ball into her fleeing back, and had been hoorawed for his great love affair ever since. Well, he thought, the men would get no more chance to devil him here. If he got into something in New Orleans, it would for certain sure be with a white woman—all white, pure white, with never a trace of the tarbrush.

Up ahead, a grinning Davy Crockett was signaling them off into a field, across which lay a sizable cotton warehouse and some other buildings. Jackson was getting the men under cover, but they were reluctant to leave the crowded, welcoming street, and some straggled to talk with admiring women. Jubal didn't bother calling them on, though some were of his company. It had been a long march and a hard campaign, marked by flat bellies and blood, crowned at last by victory. These hardy volunteers deserved the fruits of success.

Swinging down from his horse, Jubal grunted. Besides, if anybody tried to stop the celebration, the men might just pack up and head on home. Some already had. The Alabama folks had never left their own territory. Once the Creeks were whipped, they slipped off through the woods, shadowy as Indians themselves.

They fought their war back yonder because it was personal. They didn't care that the British might soon attack New Orleans. That was none of their business.

Jubal sighed, and loosened his saddle girth. Maybe someday folks would get the idea this was one country, instead of a bunch of states and territories, each going its own stubborn way. But until then, only the regulars under Major Thomas Benton came to the same count every morning, and Jubal had the sometime soldier's distrust of those who made war a way of life.

He was busy then with arrangements for his company, drawing rations and blankets, getting them bedded down in one place so he could find them again. Some old faces were gone, not run off to the mountains, but buried in Alabama, and he didn't want to dwell on them. Seeing that his horse was grained and rubbed down, he went to the house set aside as hospital and jawed a spell with Sam Houston. Sam had made it lying flat in a wagon, cussing more than some at every bump, and was getting along just fine.

"Andy gone off?" Sam asked.

"Ain't seen him since we come into town," Jubal said.

"Goin' to have him a time, roundin' up enough men in this town. You know he had to pay out of his own pocket for rations and quilts, and when he run out of hard money, he signed his name for the rest?"

"Goddamn Congress," Jubal said. "They think wars don't cost and we can win 'em with words. Your wounds leakin' any, Sam?"

"Just a mite touchy, but Andy wants to send me to Congress and make 'em stir their stumps."

"Well, you're handier at talkin' than most."

Sam Houston sat up on his quilts, face thinned and drawn. "Better at cussin', which is what them fatass gentlemen goin' to hear. Jubal, you go into the city, I'd appreciate some good whiskey and cigars."

"Proud to get 'em for you, Sam. Meant to go see some sights and buy some clothes. These here buckskins are just about to crawl on off by theirself."

Houston sank back. "Sure hate to miss out on them

Creole belles. Bed one for me, do you find the time." He grinned. "Long as you can forget your great love for that Injun maiden, that is."

"Oh hell," Jubal said, and stomped off.

In a way, he was under the command of Major Benton when Andy was off somewhere and Colonel Coffee wasn't around. But he never said more to Benton than he had to, and there wasn't any use being an officer if a man couldn't do on his own sometime. So Jubal left his tired horse, put his long gun by and rode shank's mare into town, loosening his long legs and getting the kinks out.

Men dressed pretty lifted their hats and gave him room, trying not to wrinkle patrician noses at the ripeness of him. His blackened buckskins and skinning knife and pistol marked him as one of Andy Jackson's own, and the city was well into celebrating the Creek victory. Mulatto younguns skipped around him, chattering away like squirrels and making about as much sense. All he could understand was pointed fingers and "Kaintuck, Kaintuck."

No use trying to tell them he wasn't from Kentucky, that he was a Carolinian who roamed over to join up with Tennesseans, bringing enough gold with him to outfit his own company. Carolina just got too tame, and planting and harvest was always the same. The plantation near about ran itself. even if young Abel Blaze wasn't determined to prove how good he could manage it. His brother was cut to be a planter; he didn't have Jubal's restlessness.

Here was a street crowded with stalls, where black women with kerchiefs around their heads shoved things at him to buy—sugar cakes and shiny fruits and live blue crabs, plump shrimp under layers of damp moss. He smiled his way past them and under porches whose castiron balustrades looked like black lace. Strange languages sang about his head. and swarthy seamen rollicked along, waving bottles. Cooking smells reached out to him, rich and fiery odors that had him swallowing and licking his bearded lips.

The bath first, he reminded himself; a shave and

new clothes, *then* feasting and a few drams of something more powerful than branch water. He found a barber shop and went in, ducking his great length through the arched doorway to make the perfumed, moustachioed little man understand what he wanted.

Leaving his buckskins huddled upon the stone floor, Jubal sank gratefully into a hot tub and said to the ceiling, "Damn—don't nobody here talk English?"

From another tub, a head arose, "The king's English, or the Kentucky kind?"

"How do," Jubal said. "The king ain't too kindly thought of, but it don't matter, long as we get by. Jubal Blaze, of Andy Jackson's army."

"Tom Pickett—nobody's army, nor likely to be. I'm a broker for the flatboats, when not indulging in gentler, more interesting pursuits."

The head was carrot-topped, the face freckled and pug-nosed, and a man sort of had to grin back at the lopsided smile it wore. Jubal said, soaping himself vigorously, "It's them interestin' pursuits I got in mind, after I get me some new buckskins."

Pickett frowned at Jubal's old ones. "Are you certain they're dead? I could swear I saw them move. Buckskins, *really*. I might suggest a visit to my tailor and some good broadcloth. In fact, it would be far better were I to bring Monsieur LeRoux here. That is, if you can pay cash?"

"Hard money," Jubal said, "but broadcloth ain't exactly fitten to soldier in."

"Once he has your measurements, Georges LeRoux will, somewhat regretfully, send out for deerhides, but in the meantime, to frequent certain entertaining establishments, it is better to look the part of a gentleman." Tom Pickett lifted his chubby frame from the steaming water and shrugged. "Besides, bringing a paying customer to Monsieur LeRoux will cause him to think more kindly of my own overdue bill."

So it was that Jubal, shaved to the quick, scrubbed and powdered and dressed in spanking new clothing, found himself in the company of a knowledgeable rogue. Tom Pickett seemed to know everyone worth knowing along the Rue Bourbon, the Rue Royale, and many who were not. He was fluent in the French Jubal would never master and familiar with all manner of fine foods and finer wines, so long as Jubal paid the bill.

Stuffed to the straining of his new waistcoat, rosy with brandies, Jubal leaned back in a chair and stretched his long legs in satisfaction, only half listening to his new friend hold forth on the nature of the city.

Here in the Absinthe House, war of any kind seemed far away, and maybe the British had had enough; maybe they wouldn't try for New Orleans, anyway. Content, Jubal watched the foppishly dressed Creoles come and go, skinny swords at their sides, lace at sleeve and throat. At a gaming table in one corner, voices rose suddenly, and he glanced that way, conscious of a quick, taut silence.

Leaning close, Tom Pickett whispered, "That will come to naught. If it were anyone else, there would be a challenge flung, and a meeting at dawn beneath the Dueling Oaks. But none is likely to brace Felipe de Alcantari; he has made too many trips to the Oaks. As you can see, he is still intact."

The circle of gamers had fallen back from the cold anger of a small man with the bristled air of a fighting cock. He was almost pretty, Jubal thought, but there was that about him which made the others wary. The man spat rapid, scathing French, put his hand upon the hilt of his sword, and stalked from the Absinthe House without a backward glance. Only then did muttering rise behind him.

"Looks like that un's got the Injun sign on the rest," Jubal commented.

Pickett flicked ash from his cigar and rolled a dollop of brandy inside his mouth before replying. "A dangerous man, M'sieu Alcantari, equally at home with pistols or the rapier, and all know it. Ah, that I had such a reputation; mayhap my debtors would not press me, then."

Jubal said, "You could work up to it, but I never understood this duelin' business. Back home, you just go at your man and get the job done with whatever's handiest. Gen'l Jackson now, he's dueled some."

"The *duello* should be reserved for generals," Pickett said. "Lesser mortals could settle their differences by running foot races or holding drinking contests. But these touchy Creoles—any insult real or fancied is an excuse for the field of honor, and out they go at dawn." He made a face. "An ungodly hour, fit only for ghosties and roosters."

And killing Indians, Jubal thought, or getting killed by them. "Ate so much I'm near to founder," he said. "Best we walk about some, and see the sights."

"You wouldn't be a gaming man?" Pickett asked. "My credit is yet good at a place or two, although severely limited. Or perhaps you are interested in meeting some ladies?"

Standing, Jubal said, "Ladies?"

"In a manner of speaking. Attentive females, let us say, adept at smoothing away the cares of the day."

Moving off through the crowded room, Jubal said, "Long as they ain't any part black."

On the sidewalk—*banquette*, Jubal's new acquaintance called it—Pickett said, "I am always surprised by a man with scruples, since I have none myself. Still, I would not take you for a church-going man."

"Got nothin' to do with it; just as soon mount a sow or a mare that's horsin', and I ain't particular to them, neither."

"Well," Pickett said, swinging jauntily along beside him, "each to his own taste, I suppose. I have found the mixed bloods to be superior—that delicious touch of savagery, you know. But if you will have none of them, more saved for Thomas Pickett, Esquire. Shall we repair to Madame Beauchamps' establishment, then? Her ladies are of many shades and accomplishments."

They turned into a shadowed street, narrow and dank, smelling of the river. Its thick slate walks echoed their footsteps, and grey, wispy fog drifted along it.

"Damme," Pickett said. "Should have hired a lantern carrier. But it is not far."

100

Behind him, Jubal heard the padded rush of feet, and put his back to a damp wall. "Look out, Tom!"

A darker shadow lunged at him, and Jubal's skinning knife chopped at it. The man cried out and something clattered on the walkway. Reaching for a pistol, Jubal moved along the wall, where Pickett was wrestling with a blurred form. There was a little flash of fire and a miniature thunderclap. A voice yelped hoarsely in French, and a man was down.

"Footpads," Pickett panted. "Your new clothing and lavish hand in the bistros, my friend. Ah well, Rue Gallatin has its share of such scavengers."

"Mine got nicked and run off," Jubal said. "Yours dead?"

"I suppose," Pickett answered, stooping to find his tall hat and brushing it carefully. "I felt his belly button before pulling the trigger. Shall we continue our stroll?"

Jubal looked down at the still body. "What about that?"

"The watch will find him, or street sweepers collecting other offal. Ah, there is a light ahead."

Following, putting his weapons away, Jubal felt more respect for the chubby man. For all of Tom Pickett's cheerful admission of cowardice and empty pockets, he had reacted promptly, bringing out a small derringer and putting it to good use. Neither did he seem to be shaken by the brush with danger. More to this talkative man than meets the eye, Jubal thought, and trailed him into an archway well-lighted with candles.

There Pickett stopped and faced him. "I could have been leading you into ambush, my acquaintance with the heavy purse."

"Thought of that when I put my pistol on you," Jubal said, "but you was a mite busy to be in cahoots with 'em."

Laughing, Pickett clapped him on the shoulder. "You will do well in New Orleans, my large and wary friend. If your famous General Jackson is as quick-witted, he may yet save this overripe city from being plucked.

Alors, then—let us ring the bell and bring forth the doorkeeper. The night is ours."

Inside, the big room was ablaze with light and thick with cigar smoke, singing with musical laughter and the tinkle of glasses, the quick-time scrape of fiddles. At a small but ornate bar, Jubal drank a brandy and looked around while Pickett pointed out certain ladies and named them. A big-bellied man sat with girls upon each knee; a roughly dressed fellow tried clumsily to dance with another girl. Beyond the crowd and sweating black musicians, Jubal saw the small, hard man from the Absinthe House. Felipe something-or-other. He was staring into a glass of greenish liquid and ignoring the gaiety bubbling around him.

Then Pickett was at Jubal's elbow with a pert girl whose lush breasts were overflowing her lowcut dress. She had merry blue eyes and a turned-up nose; her hair was the color of a hand-rubbed sorrel horse.

"Miss Hacker," Pickett said, bowing, "familiarly known as Bricktop. A satisfactory shade, sir?"

"Just right," Jubal said, and took a small, soft hand.

Chapter 12

Monsieur Toussaint was a grey and fidgety little man who sniffed snuff from a worn silver box. His cuffs were stained and dingy, and his bottle-green coat had seen better days. Yet he seemed a bit grand in the sparsely furnished room where Caroline sat across from him, where Kleppner lounged bare-chested at the scrubbed kitchen table.

"Eh bien," Toussaint said with a little sneeze, "this then is the *fille* you wish instructed in the rudiments of behavior and given a few words of *français*."

"Sure as hell ain't me," Kleppner said, taking a gulp of cloudy whiskey.

Peering through a lorgnette, the little man said, "But this is a *white* woman. Give me your hand, child. Eh, so—not a touch of blue around the fingernails, no thickness of the lips or nostrils, and the hair—"

"She's nigger, all right," Kleppner said. "Her mammy's a high yeller out there in the shed. Git to teachin', Frenchie; I ain't apayin' you to hold hands with her."

Toussaint sniffed, the end of his sharp nose red. "She will cause a sensation at the Ball, *mais certainement*. Now, child, this instrument is a fork; it is used—"

In swift, musical French, Caroline said, "I am well aware of tableware uses, m'sieu, and although I have never danced, I am sure I shall quickly learn."

Owlishly, Toussaint blinked. *"Ma foi,* but you startle

103

one! The accent—not quite educated, but not the *patois,* either. Tell me, where did you learn—"

Rattling his whiskey bottle, Kleppner said, "You understand her gabblin'?"

"She speaks French almost as well as myself," Toussaint said, one eyebrow lifted. "Where did you come across this jewel, m'sieu?"

"None of your business," Kleppner growled. "Just you show her how to sashay 'round and cut didoes with a fan." He stared at Caroline as if she had been keeping secrets from him, and his hand stroked the ever-present blacksnake whip.

Caroline did her best to ignore him while she concentrated upon the intricate dance steps the little man mincingly demonstrated. *"Courir le cotillon,"* he said, whirling and flicking an imaginary skirt, "a naughty dance, one understands—to run the petticoat, to show a tempting flash of the ankle. So."

Toussaint hummed a melody, and took her through the steps again and again while Kleppner grunted his scorn and she pretended to hear music. Panting, her teacher sank to his chair and reached for the snuffbox. "Much better, *ma chérie;* of course, if you wore a proper gown—"

"She'll have one," Kleppner said. "Goin' to buy it today, soon's you done, fancy shoes and stockin's, all them frills."

Sighing, Toussaint dabbed at his wrinkled forehead with a bit of tattered lace. "If I were not so old, so poor; a scholar has no chance to bid at the Ball. *Chérie*—you must practice lowering your lashes, so. Flutter them; do not stare directly into a man's eyes. They are used to *la coquette,* and frankness disturbs them. Speak softly, move gracefully; manage to brush an arm with your breast, to press a thigh with your own, *hein?"*

In a little while, pleased that this training had cost him so little, Kleppner called out to have the wagon ready, and through the window, Caroline watched Bobo hitching up the mules.

"You done fine," Kleppner said. "Prissy as all

getout, and near 'bout had that ol' bastard liftin' a hard. Yessir, time I walk you around Congo Square some, get you all dressed up, you goin' to pay off real good."

"You haven't let me see my mother," she said. "Is she all right?"

"Slickin' out pretty good, like the rest of 'em when they lay around doin' nothin' but eat." When she climbed to the wagon seat he said, "You sposed to be from up north; howcome you speak French?"

Caroline caught an overtone in his voice. "Would you be worried I'm actually white?"

Picking up the reins, he frowned at her. "Not me; everybody knows you claim a high yeller mammy."

"Still," she said as the wagon rolled, "if it turned out differently, you'd be in trouble."

Through his teeth Kleppner said, "You so much as open your mouth, tell one lie on me, and your mammy gets chopped up and fed to them dogs. You got that, bitch?"

Caroline lowered her eyes, folded her hands in her lap and sat demurely all the way into the city proper. Any way she might try to turn, Kleppner had her blocked. Certainly she couldn't prove she was anyone but Caroline Monteleone, and anyway there might be vengeance awaiting her back in Illinois. In time, she might get back to Williamson County with Solah, when things settled down, when old Senator Williamson accepted a life for a life, M'Nele for his son. They had a friend of sorts there, Caroline remembered, some nameless lawyer M'Nele had dealt with. Or was the man a friend? M'Nele had sold out all he owned, and cheaply; the lawyer probably bought it. God, she thought, was there no true black-white friendship anywhere?

He left the wagon at a livery stable, and aimed them along a bustling street without giving Caroline his arm. She hadn't really expected him to; mustees were fine to bed, but not for public hand-holding. Still, Kleppner stayed close to her, and at the doorway to an intriguing shop, pulled her near to whisper: "I'm meanin' to pass you as white here, so keep your mouth closed. They won't sell to you, do they think you're any part nigger."

The shopkeeper hesitated anyway, seeing Kleppner's rough clothes and the girl's shabby attire. She was a birdlike woman who had little use for the tight corset she wore; her greyblack hair was pulled back severely, and she looked as if she were always on the verge of sniffing. "May I assist you—m'sieu?"

Kleppner found a chair and sprawled on it, boots thrust out. "Fit her out head to toe; walkin' shoes and a street dress; fancy shoes and a ballgown, the best you got. Whatever women wear underneath."

The woman's eyebrows went up and she made a tight smile. "But of course; you have come to the proper shop, m'sieu. A ship has just arrived from France with the latest fashions."

Scratching a sulphur match upon his bootheel, Kleppner lighted a cigar and dropped the match to the floor. "Just so's she can strut with the best."

"Certainement; your—ah, ward will appear elegant indeed when Madame Jervais is done with her. Such natural beauty should be placed in a rich setting, as a jewel is."

Kleppner grunted, blew smoke, and looked at the ceiling. Madame Jervais, scenting a good sale, hopped sparrowlike about her small shop, selecting this and that, exclaiming in two languages. Caroline remained silent, bewildered and enthralled by the variety of clothing, sometimes daring to touch exotic materials with her fingertips.

In the fitting room, she reddened when Madame Jervais stayed with her, and quickly accepted underthings to cover her nudity. They were wondrously soft and clinging, and Caroline could not help pirouetting before the full-length mirror.

"Ma foi," the woman breathed, "but you are ravishing, *chérie.* It seems that he has money, but surely you can do better than a rowdy Kaintuck. There are gentlemen in this city who would give a fortune, simply to glimpse you as I do now. Such perfect breasts,

106

the flat stomach, the gentle sweep of hip—*c'est magnifique.* And your skin, opalescent, the texture of satin."

The woman had been speaking in breathless French, and Caroline whispered an abashed *merci.* Madame Jervais cocked her head to one side. like a robin. "Ah! I knew you could not be daughter to that *cochon.* And I advise you to cast those lovely eyes about, to find yourself a more suitable protector. You are wasted on one like that."

The ballgown transformed her. Caroline had difficulty recognizing herself, she looked so assured and proud in the mirror. It was a delicate green, the soft color of April itself, with no shoulders and a sinful plunging of the bodice that exposed creamy upper breasts. It snugged her tiny waist and flared just so about the hips, dropping in silken rustlings to the floor.

"Voilà!" the woman exclaimed. "With your hair properly coiffed, a touch of rouge and powder, you will turn all men's heads. Of that, I assure you, *chérie.* You like the gown?"

"It's—marvelous," she breathed.

"Eh bien; the street clothing. then; slippers for those small narrow feet, more lingerie. a scarf. My friend down the street has jewelry and perfumes; you will say I sent you, *hein?"*

Caroline liked the fit of the grey dress, too, the lightness of her shoes and the insinuating way frivolous underclothes caressed her body. "If—if he will buy them for me."

"But he must." Madame Jervais' small eyes snapped. "So gauche, that one, like all backwoods oafs, but I will explain to him. As soon as you can, *ma ravissante,* leave him for a gentleman of taste."

If only it were that simple. Caroline thought, and wondered how the woman would react if she knew she was admiring and advising a mustee. When Kleppner called, she obediently paraded before him in each dress, familiar now with the tightening of his jawline that presaged lust.

"A *chapeau,"* Madame Jervais said. "Down the

street to the left, where perfume and jewelry are also sold. Inform madame I sent you."

"More interested in gettin' hold of a nigger can fix up her hair," Kleppner grunted.

"There is a *griffe libre* on Rue Conti," the woman chirped, "a free woman of color who does ladies' coiffures."

"Free nigger," Kleppner said, not noticing the woman's frown as he flicked ashes upon her shop floor. "Hell of a thing, that. Now to money, woman—how much you want for them things?"

Caroline did not listen to the hag. Smoothing her street dress over her hips, she thought of the Ball to come, of the release from Kleppner at last. Perhaps an understanding man would buy her, certainly a rich one, possibly even a man who was clean and handsome. She would be good to him, beguiling, sensuous; she would be everything and anything he desired, so she might have her mother with her, safe and protected. At the moment, she dared not look beyond that dream.

They went from shop to interesting shop, Caroline carrying the accumulating bundles, and Kleppner drove a hard bargain in each. Men were looking at her on the street now, bold-eyed seamen, hurrying businessmen, loitering gentlemen plumed and ribboned. A woman in a carriage stared in obvious envy, and Caroline walked more proudly.

"No time for hair fixin' today," Kleppner said. "Spent enough money, anyways. Now we go on over to Congo Square so I kin get on with the sale."

Caroline's hand clenched her packages. "The s-sale? You didn't say—"

He caught her elbow. "Delkin's got the cavvy ready, but he can't squeeze hard money from that crowd like I kin."

"Solah—my mother—"

Cruelly, his fingers bit into her arm. "Just you sashay 'round so all the young bloods kin eye you, missy. You didn't 'spect me to feed them niggers forever, did you?"

She heard the drums, the primitive throbbing of jungle drums that called buyers to the slave auction, and she saw the flow of the crowd moving in one direction. Congo Square opened before her, and her heart turned over when she saw the dancers, black men and women cavorting monkeylike to the tom-toms, shamelessly posturing before the gathering of grinning whites. Showing white teeth, sweating and carrying on, they acted as if the sale were a tribal celebration, a holiday.

Chin up but her insides gone cold, she stood close to the block where Kleppner placed her, glancing beyond at the huddled cavvy, seeking her mother's face. Delkin was unshackling a black and shoving him forward.

"Gather 'round, genmun—gather 'round!" Kleppner stood upon the huge cypress block, showing his teeth. "You all know me and my merchandise. Guaranteed not a case of fever in the lot, and all good, strong niggers. Now lookee here—a young buck just comin' prime, got all his teeth. Who'll open the biddin' for five hundred, who'll say five? Ah, Mister Claroux knows a good nigger when he sees one—I got five, now who'll go six?"

Shrinking, Caroline saw men come up to feel the black's legs, to have Kleppner pry open his mouth so teeth could be checked. The crowd was jovial, boisterous, and there were very few women present. Those few were far back on the fringes, sitting in carriages whose drivers were uniformed blacks. Remote and superior, those women lolled beneath frilly parasols held by small black attendants.

Eyes were upon her, curious, puzzled eyes, and Caroline dropped her own, trying to make herself as inconspicuous as possible. She was shamed by the sale, by blacks flexing and posing upon the block, by the sly, leering comments of whites. She wished she could belong to another race, for both of these sickened her.

When she again lifted her head, the big Mandingo was on the block, and the bidding became more spirited. Tchaka stood tall and powerful, bare-chested, oiled ropy muscles glistening in the sun. There was defiance in the set of his shoulders and savage pride in his stance.

"Hey now, Kleppner," a man called, "that nigger looks like he's fresh off'n the boat."

"Just about, friend, just about. Don't see no whip marks on him, though. Might be he's got runnin' blood in him, but I'll throw in the shackles for free. Lookee that back, them muscles. Work better'n ary mule, I'd say. Eight hundred, nine? You genmun need a prime field hand—even thousand, *yessir.* Ain't that Mister Partino biddin'? Last you a long spell in the cane, sir—do I hear eleven hundred—eleven—ten-fifty, then. Thankee, sir."

Tchaka's eyes caught hers, and mutely, she tried to convey her sorrow. If he understood, he gave no sign, and Caroline looked away to the river where ships bobbed at the wharf, their sails furled. Some came from far countries across the seas, she knew, from lands where no man was slave to another. Yet some of those very countries engaged in the slave trade, sending their blackbirders to Africa to trap natives and bring them here at enormous profit. In her heart she damned them all—ship captains and crews, slavers and those who bought from them, those who used captive labor; all were equally guilty.

Kleppner said, "Here's a bargain—a high yeller wench a mite long in the tooth, but solid clear through and good for a passel of pickaninnies yet. Fact is, I'd bet my shirt she's bred right now."

With an exaggerated glance at the carriage ladies, Kleppner winked and lowered his voice. "Right good diddlin', and I can swear personal to that. She'll give some lucky genmun light-colored get, wenches for his pleasurin', bucks for house servants. Two for one, genmun, and what's the bid?"

Solah stood there, eyes closed, deep golden skin caressed by the hot sun, long hair stirred gently by a damp breeze off the river. A gull wheeled overhead with a raucous cry, and Solah opened her eyes to stare up at its white sailing. Caroline knew her mother was identifying with that circling bird and its freedom. Looking away before tears came, she watched the crowd, wanting to be certain of the name of the man who bought Solah.

He was big-bellied and wheezing; a sweating, florid face and a chewed cigar. His clothing was not rich, and there was a glint to his piggish eyes that Caroline did not like. Chins bobbing, he chuckled when he stepped forward to pay Kleppner and receive the bill of sale. A tame black came to collect Solah as she stepped from the block, and Caroline would have gone to her, but for a definite, commanding shake of her mother's head. Waggaman was his name, George Waggaman, and she engraved it upon her memory, as Solah was led away through the crowd and the auction went on.

A man sidled near, tipped his hat and spoke to her, but Caroline did not answer. The new grey dress felt stiff against her flesh, and all about her were aliens. The Mandingo was gone, her mother sold again into bondage, M'Nele dead. She had never been so alone, and after Kleppner stepped down with a jerk of his head that told her to follow him, Caroline was still alone.

Chapter 13

Chapter 13

This night, Kleppner hadn't brought the wagon, but hired a public carriage. He was reasonably presentable in an old suit whose sleeves were too short, but his shirt was clean and he had shaved. The closed carriage bounced slowly along a rutted street into the glare of many torches set sputtering into wall brackets. It pulled into line behind other rigs, and Kleppner clenched a fresh cigar between his teeth.

"Got to do this different," he said, opening the door and stepping down. To Caroline's surprise, he gave her his hand, suddenly treating her as if she were fragile and precious. "Mostly, the gals' mammys do the showin' and sellin', only they don't rightly call it by name. They call it makin' an *arrangement*." Removing the cigar from his mouth, Kleppner spat. "Light-colored niggers gittin' uppity as them *genmun*. But onct them horny Creoles catch a good look at you, they'll come arunnin' to ol' Kleppner."

Earlier that day, she had stared into a mirror and could not believe she was looking at herself. Her hair had been piled and twirled just so, with little curls hanging down at each ear and upon the nape of her neck; a touch of rouge, something dark applied to her eyelids by a chattering *griffe libre,* and she was transformed. The ballgown was a seductive marvel, the dance slippers just right, and Kleppner had even bought her a lacy shawl. She looked like some fairytale princess from a picture book, Caroline thought, beautiful but remote and not quite real.

Now she didn't feel at all regal, moving toward the wide doors of the St. Phillip Theater where men loitered for a first look at the young belles being escorted by their mothers. Holding her elbow, Kleppner steered her through a crowd of gapers and whispered in her ear: "Play it right, and you kin buy your mammy back. Don't act too high and mighty, but not like no lowdown whore, neither. Let 'em see down into your tits and smile at 'em, but don't 'zactly rub it on their legs. Higher the price I gits for you, richer the man you gits for yourself, and better chance't him gettin' you a house servant you got your heart set on."

George Waggaman, she thought, of Bayou La Fouche; an ugly fat man with beady eyes. She must get Solah back from him. Lifting her chin and fixing a bright smile upon her face, she strode lithely into the ballroom.

Immediately men homed to her, circling about and mouthing extravagant praises which Caroline acknowledged with a tilting of her head or a flutter of thick lashes. The seven traditional sets of the French *contredanse* were not difficult to follow, and she made certain that her hand lingered a bit in each passing partner's as they bowed and pirouetted to gypsy music.

Kleppner hovered somewhere in the background, a dull smear amidst the rainbow coats of New Orleanians. She sighed, and a handsome man brought her chilled wine; another offered to show her the delights of the inner garden, and two others almost came to blows over the privilege of the next dance.

Caroline was conscious of other women, lovely young girls sleek and polished; she knew that hovering mothers frowned at her, but she was strangely caught up in this lilting music, held by a certain frenzy, whirled and whirling and glittering, somehow candle flame, somehow moth.

Never had she been so admired, so sought after, and there was no crude pawing at her. Here in this enchanted ballroom, eager men accepted her for what she was, a woman of mixed blood, and still they admired her, wanted her. She found herself smiling into intense brown eyes, into yearning blue eyes; she murmured gentle answers in French and English, and felt quite giddy.

After a stately cotillon, the orchestra paused, and several glasses of wine were offered to her. Flirtatiously, Caroline accepted none, but took a sip from each. Her fingers rested lightly upon the wrist of a young blond man. He was slightly built and handsomely dressed, with merry green eyes and a freckled face. Nicolas Girod was obviously smitten with her, and anxious to be done with the preliminaries.

"May I speak with your mother? If you will but point her out—"

Her eyes fell. "My mother is not here. My owner stands near the punchbowl, the man in the dark coat."

Nicolas Girod pursed his lips. "Your owner, mam'selle?"

"This is the Quadroon Ball, is it not? I am a woman of color, m'sieu, and that one—*oui;* he carries a bill of sale for me." Caroline might have said the document was false, blurted out that she had been stolen, but Kleppner was white. She was not.

"Then I will speak to him immediately," Nicolas said.

A hand fell upon her arm, and she looked up into a different face—ah, a very different face. This one was dark and aquiline, its piercing black eyes set behind high cheekbones. He had the look of a hawk poised to strike, but he was devilishly handsome, his small pointed beard and crisply waxed moustache framing a mouth at once sensuous and harsh. Coiled power lurked within this tall, brooding man, more than a hint of edged steel in the rapier-slim body. Not for him the bright satins and flowered coats of younger gentry; he wore somber black velvet against a snowy, ruffled shirt. His jet hair, worn stylishly long, was winged with silver, and a thin scar reaching from temple to chin called attention to the fact that his teeth were even and bright.

"Mam'selle," he said, husky-throated, "I have inquired of you from your—protector. Permit me to introduce myself: I am Felipe de Alcantari."

"I am h-honored, m'sieu." Caroline tried to keep from stammering, and was glad the gypsy violins chose that moment to burst into a bouncy melody.

"So," he said, and she was with him in the dance. Fluid and deft in his movements, he made a sly mockery of the dance as one couple after another left the floor and the music to them. Probing, clinging, his eyes never left her own, and Caroline turned suddenly awkward, turned warm.

Felipe said then, "It is enough," and escorted her to the wine table. Face carefully blank, a black man filled their goblets.

"I—I am unused to wine, m'sieu," she said, glancing nervously over her shoulder. Her eager suitors seemed to have lost interest, except for Nicolas Girod and two others talking heatedly with Kleppner.

Nodding, light catching in the faint silver wings of his dark hair, Felipe cupped her elbow lightly with a possessive hand. "Then we shall speak with the Kaintuck, and you may have a breath of fresh air in the courtyard while we conduct our business there."

Kleppner frowned at their approach, but smoothed his face when Felipe suggested they gather in the courtyard. No, Caroline thought, he did not suggest— he commanded.

The courtyard was torchlit and flagstoned, heavily scented by jasmine and magnolia; a small fountain tumbled happily in the center, and stone benches waited about it. Felipe led her to one and bowed her onto the seat. Did Caroline catch a hint of irony in the motion?

"Now then," he said in accented English, "to the business at hand."

"Let's just wait up a spell, Mister Alcantari," Kleppner said, fingering his jaw. "Me and these other genmun been talkin' some, and it ain't like she's standin' on the block."

"Is she not?" Felipe said.

Nicolas Girod stepped forward, torchlight dancing upon his flushed face. "M'sieu, these are matters to be handled delicately, among gentlemen."

"Including a Kaintuck?"

Caroline could see Kleppner flinch, his hands knot. "Lookee here," he gritted, "I reckon everybody knows your reputation, but that ain't no call for you to run roughshod over us. These genmun are dickerin' fair and square for my nigger and—"

"I do not like the term," Felipe said coldly. *"Fille de couleur* is more fitting."

"Can't git my tongue around that Frenchie talk," Kleppner muttered.

"M'sieu," Felipe said very softly, "I suggest you attempt it. Now."

Caroline felt a quick tension chill the night air; the wall torches became hissing goblins and the scent of flowers turned funereal.

"Goddamnit—"

"What was that, m'sieu?"

"F-filly," Kleppner said hoarsely. "Filly de color."

Why, she thought, Kleppner—brutal, murdering Kleppner—is afraid of this man.

"Merci," Felipe said. "A butchery of the tongue, but what can one expect of a slave trader? Since that is settled, what bid must I top?"

Kleppner's shoulders were hunched, his face mottled. "Mister Girod here, he's gone to two thousand but it ain't enough. These others are kind of pressed for hard money, but they talkin' some trade, too."

Touching his moustache, Felipe said, "Three thousand in gold."

Two young men—Caroline thought their names were Abadie and Fleury—spread their hands and shrugged. Nicolas Girod said, "Thirty-five, and it does not seem proper we should bicker like tradesmen before the lady."

Kleppner shook his head. "Still ain't enough. I got a big investment in this n— this here gal; her keep for a long time, them fancy clothes, what I paid out for her in the first place—"

Caroline let out her breath. "Which was nothing, and you stole our money."

"Goddamnit, missy, I'll bust your lyin' mouth—"

"And you were paid for our keep with my body," she continued. "Has he told you I am no virgin?"

"*Peste!*" Nicolas exclaimed. "I did not realize—"

Felipe laughed, a full-throated, jarring sound. "A truthful lady, upon what passes for my soul! M'sieu Girod, I take it that you withdraw your offer, then?"

"Well," Nicolas said, "I never thought—I did not expect—"

Chopping the air with the flat of his hand, Felipe said sharply: "Three thousand it is, then. I have no such partiality to unsullied maidens."

"Now hold on," Kleppner protested, "I done said thirty-five won't do, and you're adroppin' the price."

"I have made the bid," Felipe said, "the *final* bid; understand that, Kaintuck."

Nicolas Girod hesitated a moment, glancing shyly at Caroline. The other two drew off a pace, and yet another. There were watchful faces at the tall glass doors, and again the air seemed to tighten.

Spreading his feet, Kleppner said, "We'll see about that. There's men inside be glad to—"

"You would insult me, slaver?"

Kleppner's voice was thick and shaky. "I don't know nothin' about duelin' and such, but you can't just rob a man's property."

Felipe's smile was bright and hungry. One hand rested at his hip. "Challenges are passed between gentlemen. You do not qualify, so I would simply run you through, or drive a ball through your craven belly." His hand moved suddenly, and Kleppner leaped back, arms lifting.

Caroline heard a purse clank upon the flagstones, and Felipe laughed. "Three thousand in solid Spanish doubloons. *Pick it up.*" His voice crackled like Kleppner's blacksnake whip, cutting at the man, daring him not to obey.

"Sir," Nicolas said, "the lady—"

"Precisely," Felipe answered, "the lady is entitled

117

to see the slaver upon his knees, or would you interfere, m'sieu?"

"I—I am not a coward," Nicolas said.

"Nor a fool. Kaintuck, I will not tell you again."

Shaking all over, Kleppner went to his knees and reached for the purse; metal clinked as he drew it close, as he stared black frustration at his tormentor. He carried a pistol, she knew, but he dared not make a move toward it, not against this man so deadly eager. Caroline reveled in Kleppner's shame, his helplessness.

"Bien," Felipe said calmly. "Inside there is an attorney, one Clément Laussat. You will deliver the bill of sale to him, after you have scratched your mark upon it."

Carefully, Kleppner came to his feet and swayed there. "I ain't fixin' to forget this."

"I trust not, slaver. Remember me well, for if I face you again, I mean to see the color of your blood."

Choking, Kleppner turned and plunged blindly into the ballroom. Uncomfortably, Nicolas Girod and the others followed, none looking back.

Felipe's smile softened as he bowed low to Caroline. "Your pardon, *ma chérie.* When dealing with swine, it is necessary to use the prod."

"I enjoyed it," she said, surprising herself. "I almost—almost wish he had tried for his pistol."

"Ah yes; beneath his right coattail. I watched that hand. You wish him killed for what he has done to you, and I approve a woman who knows her mind. But unless he forced me to defend myself, I could not shoot him down. The city authorities grow bothersome, and one needs friendly witnesses, *hein?"*

Rising slowly from the bench, excited and just a little weak, Caroline said, "I thank you for humiliating him."

Felipe bowed over her hand, brushing it with his lips. "We shall speak no more of him, *chérie.* Do you have a *casque,* possessions to gather?"

She dropped her head. "Only a single dress."

118

"No matter, then; there are other dresses. If you are ready, we will go directly to your new home."

Walking beside him, she said, "I am ready, m'sieu." For a chance at being a woman, she thought, for even though Felipe de Alcantari was technically her new owner and master, he was a gentleman. Already, he concerned himself with her as a person, asking rather than commanding, and she liked that.

She liked him; what woman would not? Thoughtful, courteous and handsome, strong without being brutal, he was also spiced with danger. Felipe had been ready to kill, every fiber of his being poised and ready to pounce. She had sensed it, and the other men had too, especially Kleppner.

Passing through the ballroom upon a wave of careful whispers, Caroline strode proudly beside him. Men glanced at her and swiftly looked away, for now she was under protection. Young women looked first at Felipe, then stabbed her with their dark eyes.

The black doorman bowed low and called up Felipe's carriage. He handed her up into it, and climbed to the seat beside her. A stiffness had come upon her, and she did not know why she was just a bit afraid. Certainly Felipe was to be her lover; that was why he had spent three thousand in gold pieces for the right. And it wasn't as if she were unsure of her body's delights; savage and hurtful as Kleppner was, he had taught her many things.

It seemed taking a man should be different, should be her own choice. Although Caroline was overwhelmed by Felipe at first sight, still she would like to have reserved the opportunity to say no. White woman's ideas, she thought; she would have to get them out of her head. Please Felipe de Alcantari she would, whatever his tastes. She must bind him to her with flesh and spirit, with invisible chains as strong as the slavery that held her. If he loved her, he would not deny her need to have Solah with her.

If he loved her, he would set her and her mother free.

"There is a small house," he said, as the carriage

119

lurched and creaked, "on the Ramparts. It has been empty for some time, but now it will be yours."

"You do not live there?"

In darkness, he chuckled. *"Mais non;* the ancient Alcantari house—but perhaps I will take you there one day. In the small house, there is wine and cheese; a light supper, perhaps."

His hand was warm upon her own; Caroline felt his breath stir against her cheek. "I—I will be all you wish, m'sieu."

Felipe laughed again. "I do not doubt that, my sweet. There is a wild animal within your lovely body, and tonight I will unleash it."

Chapter 14

Jubal Blaze leaned against the bar and drank tart wine. "Tom Pickett," he said, "you're right as rain about how pretty these gals are, but like I told you, I just ain't interested in takin' up with high yellows."

Pickett squinted over his lifted goblet. "You were so interested in your wine that you didn't even look around when the most beautiful girl at the Ball passed by. What a woman—tawny, supple as a sleek cat—"

"Cats got claws," Jubal said, and thought: sharp knives, too.

"So much the better, my big friend; the taming is made sweeter. And she *will* be tamed, that lovely damsel. Unless Felipe de Alcantari's luck at the tables has changed, I don't understand how he can afford a striking woman like her."

Jubal smelled perfume and sighed. New Orleans was a city that could fatten a man and turn him soft while draining off his strength. Too many pretty women, too much rich food, and trouble with the women was, a man couldn't tell from looking whether they were all white.

The certified ladies now, they were hard to reach, locked up behind iron pickets or high brick walls, and when they ventured out, usually a fat old female watchdog rode herd on them. They weren't all that interested in Americans, either. Except for General Jackson and his staff, maybe.

"Tom," Jubal said, "I got to see the general. I 'preciate you showin' me around, but comes a time when lollygaggin' stops. Andy's havin' him a hell of a time gettin' this town organized; all the folks want to do is give balls for him, not talk about any fightin' to come."

Tom Pickett drained his glass. *"Les Créoles,* bless them; so happily they do battle with each other, but as for disciplining themselves into a military unit—too much bother, you understand. And New Orleans is impregnable, the British will not attack, the sun will continue to shine and music to play, as always. And as always, *l'amour."*

Jubal shook his head. "Come on; let's us take a walk."

Wickedly, Tom grinned. "The ladies are quite tempting, aren't they? Now if *I* could afford one—any one —I wouldn't be running off to play soldier."

Outside, clearing the insinuating scent of woman flesh from his nostrils, Jubal said. "You're bad as any sashayin' Creole. We *know* the Redcoats are comin', a whole passel of 'em, and they're loaded for bear. This town ain't got a hill in sight. no high ground to fortify, everything flat as a man's hand. Andy's goin' to need all the help he can get. I reckon. There's regulars on the march down, and what mountain militia we got left, but they might not be enough."

Swinging his cane, Tom Pickett ambled along the dark street beside Jubal. "New Orleans was French, then Spanish, then French again: both languages are spoken with more ease than English, and the city resents what's called the American occupation. In Creole eyes, we Kaintucks are alien as the *Anglais."*

"Damn," Jubal said, "this country'll stay in trouble till every squabbling little piece of it quits actin' like it can go off by itself. Tennessee gettin' its back up against the Carolinas; stylish Virginians tryin' to run everything, Philadelphia sulkin' account of the capital bein' moved, and yonder in Georgia, planters actin' like they're still a royal colony."

"You surprise me, friend," Pickett said, pausing beneath a torch pole to light a cigar. "I wouldn't think you'd be so well informed."

"My pa was right bookish. Couldn't see the sense of it myself, till he about wore out a ridin' crop on me and I learned my letters. Pa kept a teacher at the house clear up to the time we was men grown, me and my brother. Didn't hurt us none, I expect."

"I expect not," Pickett said thoughtfully. "General Jackson—does he feel as you do about the weakness of the city's defenses?"

"Andy don't exactly ask my advice on how to run the army," Jubal said, "but I'd say he's frettin' some."

They approached the Absinthe House, where Jackson spent much time these days. Pickett touched Jubal's arm. "You know where my rooms are, and they're always open to you—even if your purse is empty. When next we meet, perhaps I can introduce you to some friends. I have a few left, outside the fleshpots. I think you might be especially interested in one."

"Well—" Jubal said doubtfully.

Pickett chuckled. "Oh, she is definitely *white,* my conscience-stricken friend, white as the driven snow, but hardly as pure. Still, who would choose a stolid saint over a sparkling sinner? Especially an often forsaken beauty whose old and clumsy husband has business which keeps him out of the city so much."

Jubal grinned. "Tom, you're a pure caution. Be happy to meet the lady sometime."

She could see only a dimwhite outline of the little house, and felt her way through the dark yard behind Felipe while he unlocked the door and lit a candle.

"Small," he said, "but adequate. I have had it cleaned a time or two since . . . but dust accumulates so quickly here. My pardon, *chérie,* but I did not know that this was to be my luckiest of all nights, that I would discover a rare pearl at the Ball."

Caroline looked around the whitewashed walls, at the kitchen alcove, the simple table and chairs. There was a door to the left, slightly ajar, and she realized that it led to the bedroom. A tremble skipped up her spine. She said, "It—it's very nice."

Moving to a cabinet, he brought forth a dusty bottle. "Yes, still here, but only because thieves know well whose house this is. The larder is bare, but I will remedy that in the morning. Now, if I can find glasses—"

"Allow me," she murmured, brushing past Felipe to collect glasses and carry them to the iron sink. There she worked a hand pump and waited until rust cleared from the water before rinsing the glasses. Caroline felt excitement, and an undeniable attraction for this handsome man; she was grateful for his humbling of Kleppner, but somewhere far down, there was a little bubbling of resentment, too, because he had, after all, purchased her. Could she be more than a piece of temporarily desirable merchandise to Felipe de Alcantari, or was there something more? Had he only acted within the rigid confines of a master-slave society because there was no other way?

In the light from several candles, his eyes gleamed darkly. "You move with consummate grace," he said. "I first saw only your back, and could not tear my eyes from you during the dance."

Caroline wrested the cork from the bottle and poured a purple wine. "I felt very clumsy, since I have not danced before, only in practice."

Lifting his glass in salute, Felipe said, "Perhaps uncertain, but never clumsy. No touch of awkwardness is in you. To you, my dear, and a never diminishing grace."

She raised her own glass, sitting in the chair opposite him. "If it is proper to toast oneself."

His smile was quick and bright. "The naïveté of a child in the lush body of a woman; you are delightful. Do you realize I do not know your name? There was the hurried transaction with that swine, and it will be on the bill of sale, *naturellement,* but—"

"Caroline Monteleone," she said, tasting the wine. "We—my mother and I were journeying south from

124

Illinois when the slaver took us. He destroyed our papers and robbed us."

As if he had not heard the rest, Felipe said, "Caroline; it could have been Erato, Terpsichore, any of the Nine Muses. And Monteleone? An old Louisiana name, *chérie;* I would not have thought it had reached into the North."

"My mother and father came from somewhere down here; they were free persons of color. My father was killed on the way. I—" Thinking that she might be saying too much, Caroline stopped and drank more wine. It was too soon to test this man's sensitivities, to relate the entire story. She didn't know what else might lie behind his handsome face, save the eagerness for violence he had shown with Kleppner, and his lordly arrogance.

When she looked up, his eyes locked with hers. "More wine, Caroline?"

"Only if you wish," she said softly.

"There are other, deeper intoxications," he said. "Take a candle into the bedroom. I will join you shortly."

Her hand quivered as she lifted the candle holder, and shadows danced around her as she moved through the other door. From the ceiling, a mosquito *barre* hung over the bed, and when she had placed the candle upon a small table, she drew it back. Turning down a sheet, Caroline smoothed pillows while the small bubble of resentment grew. It was inevitable that this man should command and she obey, that he seek full measure for his purchase price, but the indignity of it gnawed at her. She had never been asked, never wooed, only ordered to perform.

Her hands were behind her waist, fumbling for hooks, when he came quietly into the room and said, *"Non, ma petite;* I would expose your lovely body myself."

She felt his breath upon her neck, the warmth of him standing very close, and his fingers were adept, skipping from fastener to ribbon without a pause. With a rustling of silk, the ballgown fell forward and she caught its upper part with her hands, her breasts rising and falling rapidly.

"Step out of it, Caroline," he said, and she lifted one leg free, then the other, and stood in only her chemise. His hands played gently over her arms, her hips, and she knew with a shock that he had undressed in the other room, and now he was naked behind her.

When Felipe tugged at her chemise, she raised her arms above her head, and he drew the flimsy garment high, floated it away. Now he did not touch her, and she did not turn to him, but simply waited, her heart fluttering like a trapped mockingbird.

He breathed an oath that was not a curse, but an expression of awe. "Ahh—how can there be such perfection? The wondrous curve of your back, the carved alabaster of the buttocks, the artistic joining of the thighs, legs so sleek and slender, ankles *très* delicate, the tiny foot—Caroline, Caroline, turn for me, so that I may revel in the true fullness of your loveliness."

This time he had asked, his husky voice almost pleading, and with a new willingness, Caroline pirouetted slowly to face him, hands by her sides, her chin lifted and her eyes direct. Unpinned, her hair flowed like a midnight waterfall, and her nipples achingly turned hard.

"Beautiful," he said, "impossibly beautiful. I am indeed a fortunate man."

Now his hands moved, and his fingertips traced the modeled hills and intriguing valleys of her tense body, discovering the texture of her skin, bringing forth tiny tremblings Caroline could not control. Felipe's face lowered to hers as his arms slid around her waist, and the touch of his lips was hesitant, tentative, until her mouth opened in an involuntary gasp.

Then she was crushed against his muscled body; his teeth raked hers, and their tongues met in frantic twining as their shaken breaths were blended. Sweeping her from the floor, Felipe carried her to the bed, his mouth still fastened avidly to her own when he lowered her to the waiting sheets.

The long kiss dissolved as he lay beside her, hands

stroking and softly cupping, tenderly caressing. Then his lips were at her throat, her shoulders, tingling upon her breasts. She smoothed his hair and her eyelids turned heavy, her body rocked from side to side. Felipe's warm mouth and trailing tongue explored her rib cage, her flexing stomach, and Caroline arched suddenly when he nipped at the joining of her hip and thigh.

"What are you—no! Oh please, *no!*"

But it was too late to deny, the moment past complaint, and within a heartbeat more, Caroline did not want to resist if she could. The ceiling whirled in fairy candlelight as the bed quaked beneath her bowstrung body, and her clawing fingers tangled in Felipe's hair. Furiously, she simultaneously gave and possessed, conquered and was taken; imprisoning him in her legs, she fought she knew not what, and when the world exploded in madwild cannonadings, she disintegrated with the rest of the starshot universe.

She was warm; she was melted in furry darkness, her body flowed away to leave only the singing of her soul. Oh so slowly and reluctantly did she journey back from the far place, returning bit by bit to join herself into the whole again. Only then did she become conscious of Felipe above her, spreading her for his entrance, and Caroline roused enough to welcome the penetration, the deep, sliding reach of him.

"Oh!" she moaned, and "Oh!" again, for he knew all the secret places and found them sweetly, but with the strength a woman desired. She flamed around him, with him, and the easy rocking changed to a battering violence of her own making.

"So!" he panted, when her raking nails found his back, when her sharp teeth reached his shoulder. "What a fiery woman you are, what a triumph of abandon!"

Impaled, she was not defeated; stabbed through, she did not plead for mercy, but battled him with every fierce stroke of her rolling hips, with each enveloping motion of her grinding belly. The bed rattled; the mosquito *barre* tangled and ripped. Gasping,

127

their sweated bodies savagely interlocked, they fought on, until the fury burned whitehot and dissolved them both in the last frantic straining.

There had been no holding back with Felipe, and she had not tried to close off her mind from the voluptuous actions of her body. Solah had instructed her that a woman should not feel shame, that lovemaking was to be enjoyed. Caroline would have hated to lose that, yet she had felt revulsion each time Kleppner had roused her—until the last time, when she had succeeded in not being lifted to that brightly shuddering plateau. Now she was able to let her emotions run riot, or rein them tightly in.

Lifting from her, Felipe rolled to one side and lay upon his back, chest still heaving. Her fingers toyed with a light dusting of hair there, and Caroline pillowed her head upon his shoulder.

"La belle sauvage," he murmured. "Dressed, you could be an aristocrat, but naked upon the bed, you are a jungle beast. I have always found a touch of black blood to be far more exciting, but rarely have I been carried to such heights."

"I have never," Caroline whispered against his skin.

"The slaver," Felipe said. "In a way, I am grateful to the swine, but that one never did what I did for you?"

Face warmed, Caroline answered, "No. I—I did not expect that."

Chuckling, Felipe said, "But the other way around, *hein?* Of course, he would order that."

She hid her face in his throat and did not speak. He said, "No matter, *mon amour.* If only white women would learn, but *non;* they feel they are impure, that somehow, they are desecrated. These wives, all spun sugar and promises on the outside, empty on the inside. It is why these houses exist upon the Ramparts, the reason for the Quadroon Balls."

Softly, she said, "Perhaps one cannot command wives as one does a slave."

Felipe laughed low in his throat. "A fallacy, *chérie.* Wives are commanded, and there are times they must

128

obey. But the difference lies in a woman *desiring* to give all the pleasure she can, of her own free will. That is what the dolts do not understand." His hand found her breast and cupped it fondly. "And we are only at the start of our journey, Caroline. There are yet many wondrous roads to be traveled, and a thousand delightful resting places along the way."

She was very lucky, Caroline thought; he might have been another brute with a blacksnake whip. Felipe didn't seem to care that another man had ravished her, and he didn't speak to her as if she were a dog. If she continued to please him, perhaps soon she could ask him about buying back her mother.

"May I get you something?" she asked. "Wine, a cigar?"

Gently, he disengaged himself and sat up, putting his legs over the side of the bed. "Not now. Though it grows late, I have something to attend, a certain gaming table where the players are most anxious to recoup their earlier losses; three thousand in gold, as I recall."

Caroline drew the sheet over her body. "That was what you paid Kleppner for me."

Felipe drew on clothing. "I believe so, but if word has not reached the gamers, they will not know that." She saw him tuck a small pistol into his shirt, and after donning his coat, Felipe belted on his sword. He said, "I will send a servant with food, and you will inform him of your other needs."

Discarding the sheet, she came to him. "M'sieu—no, Felipe—"

With a fingertip, he tilted her chin and kissed her, deeply and slowly. "I would not leave you, *ma petite,* if it were not necessary. Soon we shall be together."

He was gone then, striding into the night as if it belonged to him, without fear or hesitation. At the doorway, she listened his footsteps into silence. A cicada whirred in the yard, and a nightbird whistled. Caroline looked to the next house, where a light glowed in the window, and heard laughter rise there.

Turning, she bolted the door and padded to the

table, suddenly ravenous. The larder was indeed empty, containing not a scrap of cheese, no heel of hard bread. She poured wine into her glass and drank. It had been a night never to be forgotten: the Ball, where Creole cavaliers buzzed hungrily around her, where she was beautiful in the special gown; the night which rid her of Kleppner and brought her Felipe de Alcantari, brought her hope.

Again, Caroline looked about the little house, considering the color of curtains for its small windows, perhaps a carpet to cover the scuffed cypress flooring; new glasses and cooking utensils, certainly. In the morning, she would see to the yard, for in Illinois, Solah had taught her about flowers and shrubs. In this near tropical climate, they should grow in rainbow profusion.

Carrying a candle and peeking into another room, she smiled to discover a huge iron tub, but puzzled over a system of pipes until she decided there must be a cistern on the roof, to feed down trapped rainwater.

Clothes, she thought; now she owned nothing but the dazzling gown, and how could she cook in that? When Felipe's servant arrived, she would give him a list with her sizes carefully noted. A proud man, Felipe would have her no less presentable than the women who lived on either side. Other quadroon mistresses of white men, they were, and probably quite content with their lot in life. But they had been raised from childhood for just this, trained and coached to please rich buyers.

She found a ragged towel to cover her nakedness, and went back to the table to finish the bottle of wine. She could still catch the clean scent of Felipe in the air, and the bluesweet touch of his cigar smoke. One thing puzzled her: if he was so rich as to pay three thousand in gold for her, why that remark about the gamblers not knowing it? Probably she'd attached too much importance to that; of course he could, and would, buy Solah for her.

Blowing out the candle, Caroline followed the other

line of light from the bedroom and climbed into bed after rearranging the torn mosquito netting. She allowed the bedside candle to continue its slow dance and pulled the sheet up, snuggled into a pillow softer than she'd known for months.

As shadows played upon the ceiling, she thought that Felipe owned this house, which meant another girl—perhaps more than one—had been here before her. What had happened to them? Did he tire of them and sell them to someone else, possibly a slave trader? Her mouth tightened. She could not allow that to happen to her; she must keep him eager and slake his every desire.

With Kleppner, she hadn't thought beyond a rich man who might pamper her and retrieve her mother from bondage. Turning restlessly, Caroline realized that would not be enough. However well treated she and Solah might be, they were still slaves not allowed to even dream of freedom. But freedom was somewhere out there with the whites, their rightful due.

Freedom was everyone's heritage, and those who took it from others were thieves. She could not voice that aloud, but nobody could stop her from thinking it, planning for it, and someday she would find a chink in that righteous white prison and attain it.

"M'Nele," she said, to the guttering candle, "great warrior of the Ashanti, I will not betray your memory. I will remember who you were and who I am."

Softly, she blew out the flame and lay for a long time in the dark until sleep came.

Chapter 15

Feeling ridiculous in the ballgown, Caroline opened the door to a knock and found a wizened black man. He ogled her openly, deepset eyes traveling the length of her body, but a wide grin took the sting from his inspection.

"So you the new quadroon he bought? Gettin' more taste, him. Me, I'm Turpo, and where you want this bag of vittles?"

"Bring it in," Caroline said, and on an impulse, "Have you had breakfast?"

"Just coffee; me and that fat cook, we don't get along so good, us." Heaving the bag from one stooped shoulder, he looked at her again, differently. "You willin' to cook for me?"

"I invited you," she said, rummaging through the sack. "Ah, coffee and sugar and—"

Plopping to a chair, Turpo hauled out a decrepit pipe and thumbed a pinch of tobacco into its cracked bowl. "Many fixin's as I could tote. Master, he says do like you want."

Bustling about the stove, slicing smoked bacon and putting it on, Caroline sighed at the basket of big, white eggs. How long it had been since she'd tasted eggs. "I have a list made, clothes primarily, simple dresses. And there should be more pots, some better dishes—"

"Reckon I can scrape 'em together," Turpo said.

"You 'bout the same size as Marie. Have to steal the dishes from ol' fat cook."

Putting on coffee, Caroline said, "Marie?"

"Gal here afore you; the lastest one. Smart-lookin' enough, but just a ordinary, uppity high yeller. *She* never asked me to sit and eat."

The bacon was sizzling; she moved the pan to the back of the stove, forked meat aside, and deftly broke eggs into hot grease. "What happened to Marie?"

Turpo shrugged. "Never knowed, me. 'Spect she got sold off, or lost on the turn of a card, but don't you run off at the mouth to Master I said it."

Turning the eggs, Caroline said, "You mean he might have gambled her away?"

"Done it afore. Master, he a gamblin' fool. Bet you the sun gon shine, turn around and bet you it ain't."

She served the man his plate, poured boiling coffee, and attended to her own breakfast. Being sold, she could almost accept, but to be lost at the gaming table—that showed an even more callous disregard. "You aren't certain he wagered Marie."

Eating quickly, Turpo nodded. "Ain't certain *sure* of nothin'. One day she was here, next day gone. Me, I don't ask Master what he do, and best you don't, neither." He blew on his coffee before tasting it, then spooned more sugar.

Caroline said, "Does he have many servants?"

"Ol' fat cook and me—now you; that's all."

"But surely, he has a big house."

"That's right enough; big's a barn and near 'bout that empty. Back when I was a youngun, the Alcantaris was *sumpin'*, but since the ol' folks died, and them wives—lookee here, gal: howcome you pesterin' me thisaway?"

She drank coffee. "I'd just like to know about him, all about him."

The birdlike eyes searched her. "You a funny one. Talk like you white as you looks. *Parlez-vous français?*"

"*Oui,*" she answered, "and also Ashanti."

Turpo might have flinched; she wasn't sure. He said, "My mama, she talked some kinda African, but me, I never figured it'd do me no good. Reckon you a blood, right enough. Be right careful, gal; walk easy 'round Master." He took the list she'd made for him and folded it into a pocket. "Can't read, me, but I see it gets done. *Pour le déjeuner, merci.*"

"You are welcome," she said, "and I hope we visit again."

"A funny one," Turpo muttered. "Might be, you last a spell."

When he was gone, Caroline tidied up and stored food in the larder. A big empty house and only two slaves; a proud name and a purse of gold spent on a whim. Felipe de Alcantari was the truly strange one, and worrisome. Could he be so poor there'd be no chance of buying back Solah? Yet how could he be impoverished and so casually throw down a purse of gold at the Quadroon Ball? Turpo might be exaggerating.

She tucked up her gown and went outside to inspect the fenced yard. It was weedy and unkempt, but there was a thriving, hugely leafed tree in one corner, and flowers struggling against choking grass. With a good deal of work, the yard could be attractive, like the one back home.

Home; Caroline's lips thinned. There was no home in Illinois, no smithy, no M'Nele. Now home would be anywhere she and her mother could safely be together.

"Hey, you girl! That dress too pretty to ruin diggin' in it. You don't care about clothes no more'n that, my man buy that dress off'n you."

She looked up. A light-colored woman leaned elbows on the fence. She was older than Caroline, with a chignon about her head.

"I have nothing else to wear," Caroline said.

The woman clucked. "That Alcantari man, he buy you at the Ball last night, eh? Thought I heard somethin' over here, but my man was visitin' and I was some busy. Guess you know about bein' that kind of busy, eh? Alcantari, he's a stallion, they say. Well, I

134

just be damned if you ain't blushin'." Opening a gate in the wall, she motioned to Caroline. "Come visit, girl; I give you a dress fittin' to wear."

"I don't know if I—"

"Just come and set. Ain't had nobody new to talk to for a spell. Me, I'm Narcisse, Narcisse Marigny, and maybe I can tell you how to do around here. Kept my man for ten years, and that takes some doin'."

Narcisse's house was almost identical to Caroline's, very neat and clean, and with more furniture. Fragrant coffee bubbled back of the stove, and Narcisse said, "Pour us some, time you get changed. Here's a dress that ain't much, but it'll do till Alcantari gets you some. If you goin' to start blushin' again, step on in the bedroom and change."

The woman was more full-bodied, so the shapeless cotton dress hung loosely upon Cissy, but it was more appropriate than the lovely ballgown. Folding the gown carefully, she brought it back into the kitchen and placed it upon a chair, beside the fancy shoes. Barefoot, she felt more at home.

"There," Narcisse said, "now you look like you belong on the Ramparts. Reckon you been to your last Ball, like the rest of us, so you might's well sell that pretty dress."

"But it's so lovely," Caroline protested.

"No prettier'n you, *chérie,* and the men, they more interested in naked than dressed, eh?" Narcisse's face was smooth and lively. "Me, I recall when my man brought me here. Scared, I was, and tremblin' all over like with fever. *Maman* had me ready and I knew what to 'spect, but there was still that scare, no? Sixteen years old, with my maidenhead saved for that night." She laughed, throwing her head back; light glinted from looped earrings. "Now I know Felix— that's my man, him—Felix was scared as me, eh? Just as young, not real sure he could handle a quadroon."

Sipping strong coffee, Caroline said, "I thank you for the dress, and the coffee is delicious."

"Baton Rouge, Mobile?" Narcisse asked. "Not from this town, for sure."

135

"North," Caroline said, and the woman's eyes narrowed.

"Free country?"

"It's not all free," she replied, "but there are free blacks."

"And you down here. Tell me about it."

Caroline hesitated, but once started, the story came tumbling out: the killing and their desperate flight; their capture by Kleppner, her mother's sale on the block, her own purchase by Felipe.

Narcisse got up to pour more coffee. "You better off here, girl. Maybe Alcantari get your *maman* back and papers for you sometime. Do he set you free, they get copied at the courthouse, those papers, and your babies, they be free, too. *Oui;* you better off here."

"You're not a slave?" Caroline asked.

Again Narcisse laughed. "I was born *gens de couleur. Maman,* she lived on the Ramparts, too."

"Then why—I mean, you're still here—"

"Where else, eh? I got plenty to eat, a white man, he don't beat me. My two babies, they go to *le professeur* to read and write. What you want, me to be like them tacky *griffes libres* runnin' hair salons, maybe washin' clothes? Not for me, girl, and not for you, pretty like you are."

Caroline shook her head when the coffee pot was again offered. "Are you married to him?"

"Married? *Sacre,* no! Girl, don't you know nothin'? White man marry an octoroon? They hang us both."

"But if he should leave you?"

Narcisse made a quick sign in the air with her hand. "For the bad spirits, you understand. I buy good spells from the conjure woman, but even the best *gris-gris* don't stop it from happenin', do it get said too much. Me, I got a tight hold on Felix; ten years, like I told you. I don't get fat and I please him good. Ain't no cause for to leave me, him. If he picks another girl at the Ball, buys one at the Square, he still come to me 'cause I do him so good."

But Caroline had caught the thin echo of fear in her voice, the troubles unspoken, and knew how it was on the Ramparts. Each woman here, mistress bought outright or simply supported, wanted to believe that her white man would prove an exception to the rule of desertion. She said quietly, "Felipe de Alcantari had more than one woman in his house. Like Marie."

Narcisse tossed her head. "She run off, that one. No sense to her atall, always carryin' on behind his back. Lucky he never caught her. Yell at him like a white girl, don't have gumbo on the stove when he come, runnin' up bills for dresses. One night she run off, just like that, and that yellow nigger Joseph, him from the vegetable market, he gone, too."

"Did Felipe look for them?" Caroline asked.

"He don't say nothin', just send his man to clean out the house, *tout de suite,* and don't come around no more. Until last night with you. Me, I'm glad to have you for company. Don't get along so good with ol' Lisette down the street, and the other house past you—that's good to stay away from."

Caroline said, "I'll be glad for company, too. I have only Felipe, and no friends."

Putting one hand upon hers, Narcisse said, "I be happy to be your friend, me. You tell about up north, I tell you how to get along down here, how to keep your man—like me."

It was the first of many mornings, many days when Caroline was to learn of the loneliness in the white-washed houses, the thread of fear that bound them all together. She was to know the children without fathers who claimed them, the tension that built with each unvisited night as each quadroon mistress wondered if this was *her* time.

But now there was much to do at her own place, and she went to work brightening, cleaning, washing until the house glistened and the yard was clean. She made a savory soup with supplies Felipe had sent, and had potatoes ready for baking, a salad waiting its sauce. Freshly bathed, her hair washed and combed loosely down her back, new candles going, she waited

137

for Felipe to return. A bottle of wine also waited, in cooling water.

When he did not come by supper time, Caroline dined alone and thought about him, what she felt for this man who had come so suddenly and providentially into her life. He had delivered her from Kleppner; he had also reached some blazing core of her with his combination of gentleness and fierceness, his practiced knowing. She was his property, listed upon a bill of sale, his slave. Would she have chosen him if she could, if there had been suitors for her hand, if she was white?

Caroline could never know that. She did know there was a dark strain in him, more than a hint of danger, but perhaps that was reserved for animals like Kleppner. Felipe was an aristocrat, a man of pride and passions, and she had seen but the surface of him. In time she would know him better—and concentrate her very life on pleasing him?

Like Narcisse, she must. All the Ramparts women must. As Narcisse said, when the liaisons were done— always others, never for Narcisse—most often the notification arrived by letter, cold and formal. What matter that the woman usually received the house and its contents, that the children were free? Already, Caroline sensed the rigid social barriers among *gens de couleur:* octoroon and mustee at the top, other mixes farther down, according to the shade of their skin. Abandoned, the mistresses of the Ramparts must search among their own kind for permanence, for love. It would not be easily found, Caroline thought.

She uncorked the wine and poured herself a glass, halfway listening for the beat of quick, confident boots along the walkway. She heard small sounds of the night, the whirr of courting locusts, a muted cadence of tree frogs begging rain, and from the house on the right, a peal of young laughter too soon cut off.

Where was her mother, where was Solah? That gross man with the piggish eyes—had he taken his newest slave to bed? That one would be brutal, Caroline thought, and hoped Solah knew the trick of standing aside from her body, that she would not suffer beyond the humiliation.

For some reason then, she also thought of Tchaka, the big Mandingo. He had saved her life and she owed him for that, but how could the poor repay the poor? He was strong; with luck, he would survive the cane fields and the killing labor there, the heat and insects and the many faces of death.

Closing her eyes, she saw her father's face imposed upon the Mandingo's, for they were the same kind of men, powerful and filled with pride. M'Nele would not have toiled long in the cane, not long accepted the lash. He had escaped, and maybe Tchaka would, also. Maybe he too would die in the attempt, and was that all bad?

Caroline looked at the window. She could walk out of this house right now, carrying a sackful of food. No iron shackle held her; no vicious hounds stalked the yard; no slaver's gun and whip awaited her. But where would she go, how long could she survive, and where, how, would it be possible to find her mother? Yes, she wore chains. They did not clank or cut into her wrists and ankles, but she was bound by them, and although they could not be seen, their color was black.

Restlessly, Caroline got up and walked to the door. When she opened it, there was a drift of flower smell from the house on the right, and a strain of music, the lilt of a gay song. On the left, Narcisse's home was dark, but for a single candle in the window. Warm air, silvered by the rising moon, caressed her bare arms.

She was new; she did not have ten years of intimacy with Felipe, and he had no husbandly obligations to fulfill, no white, legal wife to sup with. She listened to happiness in the other house, and saw the outline of a carriage out front, the bored stamping of the horse. *That house was good to stay away from,* Narcisse had said, and Caroline wondered why.

One more glass of wine, she decided, so she would sleep easily. The bottle neck rattled against the glass when she heard the footsteps and turned quickly to see him in the doorway, tall and arrogant and smiling.

Running to him, she flung her arms about him and pressed herself close, heart at a gallop. "Felipe, oh Felipe—"

His kiss was abrupt. "I am hungry," he said.

Chapter 16

There were times he stumbled in so drunk that Caroline had to undress him and put him to bed. There were nights when he did not appear at all, and others when she wished he hadn't. That was when Felipe lost heavily at the gaming tables, and his temper was foul. But when he won, he was all cheer and levity, and it was almost as if they were newlyweds.

Felipe didn't abuse her physically, but Caroline was fearful of him when he was in one of his black moods. He never lifted a hand to threaten her, but the flat, icy look in his dark eyes was chilling.

"No," he said, when she first broached the subject of Solah. "Later perhaps, but for now, it is impossible."

"My mother is not well," she said quietly. "There may not be a later time for her."

Slapping the table, Felipe said harshly, "I did not buy your mother. I am not responsible for her, do you understand?"

Caroline fell silent, her heart sinking as she went about her duties and prepared his supper. Felipe was thinner of late, the thin scar along his cheek more pronounced, flaring red when he was angry.

There was always enough to eat in the little house, simple foods she had learned to make tasty through recipes given her by Narcisse Marigny. Sometimes there was no wine, and Felipe pretended not to notice, making do with coffee flavored by chicory. Often candle stubs had to be melted and reshaped into usable tapers, but she had a small wardrobe of plain clothing and two pairs of practical shoes. And lately, rather than sending the servant Turpo with victuals, Felipe had begun giving her a little silver, so she could shop the markets for bargains.

Now she was on one of those holidays, excited at being able to move about unattended, to stroll freely among the stalls and pause at each display. Narcisse was with her, and the day was bright, its early fall heat pleasant, the market raucous with sound and brilliant with color. Free blacks and mulattoes hawked their wares beside white farmers and traders, and threading the crowd were sailors of many nationalities —a few primly dressed seamen of the American navy, swaggering corsairs, intense Spaniards and Frenchmen and blond Nordics.

"Not that crab," Narcisse said, poking in dampened moss padding with a careful finger. "He don't move so good, him—this one, and that fat fellow." She put half a dozen into her basket, insisted on some of the Spanish moss as *lagniappe* to keep them alive and healthy, and weighted down her purchase with two long loaves of bread.

Walking with Caroline, she said, "You do like I say, and scrape out that yellow fat to mix in the gumbo?"

"Yes," Caroline answered. "It makes the soup richer, and Felipe likes it. Have you seen any good okra?"

"Okra about gone," Narcisse said. "Winter time, got to use more dry tomatoes and green peppers. Don't taste the same without okra, though. Look yonder; that man got nice soup bunches."

They were beyond Congo Square, between it and the river, and Caroline paused, hands tightening upon her basket handle as a cavvy of slaves shuffled past, swaying dully in lockstep, their heads down. She heard the crack of a whip and flinched, but the slaver driving the group was not Kleppner.

"Down thisaway," Narcisse urged, moving from the

142

stalls into a dank and narrow alley. "Me, I must know my fortune and buy a new amulet."

"Narcisse," Caroline said, "I don't think—"

"Shh," Narcisse warned as she stopped before a closed door hung with three polished bones and a swatch of black feathers. "Madame Zozo, she don't like much noise. Disturbs the spirits, eh?"

Inside, the shop was dreary and dim. It smelled of musty things, of ancient dust and dried skins. Caroline stifled a gasp when her head brushed against down-hanging, stiff bat wings, and almost screamed as something long and dark slithered across the floor. Candles flickered farther back, and Narcisse led her that way, where a crone huddled upon a raised platform, surrounded by charms and earthen pots of eerie ingredients.

"Madame Zozo," Narcisse whispered. "It's me, Narcisse. You read my fortune for me?" She held out two small coins.

A withered black hand clawed them from Narcisse, and the head lifted. Caroline had never seen anyone so very old; the face was hardened parchment, wrinkles piled upon lines, shrunken and worn by countless years. But the eyes were live embers set far back in their dark pits.

The taloned hands moved, rattled something, and Caroline saw bones spilled upon a stained rug. The crone mumbled, rocked back and forth, and began to chant as she stirred the bones. Caroline frowned, then put down her market basket and leaned forward to listen, for the old woman was singing in Ashanti.

The song stopped, and Madame Zozo said in French: "Your man will remain; his wife knows, but pretends she does not. You come for a new amulet, because you have been careless and damaged the old one."

Narcisse drew a sharp breath and nodded.

"This *juju* bag is more powerful," Madame Zozo hissed. "It holds the skin of *Damballah* the snake, and blood of the roosters, white and black; the eye of a spider, and dust from the grave of a virgin."

More coins passed between them, and Narcisse whispered, *"Merci,* madame. Now my friend here—"

The conjure woman gathered the bones, dropped them again and peered down at the new pattern. Candlelight touched a scattering of thin grey hair around an almost bald skull. Redcoal eyes glittering, she looked up at Caroline. "What you do here, woman? I do not read the bones for whites."

In swift Ashanti, Caroline said, "Grandmother, I am not white, and if you are truly one who speaks with spirits, tell me if my mother is well, if I will have her beside me."

Madame Zozo drew back, claws held out protectively. "You have no mother, Ashanti-who-is-not. You have no father. My—my head spins; I cannot see clearly—but there is death."

"You are a false prophet, old grandmother," Caroline said, "for my mother is Solah, daughter of the Ashanti. She is—" Caroline stopped, a band of fear encircling her heart. She didn't *know* her mother was still alive. Picking up her basket, she stepped back, hating the old woman for planting doubt in her mind, hating the voodoo trappings and this dreary, depressing room. "Let's go, Narcisse."

"The scorpion," the crone mouthed, "it will sting itself to death, also."

Narcisse fled the shop trembling, and outside said, "What that was you were talkin'? Madame, she got mad at you, eh? It don't do to make no conjure woman mad. And what she mean, you white?"

Caroline didn't answer right away, for the band pressed tighter around her heart. The scorpion; why did the old woman speak of scorpions? Kleppner might have noticed, and Felipe certainly, for he had remarked upon it, but there was no possible way for the conjure woman to know.

"She—she's a farce," Caroline said. "She chanted in Ashanti, and we spoke in that language. It startled her so much, hearing a tribal tongue from one she called white, she didn't know what to say."

Narcisse's face was puzzled. "Madame Zozo, she

144

the best *gris-gris* maker there is. I still got my man, ain't I?"

"The charms work because you believe they do. If that old hag was real, I'd have her charm Felipe into buying back my mother."

"Takes gold to do that," Narcisse said, glancing back over her shoulder and hurrying from the alley. "They say your man, his purse is empty, but maybe he gets lucky some more. Don't you fret none, *hein?*"

Caroline didn't tell her the woman had said she had no mother, didn't inform Narcisse about the scorpion. Her friend was still a little nervous when they parted at the gate. Denying the very existence of *juju,* Caroline prepared a gumbo and a salad of fresh greens and tomatoes, sprinkling it with vinegar, the way Felipe liked it. No, she thought; Solah was alive; the crone lied. That talk of scorpions—on other visits, Narcisse might have gossiped about the faint birthmark on Caroline's left hip. She might have seen it when Caroline was bathing.

Horses neighed in the street, and she stopped cooking to look out at the carriage before her other neighbor's house. A beautiful young girl alighted from it, laughing upon the arm of a swarthy, bearded man. There was another woman in the house, Caroline knew, older and shy; she had seen a face peeking through curtains. Now this lovely child—was it possible that white men kept more than one mistress under the same roof? Caroline chewed her lip and returned to the stove; with these men, anything was possible. If Felipe did the same thing, she would have no choice but to accept it.

Stirring the gumbo, she admitted he was still kind to her, that when she went to bed with him, there was the same fierce need between them, and it wasn't at all unpleasant for her to do to him, and for him, the intimate things which had been so repulsive when she was being taught them by Kleppner. If only he wasn't such a daring gambler; if only the Alcantari fortune was yet intact, and he could bring Solah to her, then Caroline would be almost content. She would never be *completely* happy until the whole order of things was changed, and she could call herself a person, free to come and go without permission, free to love whomever she chose.

That might be never, she told herself, but it would not be for lack of trying. She moved about the room, lighting candles, wondering if Felipe would come tonight, or if he was making the rounds of the cafes. Putting water on for the coffee, Caroline had another thought. Since they had been together, she had heard no word of Felipe meeting anyone beneath the Dueling Oaks, and she would have picked up at least a whisper, for the houses along the Ramparts were a hotbed of gossip. All except the one to her right, the neat house she had been warned away from.

Felipe had faced many men, it was said, and each time, he left his opponent dead in the dawn, not satisfied to simply draw blood. Perhaps she had some gentling influence upon him; Caroline fervently hoped so, for she had no idea what would happen to her if some grey morning, it was Felipe who lay dying upon the grass, felled by rapier or pistol. Would she be passed along to an heir, with his other property, or be turned over to some creditor's claim? She clenched her hands. She wasn't chattel; she *wasn't*.

At that moment, she heard the thudding of a horse's hooves outside, and went to the door. Although she'd never seen him on horseback, it was Felipe who dismounted laughing and tossed the reins to a panting, well-sweated Turpo. He must have won, she thought, and her mind went racing, echoing her mother's name.

Sweeping off a plumed hat, he bowed to her. "My lady. Is that ambrosia I smell? Is it the very nectar of the gods? No matter; I have brought champagne and truffles. Turpo!"

She stood back to let him enter, but he swept her into his arms and planted a hearty kiss upon her mouth. *"Alors,* my dear! This day all Rue Royale— *oui,* and Rue Bourbon, Rue Dumaine, also—rings with the name of Alcantari. Oh, what a beating I gave them, *mon amour.* I could do no wrong, but that is only as it should be, yes? Come, my dove, my beautiful pigeon; let us celebrate my outstanding luck."

In this mood, Felipe was gay and charming, his laughter easy and quick, and she could not help but laugh with him. He did not mind that she brought Turpo a bowl of food so the wizened little man would not pout sullenly outside.

Caroline wanted to ask how much he'd won, if it was also enough to buy Solah, but one did not pry into Felipe's personal affairs. His good humor could swiftly vanish before a thundering black storm of anger, and she did not dare challenge him. So she celebrated with him, becoming a bit giddy on champagne, and was glad when he sent Turpo away with the horse.

Lying across the bed, propped upon his elbows, Felipe said, "Undress very slowly, *chérie*. I never tire of watching your lovely body expose itself inch by glowing inch."

"I hope you never will," she said, and stood before him, obediently removing the dress, showing a flirtatious leg, turning to tease him with the back of her shift. Flicking the ribbon from her hair, Caroline allowed it to spread softly down her back, where it reached her hips.

"*Magnifique,*" Felipe breathed, and peeled away his shirt.

His nearness always excited her. Deep down, she had always been proud of her body. He had helped her not be ashamed of its fires, and she posed for Felipe now, drawing the shift over her head. Pirouetting slowly, Caroline showed him every angle of herself, advancing step by gliding step toward the bed as she did so.

"Only a single blemish," he said, "and that a small one, calling attention to the delights of its framing, as ladies apply beauty patches beside their mouths. Turn so, *bichette*—ah yes, so I may kiss the mark."

As his lips brushed her buttock, Caroline fought to keep from going taut, for the conjure woman's warning came rushing back: *the scorpion; it will sting itself to death, also . . ."*

Hands caressing her waist, Felipe drew her to him. "The birthmark has a certain shape; *mais oui*—the stinging one." He laughed and pulled her closer, burying his face in her belly. "The proper mark for your *derrière*, Caroline. Often, you use it as if you are striking, striking. . . ."

Drawing her down upon him, Felipe made slow and deep love to her, bringing her deftly to shivering heights and holding her upon them for roaring, foaming eternities. She devoted herself to him, always in the back of her mind the thought that perhaps tomorrow she could speak with him again about Solah. Surely, in this timely run of luck, he would not refuse her. Felipe was always generous when he was winning. It would be so wonderful.

At last sated, he turned his back to her and Caroline drew the mosquito *barre* around the bed, slipped out to fold his clothing and blow out the candles save one. In the kitchen, she quietly removed dishes and wine bottles, and saw that kindling was at hand for the breakfast fire. In a wrapper that had belonged to one of his other women, perhaps to the vanished Marie, she was restless, the sparks of passion dwindling slowly within her. But that alone was not the cause for her sleeplessness; she thought of her mother, somewhere out there in the night, slave to a ferret-eyed white planter.

Solah could sleep here upon a pallet, or in the bed when Felipe did not come. They could plan for the future, talk of their pride in M'Nele. There were many things she could yet learn from wise Solah. If only Felipe would listen, if he would smile at her teasing and agree she could have this thing so dear to her.

The creamwhite smell of jasmine came floating through an open window, and Caroline went out to stand in the yard, to stare up at the stars and wish she knew proper prayers to reach the old gods of the Ashanti.

Only a whisper, the voice reached out to her in

the night: *"Pardon,* madame. I cannot sleep, and if you allow me to join you—"

"Who—who are you?" Caroline asked.

"Catherine," the girl said, "Catherine Villars. My sister lives here beside your house, and now, so do I."

Caroline moved to the fence where the small shadow waited. "It was you in the carriage today."

"Yes, madame. He—my sister's man brought me. Pierre says I must remain here awhile, as there is some trouble in the city."

Impulsively, Caroline reached to take the girl's hand. It lay small and warm within her own. "We all have our troubles, Catherine."

"I know," Catherine murmured. "Marie has told me you are mistress to Felipe de Alcantari, a most handsome man, but a man not so easy to live with."

Caroline suppressed a chuckle. "You're a bold child."

"It disturbs my sister," Catherine said. "But I am fourteen years old, and not really a child."

"So old?" Caroline felt an immediate liking for the girl.

"My sister was only a bit older when Pierre brought her here. We of the blood mature quickly, is it not so?"

"I suppose," Caroline said. "But then, we do not know; they do not allow us the time."

Catherine squeezed her hand. "It is not all bad, madame. There is true love to be found; this I know."

Chapter 17

Jubal made his way into the smoky, clamorous confines of the Absinthe House. Men sang and joked and pinched the bottoms of giggling barmaids, and a card game was going full force in one corner. At the bar, Jubal passed up the bitter, licorice-tasting absinthe for a glass of decent whiskey, lighted a fresh cigar, and looked about the room.

Pickett was right; these Creoles had no thought beyond the pleasures of the night, the next glass of wine, the next delicious meal, the next beautiful woman.

There was still a mighty lot of soldiering to do, and little help these popinjays would be, time British warships hove to in the Gulf of Mexico, or worse yet, in the Mississippi itself. Once the city came under those guns, it would be a different tale; a few redhot cannon balls would change all this frivolity to panic. Then it would be too late to enlist companies, for Redcoat bayonets would soon be probing the burning streets. His smile was cynical; no hardhead British dragoon would play dueling games with Creole swordsmen then; musketball and grapeshot would answer any strutting challenge.

And the Tennessee, the Carolina volunteers? They'd do a heap better, Jubal figured; most had seen action against the lobsterbacks at one field or another, and knew the mettle of the English soldier. It was some different going against them than meeting Creek Indians. Stung by several walloping defeats, the British would be out for blood and glory here.

Detaching himself from the bar, Jubal moved slowly through the roistering crowd to the door in back where a blue-coated sentry stood guard. He was looking at the man's regimental facings and didn't see the little Frenchman until his elbow spun the man aside.

"Beg your pardon," Jubal said, and kept going.

A quick hand caught his coat. "A moment, m'sieu." Jubal turned. "Already said excuse me, friend."

The man was small and a dandy, hair curled and lace at his throat, a maroon waistcoat and pantaloons, white silk stockings. He carried a long cane. "You did not sound sincere, Kaintuck. I demand a loud and sincere apology."

"One," Jubal said, "I ain't from Kentucky; two—I bumped you accidental, and that's all there is to it."

The bar had gone quiet, and interested faces were turned to them. The little man puffed his chest and held his cane in both hands. *"Cochon!* All Kaintucks have the manners of pigs, and should be stuck like them."

At the card table, someone laughed; the faces were expectant, hungry-eyed. Jubal said, "Little man, go find some half-grown youngun to play with. You just ain't cut out man size."

The cane came apart in the Frenchman's hands; with a snicking, wicked sound, a long, thin blade sprang forth, and its keen point flashed to within a hair of Jubal's throat. Pinch-faced and hard in the eyes, the Frenchman said, "Then I shall have to trim you down to my own height, Kaintuck."

"Oh hell," Jubal said, and kicked the man in the kneecap. The sword cane flew up, and Jubal scooped a wooden chair in one big paw, to catch the point when it came ripping in again. He twisted, and the blade snapped. He dropped the chair and took a long jump to catch the stunned little man by the scruff of the neck.

Jerking him off his feet, he wheeled him above his head and hurled him across the room at the card table.

151

The Frenchman hit it with a flurry of arms and legs. Two other men were bowled over like tenpins, and the table shattered with a raining of cards and coins.

Feet apart and long arms spread, Jubal said, "Anybody else yonder think this is so damned funny? You, you little French pissant—if your back ain't broke—be happy I don't shove that trick sword spang up your ass. I'll sure as billy hell do it to the next popinjay even shows one to me."

The silence held as he walked to the sentried door. The guard grinned at him and said, "Pass, cap'n. The general's halfway expectin' you."

Only after the door closed behind him did the muttering arise. Down a bricked hallway and up a half flight of stairs was Jackson's sometime office. Colonel Coffee, coatless and harried, was bent over a table of papers; Major Benton, powdered wig in place and his brass buttons shined, lounged in a chair with a flagon of wine before him.

Jackson said, " 'Bout time, Blaze. Where in hell you been?" The general looked tired, and cupped his injured arm with one hand. "You have anything to do with that ruckus out yonder?"

"Some," Jubal admitted. "Fella waved a sword at me."

Major Benton coughed. "We're having a difficult enough time here, without antagonizing the people. We're having to restrict the troops to camp, and I hope we don't have to do the same for junior officers."

"The men won't take kindly to that," Jubal said. "A heap of 'em would just as lief be home, anyway."

"Deserters," Benton said scornfully.

"No," Jubal said, "just farmers and hunters that ain't got a passel of slaves to do for their families."

Jackson thumped the tabletop. "Goddamnit, I don't have time to listen to squabbles. Cap'n, Colonel Coffee tells me your company's the best fed, best clothed in my command. That means you're a good forager and just about halfway horsethief. So until the fight, I'm assignin' you to Quartermaster under Major Benton, so you can—"

"Quartermaster?" Jubal's shoulders hunched. "That's for storekeepers and them that can't stand to dirty their hands."

"Sir!" Benton said. "Are you calling *me*—"

Jackson roared: "Shut the hell up! Goddamnit, *I'm* runnin' this shebang! I'll have no duelin' tomfoolery 'twixt my officers. Both of you'll goddamned well do what you're told or I'll hang your hides out to dry. Cap'n, your job is to find us musket flints, just as many as you can buy or steal. We're woeful short on flints, and there ain't any comin' from Congress. That bunch can't find their asses with both hands, much less get me what I need for this here battle. So it's up to you; I don't care how you supply me with flints, just goddamned well *do* it—understand?"

"Yes, gen'l," Jubal answered.

Scowling, Jackson said, "Well, you tied to a stump or somethin'? Get on with it."

Jubal ignored Major Benton's smirk and wheeled about. Where was he going to find suitable flints for the army's muskets? This was flat and marshy land, without so much as what could be called a decent rock in its black dirt. But the Creeks had used flint arrowheads, and they got them somewhere. It was a hellish long ride back to that part of Alabama, and damned few Creek survivors left there to pass out information. Still, Andy Jackson didn't cotton to excuses, and you couldn't very well fling excuses at the British when they landed.

Frowning, he went back into the tavern, and again the talk stopped itself at sight of him. The little Frenchman was gone, toted off somewhere by his friends, but others stared at Jubal, and more than one hand fingered a sword hilt. Be damned to them, he thought; next time some mincing peacock got in his way, he'd go whole hog and tear the whole place down around their heads.

Nobody blocked him. He reached the *banquette* and hurried along it to find the livery stable and his horse. Tom Pickett, he thought; Pickett knew everybody and near about everything around New Orleans.

153

Maybe Tom could get word to one of the flatboats coming downriver to pick up a supply of good flints; maybe he knew of banks to the west or north where the stone could be mined, or if the swamp-haunting Choctaws had any. From the few he'd seen, they were a raggle-taggle bunch, nowhere near warlike as the vanquished Creeks, but they had to cut meat with *something,* had to hunt and make fire with *something.*

Almost reaching the stable, Jubal suddenly changed direction and trotted back into the heart of the city. He'd see Tom right off and tell his problem, because there was precious little time to spare. Andy Jackson didn't know exactly when the British would land, but he certain sure knew they would.

All these duelers, Jubal thought; there were pistols aplenty in New Orleans, and if he had to, he'd bring in troops to search every house and confiscate every man jack's sidearm, every fowling piece, to strip them of vital flints. Let the Creoles squall and be damned.

Outside a tavern, he hired a black to carry a lantern ahead of him, and hurried the man along to the ramshackle building where Pickett lived. They were at the door when the black yipped and dropped his light, but Jubal could make out the figures coming at him in the dark. Three shadows ducked in low at him, like wolves looking to hamstring.

His left hand snapped the two-barreled pistol from under his coattails, while his right whipped the skinning knife around to catch the first one solid across the throat. The pistol went off, but something caught Jubal a hard lick on the head and he went down.

He knew enough to roll away, and the skinning knife wheeled up in reflex. But Jubal couldn't see worth a damn, and somebody was chopping down at him. He caught a heavy blow on his shoulder, another along the back, and bellowed in outrage. Another man was hollering, too, probably the one he'd got to with the knife, and the sounds rang inside Jubal's head.

Then boots were astride him, and a pistol exploded, a man yelped, and hands were tugging at Jubal's coat.

Blindly, he struck at them, and Tom Pickett said hoarsely, "Damn it, Jubal!"

Jubal quit fighting and got himself to one knee, shaking his head to clear it, blinking away the fog. The lantern lay where the black dropped it, sending out feeble light that showed one ragged man curled upon the *banquette,* hands gripping his belly. Another was staggering down the street, and a third had fallen halfway across, arms flung wide.

"Inside," Tom said. "Come on, Jubal, before the watch arrives."

"Son of a bitch hit me a lick with a singletree," Jubal grunted. Swaying to his feet, he allowed Tom Pickett to steer him into the building and plop him onto the bed. "What the hell they jump me for?"

"Footpads," Pickett said, turning up the lamp and inspecting the side of Jubal's head. "Hold still, now."

"Meant to do me in," Jubal muttered. "Wasn't just after my purse, the way they come at me. Ow, damnit! Go easy with that rag."

Pickett stepped back. "Not much of a cut, but you've already got a lovely lump growing there. How do you feel? Do you see two of me?"

"One's enough, 'specially when you come barreling out to save my hide. My head's right thick, I reckon, but I feel like I been kicked by an ornery mule."

"Here," Pickett said, proffering a glass of whiskey. "Now give me your coat and I'll try to get the mud off it."

"My pistol," Jubal said as the whiskey took hold. "Must of dropped it."

"Then it's lost. The watch won't know whose it was. You provincials—holding to that great bloody knife and losing the pistol." He took a drink himself. "If those weren't cutpurses, then why should they attack you?"

Jubal shook his head and winced at the mistake. "Don't know, less'n that little Frenchie pissant sent 'em." Holding out his glass for more painkiller, he told Pickett about the affair in the Absinthe House and the man with the sword cane.

Pickett nodded. "Yes, that would do it. We Kaintucks aren't liked in New Orleans, your famous General Jackson notwithstanding. When you manhandled that local swordsman before his peers, you embarrassed him greatly. Since you didn't react like a gentleman and challenge him, he sent hired thugs after you."

"Should've broke his back," Jubal said. "Will, the next goddamn *gentleman* waves a sticker at me."

There was a clattering outside, and raised voices. Through a window, Jubal could see flaring lanterns. Pickett said, "It's best you don't get involved. Can you walk?"

Jubal got up and put a hand to the wall to steady himself. "Sure can."

"Put on your coat. It's damp, but it will pass, should we be stopped. And do put away that knife."

Down the dark hall and out back they went, Pickett leading. They crossed a courtyard and found a heavy iron gate set into a brick wall. Passing through, Jubal found himself on another street, one where torches still sputtered. Head throbbing, he followed his friend, glad that Pickett knew where he was going.

"In here," Pickett directed, and they went through another ornate gate that swung noiselessly on its hinges, into a courtyard thick with foliage with a fountain bubbling in its center.

Jubal stopped suddenly when a huge black towered from the shadows, but Pickett gave his name and the giant faded back without a word. Jubal took his hand from the hilt of his knife as they mounted a circular castiron staircase to an upper level. Another mammoth black sat before an oaken door.

Inside the room, a chandelier blazed with many candles upon walls rich with tapestries, lined with polished, delicate furniture. Shabby Tom Pickett walked through the room as if he was most familiar with it, tapped upon a small door nearly hidden in the far wall, and waiting an answer, pointed toward a stock of bottles. Willingly, Jubal went to them and selected whiskey. Pouring the goldenbrown liquid into

156

a stemmed crystal glass, he almost spilled it when the woman came into the room.

"Friend Jubal," Pickett announced, "this is Madame Lisette de la Rassac; Lisette—Captain Jubal Blaze, of General Jackson's staff."

Jubal stared. From the crown of her glittering head to the tips of her tiny, jeweled shoes, Madame de la Rassac looked as if she had been dipped in molten gold and carefully, lovingly polished. Emerald eyes smiled at him from lowered bronze lashes, and her generous mouth was dewy rosepetals.

"Capitaine," she murmured, dazzling Jubal, warming his skin. He was suddenly very conscious of his appearance, the discolored lump on his head, his raddled coat and muddy breeches.

She held out her hand, and awkwardly Jubal took it, wondering at its fragility, its whiteness. One foot forward, very sweet and poised, she stared up at him, and he realized belatedly that he should kiss her hand. Nothing loath but wishing he had the style and flair, Jubal pressed her hand to his lips, then didn't want to let it go. "Madame," he said.

"Do call me Lisette," she said. "How nice of Tom to bring you." She didn't move back from him, and there was a disturbing power in her closeness.

From the array of bottles, Pickett said, "I've been meaning to introduce you, but Captain Blaze has been busy with the general and—a few other things. But tonight he was set upon by footpads, and since we have no wish to become involved with the authorities, I hoped you would be so kind as to offer my friend a temporary shelter. Your husband is traveling again, I presume?"

Lisette floated away, leaving an emptiness behind. Pickett furnished their hostess with a glass of sherry, and she flicked a glance over a cunningly rounded shoulder at Jubal. "But of course; poor Michel and his business. And *naturellement,* I will be more than happy to provide hospitality for one of General Jackson's heroes."

It was strange, Jubal thought, how a voice could

be both furry and silken. He gulped his drink, and she noticed his bruised head. With a little gasp, she swiftly came to him again, her butterfly fingertips fluttering scented and tender across his skin. "But you are injured! How terrible. Tom—call my maids; *m'sieu le capitaine,* sit you here upon the couch so I may remove your coat. Ah, so; those brutes, those *cochons,* to do this thing!"

Retreating behind closed eyelids, Jubal tilted back his head and tried to relax. He peeped at the serving girls, both mulattoes, and at the rounded swell of a small but beautifully sculpted breast when Lisette leaned above him. She was no bigger than a child, he thought, but never had he seen so much woman packed into so little frame.

From the maids' trays, she applied perfumed soap and water. Gently, she rubbed in soothing unguents, and Jubal was hard put not to plant a lingering kiss upon the tip of the cunning breast that so closely tantalized him. He would far rather take the entire lovely globe into his mouth, shining gown and all, and resisted temptation by digging his fingers into the couch.

"Pardon," Lisette said. "I have hurt you."

"Oh no, no," Jubal lied, for the pain was not in his head, which he wished more woefully wounded so that she could spend more attention upon it. The pain was deep and low in his groin, and manfully he fought against the stiffening.

"Out, out, and prepare the tub," Lisette commanded the serving wenches. "Tom, this gentleman must rest and recover. Another whiskey, *capitaine*—"

"Jubal," he said weakly.

"Another whiskey for M'sieu Jubal, then take yourself off, so I may watch over him. It would not do to allow a savior of our city to languish unattended."

Tom Pickett smiled, and Jubal thought he caught the wink of a roguish eye. "Of course, madame. We shall be forever in your debt."

When the woman turned from the door, Jubal saw she had more lovely facets than the gleaming chandelier above. The flash of an appealing ankle beneath the trailing dress, the fluid roll of a perfect hip, the animation of her golden cameo face—it was too much for a man to absorb all at once, but he tried, he tried.

"Allow me to help you," she purred, and he felt like a great, clumsy bear when she braced his elbow, when one breast snuggled searingly to his forearm and would certainly char his shirtsleeve. "The maids have drawn a hot bath, and I will see you to it. Then I will prepare your bed—ah, m'sieu, that such a thing should happen on the streets of *Nouvelle Orléans. A bas* such dogs!"

Tactfully, she withdrew when he faced the largest tub he'd ever seen, and fluffy white towels the size of blankets. In the water, his hand trembled upon the very soap that had caressed Lisette's nude body, that had exchanged intriguing scents with her flesh.

Deep in the water, he wondered how a near bankrupt flatboat broker could know such a woman, what stroke of fortune had brought together Pickett and Lisette—Lisette; he rolled the flavor of the name upon his tongue. No doubt something to do with the husband's business. Jubal blessed the trade that took a man far from so attractive a wife, and hoped the business prospered farther afield.

But could such a polished lady be drawn to a crude backwoodsman? She had called him hero and stressed his military rank; perhaps that was an honor that would lift him to her level. So golden, like a new dandelion in July sun, yet somehow spilled moonlight would suit her better—or candlelight pouring softly over the sensuous curves of that small, wondrous body.

Hastily, Jubal abandoned the tub and dried himself roughly, knowing now he had been struck solidly in several places with a club. He was lucky it hadn't been a broadsword or an axe; then he would never have met Lisette.

Donning breeches and shirt, he brushed hopelessly at his shock of hair, very carefully around the darkening lump. In the field, a soldier expected trouble and was on guard against it. Here, he was a fool to relax, and it would not happen again. There was some satisfaction at reaching the first man with his knife, but without Tom Pickett, he'd have been a goner. For a self-professed coward, Pickett had done all right. That damned little Frenchie, Jubal thought; if he ever saw that pissant again, he'd knock him flat and stomp a mudhole in his ass.

Discreetly, she tapped upon the door, and Jubal jumped at her husky whisper: "Do not dress fully, m'sieu. Your bed awaits."

The top of her head came only to his chin, Jubal realized, and her thigh brushed his knee. He could look down into the delicious cleft of her breasts as they walked together, and envy the shimmering cloth that so lightly held them.

"Ici," she said, "here in my own bedroom."

Jubal swallowed. "Madame—ah, Lisette—I can't turn you out of your bed. The floor, a couch, anywhere will do."

"Mais non," she scolded. "My husband's room is being aired and is not ready, and the guest rooms are being repainted. So you will have to make do with my poor bed. See, there are whiskey and cigars beside it."

The entire room was vivid scarlet, thick drapes, deep carpet, a sitting area, even the satin coverlet upon the bed itself—a compelling, blood-leaping red. Jubal could only stare and wonder.

"You will not give away my secret?" Lisette asked. "To be a proper lady always is such a bore. Here I can be my true self; here I am *alive.*"

"Yes," he whispered, "oh yes," and lowered himself gingerly to the bed while he picked up the whiskey glass. "But where will you sleep? You've already been so kind, and I just don't feel right—"

"Do not worry, Jubal." Her lush lips fondled his name. "I shall be content, rest assured." Her deep green eyes skipped up and down him. "So large, you are, but not—how do you say?—out of balance."

Jubal tossed back the whiskey; it was no stronger than creek water. He didn't know what to do with his hands, and tried to discipline his eyes.

"For a while," she said, "please leave the lamp turned up. I would look in upon you."

He mumbled something, and watched her sway through the door, then stared at the closed panel as if he could still see her outline. Sighing, he drank from the bottle and drank again. His head throbbed and his shoulder and back ached, but worse was the gnawing in his belly. Madame Lisette de la Rassac was a great lady who was only being kind to the friend of a friend; he'd been a fool to expect more.

Bootless, he lay back upon the bed and sniffed at her pillows. Pickett had mentioned a lonely wife whose inattentive husband spent much time upon the roads, but surely this couldn't be the same woman. Tom was probably right now soothing that other wife.

So much for the vaunted octoroons, and for dusky Creek squaws; Lisette's golden loveliness shamed them all. Jubal closed his eyes, crossed and uncrossed long legs, then came to one elbow to have another drink. Thumped about and somewhat tired, he would still play hell sleeping peacefully in this soft, perfumed bed. It was filled with Lisette; each rustle of the coverlet was the enchanted caress of her petticoat against slim, gliding legs.

Damn Tom Pickett for bringing him here, for exposing him to this unattainable beauty. They should have gone to the whorehouse, to an inn, anywhere but this sweet torture chamber and its eiderdown rack. Jubal drank again and his head buzzed.

He didn't hear the door quietly open and close, but when she stood above him in a gauzy nightdress, scarlet, of course, Jubal could see every beguiling line of her tiny, superb body.

It was amazing how his single hand cupped both her rounded buttocks, how stiff was her strawberry nipple between his lips. And when he knew the full flavor of that, Lisette's mouth gave him a bright new taste, a roaring wildness that raced through every vein of his taut body. At first, he was afraid he might hurt her, but there was a savage strength in that whipping

161

little body, a desperate need in its flailing, encompassing legs.

"Harder, *mon amour!*" she gasped against his teeth. "Ahh—*oui!* Harder and deeper—you are truly a giant! Tear me open with it, rip me wide, lover! Yes, yes—ahh! Ahh!"

She bit and clawed; she writhed and heaved, and she accepted all of him, battering greedily against him. Hissing into his mouth, her tongue a softwet whiplash, she devoured him. Jubal had to pin her down, to strike within her bucking flesh until the great, wracking shudders rolled over them both.

Still held down by his weight, her sweated belly swung tic-toc, tic-toc, like the feathered pendulum of a clock, and her legs clutched him fiercely.

"See, *mon chéri?*" she said into his chest. "I said I would be content, and I am. For now, my huge bear, only for the moment."

Chapter 18

This time, Felipe walked home. He moved slowly through the doorway with the stiff-kneed gait that told her he was carrying too much wine, and his waistcoat was stained, his usually spotless shirtfront rumpled. Saying nothing, he flung off his hat and stood his sword in the corner, then sat heavily into a chair at the table. Fumbling for a cigar, he also brought out the wicked little derringer and placed it upon the table.

Biting her lip, Caroline knew he had lost, that there would be no chance of having Solah with her; not this time, and maybe never. She busied herself at the stove, dipping a bowl of steamy *pot au feu*, breaking off an end of crusty white bread to place before him.

"Bastards," he said thickly. "Stinking shopkeepers, greedy bankers, lowly tradesmen—scum, all of them. Not fit to game with a gentleman."

"Yes, Felipe," she said, and filled a coffee cup for him.

He glared into the soup. "But at least one will regret it. That miserable ship chandler Croquère had the audacity—*audacity,* I say—to intimate my note would not be good. Of course I slapped his fat jowls, and the fool squealed out a challenge before he could regain his senses."

"You—you'll duel him then?" Caroline asked.

He dug his spoon into the soup, brought it to his mouth. "I will kill him at dawn. Hah! Croquère chose

163

broadswords, knowing I am not familiar with that weapon and hoping to save his precious skin, but I will kill him, nonetheless."

Crossing her arms over her stomach, Caroline squeezed hard. "Will your head be clear?"

Felipe put aside the spoon and drank directly from the bowl. When he lowered it he said, "How touching that my mistress frets for my life, and therefore her own. Yes, my head will be clear and my hand steady. That is not the problem. I have only one second and the code calls for two. It seems the grubby shopkeepers have no taste for the sight of blood, and the gentlemen of my own class contrive to be unavailable, damn them." He ate bread with his coffee.

"Do you want anything else?" Caroline held her voice steady with an effort.

"More coffee," he said, and caught her wrist. "It is not late. Go speak to that one next door, that Pierre, or his brother, if Pierre is not home. They are both familiar with death, though hardly with honor. Do not tell me you are not known in that house; I know you visit the women; I know everything you do, Carrie."

Caroline returned the coffee pot to the stove. "But I cannot just—"

"You can," he said, "and you will." His eyes were hard, his mouth ugly. "Say it is necessary to use his carriage, also. My own is—being repaired." Speaking into his cup, Felipe said, "The thought firms in my mind—ah, yes. This will be the opportunity." He looked up at her. "Why do you hesitate, wench?"

There was no standing to him, and she knew it. A shawl about her shoulders, she walked to the next house and knocked. There was movement inside, and a man's voice rasped, "Who's there?"

She called her name, and a heavy bolt slid back; the door opened but no one stood in it. Caroline stepped in, and the door swung shut; Catherine rushed to her, and she saw Marie Villars across the room. Only then did the man step from behind the door, sliding a pistol back into his waistband.

"In darkness," he rumbled, "one never knows. My apology, madame."

Catherine said quickly, "This is my friend, Pierre—the one I spoke of. Marie knows her, also."

It was the first time Caroline had seen him up close, and he was not handsome. There was a cast in one eye, and he was dark, a square, heavy-shouldered man who walked with a rolling gait, but lightly. "M'sieu," she murmured, "I—I would not trouble you, but my—Felipe de Alcantari bade me come."

His smile was pleasant, and he swept a furry hand in a near bow. "Alcantari, yes? Be seated, madame, and tell me what that great gentleman wishes of my humble self. Marie—wine for our guest, for she looks pale."

Catherine sat beside her as Caroline stammered out the request. The house went still, and Pierre held up his glass to watch lamplight play in its depths. "So; and Croquère the chandler is the victim this time. A good thing he has a partner, Marie; our ships will not lack good fittings."

Marie Villars said softly, "Is it wise, Pierre?"

He lowered the glass, and said to Caroline, "Your pardon, madame, but Alcantari has misled you. There is no lack of out-at-the-elbows *gentlemen* who delight in attending such meetings, even to allying themselves with him. He must have a reason, that one. *Bien;* I will be his second and discover the reason. Madame, you will please inform M'sieu Alcantari that I, and my carriage, are at his disposal."

After thanking him, Caroline went out onto the porch with young Catherine close behind. She said, "I hope I have not brought trouble upon your sister's man."

Catherine touched her shoulder. "Pierre was born to trouble." She sighed. "And so, I fear, was Jean."

"The brother Felipe spoke of?"

The small hand trembled upon Caroline's shoulder. "Oh yes; you have not seen him, but he is—he is—"

"An older man who does not see the woman in you?"

165

"He will," Catherine said fiercely. "I will *make* him see."

Felipe might be angry if she dallied, so Caroline patted the girl's shoulder and promised they would talk soon. Then she hurried home.

Empty, the coffee pot sat before a morose Felipe. He did not brighten when she told him Pierre had accepted, but said, "Of course; it is an honor for his kind. That Croquère and his broadsword; a butcher's weapon, and he will use it so, but any sword has a point, my mustee." He raised his head. "I will sleep while you sit here. At first cock's crow, waken me, and be ready in a cloak."

Caroline stared at him. "You mean for me to go with you?"

Kicking over the chair and standing up, Felipe laughed. "It is not done, *hein?* But I have been thinking of many things that are not done, *divertissements* that will keep their small minds from money matters, and you are important to all. So at dawn we begin, you and I."

During the night, Caroline kept a small fire going and made fresh coffee. She thought of the blacksmith shop in Illinois and the small house there, of M'Nele's broad chest when he pounded glowing iron into horse-shoes, of Solah's quiet and worried counsel. They had labored so hard and so long to protect her. Then because of her, they had put themselves back into danger. M'Nele had died for it, and Solah—

The scorpion stings itself, the conjure woman said. She had not said the poison would strike all things close and dear.

Felipe; what would happen to her if the other man killed him? She might be put on the block in Congo Square, a sacking dress lifted from her body to exhibit it to leering farmers, her adeptness in bed extolled, her breasts pinched, her buttocks handled.

The Quadroon Ball was more subtle, but the same merchandise was on display, the same speculative buyers at hand. Would she be passed from man to man as each tired of her, and be sold at last—as shopworn goods—to a house of prostitution?

"Stay alive," Caroline whispered. "Stay alive, Felipe. Not because I love you, but because I need you."

She must have nodded, for she jerked awake at the rattle of the carriage at the door, and leaped immediately to shake Felipe from his sleep. He splashed water over his face, donned a clean shirt and tied his stock with steady fingers. "Have you seen a man killed, wench?"

"Yes," she answered.

"Oh?" His eyes were bright. "But never so precisely, I wager. Come then; we must not keep Croquère waiting, nor Pierre Lafitte."

"Lafitte?"

Mockingly, he bowed to her. "But of course; did you not know? I have availed myself of the services of a smuggler chieftain; not *the* leader they call *le Bos;* that dubious honor is reserved for his brother Jean, king of the Gulf corsairs. But Pierre will do nicely." Then his fingers bit into her arm and she was pushed ahead of him to the carriage.

Inside, when Pierre recognized her, he drew in his breath. "M'sieu! A woman at a duel?"

"A quadroon at that," Felipe answered, "or mustee, if you prefer. Another blow in their fat faces, I think. You are not ashamed of your own *gens de couleur?*"

"No," Pierre said shortly, "and I do not subject them to such as this." Settling back, he said no more, and Felipe stared out the carriage window toward greying light. "The other one will meet us at the Oaks," he said.

Inside her head, Caroline repeated, Stay alive, stay alive. I am beginning not to like you, Felipe, but you must stay alive. And she knew this was also condemning another man to death, but that was not her doing.

When the carriage rocked to a stop, the horses snorting and the black coachman calling softly to them, she shot a glance at Pierre Lafitte from the corners of her eyes. She had heard the name whispered in the marketplace, sometimes gaily, sometimes warningly;

Lafitte: smugglers who avoided customs with contra-
band fineries and war-blockaded luxuries so dear to
Creole hearts. Everything from Chinese silks to Haitian
slaves, it was said. It was also rumored that the Lafitte
brothers and their motley crew of seamen, operating
from the trackless marshes of Barataria, were no more
than cutthroat pirates. No, said others; Jean Lafitte
carried a lifelong grudge against the Spaniards, and
took as prizes only treasure-laden galleons of those
arrogant and rapacious dons.

But even talkative Narcisse had not told Caroline
she lived next door to Pierre Lafitte; perhaps, with her
belief in voodoo, the woman had been afraid to invoke
the name. Here the man was to be Felipe's second,
standing now upon dewy grass to offer his hand and
help Caroline down.

Felipe was striding ahead to the little group of men
clustered beneath two giant liveoak trees, and Caroline
thought how different they were, Pierre and Felipe. To
Felipe she was a possession, no more, but Pierre
treated her as a person, with the same deference he
might show a white lady. Yet Felipe was an aristocrat
and Pierre a pirate; where was the difference?

Pierre would have left her standing far back from
the oaks, but Caroline said, "Please—he will be angry
with me," so he brought her closer. Heads turned her
way, and the men huddled to whisper to each other.

"Eh bien," Felipe said loudly, "the sun is rising, gentlemen—and M'sieu Croquère—so let us be on with
it."

A somber man tendered two wide swords, and Felipe mockingly bowed, giving his nervous opponent
first choice of weapons. Caroline saw a chunky man
with a paunch, coatless and trying not to shiver in the
dawn wind. He looked old and as if he had not slept
and was very afraid.

One of his seconds said, as if the words were difficult to pronounce, "M'sieu de Alcantari, we would
count ourselves satisfied at first blood."

"And I will not," Felipe said. "The only way this

shopkeeper can avoid his death is to humbly apologize to me—upon his knees."

At Caroline's ear, Pierre whispered, "He presses. No man can do that and remain a man."

Croquère shuddered visibly, then threw back his shoulders. His voice was not strong: "D-damn you, Alcantari! Let us fight."

Grey fingers of light brushed Felipe's face as he stepped back, his ruffled shirt crisp, long hair flowing in the breeze. There was the awful eagerness in it, that look Caroline had seen once before, when he had threatened Kleppner. Now his profile was that of a hungry hawk, sharply defined, all hard planes and angles.

"En garde, m'sieu."

Croquère's rush was clumsy and desperate, the heavy sword swinging in a dully shining arc. Casually, Felipe parried and the blade rattled, passed him harmlessly. His arm straightened with a snap, and Croquère fell back with a dark spot spreading upon his left shoulder.

"Come now, shopkeeper," Felipe called. "A little *touche* like that does not cripple."

Gasping, the man wheeled his sword high and brought it whistling down, but Felipe dropped to one knee and Caroline saw his blade flick at Croquère's thigh. The chunky man grunted with pain and staggered, his swordpoint *chunked!* into the earth.

Felipe's laugh was shards of glass rubbed together as he lithely slid up and away, all fluid and deadly grace. "Do not hurry, shopkeeper! Recover your blade; there is plenty of time to die."

Caroline's stomach turned. This was cruelty, meaningless and savage. Felipe was playing with the bleeding man, torturing him mercilessly. She saw Croquère's whitely sweating face, the spread mouth pulling for air, and the rising sun showed his wounds.

"No!" she cried out, and pressed the back of her hand against her mouth.

Felipe ignored her, dancing in and gliding back out,

169

his point red now. Croquère's arm sagged and he wobbled, his paunch heaving.

Beside her, Pierre Lafitte said hoarsely, loudly: "Enough! Enough, you hear? Be done with it."

Gathering himself in a final despairing effort, Croquère stumbled at Felipe, hacking with the broadsword. There was a darting moment when the men strained together belly to belly, and a grunt.

"Oh, very well," Felipe said, and stepped back, withdrawing his blade so that Croquère could fall. Laughing, he flipped the sword into the air and caught it by its slippery steel, presenting the hilt to one of the dead man's seconds. "A passing fair blade," he said. "Too plebeian for my liking, but passing fair."

Another man kneeled and opened a satchel; the doctor, Caroline thought, but too late. Sickened, she held hard to Pierre's knotted arm and turned away her face.

"Come, my dear," Felipe said, approaching them and walking on by. He did not thank his other second, did not even mention the man's name, but left him standing with the others, one now with his enemies. But in the carriage he said to Pierre, *"Merci,* although it was hardly worth the ride, *hein?"*

Pierre said slowly, "Even a pig should be dispatched quickly."

"A schooling for the others," Felipe said, sinking back against the cushions as the carriage pulled off. "A lesson for all the city."

"If the professor also learns, m'sieu. A desperate man may overcome skill one day. I have seen it."

In high good humor, Felipe said, "Footing is uncertain upon the sea."

"Life is uncertain," Pierre said.

"And so, worth the living, *oui?* Otherwise it would be such a bore." Felipe leaned forward. "I would speak of business with you."

Pierre shook his head. "Not before the lady. I have made it a rule to keep my ventures from my own lady, and I trust you to do the same."

"Lady?" Felipe asked, then chuckled and shrugged. "No matter; what I have to discuss will be of mutual profit to us, and we can speak of it over brandy, as friends."

The carriage stopped before Pierre answered. "The Lafittes wear their friends at their sides, m'sieu. But I will drink with you and speak of profits."

Again it was Pierre who helped Caroline down, and she wished she did not have to go into the house with Felipe. If he lay with her today, she would scream.

Chapter 19

The difference, Jubal thought, wasn't so much in the food or the money, but what was done with both. Back home at Tarboro, they had smoked ham and fresh eggs, too, but Lisette's cook worked some kind of magic with seasonings and sauces. Carolina coffee wasn't fixed this way, with chicory to cut the bitterness, and nobody there had even heard of flaky, sugared *brioches,* much less served them for breakfast.

On the Tidewater, plenty of folks had plenty of money, fancy houses and servants. But inland a little, everything changed; things got plain and sturdy, and no matter how many acres a man planted, he kind of turned up his nose at satin knee breeches, powdered wigs and the like, and at folks who wore them.

But here—Jubal leaned back from the table and took the mild cigar Lisette de la Rassac stood ready to light for him. Rolling fragrant smoke in his mouth, he eyed the way her lissome body swung appealingly as she went to pull the bell cord. Here, these Creoles made the most of everything, and that included lovemaking. Lisette really knew how to build a man slow and easy to his short rows, and just when he thought he had no more strength left, she found ways to bring him back hard and eager again. A whole lot of woman, Lisette, not about to get herself lonesome while her husband was on his travels.

"How is your head this morning?" she asked, when the serving maids had cleared the table and gone.

Jubal grinned. "Clean forgot about it last night, and if I didn't have somethin' to see to for the general, I reckon you could make that knot plumb disappear afore the day's out."

She leaned to kiss him, trailing perfumed hair across his cheek, brushing his shoulder with a ripe, firm breast. "Hurry, always hurry with you Kaintucks. Tom Pickett is coming for coffee; at least, wait for him. Will you be gone long, *chéri?* If so, I shall be devastated."

"Don't know; till I get the job done, I reckon." Jubal looked at the ash on his cigar. "Don't even know where to start good."

An outside bell rattled, and Tom Pickett came freshly scrubbed and smiling into the room to kiss Lisette's hand and thump Jubal on the back. A mulatto girl trailed in his wake, bearing fresh coffee and *brioches* on a silver platter.

"A fine morning," Pickett said, eyes twinkling at Jubal, "and rightly so, after a fine night. I inquired after a certain small man and his *colchemarde;* it seems both he and his sword cane departed the city. Lisette, as always the coffee is superb, and as always, you are stunning."

She made a little curtsey, her fine breasts jiggling. *"Merci, mon ami.* But turn your charm upon your friend, who insists upon leaving me."

Jubal wished he could turn phrases like they could, that he could talk like people in books he'd read. He felt clumsy. "It ain't that I *want* to go, Lisette; you ought to know the truth of that. But I got my duty, and ol' Andy Jackson, he don't take kindly to dawdlin'."

Pickett said, "Perhaps I can help. I'll never be a military man, thank my lucky stars, but if it's to do with supplies—"

"I been thinkin' on that," Jubal said. "If'n you finish chewin'—"

"Do not let me disturb you," Lisette said. "I must see to the servants, but Jubal—you will not leave without saying *adieu?"*

"Never," he promised, and enjoyed the motion of

her long legs beneath the silk gown as she left the room. To Pickett he said, "I need flints, Tom; many as I can lay hand to, and nothing like to crumble after they get snapped a time or two; I'm after good, hard flints."

"For muskets," Pickett said, and put down his coffee cup. "And by the look of you, I'd say the lack of flints is vital to the defense of the city."

"Didn't say that," Jubal denied. "But I figured, what with you knowin' the flatboats comin' downriver, and the country hereabouts—"

Pickett looked thoughtful. "Yes, I think I can help. But it will take some doing. You understand, very few flints come down on the flatboats, just enough to supply local needs. But farther north, there just may be a ledge of decent flint near Natchez. I've heard rumors of it."

"Andy didn't say how much we can pay," Jubal said, "but I reckon it'll be somethin'. Congress ain't all that quick with money, and he's put himself out of pocket more'n once on this campaign."

"The general's word is good," Pickett said, "although it will take ready money for the transactions."

Jubal nodded. "Comes down to it, I 'spect I can handle it. Been totin' a letter of credit halfway across the country, case I needed it."

"Oh?" Pickett's eyebrows went up. "From the Congress?"

"Not hardly; from my bank in Carolina."

"Well," Pickett said, "it seems our roistering Kaintuck is a man of means."

"Wouldn't say that, but I can get by. Now about them good flints—"

Pickett stood up. "Travel arrangements must be made, supplies gathered, and how I detest thumping along astride a horse. But the Natchez Trace is no place for wagons, unless accompanied by an armed escort. If we succeed in acquiring the flint, it can be shipped here by flatboat. Natchez is a waystop on the river and boats can always be found there."

"Better get on to the bank, then," Jubal said. "I

can put this letter through and take some of it in gold. Got my horse to see to, and a heap of things. Tom, I 'preciate this."

Pickett sighed. "No more than my duty, I suppose. I mean, the Natchez Trace is probably safer than staying in New Orleans, beating off Jubal Blaze's attackers. You do seem to draw trouble, friend."

"And you been handy twice to help out. I ain't forgettin'."

"Accidental, I assure you. Normally, I flee violence as the plague; gaming and wenching are far more to my liking and much easier on the skin. But we Anglo-Saxons must stick together, since your general is not having much luck with the Creoles, and who knows exactly when the British will strike."

"Too damned quick, I reckon," Jubal answered as he rose regretfully from his chair. "So we'd best take to the road while Andy Jackson keeps talkin' and beggin' for volunteers."

Moving to the door, Pickett said, "He'll round up a few, I presume. There are always those who treat a battle as a holiday, but most of the population hopes, rather wistfully, for return to French rule."

"That won't never come off. We bought and paid for the whole of Louisiana, and bigod, we'll fight for any piece of it."

"Of course," Pickett said. "Some will, and some won't."

In the living room, Lisette waited, looking so fresh and dewy Jubal could hardly believe what had taken place the night before. He thought of silken sheets and woman skin just as soft and slick, then of nights sleeping on the cold ground, and knew damned well which he'd choose, was it up to him alone. Diplomatically, Tom Pickett went on ahead, and Jubal took the woman's hand.

Lisette would have none of that. She pressed tightly against him, her hands roaming, her belly reaching. "*Mon amour,* you will hurry back?" She gave him no chance to answer, her mouth damp and hungry upon his own.

At last he pulled away. "You don't turn me loose, I'll never get to leave. I'll come back soon as I can."

He left her with promises and with the scented warmth of her skin still upon him, joining Pickett upon the *banquette* outside. "What a woman," he said. "More I owe you for, friend."

"Not for Lisette; I am no procurer, Jubal. I simply thought you two would be good together. Alas, she has no such time for a ne'er-do-well like me, although I amuse her."

Across Rue Bourbon, dodging between carts and black women carrying baskets upon their kerchiefed heads, they found a grocer who would deliver travel supplies to Tom's rooms, and down toward the Ramparts Jubal paid for a horse and saddle for Pickett. It was an ugly, sullen beast, but looked sound and sturdy.

"He will trample me first chance," Pickett grumbled. "Did you see the vicious glint in his eye?"

"Deep chest, wide barrel and good legs; he can run if'n he has to," Jubal said, "and from what you say about the Natchez Trace, he might just haul your tail out'n trouble."

"Just being near that animal makes me uneasy. A steadying drink, Jubal? We can't start until morning, anyhow."

"Just one," Jubal agreed. "Then I got to hightail it out to camp and get my gear together, let some of the boys know what I'm up to."

The cafe was at the far end of a flagstone court-yard, cooled by what Pickett said were banana trees and climbing vines that bore grapelike clusters of purple flowers. Jubal sniffed the small glass of green liquor Pickett ordered and didn't like the smell of it, contenting himself with brandy and coffee.

He was looking out at the street when the man and woman stopped. Jubal stared openly, his jaw sagging, for the sight of her hit him low in the belly like a mule kick. She carried sunlight with her, haloing a softly curling wealth of blueblack hair that spilled with enticing abandon down her straight back. She was slim in the waist and filled where a woman ought to be, and she didn't have to call attention to those curves by tricks of dress; they spoke for themselves. Or hollered out loud, Jubal thought.

Proud as a blooded filly, she stood there in a simple dress that made a man jealous of what-all it touched, her kind of square chin up and her dark-lashed eyes wide. Jubal tried hard to fault her and couldn't, for if her ripe mouth was a mite too wide, it kind of matched up with those big, brown eyes. He didn't even notice the man with her, just knew he was there.

"Easy, my friend," Pickett murmured. "Stare too long and you'll be looking into the muzzle of a dueling pistol, or having a very quick look at the sharp point of a rapier."

Jubal swallowed wine. "Maybe she ain't all polished-up beautiful like Lisette de la Rassac, but migod—she makes a man's whole hide fair itch."

Pickett said, "No doubt, but I have too much respect for my own skin to even think of scratching. That's Felipe de Alcantari, who only yesterday killed his latest man beneath the Oaks. And that's his new mistress, the one he—but why is he parading her down the streets this way? Unless he means to use her as bait, to tempt brash and outraged gentlemen into making mention of her presence."

Now Jubal glanced at the man, a lace-cuffed dandy in a plumed hat. He had seen him somewhere before, Jubal thought, and noticed the familiar ornate hilt of a sword he wore. The man looked their way, and Pickett found sudden interest in his glass of absinthe, but for a long moment, Jubal locked gazes with Alcantari. It was like eyeballing a moccasin, he thought, that cold and that watchful.

Then the pair was moving, crossing the street and stopping before another cafe. Pickett let out an audible breath and shook his head. "Alcantari must be deeper in debt than usual; but flaunting her like that, escorting her into shops—"

Jubal drank, not tasting the stuff. "Ain't all these Creoles rich? They sure act like it."

"Ah, there you have put your finger upon it: the

acting. Alcantari *acts* as if the old estates have not been sold off, as if most trappings of the family mansion have not gone to satisfy creditors. True, his performance may go on for a long time, for his reputation is such that few shopkeepers dare press their bills. A touchy one, Felipe, and far too deft with rapier and pistol. Let me see, he has met fourteen—no, fifteen—men under the Dueling Oaks, and only one recovered."

"Sounds like so much foofaraw to me," Jubal said, trying not to stare at the golden, poised girl. "If men mean to fight, why not go right to it where the trouble starts?"

"New Orleans society is not so simple; there are traditional formalities, the challenge made and answered, weapons chosen, seconds picked. It's like a dance, every step planned."

The man was posing on the sidewalk, keeping the girl at his side, and Jubal just had to look back. "Damned bloody dance, I'd say. You ever been challenged, Tom?"

Pickett laughed. "Not me; gentlemen only challenge other gentlemen, and I'm just a threadbare Kaintuck. Besides, I stay out of their way. Where Alcantari is concerned, I'd swim the river to avoid giving him offense."

Had the woman's eyes touched his and lingered ever so briefly? Without interest, Jubal said, "That a French name? Don't sound like it."

"Old Spanish; very old Spanish. Alcantaris were noblemen here when the city was a collection of huts, but the family luck has run out. Felipe is the last of his line, a notorious rakehell who squandered his own fortune and those of two wives he outlived. Perhaps, after he has worn the bloom from that ravishing beauty—but hell; I gossip too much, especially since most young blades are careful about even mentioning his name."

"He ain't married to her?" Jubal asked. He watched Alcantari seat her at a sidewalk table.

"No; he would not—Jubal, are you such a stallion

that one lovely woman at a time is not enough for you?"

"What's her name?"

"I don't know, but if you insist upon being a fool, I will find out." Pickett looked across the street. "She probably lives on the Ramparts, but again I ask you take care. Alcantari is very dangerous, and—" He stopped talking for a second and rubbed a hand across his chin. "And I see he is keeping other company. If I am not mistaken, that is one of the Lafittes walking away from Alcantari's table."

"The pirate?"

"Shhh," Pickett warned. "You seem dead set upon offering up your fair body to the code of the *duello*. What happens to the flints then, and the defense of the city? Officially, the Lafittes are respectable businessmen; brother Pierre even keeps a blacksmith shop, while brother Jean—let us say he receives shipments of merchandise at his establishment on Barataria. A place extremely well-armed and guarded, but that is only natural, since so many corsairs ply the Gulf these days."

Jubal put down his wine glass. "And British men-of-war, as well. That girl—he's taking her on down the street."

"To my quiet cheers," Pickett said.

"I just never saw anybody like her," Jubal muttered. "It ain't that I'm such a stud or that Lisette ain't enough for any man, but that girl—"

"Will innocently get someone spitted upon a blade of Toledo steel," Pickett cut in. "Some idiot will allow his resentment to overcome logic, and a challenge—I wonder what Alcantari and Pierre Lafitte have in common. No matter, friend; let us be off on our mission. Shall I meet you at the camp?"

Jubal stood up, squinting after the pair as long as he could keep them in sight. "Best I meet you at the livery stable come daylight." He placed a gold coin on the table. "See can your tailor—that LeRoux fella —fit you with buckskins. Them clothes you're wearin' will bust out at the seams in the woods."

179

"I shudder to think of it," Pickett said, deftly palming the coin, "but I will be ready."

Walking off, Jubal kept peering along the street for the girl, but didn't see her again. It was the damnedest thing, he thought; here he was, fresh from the sizzling embraces of Lisette, and hankering after a strange woman like he hadn't been bedded for a lonesome, randy year. If she acted like that on him from afar, what effect would she have up close?

He dodged a lumbering wagon and stepped around a mudpuddle, heading for camp. She hadn't even looked his way, but he'd felt the heat of her, something powerful that stirred his loins and set his blood to racing. Jubal tried to remember the shade of her skin, but all he could see behind his eyelids was the color of sunshine, the glow of her. Her eyes; he would never forget them, nor the shape of her mouth. Was it a bit too wide? Lush and beckoning, certainly. And she stood straight as any black woman balancing a load upon her head.

Walking rapidly, unmindful of the heat of the day, Jubal pressed on toward the camp where the fattening, bored army waited. How tall was the girl? Would she reach to his shoulder? All that glistening hair, sleek as a black cat's, tumbled loose instead of bound up in curls and doodads the way other Creole ladies wore theirs. Yes, there had been a ribbon across it, just over the smooth forehead, but for the life of him, Jubal couldn't bring back the color of the ribbon.

Mistress. The word jumped in his throat. A girl like her, somehow bound to that Alcantari man who strutted her as if he owned her outright. Jubal was by no means familiar with the strange customs of this mixed-up city, and had no idea what could have brought about such an arrangement. But he knew a guilty kind of joy that she wasn't legally wed to Alcantari, and he just didn't give a good goddamn that all New Orleans knew they were living together.

A dangerous man, Alcantari; that's what Tom Pickett said; a duelist. Well, to hell with that; the codes and posturing and flinging challenges were for Creoles,

180

not Carolinians. He'd just have to take his chances with Alcantari, if the matter ever came to a head.

First off, though, Captain Jubal Blaze had to get his job done, find enough good flints and get them back afore the Redcoats came storming up the river to take the city.

Next thing, he had to talk to that girl. Could be, she might just spit in his eye. Jubal walked faster, then broke into a trot. Somehow, down deep in his innards, he felt she wouldn't do that.

Chapter 20

If he had taken her on a grand tour of the city out of pride in her, if it had been almost anything but what it was, Caroline might have enjoyed herself. As it was, by the time she was returned home, she was drawn tight as a fiddle string.

All those dark and startled looks, the shock and frowns, men pulling aside to leave a little pool of aloneness around Felipe and Caroline; it had been awful. Not only had she been in constant fear of the nasty word and the challenge sure to follow, but it hurt, being made an object of scorn, a black woman treading hallowed ground, invading the private precincts of godlike whites.

Angrily, she gulped wine and sat at her own table with shoes kicked off. At the Quadroon Ball, she'd been admired, wanted, followed by Creole gentlemen. Any of them would gladly kiss her, fondle her body, take her to bed for the most intimate caresses. Yet she was not allowed to sit at table with them in public, to drink from uncontaminated glasses, and even the brushing of her skirt was somehow foul.

"Damn them," she said aloud. "Damn them for hypocrites and liars. I wish—almost—that somebody would have faced Felipe because of me, and gotten his leering face slapped—"

But she remembered the cruel, bloody scene beneath the Dueling Oaks and shivered. She could not carry a death such as that upon her conscience, even if it was in some manner deserved.

Caroline looked through her window at the Villars house, or Lafitte house, no difference. Felipe was there now, making final arrangements with Pierre Lafitte, plans that would prop up his sagging fortunes. Since he usually talked as if she were not in the room, Caroline had heard most of it, enough to understand what Felipe was getting into. The Alcantari house, long since stripped of its most valuable furnishings to satisfy Felipe's gambling creditors, was to be used as an outlet for smuggled goods brought up from Barataria.

Brazenly, Felipe would invite buyers to inspect bolts of silk and brocades, kegs of spices, and precious jewels, recently "discovered" in the old house's storerooms. These were all goods that luxury-loving Creoles were being denied by patrolling British warships, lovely things that had they been in great supply, would still be subject to the customs tax, and thus far more expensive.

And what official would dare voice his suspicions of so much newfound Alcantari wealth? None but a fool would risk Felipe's immediate, and fatal, defense of the family honor. Besides, creditors aplenty would be too happy to look the other way, so long as they were paid. It was a good plan, profitable for Pierre Lafitte, who would have a speedy and legitimate outlet for his smuggled goods, profitable for Felipe de Alcantari, who could return to the gaming tables.

But now Caroline knew that only a large and lasting stroke of fortune would ever lead him to buy back her mother. Even then, she might have to appeal to his sense of caste by pointing out those women along the Ramparts who had servants of their own and let him consider that an Alcantari mistress should be no less.

Getting up, she moved to the stove. Would he want supper, after touring the cafes all day? In one cafe, set back in an attractive courtyard and seen from across the street, there was a huge and bearlike man, with a shock of sandy hair and clear blue eyes that had stared and stared until she met them for a moment.

Was he another of those who knew she did not belong on the arm of her protector in public? Angered by her black presence, had that one also sat scorning her? She had not felt that, but it must be so. A slender man sitting with the blond bear had leaned close to whisper, but the big man continued to stare until Caroline looked away. Even then, the impact of his eyes followed her down Rue Bourbon.

No matter; he was white and she was not, and she belonged to Felipe de Alcantari.

A timid rapping called her to the door, and Caroline opened it to Catherine Villars. The girl's black eyes were shining, her cheeks flushed. "Oh, Carrie—he's coming today."

"I thought Pierre was already there."

"Not Pierre," Catherine said, *"Jean.* You have never seen Jean, and you must promise me you will not fall in love with him."

Caroline laughed. "What is love, little one? Whites do not love us; they use us. And if we love them, we are fools."

Catherine's hand flew to her mouth. "Oh no; do not say that. If I believed that, I—I would *die."*

Touching the girl's shoulder, Caroline said, "You care for this Jean Lafitte so much, then? And does he return your love?"

Blushing, Catherine murmured, "He does not know. *Le Bos* thinks of me as only a child, but I will make him see; I will force him to open his eyes. Oh, Carrie, he is so handsome, so gentle and kind—"

"And a pirate, they say."

Catherine's eyes flashed. "If so, it is because the Spaniards hurt him so. His wife, *mon ami;* his child —both dead at Spanish hands, and m'sieu himself starved, tortured. Ah, they do not know, those who whisper pirate of *Capitaine* Lafitte; they cannot know him as I do."

"Perhaps no one can," Caroline said, drawing the girl close to comfort her. But Catherine struggled from her arms and said, *"Ici!* He is here. Look, he descends from the carriage. Isn't he just beautiful?"

No, she thought, Jean Lafitte was not beautiful; what man was? But he was tall and slim and graceful as he moved. There was that about him which suggested great strength. His hair was long, sleek and black as Caroline's own, and as he turned his head for a moment, she caught a glimpse of sparkling black eyes and a moustache and sideburns. This late afternoon he wore a widebrim hat with a gold buckle and a dark blue sea captain's coat; an ornately hilted sword swung at his right hip and jackboots reached high up muscled legs.

"Someday," Catherine Villars whispered, "someday."

"If you wish," Caroline said, watching the man go into the house and seeing something else, a pair of swarthy ruffians lounging beside the waiting carriage, heavily armed men who looked born to violence. "Come, Catherine; have a sip of wine with me."

Sighing, the girl nodded. "My sister leaves the room when they speak of business, and so must I. But perhaps he will stay the night; sometimes he does."

"And his guards, also?"

Catherine sat at the table, very young and smooth faced and with her eyes lighted from within. "If there is no danger, m'sieu sends them away. One night, he will call to me, and I will go to him. It must happen; it has to; the voodoo doctor said—"

Voodoo and conjure and *juju;* wrinkled hags who mumbled of scorpions and death; Caroline said, "Surely, you have too much white blood to believe in—"

Catherine looked up, dark eyes intent. "But of course; Doctor Dambah's charms are known to every *griffe libre* in New Orleans. My sister has been helped by him for years; because of the *juju,* Pierre would never leave her."

It was what Narcisse claimed for her conjure woman and her man. Caroline said, "Perhaps Pierre is simply a good man who cares for Marie Villars." She would not say love, and why was she now thinking of scorpions, why did the mark itch upon her buttock?

185

"I will take you," Catherine said, "so you may get a special charm of your own."

For Felipe de Alcantari's undying love, or a *gris-gris* so he should not parade her in hopes of a duel, an amulet to shield him from sword and pistol ball, so she might continue to live without whips and chains?

"Someday," she said, echoing Catherine's words, but not the hope in them.

And later, when the girl flew across the yard because Jean Lafitte remained and his brother departed with Felipe and the fierce-looking corsairs, Caroline set about preparing a lonely supper. Books, she thought; she would have to ask Felipe for books, if the idea of her reading did not offend him. The dark closed in upon her and candle shadows hovered on the walls. Felipe had not said *adieu;* the master, he came and went as he pleased without announcement, but she must always be at hand.

Tidying the house, she bathed and drank too much wine and went to bed to lie sleepless for a long time, listening to wind rise, to a ring of laughter from another house. Felipe had not lain with her since the duel, and she told herself she was glad, but that did not stop the loneliness.

Sliding at last into sleep, she dreamed of a vicious, threatening scorpion, and came suddenly, chillingly awake at the rattle of its scraping claws. Covers drawn around her trembling body, Caroline tried to shake off the nightmare, but the sound came again—scratching, scratching. It was at the back door, trying to get in!

Caroline fumbled for a sulphur match and struck it to a candle. In the kitchen, she picked up a knife and stood uncertainly, not sure if the noise had been dreamed.

"Carrie—Carrie—" Her name came dry and leaf-stir soft, pleading through the door.

She unbolted it, drew it back. Held high, the candle shed its faint and skipping light upon a kneeling figure —*Solah!*

"Mother! What—oh, let me help you in; here— that's right, give me your hand—mama, you're hurt!"

186

Struggling, she got Solah into the house and into a chair. Candle on the table, hands shaking, she poured some of Felipe's brandy and held it to her mother's lips. "Drink this, mama; another swallow; one more, please—"

One of Solah's eyes was swollen shut, and dried blood clung to the corner of her mouth; her skin was ashen and an angry bruise marred her cheek. She sat hunched over, elbows propped on the table, bent against a desperate pain, her dress torn and dirty.

"Mama," Caroline said, "hang on. I'll send for a doctor."

One eye a bit brighter, Solah wobbled the brandy glass to her mouth and drained it. Her cracked lips moved. "N-no; a doctor will do no good." She spoke in the old tongue, in Ashanti. "I am hurt, my daughter, and there is no time."

Caroline refilled the glass. "But there must be. You —you are here and I—" She turned for water and a cloth. "How were you hurt? How did you find me? The bed—come, I'll put you in my bed and get some-one—"

"No," Solah whispered. "He—he broke something inside me, and my time runs out. There—there was a—" Her head dropped and Caroline bathed Solah's face in cold water. "A conjure woman," Solah went on, voice stronger now, "she knew of you. It was a long journey, my daughter—a very long journey."

"You mustn't talk; you need rest." Caroline's hands were gentle in their probing. "Your ribs, do they hurt here? That white man, that George Waggaman, did he do this to you?"

"I must talk," Solah insisted, "for I have much to say. More drink—it strengthens me, and there is so little time."

"You ran away," Caroline said, "you escaped from the planter and came here to me. Oh, mother, I'll hide you, I'll beg my man into doing something."

Solah's good eye fixed upon Caroline. "Understand this, child: I am dying and no one can help me do that. Each of us—each dies alone." Her head bobbed,

187

recovered. "Yes, he who called himself my master did this to me, but never to another woman. He lies with a knife in his belly."

When Caroline would have said something, Solah shook her head. "Listen closely, daughter. I come to beg your forgiveness, so I may meet the old gods without shame."

"My—*my* forgiveness? Mama, mama, after all the trouble I caused you?"

Brandy drooled down Solah's chin and Caroline wiped it away. Solah said, "I did you a great wrong."

"Never," Caroline insisted. "You and M'Nele gave me everything; I brought all this evil upon *you*. Mama, my mother—"

"No," Solah said. "This you must understand, child. I am not your mother; M'Nele was not your father."

Staring, Caroline tried to say something and could not.

Swallowing brandy and coughing, Solah went on: "You—even your name is a lie, girl. It is not Caroline Monteleone; M'Nele and I, we never had a white man's name."

"Mama, your head—"

For the space of a fleeting moment, some of the old fire blazed up in Solah, the Ashanti words rang sharply. "My head is clear. Listen to me and do not deny, do not speak, for what I tell you is true. You are—you were—called Justina, Justina LeCroix, the daughter of Xavier Rigaut LeCroix. Remember that name, child; write it upon your soul so you may never forget. It is your birthright, that name, and I pray we may be forgiven for taking it from you."

Caroline tried to bathe her mother's face again, but Solah pushed the rag away. "Listen—M'Nele and I, we were desperate to run; they were going to sell me, breed me to another man. So we ran, escaped to the North, but to protect ourselves, to keep the patrol off, the slave hunters back, we took a hostage. The gods help us, we took a baby hostage. *You,* girl; I carried you upon my hip, and the old master knew if the dogs caught us, *his* child would also die. It was a bad thing to do, an evil thing, but you must understand how it was. M'Nele was my man and I wanted no other. We *had* to be free."

"No," Caroline said sharply. "My father would never —M'Nele could not—"

Solah's hand tightened convulsively upon Caroline's, and the woman's head rocked loosely upon her neck; fresh blood stained her mouth. "He could not," Solah agreed, "because he was a warrior, not a butcher, and because—you became more ours than LeCroix's. The forest, the cold and heat and starvation—our child was brave and did not cry. I—I came to love you, girl. And in time, so did M'Nele. You were—you were much like our own baby, dead at birth back there on the plantation. But for your color, you were Ashanti, and we were proud of you."

Eyes rolling, Solah slumped forward, and Caroline cradled her mother's head to her breasts. She felt numb, bewildered; had her entire life been a lie? If she was not Solah's daughter, if her true parents were—

Struggling erect, Solah fumbled for strength in the brandy glass. A soft moan hissed from her. "We—were punished. We kept you from the world, from your own blood, and M'Nele died for it, as I also am dying. Justina—ah, that name has been long in my mind and never upon my lips—there is proof. The lawyer in Illinois, the one who sold M'Nele's shop for us—he has it all on paper. Even—even the notice spread far and wide by Xavier LeCroix offering a reward for word of his daughter. It tells of the birthmark upon your left buttock, the sign of the scorpion. Mister— Barker; Marion, Illinois; Artis B-Barker. He has the papers, the papers that are proof—you are white, child —*white!*"

Caroline caught the woman as she slid from the chair, lifted the slight form easily and quickly to carry her to the bed. Solah lay so still and pale, but her chest was rising and falling. Caroline crouched upon the edge of the bed and held her hand, dabbed blood from the gaping mouth.

Waggaman had done this; the planter beat her

mother, beat Solah to the point of death. Caroline wished he were alive, that the knife weren't in his fat belly, so she could twist it there herself.

"Mama," she said. "Mother—*you* are my mother. I love you. Do not leave me now. Please hang on. We are together, and I will care for you, protect you as you did me—"

Eyelids fluttered and Solah looked up. "Do not—do not let them find my body here. Hide it, then seek the lawyer; claim what is yours and—and forgive me."

"There is nothing to forgive," Caroline said. "I am Ashanti, not white. I am—mother! Oh, my god—mother!" Although she held tightly to Solah, she could almost see the life leave, feel the collapsing of the poor, tortured body in her arms. Burying her face into the hollow of a throat where no pulse throbbed, Caroline cried for all that had been, all that never was. She cried for Solah and M'Nele, for Caroline Monteleone, for all the Ashanti, Mandingo, Bantu, all those who had no control over their own lives. She did not think to mourn for a white planter and his wife, a man named LeCroix who had his baby stolen from him by escaping slaves. She did not care for someone who was only a name, for whatever his other misfortune, Xavier LeCroix was white, and that overcame all troubles.

The candle flickered low when at last Caroline rose from Solah's side. When she heard something rattle at the front of the house, she went to the door and peered out, but it was only the wind. It was only candle smoke she smelled, not Felipe's cigar. She was glad he had not come home, had not seen Solah in her last hour.

Solah was right; her corpse should not be found here, for there would be questions, official inquiries that might anger Felipe. But what was to be done with it? There should be drums and mourning, ashes smeared upon faces and arms traditionally slashed, so that Solah's spirit might depart in peace. But already the night was short, and there was much to be thought out.

Caroline closed the dead eyes and placed Solah's arms at her sides, then wrapped the body in a quilt. She left it upon the bed and took a spade to the far corner of the back yard. Oleander bushes grew high there, and Caroline dug for a long time near their roots. When she was done, she carried Solah there and lowered her gently into the grave, whispering the Ashanti prayer of the Long Journey. By the time she had finished patting soil back into place and spreading fallen leaves to hide its freshness, a pale and mocking dawn had begun to light the sky.

Moving stiffly, Caroline washed herself in cold water, and also washed the brandy glass, her fingertips lingering along the rim Solah's lips had touched. *White;* the word echoed through her mind—*white!* A plantation owner's daughter, stolen as a baby and carried north; raised by two blacks as their own, with love. Ah yes, with love. It had brought Solah here, dragging her broken body, to expiate an imagined sin. But what did it all mean to Caroline, or to this newly discovered Justina LeCroix?

If proof existed that Caroline Monteleone was indeed Justina, it was far away and might forever remain hidden, for she was owned by Felipe de Alcantari, and *that* proof was certain in a bill of sale. In the eyes of all, especially the law, Caroline was part black without manumission papers, and therefore a slave. Everyone in Marion, Illinois, would remember black M'Nele the smith and his light-colored wife, their yet lighter daughter. And vengeful Senator Williamson would certainly see that no favors were done for the family of his son's killer.

Because the morning held a hint of chill, Caroline made a fire in the stove and put coffee water on to boil. She sat at the table, her mind refusing to accept all Solah had said, trying to think why her mother would lie. The mark of the scorpion; that was her identification, described in an old reward flyer in a lawyer's office. It was also her *gris-gris,* a poison that had destroyed two people she loved. Hand straying to caress her hip, Caroline shivered.

The door slammed back and she jumped. It was unusual for Felipe to visit so early, unless he had been carousing all night, but by the look of him, he was sober.

"Up so early, my love?" There was withheld excitement in him.

Her voice sounded thin and strange to her. "Sleep was difficult."

He strode to the stove, looked at the coffee pot, walked back with quick and eager movements. "I have business and will not see you for a while. Here is a purse, enough money for whatever you need. But stay close to this house, *chérie*. Do not wander afar—the markets, visits nearby, that will be all right."

She said, "I do not mean to wander. Where would I go?"

He dropped into the chair opposite her. "There are affairs I must conduct with Pierre Lafitte, you understand; some will take me on long journeys, but I will always return to you." Felipe's dark eyes gleamed. "Perhaps when you least expect me."

Caroline looked at him. "Neither do I mean to betray you. I am your property."

"So long as you remember that," he said. "But even if you do not, others will. Who would trifle with the mistress of Felipe de Alcantari?"

"Who, indeed?" Caroline said.

He stood up. "Forget the coffee and come to bed. It will be a long time before I know your body again."

Wetting her lips, Caroline said, "Please, Felipe; I—I do not feel—I would rather not."

"You would rather not?" Felipe's face went tight and dangerous. "You forget your place, wench. Move, I say—and if you do not exhibit your usual fire, I will scar your other buttock to match that of the scorpion."

Sickened, approaching the newmade bed where Solah had drawn her last breath, Caroline felt her growing dislike of Felipe turn into cold hate. Biting her lower lip so hard she could taste blood, she bared her body and lay back with closed eyes.

It was odd, but only once before had Felipe likened her birthmark to a scorpion.

Chapter 21

The river was big and muddy as all getout, and although the flatboat didn't seem to be moving all that fast, a look at the near bank whipping past told the Mississippi's power. That, and the swirls of brown water apt to suck under a floating log without warning, only to spit it up later on. One granddaddy of a river, Jubal thought, poison mean as some old codgers were apt to be, and a heap more dangerous.

Moving away from the side, he made his way toward the stern. Their horses were tethered there, rolling their eyes and eyeing the river suspiciously. Jubal glanced around to find Tom Pickett, and saw him talking with one of the flatboaters, a hairy, sullen man who looked more like a pirate than those pointed out to him in New Orleans. The captain had one eye gouged out and scars trailed down his cheek, and it looked like somebody'd come close to scalping him.

The long ride up to Natchez had been a bust. With Pickett's help, he'd scoured the town for decent flints, and come up with only a sackful of some that wouldn't last more than two, three snaps in a fight. Where the hell had they all gone? Nothing coming downriver, according to Pickett's information, and it was like somebody'd put hounds after the Indians and run them away off in the woods. The one Natchez they'd scraped out of a saloon alley swore he knew where a ledge of good flint was, but time they hightailed it all over the forest and the Natchez got drunker by stealing Pickett's flask, he couldn't have found his fleabit ass with both hands.

Then there'd been one stop after another at scruffy places in Natchez-under-the-hill, those smoky, edge-of-trouble hovels that catered to flatboatmen, riverboat gamblers and the like. In every one, Jubal put his back to a wall and kept one hand on his knife while Pickett sounded out besotted, surly men about flints. Green whiskey and food which tasted that color just about turned Jubal's belly, as did the bedraggled whores who came whining at the clink of silver.

Twice during their wanderings through the muddy pigsty alleys, Pickett had made what he thought was a good lead and asked Jubal to stay behind while he went to see. Twice, he'd come back shaking his head and with empty hands, saying all he'd found was two more liars.

Talk in the taverns and on the flatboats was of the fight coming at New Orleans, and the stories got bigger from one mouth to another. Still, they were enough to make Jubal fidgety, and he told Pickett so, insisted they start back for the city and figure out some other method for getting the flints. Time, Jubal thought, was closing in fast upon him, and upon the riflemen who would face some of England's best troops.

"A flatboat," Pickett said, "is the fastest way down. I'll see to room for us and the horses—if you'll furnish the cost, my friend. As usual, my coffers seem to have sprung a leak."

"In a way," Jubal said, "I guess you're workin' for the army, so I'll try and get back my money from Congress."

So now they rode the loaded barge, one whose belly carried bales of hides and barrels of flour, tobacco and bolts of calico—all very important to the war, Jubal thought bitterly. The thing ought to be wallowing along, laden with powder and shot and flints, but it was the damnedest job, trying to get the whole country to pull in harness. Seemed like every state or territory, and every hammerheaded representative of each, was flat out determined to haul their own way and devil take the hindmost. No wonder the Redcoats and the Spanish in the Floridas and everybody else got big ideas about chawing a mouthful out of the fledgling United States. Hell; even that chief Tecumseh was trying to switch all the tribes over to the British, hoping somehow to get back all the land. As if it was likely they'd turn loose *anything* they got their greedy paws on.

Frowning, Jubal watched the dirty water and thought the Redcoats would have a fine chance to grab off a goodly chunk of the country if they took New Orleans. They'd already put the torch to Washington in this war, and although they'd got their lobsterback asses kicked some, it would be another story when they looted New Orleans and brought their men-of-war upriver to cut off commerce.

Jubal shook his head. It was a damned shame a passel of riflemen couldn't just take some boats clear over to England and run the king right on off his throne. Grinning, he pictured the monarch skedaddling through his palace with a bunch of yowling woodsmen after his scalp. It would never happen, though; the men who started wars didn't have to fight them. Be a heap fewer wars if they did.

Tom Pickett came up beside him. "These river men —a wild crew. I imagine it's because they've had to fight off so many attacks by river pirates."

"Look like pirates themselves," Jubal said. "Every time I turn my back, I get this itch atween my shoulders."

Pickett nodded. "It's been known to happen, passengers vanishing during the journey, and the boatmen turning up with more money to spend in the bordellos of New Orleans. It's difficult to trace, of course, since the men are paid off there and the flatboat sold for its timbers. Someday, I foresee ships going both upriver and down, and the barges will be done with. And the ships won't be captained by men like One-Eye there, nor will they be powered by sail."

Jubal grunted. "Too damned far to row, and the wind makes up its own mind."

Pickett looked toward the stern, then back at the

hurrying Mississippi. A wide bend in the river was fast approaching, with a heavy cloaking of trees marching down the bank to soak their gnarled roots in the water. He said, "In England, they've been experimenting with steam engines. Maybe the future will see those engines in ships. Imagine fleets that don't have to depend upon the wind, that can change course at will and plow head-on through a gale."

Propped against the low rail, Jubal turned. "Sounds like you know somethin' about navies. Never got impressed to serve on one of them warships, did you?"

Pickett chuckled. "I never gave the press gangs an opportunity. Too fast on my feet. Oh, Jubal—don't I see your horse working loose from its tether?"

"Damn!" Jubal said. "If'n that jughead gets loose on this boat—"

He felt rather than saw the rushing shadow behind him, and grabbed one-handed at the rail as he turned to meet it. Something crashed into his head and he staggered, a heartbeat too late in bringing up his knife. Then the chill waters of the rushing river closed over Jubal, rolled him over and over and down, down. Choking, he flailed at strangling water and kicked strongly.

His head broke the surface, and his right arm struck something—a floating tree. He caught at it, but wet fingers scraped along its slippery length and it was whipped away. Treading water, Jubal coughed muddy liquid from his throat and sent a roar after the flatboat, already turning the bend ahead, its stern sweep working steadily. He could see a knot of men on the stern, but couldn't make out what they were doing to Tom Pickett.

The current sucked at his legs, and a sinkhole threatened to pull him down. Fumbling for the scabbard, Jubal thrust his knife safely into it and started to swim. Younguns in the Carolinas learned to swim near about soon as they could walk, but he'd never bucked a river like this. It was so damned big and strong, jerking a man this way and that like it had a mind to drag him right on down to the bottom and wallow the life out of him.

Pickett; had they beat old Tom over the head or put steel to him? Could be, Jubal was better off in the water, if that Cap'n One-Eye son of a bitch was so hungry he'd kill a pair of men for their horses and the little in their purses. Maybe they'd throw Tom's body into the river, too, soon as they went through his pockets. The river rats probably went for Jubal first because he was big enough to make a mess of trouble for them.

He swam on, keeping a wary eye out for driftwood, for a submerged log that might knock in his ribs. The boat was out of sight now, gone around the bend, and he looked for what might be a bobbing head, but couldn't see anything. Jubal felt guilty about Tom; the man was only helping out; he wasn't any part of a soldier, just a man who tried to keep his skin whole and now he was dead, like as not.

The river kept pushing him, and Jubal angled over toward the near bank, riding the current instead of fighting it, but working off to the side. The way he figured it, he was a far piece from New Orleans, and if he made it to shore, all he would be carrying was his skinning knife. But he was lucky, anyhow; the blow that was meant to mash his head had only stunned him, and he could thank the thick Blaze skull for it.

For a long minute, he battled a stretch of circling water that was almost a whirlpool, and fought on some more to cross an undertow that threatened to pull him back into the middle of the river. In quieter water, Jubal tried to clear the taste from his mouth; the damned stuff was flavored like a mucky barnyard smelled. Turning over onto his back, chest heaving, he gulped air while the backwater rocked him gently. Then he rolled to one side and caught hold of a cypress root, held on and got his leg around it. When he could breathe easy, he pulled himself up and into some cattails, mashing them flat with the weight of his body and not much giving a damn if he happened onto a nest of water moccasins. Tired as he was, the snakes would just have to get the hell out of his way.

The sun dried part of him as he lay there, but the rest of him was clotted with dank mud. Somehow, his pistol had stayed with him, but the charge was wet. The knife had to get him past whatever lay ahead, sneaking Choctaws, highwaymen working the Natchez Trace, some black bear with a burr under its tail, anything. Jubal waited awhile where he was, staring down the river, hoping for some sign of Tom Pickett, and when he found none, he climbed up the slope and pushed through willows.

For a mile or so, he stayed close to the river, even though brush and brambles were thicker there, so heavy at times he had to hack his way through. He wanted to check the banks, look over the sandbars for the body of Tom Pickett. It wouldn't be natural for the corpse to rise yet, but there was the off chance it might get spit up and hung on something.

Hell of a way to die, he thought, down there in dark water where snapping turtles and catfish and conger eels fed on a man like he was Sunday dinner. Damned if Jubal wouldn't just as lief get his hair lifted, long as the brave tomahawked him good first, or put a bullet through his brisket.

"Sorry, Tom," he muttered, and cut inland some, jogging along until his moccasins got dried out, then lengthening his stride to a ground-eating lope. There was a wagon road of sorts along here, not used much by the look of it, and when it petered out, plenty of deer runs.

Jubal fixed the face of the one-eyed flatboatman firmly in his mind, and remembered what the helmsman looked like, too. They'd be middling easy to find, if they stayed around the docks like Pickett said. Damn; he was going to miss Pickett, and he'd have to tell Lisette de la Rassac about it, he reckoned. Tom didn't have any kin that Jubal knew of.

He trotted beneath ancient liveoak trees whose twisted branches dripped greybeard moss, past clumps of weeping willows with driftwood high in their looped limbs, flotsam that showed what happened when the old granddaddy river got riled and came roaring out of its banks.

One thing bothered Jubal: how come they'd chunked him overboard without taking his purse? Might have happened too quick, what with him bringing out the knife and all, but a half-smart thief ought to have thumped him again. Wiping sweat from his face with his sleeve, Jubal ran on, still puzzling over that until remembering the flints drove everything else from his head.

Andy Jackson was going to be some upset about not getting any flints, about Jubal skittering off hither and yon to no good purpose and getting a helpful civilian killed in the bargain. Maybe he'd better not even see the general, maybe he'd better find him a good horse with a whole lot of bottom and head on out toward Tennessee or Illinois, like he should have done right off.

Major Benton was bound to snicker, and one more aristocratic, Tidelands smirk from that bastard would be too much. Jubal slowed to a walk and thought he'd make it to Pickett's rooms, see Lisette, then light a shuck north. Might take two horses and change off; he could use a fresh one as a pack animal on the way back. Picking up the trot again, Jubal knew damned well that was foolishness. The smart thing to do was get his own flatboat and crew, load it with what-all flints and supplies his letters of credits would bring, and come helling back down the Mississippi. The thing was to get up and back in time.

He hit a good road, and began running easy, to surprise a family in a wagon when he went by. The man half lifted an old fowling piece, but lowered it and called out something in French. Jubal just waved and ran on. He didn't find a horse until near sundown, and paid too much for it. The old mare wasn't much faster, but he was tiring some by then.

Street torches were lighted when the horse wobbled into the city, and he was glad enough to slide from her bony back and turn her over to the liveryman. It felt like his empty belly was stuck to his backbone, when he made off up the street. Folks gave way for him, made plenty of room for a big, wild-eyed man in filthy buckskins who reeled drunkenly along the *banquette*. Jubal wanted to laugh at the expressions on their startled faces but he just didn't have the strength.

Pickett's door was locked, but a running start helped knock it open, and Jubal plunged inside to fall across the rumpled bed. Getting to one elbow, he blessed Tom's spirit for leaving a bottle of brandy close by. When it was half gone, he got up and found a slab of cheese, some hard bread. He finished that with the rest of the brandy and pillowed his head upon some clothes. As sleep claimed him, Jubal remembered being dimly surprised that the clothing—Tom Pickett's clothing—was damp.

Light and sound together brought Jubal up with a snap, the skinning knife flicking from its case as he rolled off the bed and landed with his feet spread, ready for anything.

Anything but the sight of grinning, yelling Tom Pickett and the mad dance the man caught him up in. "You big bastard! How'd you get out of the river— where'd you come from—how—"

"And you," Jubal said, almost crushing the slighter man in his arms. "Thought those damned pirates knocked you in the head, too. What—"

"They did," Pickett said. "Let me go, man—before you break all my ribs. But those brigands threw me into shallow water, almost on a sandbar. But you—out in the middle of the river—you've the devil's own luck, Jubal!"

Jubal found the empty brandy bottle and shook it. "They didn't take time to grab my purse. I'll refill this. Needed it bad when I got in."

They exchanged stories, and Jubal found Pickett had been fortunate, making it to shore quickly, then catching a ride into the city on a wagon. He'd been out scouring the town for the villains who'd robbed them both, Pickett said.

"Have you been to see Lisette?" he asked.

"No," Jubal said, "nor the gen'l, either. Best not let Andy know what a fool I've been."

"Time *is* short," Pickett said, "and it would not do to pay Madame de la Rassac a visit just now; her husband is at home."

"Hadn't meant to," Jubal said. "If'n I can scrub off some of this river mud and take care of one little chore, I mean to go get them flints, do I have to ride clear to Tennessee for 'em."

Pickett frowned. "Will there be time? I understand warships are gathering in the Gulf, that even Lafitte's pirate fleet is staying close to home."

Jubal put coins on the table. "See can you find us somethin' to eat and drink, whilst I wash up. I'm thinkin' it's too bad ol' Andy don't have him all the ships that pirate's got. Might block off good landin' places for the British, at least."

"Yes," Pickett said thoughtfully, "I suppose there are others wondering the same thing. All right, friend —I will find us warmth for the inner man. You're not changing back to your broadcloth?"

"Uh-uh; got me some kind of long ride ahead."

"You're determined to go on, then?"

Jubal looked at Pickett. "Got to. Meantime, I'll send word to Major Benton he's to confiscate every spare flint he can find in the city, but most of 'em's got to come from me."

His buckskins were still damp when Jubal ventured onto the street with Pickett some time later, and he kept a wary eye out for any of Jackson's staff. At the door of the Absinthe House, he collared a lounging Tennessee rifleman and sent him upstairs with a written message for Benton, then hurried away.

Tom Pickett had another idea, it seemed. He would speak with Jean Lafitte, if he could find the corsair chief, and ask about the possibility of buying flints. It just might be that Lafitte had a surplus store tucked away in his Barataria fortress.

"Good enough," Jubal said as they headed for a cafe, "but I'm about to hunt up some good horses, anyhow."

Snapping his fingers, Pickett said, "We're in luck again. There he comes, *le Bos* himself. Best you step into the cafe, Jubal; leave me to deal with this freebooter. I understand his language."

The pirate was a tall man, Jubal saw, and wondered if he'd picked the rich suit he was wearing from some merchant captain's sea chest. There were bulges beneath the coat that were certain sure pistols, and a serviceable blade swung at the man's side. Walked something like a cat, Jubal thought, and had eyes just about as watchful. He stepped inside the cafe and left Pickett to approach Lafitte.

The absinthe had a green stink to it he didn't like, so he ordered honest whiskey and a cigar. When he'd lighted the cigar, Pickett came to him. "He says no, that he needs what he has."

"Wasn't much of a talk," Jubal said.

"He isn't much of a talker," Pickett answered. "Still, I may be able to persuade him. Let me try."

"It's the livery stable for me," Jubal said. "If'n I can't find good horses there, I'll scout around some. Got to get my gear together, too, and that'll take a spell." He stepped out onto the *banquette* with Pickett. "But tomorrow for sure, this hoss means to be on the road north. You make a deal with that pirate, well and good, but I aim to make sure that when we throw down on them lobsterbacks, sparks jump into the pan and them rifle balls find a home."

Two more long strides he took, then stopped so quickly that a chimneysweep caromed off his shoulder and apologized profusely.

"What is it?" Pickett asked.

Jubal swallowed. "There, bigod—across the street yonder; it's her."

Pickett stared. "Who?"

"Don't know her name, and if'n some Creole hecoon gets his back up about it, I sure as billy hell mean to find out, Dueling Oaks be damned."

"Jubal," Pickett said, "wait; don't just go blundering—"

He left Pickett behind and plowed straight to the

two girls, one small and bright-eyed, the other medium tall and slim, with that look of a sure enough queen about her. Jubal had enough sense to take off his hat. It mashed between his hands as he blurted out a greeting, told her his name and tripped over his tongue to fall silent and redfaced, waiting.

The little girl whispered something, and the tall one looked dead into his eyes with a power that reached clear down to his belly. When she said her name, it was the first time Jubal knew that sunshine and moonlight and flower smells could mix themselves all up together.

Chapter 22

Caroline was glad for the company of Catherine Villars, needing someone to talk with, someone young and alive and filled with hope. Nothing would make her forget the secret grave in the back yard, but being with the lovely, sparkling girl took her mind off death.

"Felipe is gone?" Catherine asked.

Caroline nodded. "On a journey; something to do with the business between him and Pierre."

Lifting an eyebrow, Catherine said, "Oh? I did not hear Pierre speak of this, but then he keeps many things to himself. Carrie my friend, I am sorry to say this, but Pierre—I do not think he values your Felipe highly."

"That's all right," Caroline said. "I have the same opinion." If he had known, would Felipe have forced her? If she'd told him she had just buried the only mother she had ever known, would he still have insisted upon lying with her? She thought so; Felipe could not tolerate opposition, certainly not from his mistress, particularly not from a black and a slave.

"Come," Catherine said brightly, "you may be my guardian today; we will go to the markets, and to consult with Doctor Dambah. If any man flirts with me, you must look stern and forbidding. Of course, I will not smile at any of them, but it is nice to know they think me attractive."

"They would be blind not to, Catherine."

The girl pushed out a ripe lower lip. "One *is;* but

perhaps not for long, *hein?* The charms become stronger, and soon he cannot resist me."

Carrying her market basket and somehow feeling as if she were deserting Solah, Caroline followed the irrepressible girl along the Ramparts. There were coins in the pocket of her apron, and she wore the chignon, the kerchief around her head that would mark her for what she was, a woman of the blood. She wanted to be identified so, needed to be, despite the story held locked inside her jumbled mind.

She was Caroline Monteleone, not someone named Justina LeCroix; she was proud of her black blood, for she had known nothing but shame and cruelty from her white heritage. There was so much to think through, to weigh and consider. It would be impossible for her to reach the Illinois lawyer; Felipe would not allow that, even if she dared tell him. Three thousand in gold he had paid for her, and he would wring the worth of every picayune from his purchase.

Yet, might it not win her true freedom, to be accepted as wholly white, legal heir to Xavier LeCroix? If solid, undeniable proof could be found, Felipe's bill of sale would be void; one could not buy white girls—not outright, anyway.

"That Turpo," Catherine whispered. "Felipe has set the little weasel to spy on you. *Non*—do not turn and look. He remains far back, watching you. But no matter; we will lose him in the market."

Was Felipe jealous of her as a woman, Caroline wondered, or simply because she was his property? He might be using her again, tempting unwary men with the bait of her desirable body, so he might challenge them and spill more blood beneath the Dueling Oaks; so that others would not press to collect debts or deny him credit.

Tugging her arm, Catherine said, *"Ici*—here beyond the oyster sellers and around the vegetable wagon. So; we stand here in the shadow until Turpo sniffs past and discovers we are not to be found."

"I do not care whether he sees me," Caroline said.

"But *I* do," Catherine murmured. "I would not have

Jean know I visit the conjure man. I think he avoids me because he resists encirclement, entrapment. He does not realize I will not bind him, but travel at his side, fight at his side. I will be as good a lieutenant as Dominique You, better than the rat-eyed Gambi. *Vite, vite,* Carrie; hurry now—we go that way."

The market boiled with shouting colors, seethed with busy scents and laughing, haggling people, most of them various shades of black and brown. Here and there bearded fishermen hawked their silverpink wares; an occasional white lady stood with parasol over her head and lace handkerchief at her nose, while her servant gathered victuals.

And as Caroline passed through a crowded alley with Catherine, she heard snatches of talk concerning the sale of very special goods at the house of Alcantari, news passed along with a finger laid beside the nose or the knowing wink of an eyelid.

Catherine stopped and pointed a slim finger. "There, above the bakery; the salon of the fencing master. Jean Lafitte also does not know I practice there. Of course, Pierre does, since he gives me the money, but that one laughs to think a mere girl should be interested in the foil, épée, saber. And he does not tell his brother. One day, I shall surprise them both."

Bits of jewelry gleamed from the window of a silversmith; tantalizing perfume beckoned from another shop, but that display was small.

"The British," Catherine explained. "Their warships patrol the coast and take merchantmen as prizes; shops here will soon be bare. Only *le capitaine's* vessels know how to slip past the English frigates, and *le Bos* fears them not. Down at his port in Barataria, there are many cannon and strong breastworks, with savage fighters to man them. The British, they avoid my Jean, you may be sure. Ah—here is the alley; it is very narrow, so you must follow me along it."

Brick walls were close and smelled of mossy age, dampened and forbidding; something scuttled in the shadows, and Caroline drew back from the hairy, many-legged clot of a waiting spider. Boldly, Catherine

Villars turned right and pushed upon a heavy oaken door; its rusted hinges grated shrilly, echoing down a black tunnel.

As they moved through heavy darkness, the muted throbbing of a drum reached Caroline, seeming at first far away, but growing closer and louder. Catherine took her hand. "A bad time for us, but now we cannot go back. The door will be bolted from outside, as well."

"What—what is it?" Caroline whispered.

"Danse Calinda, a voodoo ceremony of the Magnian sect. They worship the serpent Damballah; it is from that one Doctor Dambah takes his name. Shhh! Follow me closely."

The tunnel opened into a big room, and Catherine led them slowly, quietly along one wall, keeping to shadows cast by greenish flames leaping in a brazier set upon a wide altar. Smoke was pungent and strangely cloying, and Caroline saw the swaying, naked figure of the drummer, the muscled, oiled black body whose hands stroked mesmerizing rhythm from a skin tom-tom.

There were other movements, a swaying of people who could not be plainly seen, men and women who muttered and clapped to the pounding of the drum, the leaping of green fire. A hooded shape towered upon a dim throne at the far end of the platform, and as Caroline's eyes grew more accustomed to the half dark, she made out two statuesque women posed beside it. One was black, one seemed white; both were nude.

As she watched, they moved forward in a gliding, undulating dance, carrying something between them, something long and sinuous. Caroline choked back a gasp; it was a monstrous snake, scaly and with beady eyes that reflected the poisonous light. A moan went up from the chanting crowd: "Damballah! Damballah!"

Now the man rose from his carved throne and threw back his hood. He was bone-thin, his shaved head an ebony skull, but he strode into the circle of light from

207

the brazier with a curious majesty, a rippling walk not unlike the looping of a serpent.

Hands outstretched, head thrown back, he called something in a tongue Caroline didn't understand, and his priestesses passed the wriggling snake over their sweaty bodies, across high, bobbing breasts, between glistening thighs. The crowd's moaning turned frenzied, and the man hissed back at them, exhorting them, commanding.

At her ear, Catherine whispered, "This thing is *ours*. There are whites here, but they pay respect to Damballah and his priest, and can never truly understand. See—they pass the *rafia,* rum which is mixed with the blood of a black rooster and a white one."

Shuddering, Caroline saw the gourds spring from hand to clutching hand, the naked bodies overlapping, blending. It was a different world, a teeming hidden life unsuspected by the workaday world outside, and although she fought its compelling power, she found herself swaying to the drum. Here no slave waited upon master; here Damballah ruled black and white alike, and did not distinguish between them.

They tangled upon the floor, writhing women who locked ivory legs about the thrusting bodies of black men; white men who fitted themselves into greedily veed thighs of black women; black upon black; white upon white—a gasping, panting mass hearing only the drum, seeing only the serpent god. They did not think, for there was only the need to *feel*.

Slowly, Caroline realized that Catherine was tugging at her arm, that she was being led stumbling along another dank corridor, this one behind the altar. Her head gone light and senses reeling, she sank to her knees upon a plaited reed mat, while the grip of Catherine's hand held her to reality.

Behind them, the tom-tom reached a hammering crescendo and fell away. Catherine whispered, "He will be here soon. He always comes to meet me, for he knows my love will someday let me stand beside *le capitaine.*"

Caroline shook her head and breathed deeply; the

very air in that other room had seemed drugged, slowing her mind while causing her blood to race. Now she was taking hold of herself again.

Doctor Dambah appeared suddenly from behind a curtain, wrapped again in his hooded cloak, narrow face shiny with sweat, eyes red and sunken.

"This is my friend Caroline," Catherine said as the *juju* man sank cross-legged before them. "I am here to strengthen my love charm, and she to have the path of her life told."

The witch doctor's face shrank back inside his hood. In the singsong patois of New Orleans slaves, he said, "This lady—I don't know about her, me. Who say, she white, she a little black?"

Caroline answered in Ashanti: "I do not know the tongue of the serpent, spirit talker. Do you know mine?"

His French was near flawless. "If I do, it is impolite to speak it before Mam'selle Villars. But still I do not know; I cannot see clearly. My eyes tell me white; my ears hear Africa. Give me your hand."

The touch of his skin was dry and chill; Caroline willed her hand not to tremble as he droned, "I see—many things not clear. Trouble, certainly—much, much trouble. There is fire and there is blood." The man rocked, his lean fingers coiling about hers, hissing now: "And if both be strong, you *and* your man, I see love."

Caroline tried to take back her hand, but his grip was steely, serpent-powerful. She said, "I do not believe this, voodoo man."

"A change," the flat, hissing voice went on, "very soon a change in many lives, but most of all, in your own. You question yourself, woman; not me. You even question your name."

She twisted her hand free and backed away from him. "For those who believe, for those who are simple fools, also—but this is not for me. Here is your silver."

Doctor Dambah did not pick up the coin. He swiveled to Catherine Villars and accepted a tiny skin bag from her, reached to a gourd filled with some oily aromatic substance and dipped it there.

"You, little one," he said. "It will not be long. You have waited, and the cloud will fall from his eyes."

Catherine glowed. *"Merci;* oh, how I thank you!"

Restless, the taste of green fire still caught in her throat but the images of the orgy fading now, Caroline stood up. In a moment, the girl was beside her, taking her cold hand, speaking of another door, a secret way into yet another alley. Eager to be gone, Caroline turned from the squatting man.

Like something long and slim passing through dry leaves, his voice followed after: "The scorpion—perhaps it is to be feared; perhaps it is to be used."

Hurrying, Caroline gasped out into open air, into cleansing sunlight. She leaned against a wall, letting bright day wash through her.

"Scorpion?" Catherine asked. "What did he mean?"

"I—" Caroline rubbed a hand over her face. "Forgive me; the smoke in there—"

How did he know and what *did* he mean?

"You are ill," Catherine said. "I am sorry, Carrie; let me help you."

"I will be all right. Just a moment—it must be late in the day. We were in there so long."

"Only a few minutes," the girl said. "Do you want to go home?"

"No; there is food to buy."

Walking slowly, they turned the corner of Rue Dumaine and circled back toward the marketplace and its bustling stalls. Caroline welcomed the noise and swirling crowd, welcomed known sights and odors and most of all, the brightness. Here were no snakes, no drinking of blood mixed with raw rum, no orgy or dark prophets with baleful eyes that pierced clothing and perhaps reached the soul.

Caroline forced herself to concentrate upon shopping, to pick the best melitones and cayenne peppers, to haggle with an oysterman. Beside her, Catherine Villars was ecstatic, believing in her fortune, looking forward to her love being requited by the corsair chieftain. And then what, she wondered; would the child be moved into yet another house on the Ramparts, or would Jean Lafitte carry her off to the pirate stronghold on Barataria? Was it truly possible to be happy, knowing a white man would never, *could* never, recognize his mistress of the blood as anything else?

But if a woman was white and free, the rules would change. She could demand certain rights, without fear of being sold off, without dreading the iron manacles that always awaited unruly slaves. Caroline rolled the name upon her tongue—Justina LeCroix.

Justina's father had sent printed broadsides far and wide, seeking his missing child; he must have wanted her returned. Was Xavier LeCroix still alive? Had he long since given up hope of finding his lost daughter? Caroline balanced her market basket upon one hip and followed the ebullient Catherine through the crowd. She did not really believe she was Justina LeCroix, so how could the man? There was this nagging thought that would not leave her, that Solah had, for some mysterious reason, lied with her dying breath. Perhaps it was to make Caroline act white, be white, receive all the good things that would come her way simply because of the legal color of her skin.

Solah had been her mother in every way, with love and tenderness and knowledge, trying against odds to educate her, seeing she learned French, teaching her Ashanti. Why Ashanti, if she was actually so lily-white?

Catherine held her arm. "He is passing down the street. Oh, how handsome he is, and see how other men defer to him."

Again Caroline got a good look at Jean Lafitte, the quiet elegance of his dress, the sure way he walked. There was another man with him, a man talking rapidly, gesturing, but not for long; Lafitte said something and the man stopped to turn into a cafe.

"Will he cross over to greet you?" Caroline asked.

"Mais non," Catherine breathed. "That would not be proper, and there are too many eyes upon him as it is. I wish he would not walk alone, that his men watched over him, as they do Pierre. But no; *le capitaine* must show he is fearless."

"One man walked with him," Caroline said.

Shrugging, following her hoped-for lover with longing eyes, Catherine said, "That one; a Kaintuck, perhaps an Anglais, a nothing."

As Lafitte passed and lesser men gave way for him along the *banquette,* the same Kaintuck came out of the cafe and stared after. With him now was a huge man, a shambling bear of a man with shaggy hair. Caroline dimly recalled having seen him before; of course—the one with boldly staring eyes when she was being paraded by Felipe some time ago. But he was dressed differently now, in buckskins and moccasins, a great knife swinging at his belt.

"Come, Catherine," she said, "let us go home."

But it was too late. Plowing through the crowd, oblivious of men spun from his path, uncaring for their frowns, the big man was crossing the street, coming directly toward them. His light eyes were fixed upon Caroline, his bearded jaw set in determination. Trailing behind came the other one, the man Catherine called a nothing.

Sweeping off a coonskin hat, the big man looked down at her and rumbled, "I reckon this is the wrong way to go about meetin' you, lady—but I ain't about to let you get away from me again, and if it costs me my front seat in hell, why so be it. My name is Jubal Blaze, captain in Gen'l Jackson's brigade."

It was as if she had been surrounded, as if all escape were cut off and there were no place for Caroline to run, although in truth the sidewalk was clear. She stood quite still, craning her neck to stare up into the intent, uncertainly smiling face.

Behind her, voice the barest whisper, Catherine Villars said into her ear: "Ah! It seems we both are involved with *capitaines.*"

Chapter 23

Catherine skipped beside her, eyes bright. "I have never seen you look like this, *chérie;* certainly not when you speak of Felipe."

Caroline turned into her own yard and the girl followed. "I just don't know," she replied. "It's so strange —as if I have been waiting for him all my life, as if I somehow knew deep in my heart that he would come along. But that is fantastic, impossible."

"Is it?" Catherine Villars asked. "That is what my sister says of my love for Jean. But I *know;* oh yes, I know very well."

They were around the house and into the kitchen then, where Caroline set down the basket of food. "But you can wait; you are not owned, as I am. And Felipe —oh *mon Dieu*—Felipe would kill us both, if he so much as suspected that I would betray him."

Settling herself at the table, Catherine said, "There is master and slave; then there is *amour*. It occurs, my lovely friend, even here along the Ramparts. Not often, I will admit, for so many of the *gens de couleur* are not willing to gamble their futures, their very lives, for that one marvelous moment. But it occurs."

Caroline tried to laugh. "You are an incurable romantic, girl. While I—" She paused, seeing again the shaggy, intent man, feeling once more the impact of him, knowing the clear depths of his eyes.

"Oui," Catherine prodded, "while you are—what?"

Putting away vegetables, Caroline said, "Even if I

were such a fool, there is no way for me to meet him. Where could it happen—here, where all eyes would be upon us? Never."

Catherine giggled behind her hand, black eyes mischievous. "I whispered a meeting place to him, you know."

Whirling, Caroline said, "You what?"

Nonplussed, Catherine said, "I saw the flame leap between you two. I saw the way you looked upon him, and he upon you. So I whispered a certain address to him, and if you do not dare to meet him there—although it will be perfectly safe—why then, what is the harm? He will simply go away broken-hearted, and you will pine away here, being the good and faithful slave."

"Why did you—he—I cannot possibly—Catherine, you are a vixen!"

"I know," the girl said complacently. "And your cheeks are flushed, your eyes shine. It is the way I feel when I see my *capitaine,* my Jean. And the house is one of Jean Lafitte's, a place he sometimes stays when no one is to know he is within the city. Ah, it is the very place where he will soon take my maidenhead, but I do not mind your using the house first, Carrie."

"Vixen," Caroline repeated, "child of the devil; you are enjoying this arrangement, this—this assignation."

"But of course. Will you eat first, or bathe first? When I go to my Jean, I hope it will not be with a full stomach. I am sure to get so excited I might become ill. It would be so gauche."

Taking a deep breath, Caroline said, "I will heat water for my bath." A tremble shook her, rippled through a body gone warm and soft and expectant. Did she really dare to do this, to go to Captain Jubal Blaze as if she were a shameless trollop, as if she had no commitments, no bonds—or as if she were white and could freely make a choice?

If Felipe actually was what he had seemed at first to be, if he had used only a little of the money he

214

passed over the gaming tables to buy back Solah, would she even be considering another man? Would all-white "Justina LeCroix" secretly meet with a lover?

"Let me wash your hair," Catherine insisted. "You are sure to tangle it. And I will bring over some jasmine perfume, a brooch for your dress. Oh! What will you wear? The ballgown?"

"Only if you can lend me a cloak," Caroline said. "It is too much, or too little, to wear on the street."

Then she was very young again, almost pure again, excited with Catherine, chattering and laughing and making a dozen crazy plans all at once. The house—of course it was safe, with a special courtyard entrance through which one could slip, if one desired to be unseen; oh, a veritable house of Cupid, Catherine swore, or it would be, once a woman's touch was applied to its decor. And *certainement, le Bos* would not mind, even if he were not off in Barataria with his brother. They had not a high opinion of Felipe de Alcantari, the Lafittes, although business was business and they dealt with him now.

After drying her hair and sitting still so Catherine could brush it, Caroline had an impulse to tell the girl about Solah, and the hidden grave in the back yard. But she thought it would seem only an excuse for infidelity. Could a mistress be unfaithful? A white one might; a mustee only obeyed, or ran away, or—

"Do you think he knows?" Caroline asked suddenly.

Brush in hand, Catherine paused. "That you are of the blood? *Mais non;* these Kaintucks, they are not like Creoles. You look white, therefore you are, *n'est-ce pas?* Oh, but this is delicious—a secret within a secret. I shall burst."

"I should tell him," Caroline said.

Catherine's brush tugged painfully at the raven hair. "You will not! For me, it does not matter; my love will adore me when the time is proper, as Pierre adores my sister. But you and this great bear—are you not already tired of being owned? What if he approached Felipe and tried to buy you? There would be ugly suspicions, upon my soul, and a challenge sure to follow. What if this red *bassier* is one who only sharpens his claws on blacks?"

"Then he should know," Caroline said, "before it is too late."

"Peste!" Catherine hissed. "More the fool, you. If this one is truly your heart, first bind him close and *then* confess, if you must. I swear, Carrie, there are times when I think I am much older than you."

Caroline sighed. "Or at least wiser; we shall see. I will not tell him." She turned upon the chair to take the girl's hand. "You will go with me?"

Smiling, Catherine said, "But yes; who is to show you the way and furnish the key? Only I will not remain to hold your hand, although if I did, it might be very—instructive."

They laughed together, rocking in each other's arms, and concocted all sorts of unlikely stories, should Caroline be found out by someone. Each step seemed so delightfully sinful, applying perfume, fixing the glittering pin into place where it would call further attention to the creamy swelling of her breasts in the lowcut gown, trying on the dark and hooded cloak. But sunset was upon them before Caroline realized, and suddenly she was afraid.

"The streets will be dangerous for women alone," she said.

Catherine pressed the carved, golden hilt of a dagger into her hand. "Take this; Jean gave it to me long ago. I have another, and although it will not reach out like a rapier, up close it will give pause to a footpad. There; tuck it beneath your skirt—so. Come now; we must hurry before it grows too dark." The girl hesitated. *"Chérie,* is it the streets you fear, the man, or yourself?"

Pulling the hood about her face, Caroline said, "I have already come too far to be afraid of anything."

"Alors, come," Catherine said. "We depart."

As dusk gathered upon the city, people were moving homeward, and lamps were beginning to glow in shadows. It was yet too early for nighttime revelers to set forth upon the *banquettes,* so they passed only an occasional man late for supper, or a hurrying black who did not lift his eyes to them.

Head close to Caroline's, Catherine Villars said, "It is the perfect time to travel, as dawn will also be perfect for you to return. Here is the crossing of Rue Conti and Rue Burgundy; we turn to the left here. Now, down along this wall and another turn. Here is the alley; not far from the Ramparts, as I told you."

Caroline flinched at the silent opening of a tall iron gate, and slid through. "Stay here in the garden," Catherine whispered. "Your lover may arrive at any moment. I will open the door and light candles."

"Catherine—" she whispered back, but the girl was gone. Drawing the cloak closely about her, she moved uneasily along a path of sawn cypress blocks, between flowered bushes. She looked up at the surrounding wall, and faintly in the twilight, saw the barbed spikes embedded atop it. With the iron gate closed and barred, she and Captain Jubal Blaze would be locked away from all others, alone in a small world of their own, two strangers drawn together by nothing she could name.

Catherine was at her side again. "I have put wine into the well basket to cool, and Jean always keeps hams and cheeses in the larder. The candles are lighted and—be certain to close the gate, to bar the door, although I do not think any Orleanian fool enough to trespass upon *le capitaine's* courtyard. My friend, my sister—be happy."

Swallowing, Caroline said, *"Demain*—tomorrow, Catherine," and said it to a quick shadow flitting beyond the gate.

She clenched her hands, and the metal of the sharp dagger beneath her skirt pressed against her, warmed by her flesh. Once before she had waited for a man beside a river. He had paid dearly, but had cost her so much more: M'Nele, Solah, her freedom. Fretfully, she moved about the yard, to the well and back to the gate. Suppose this one did not come, that it was all a cruel joke—or worse, a bait put out by Felipe de Alcantari? It was late to think of that, for surely the hidden hook would be sunk into her, anyhow; her presence here was betrayal enough.

Huge and hulking, a shadow blocked the gate. Caroline took an involuntary step back, and the shadow came closer. "Miss Monteleone?"

That voice was more used to roaring than being dropped to a husky whisper, and the way he pronounced her name in hard syllables—"Captain Blaze?"

A mountain, he cut off what light was left in the soft sky. After closing the gate, she turned and walked past the well with an assurance she did not feel, to the door cracked to let out a golden sliver of candlelight. She felt him lumbering behind her, but could not hear his steps; the size of a bear, yes, but he moved with the silence of a great cat.

The room she entered was small but richly furnished, its walls tapestried, its floors carpeted, and silver goblets shone upon a table of dark, exotic wood. Dropping her hood, she faced him. "If you will be seated, m'sieu; the wine is cooling and I shall fetch it."

Uncertainly, he stood blinking in the light, buckskins so new she could smell the tannery, moccasins upon his feet like an Indian, furry cap being mangled by his great hands. "Miss Monteleone—ahh—"

Removing her cloak, she dropped it across a chair and heard the quick intake of his breath. Caroline hoped her own unsteadiness did not show as she lifted her skirts and swirled back out into the courtyard for wine bottles. Heart threatening to run wild as a runaway horse, she managed to bring up the basket and not drop the wet bottles. Back inside, she placed wine upon the table and barred the door; the sound of the heavy bolt had a finality to it.

Her voice was only a bit odd as she said, "There is cheese and ham."

Sitting upon the edge of his chair, Jubal Blaze said, "Couldn't down a thing, I swear."

"Nor I," she said honestly, "although if your throat is dry as mine seems to be—"

"Didn't say I couldn't use a drink," he said quickly. "Might as well admit I'm some edgy, bein' here with you like this."

Uncorking a bottle, Caroline poured golden wine into goblets. "It was what you wished, rushing at me in the street like that?"

Jubal nodded. "Just had to do it. I mean—well, I never had anything hit me like that afore—like you, that is. Oh hell; looks like I'm goin' to keep trippin' over my tongue. Know what I want to say, but it don't come out right."

"What do you want to say?" She repressed a shiver when her fingertips brushed his hand as she handed him the silver cup.

He drank off the wine at a gulp and hid his eyes from hers by peering into his goblet. The moment gave her a chance to closely examine his face and decide that Jubal Blaze was not exceedingly handsome. Yet his features were not coarse, and there was a certain appeal to them, a small-boy quality that lurked behind the strong, bearded jaw and straight mouth. His hair was more golden than red, she decided, and his beard more red than golden, his corded throat like a column, his skin roughened by sun and wind. Then he looked back up at her, and she had to hang onto the table to keep from falling forward into his eyes, lake-blue, skyblue, but shaded by flecks of April green.

"Want to say I'm sorry for comin' at you on the street thataway, but if I hadn't, you wouldn't be here and I'd be gone with you fillin' up my head."

A sip of wine helped, and she said, "Oh; you are going away?"

"Business for the gen'l, but I'll be back soon's I can. Miss Monteleone—Caroline—" the words poured out in a rush then, "—damnit, I can't talk pretty like you're used to, but I know you're so pretty it plain hurts a man's eyes to look on you, and there's a stirrin' in my blood like I never felt afore. But—but it's wonder enough to set here and be near you, and I wouldn't hurt one shinin' hair on your head."

She said his name to him, rolled it along her tongue and tasted its flavor: "Jubal, if I feared you, I would not be here."

"I wanted to do this right," he said, "however you all go about it down here, introductions and the like, but there just ain't the time."

"You did just fine," she said softly. "I am not married, Jubal, but there is an—arrangement. If I loved him, I would not be here."

"Reckoned you to be a woman who knows her own mind. I—" He stopped talking and just stared at her, naked hunger brimming in his eyes.

Caroline didn't know the way to a bedroom, so she poured Jubal more wine and moved away as if she did, looking. There, beyond a door opening off the sitting room, a great bed waited, coverlet turned down, silken sheets beckoning. Catherine Villars had placed a lighted candle beside the bed, and silently Caroline thanked her for it.

She did not call him, but moved into the center of the room and began to undo her dress, her single beautiful dress. As if he heard the whispering of satin, Jubal came to stand in the doorway. Caroline stepped from the gown and placed it carefully aside, standing before him in only a thin shift. Locking eyes with him, chin lifted, she slowly removed the last bit of clothing.

"Your hair," he said in a choked voice, "it's like a summer thundercloud floatin' down your back. Migod, but you're some beautiful, all over beautiful."

"For you," she whispered, stroked by his eyes. "I am glad to be beautiful for you."

He made a sound in his throat, and suddenly she was lifted in powerful arms, the length of her body pressed to his own, held tenderly there as if she was so fragile the gripping of his fingers might destroy her.

As Jubal carried her to the bed, she tasted the warmth of his throat, nuzzled into the soft curlings of his beard, explored the corner of his mouth with nibbling lips. She felt his hands roaming her back, her hips, her breasts, gently, ever so gently.

Because he was awkward, because the awe in him would not allow him to release her even for a moment, Caroline caught fistfuls of his hair and turned his face down to her own, a small, happy cry escaping her lips as his mouth found them. The flavor of him was that of a fresh, wild wind whipping down from some towering height, a wind spiced by the crossing of green slopes blanketed with spring flowers, a mighty gust that caught at the core of her being and carried her along in its majestic force.

Shaken, her tongue drinking of his, Caroline somehow worked at his buckskins, hands darting, pulling, insistent. When the barriers were gone, she burrowed her mouth into his chest, drew it along the ropy muscles of his arms, and her questing hands found the staff of him, so mighty and throbbing, a tremendous strength to caress and encompass. Unrestrained, her body flamed against Jubal, belly striving against belly, then higher because she had to know every inch of him. A moan hung in her throat when his lips fondled a rigid tip, when his big hands spread tenderly over her haunches.

She could not, would not, wait a moment longer. In a frenzy of seeking, Caroline fitted herself to him, and this time the sob broke free as she took him into her body. Deep, oh *deep,* and so natural, so very beautiful, moving together in a slow and loving minuet, to this secret music whose tempo changed, quickened into the driving fury of voodoo drums. Thundering, the crescendo broke over her, over him, and Caroline melted down into a clinging, velvety darkness.

But she held to him desperately, for if she did not, she might dissolve into glowing droplets that would pass through the shuddering bed, down through the flooring, and be absorbed into the heaving womb of the earth itself.

Muffled into her hair, the voice drifted from far away, saying: *woman, woman,* and Caroline answered it, heartbeat by heartbeat, pulsed toward the source in upward leaf-spiralings until the light was not a bursting star, but a joyous candle.

"Woman," he said into her breasts.

"Yes," she answered him, "oh yes, yes!"

Chapter 24

Never had Caroline's lovemaking been so abandoned, so unhampered; she gave freely of herself and the learned arts of her experience, thrilling Jubal Blaze and delighting him, although there were times when she feared she might also be shocking him somewhat. But those uncertainties soon passed for them both, and it was only when they were sated, their need for each other filled for the moment, that she could loose her mind from her excited body and think clearly.

She must leave him at dawn, and already the sun was too close. Lifting up on an elbow, she watched him in sleep, the strength of him stilled for now, his craggy face relaxed. Such a giant, she thought, and yet such a boy, in turn demanding and youthfully fumbling. Silently, she thanked her mother, thanked Solah for kindling the Ashanti pride in her body. For in making Jubal happy, she also found a deep and abiding satisfaction for herself.

It was so different, not at all like the mauling Kleppner had given her, not even like the deft and practiced caresses of Felipe. This was an all-pervading desire, a tenderness that wrapped her soul in moonlight and a wanting that would be ever keen, ever needing fulfillment.

He would come back; he *must* return from this army business that was his duty now. The city had to be defended, and surely Captain Blaze's presence would be needed. Caroline gnawed at her lip; what if he fell in battle? No; no; maybe she should pray he didn't return until after the fight. If anything happened to this gentle red bear, Caroline Monteleone could not live.

Nor, even if she was real, could Justina LeCroix live. She lay back upon the pillow, careful not to disturb the sleep of her lover. Suppose she was in truth a LeCroix, all white and long lost from an old, aristocratic family, as Solah had sworn with her dying breath?

Would that mean she could, upon receipt of proof, simply walk away from Felipe de Alcantari? He had a bill of sale for Caroline, a mustee, but nobody could own a single hair upon the head of Justina LeCroix, an unmarried white woman.

The name of the lawyer Solah had gasped out—Barker; Artis Barker of Marion, Illinois. Documents, Solah said, proof that a child had been stolen from Xavier LeCroix and taken north many years ago. Part of her resisted the idea fiercely, denying she did not carry Ashanti blood, while a more logical part insisted that this was the way out, the road to freedom and a future. With Jubal Blaze, she thought.

He rolled over and Caroline lifted from the bed to dress herself. Grey was stroking the windows of Jean Lafitte's house, and the candles had guttered out. She wanted to cook him breakfast, to make his coffee and light his cigar and stroke the shaggy mane of hair, but there was no time. The streets were deserted now, but would not be for very long, and she had to hurry back to the house on the Ramparts, hoping every hurried second that no acquaintance of Felipe de Alcantari recognized her. And there was Jubal's duty. The clock was enemy to them both.

The ballgown seemed out of place now, and she covered it with the dark cloak before leaning to kiss Jubal's cheek, to kiss his ear and throat.

Waking blurry-eyed, he reached for her, and oh, how she wanted to snuggle against that great, furry chest. But Caroline slipped laughing away. "Your general awaits you, Jubal. And as for me—I must go quickly."

224

Rubbing his face and sitting up, Jubal said, "This ain't your house, then?"

"Only a meeting place, *mon cher,* but one I shall never forget. When you return, you will not forget where it is? A message can be left in the gate for me. The times I cannot come, I will send someone."

"Your servin' girl," Jubal said. "A right pert little thing. Wasn't for her, you might have just walked on off down the street, and I'd never—" he broke off, then said: "Caroline, whatever it takes, if'n I have to whip the whole Redcoat army by myself, I'll see you again."

Strangely embarrassed, she put her back to him while he got dressed. "Jubal, if you can tell me, do you ride north, far to the north?"

"Not all that far," he said. "I mean to slip by the camp and pick up some help. Reckon Kentucky'll be far enough to find what we need."

Hearing him moving, Caroline turned. "Paducah, perhaps?"

He looked at her. "Might be."

Crossing her arms over her stomach, she said, "Just a bit to the north, a town called Marion, Illinois. There's a man, a lawyer; he has papers very important to me. Oh Jubal, if you can find Mr. Artis Barker and get those documents, it will mean—mean so much to me."

His clear blue eyes held hers. "Maybe important to the both of us?"

"Yes, yes!" She spun to look in the secretary for quill and ink, found them and quickly scratched the names. "Caroline Monteleone—or he may have them listed for Justina LeCroix; if Mr. Barker does not trust you, mention these others to him: M'Nele, Solah; remind him of the smithy." Spilling sand over the paper, she returned it to the box and folded the list.

Jubal tucked his belt around a waist amazingly narrow for so large a man. "You don't have to tell me any secrets, but has this got anything to do with your—arrangement with that man?"

"Everything," she answered. "When you return with

225

the papers, I will have no secrets from you, Jubal. And I will be free of him, forever."

He reached for the paper. "Then you can be certain sure I'll get 'em."

She was against his body, enfolded and warm and protected. It would be so good to stay there forever. Somewhere in the house, a clock struck the hour, and Caroline knew it could not be so, not yet. Regretfully, she drew back from him. "Go, Jubal Blaze, as I must."

He held her hands a moment longer. "When I get back, I reckon I'll have somethin' to say to you." Lifting her hands, he kissed them. "Goodbye for now, Caroline; for now, woman."

Cat-quick, he was gone from her and she listened him to the door and through the iron gate beyond, her heart calling after. And when there was only the lonely echo left, Caroline sighed and raised the cloak hood over her head. A few more ticks of the clock, and she was also through the court and had locked the gate behind her, its key cool in her palm.

Moving almost at a run, she sped through empty streets, seeing only a few curlings of smoke from breakfast fires rise above slated roofs, only a black man yawning himself down an alley, a dog that eyed her suspiciously. The sky was still grey when she reached the Ramparts, but there were hints of pink in it, and over at Narcisse Marigny's little house, someone was already moving about. Inside the gate, Caroline looked to her left: no, nothing at the Villars place, no horse tethered or carriage waiting for Pierre Lafitte.

Hesitant steps took her to her own door. Cracking it, she listened, knowing it was far too late for hope if Felipe had returned and found her gone. But the house was empty, and she could not smell cigars or spilled wine. He was still away; Felipe was not yet in the city, and a held breath gusted from her in great relief.

Quickly, she peeled off the ballgown and returned it to its hook in the small *armoire*. Donning a simple house dress, she rumpled her bed, feeling guilty *because* she felt guilty. She had given no promise to Felipe and he expected none; the bill of sale from

Kleppner was all he needed, naming the master and establishing the slave. But perhaps not for long, not for long.

Suddenly ravenous, Caroline recalled she had eaten no dinner. She started a fire in the stove and put on coffee water, larded the skillet and sliced bacon from the side hanging in the larder. She made biscuits as Solah had taught her, and when the oven was hot, slid in the pan. She wondered that she could do all these small things, that she could remember even the simplest of movements, because she was so filled with the wonder of Jubal Blaze.

Still, she devoured the food and was pouring a second cup of coffee when Narcisse Marigny came through the kitchen door.

"Narcisse," she said, "we are both up early. Pour yourself some coffee."

The woman's face was drawn, but puffy around the eyes, as if she had been ill, or crying. Silently, Narcisse found a cup and filled it, sat at the table to spoon sweetening into it. "Seen you come in," she said.

"I—I couldn't sleep."

"No business for me, but best you take care, gal. Your man will kill you, I think. The other woman he had, that Marie—a different Marie from the Villars woman—I think it happen to her. Who cares what happen to a goddamn nigger?" Narcisse's eyes puckered, and she brushed angrily at them.

Gently, Caroline said, "What's the matter, my friend?"

"I don't cry for your man's quadroon, me; cry for myself, for goddamn nigger Narcisse. He—my man—non!—not my man no more; he don't even tell me to my face, him; just send somebody with a paper what says I can keep the house. Like I care *merde* for that!"

Caroline reached to take the woman's hand. "But Narcisse, the children—"

"Oh, they free, 'cause I'm free—whatever that mean, and he don't care no more for them, for me. Maybe his white wife catch a baby; maybe he find another yellow woman. So me, I got a house and chillun and

227

no way to feed 'em. Have to find me work or sell the house."

She held to Narcisse's hand. "I'm sorry."

Pulling away her hand, Narcisse drank coffee, and when she put down the cup, seemed more settled. She said, "Gal, don't you get yourself fixed like me, *non*. Be smarter than Narcisse, you. What good it is to be faithful, when he goin' to drop you anyway, sometime. But I tell you this—your M'sieu de Alcantari, he is *dangereux*, and you be careless, you wind up like that Marie gal, in the river."

"Careless?" Caroline asked. "What do you mean?"

Narcisse's fingers strained around the coffee cup. "Me, I see a woman come in your house, but I don't see her come out. That same night, I see your man arrive twice, *two* times, you understand. The first time, he is quiet like a snake; next time he comes with noise, so you know he here."

She looked down at her own fingers and found them knotted. The night Solah came dying, was that the night Felipe had sneaked up on them? Had he been listening when Solah gasped out her story? He never said a word about it.

Narcisse said, "Now you come slippin' back at daylight. A dangerous game for yellow woman to be playin', but long as you don't get yourself caught, you more better off than me, *hein*? Your man, he send somebody with papers, you got you another man on the string. Only one thing: last time, that Felipe, he don't send no papers; he send to the river."

"Thank you for telling me," Caroline said. "You are a good friend, Narcisse."

"But one without strength, so better you stay close with Villars." Narcisse fiddled with her cup. "I say nothin' to nobody else, me. But I got this itch. The woman came to see you, she stay or she go?"

"She went," Caroline said, then tried to offer what comfort she could, but there was nothing she could really do to help Narcisse, nothing anybody could do.

It was so unfair, so brutal. Narcisse had given her white man everything—cheer and love and children,

228

several years of her life. In return she received the deed to a small house. If she didn't find a *griffe libre* to move in with her, a free black man with a job of sorts, or perhaps a small business, she would have to struggle to feed her young. She might have to go on the streets, or bring drunken seamen home, while her babies waited hidden in a corner. So damned *unfair.*

Narcisse departed, cried out now. Caroline frowned into her cup for a long time, trying to sort things out. Had Felipe sneaked here to spy on her, believing she might take another man to her bed? Had he overheard Solah's talk of documents and the lawyer, and did he know that her mother was buried in the back yard beneath oleander bushes? Thinking back, she remembered being startled by a sound and going to see but finding nothing.

And not long afterward, Felipe left the city on business, with the Lafittes, he said. But Catherine Villars never mentioned the brothers traveling with Felipe, and that young girl knew every move made by her lover-to-be; she kept a close watch through her sister and Pierre.

Caroline went to the back and looked to the left, to see movement in Lafitte's house. She was trying to decide if she should go over there, when Catherine came bounding across the yards with skirts flying.

"Tell me, quickly!" Catherine panted. "Was he wonderful? Are you in love? Oh—I know he *must* love you, but do you return it? Carrie, please—"

"Sit down," Caroline said. "There; now let me see if I can answer all those questions. Am I in love? I—I don't know, Catherine; I know only I have never felt like this about a man. And he did not speak of love to me, but I am certain his eyes and his body said so. It was a night of wonder, *chérie,* a magic night in an enchanted house that I thank you for, even if there is never to be another."

Face gone sober and dark eyes widening, Catherine said, "But there must be another; of course there must be. Love does not pass in a single evening. It lasts forever."

Caroline spread her hands. "Sometimes you are wise, and sometimes a child. Did Narcisse's love last forever?"

Catherine's ripe young mouth tightened. *"Mine* will; I shall make certain. One must have faith and believe, and try very hard."

"Other things may get in the way." Caroline said, "other events and people over which lovers have no control. *Chérie,* tell me—Pierre and *le capitaine* are away; is Felipe de Alcantari with them?"

Shaking her head, Catherine said, *"Mais non;* they do not like him nor trust him."

"Yet he is gone," Caroline mused.

"Shall I find out for you?" Catherine asked. *"Le Bos* has eyes everywhere; he must, to protect his back from traitors and those who wish him ill. Since he is doing business with this Felipe, *naturellement,* he will observe him closely." Eyes dancing again, shifting quickly in mood, the girl said, "Are you planning to run away with your Kaintuck? Is that why you must know Felipe's whereabouts?"

It rose in Caroline's throat, the urge to tell this girl all, to admit she had sent north to discover if she was white, or if her black mother was only trying to protect her. She wanted to share the secret with someone, to speak of the grave out back, the hope rekindled in her breast by a single night spent making love with a strangely tender man. But she held it back, bit off the disclosure because Catherine might not understand, might not be her friend any longer, if there was suspicion Caroline was not of the blood.

As things stood, she had at least some support from others of her kind, and if she denied her blackness without proof, they would not trust her. With the proof, they would trust her even less, for she would become the enemy.

"Perhaps," Caroline said. "He also travels, for his army, but he has promised to return and leave a message in the iron gate."

Catherine clapped her hands. "Wonderful! Already I like him far more than Felipe. I will ask my sister to ask others, and we will discover when Felipe left the city, which road he took."

And that, Caroline thought, would only tell her a bit, not *why* Felipe left.

hereiff, however long it took, rain, or shine, and be
damned to whatever kind of arrangement she had with

Chapter 25

Taking a look behind, Jubal had to grin. Of the four
men following, Mason McGee looked as if he'd never
sat a horse before, and he was all over the saddle,
flopping ungainly as could be. He'd be more than a
mite sore, time they got to the end of the line, and
damned glad to ride a flatboat down.

There was Barton Roberts, that lived down the road
from the Blazes in Carolina, and two Tennessee men,
Daniel Smith and Cody Youngblood, none taking pity
on poor McGee. That lanky old boy would come,
though; said he was some tired asetting on his hind
end and waiting for the war to run up on him. And
Mason was a good man afoot; Jubal recalled his coolness during the Indian fight.

He'd a heap rather be traveling alone and faster,
but the way things were along the Natchez Trace, a
man to himself was apt to get waylaid. But five well-
armed men together was a chaw too big for road
agents to bite off, and Jubal's time was getting cut
nigh to the bone. He couldn't afford any more misses;
he had to find flints and get them back.

That much Jubal had settled in his mind, but what
bothered him was last night, that long, storybook night
and Caroline Monteleone. If there wasn't a battle coming, if he hadn't given his bounden word to fight in it,
he might just turn his horse's head and ride lickety-
split back to New Orleans. He might just set there
in front of that iron gate and wait until Caroline showed

herself, however long it took, rain or shine, and be damned to whatever kind of arrangement she had with that fancy Creole.

She'd never said a name, of course, but that's who it was, Jubal figured, that strutting popinjay he'd seen her with, first time he laid eyes on Caroline. Alcantari, that was what Tom Pickett called him, and all that talk about that peacock killing men in duels. When Alcantari could be with Caroline—and the picture of that made Jubal twist uncomfortably in his saddle— a man would be a fool to go out dueling.

Jubal frowned, and ducked beneath a low-hanging limb festooned with grey moss, while the other men hoorawed each other about their doings in New Orleans. Behind him, they kept at each other, sounding like a bunch of damned old bluejays. Jubal squeezed his horse and moved farther ahead, feeling the change in the weather, the hint of cold coming.

There was a fireplace in the house behind the iron gate, and he could see Caroline before it, head turned so light stroked her golden skin. The image ate at him until he let it go, but not before his mind's eye watched fire reflected in her softblack hair, until he'd seen it kiss the perfumed valley between her fine, high breasts.

Turning, Jubal called back, "You all chatter much as you want. I'm movin' on ahead, scoutin' like. See can you stay to the trail and not fall in the river."

And Barton Roberts hollered out: "Be right careful you don't run up on no Injun gals, cap'n!"

Jubal rode on, their laughter ringing in his ears. He passed a fisherman's shack, and a mite up the road a cool wind blew from a browning garden patch while a dog yapped. The house wasn't hers, Caroline said; hadn't said it was Alcantari's, either. He hadn't picked at her about her doings with the man, because he was just too damned glad to be with her. But a lady like her, educated and all, how come she lowered herself like that, when she could be married to any man with eyes in his head and juice to him?

"Damn," Jubal said aloud, "maybe that's it. Could

233

be she *is* married, and diddling around with that uppity Creole on the side."

Not liking that idea either, he considered it and discarded it. There was depth to Caroline Monteleone, and honesty; if she was only interested in a night's fun, there was no cause for her to mention her ties. Somehow, Jubal had the feeling that once she gave her word, she'd cleave close to it. Something was all mixed up, and he couldn't unravel it.

Were she a widow, wouldn't be a speck of trouble for her to marry again. She wasn't poor and being took care of; look at that fancy dress she wore. What the hell was it, then? When Jubal got back, he meant to find out, and if there was anything he could do to change her affairs around, he surely would.

The road bent itself, and Jubal pulled his horse to one side so a loaded wagon could creak by, heading for the city. The black driving it bowed his head and mumbled a greeting, which Jubal answered shortly. Suppose Caroline didn't want changes made, and was happy just like she was? Couldn't be, he told himself; there was sadness to her, a sorrow lying deep inside. That much and more, he'd sensed.

The word love hadn't passed between them, but it might have been said by their bodies. Jubal pulled in a deep breath of pine spiced air and remembered Caroline's perfume, no more compelling than the exciting musk of her woman sweat. Damn! How did a lady learn all those tricks? It wasn't that what she did just about turned him inside out, it was the shock of it, at first. There'd been whores done it to Jubal, but they didn't go about it the same fashion, like she enjoyed it much as he did. When she ringed him with her mouth, he about busted right through his hide, and for a second there, he was repelled by her doing it. Only a second, though; after that he got lost in the giving of Caroline, the sweet, scorching attention paid to him by all parts of her magnificent young body.

Was that love? Damned if he knew, but Jubal was sure he didn't want to think on her doing all that with Alcantari or anybody else. He rode on, going back over every detail of that wondrous night, reliving every vital moment, and there was a dreamlike quality about it all. The overlapping images bothered him so that he spurred his horse into a gallop to shake them off, leave them behind.

After a spell, he quit that because the horse was blowing and he couldn't run away from Caroline anyhow. Stopping to let his horse rest, Jubal listened behind, but couldn't hear his men. He'd outdistanced them with his tomfoolery, but no matter; they'd keep behind him on the trail, and he'd just as lief be alone right now. When he moved out again, it was through a dense grove of water oaks, with towering cypress trees beyond them, and scuppernong vines reddening for the first bite of frost, rich golden grapes heavy upon them.

Jubal's belly reminded him he'd passed by supper and had only coffee for breakfast, whilst he was stirring around the camp getting volunteers for this trip north, and keeping from sight of the likes of Major Benton. He leaned back to a saddlebag for a chunk of dried meat, but took back his hand when up ahead he saw the sprawling clapboard shack. The wobbly sign on it said Inn, so Jubal steered his horse off the road to where the house was set back.

Didn't look like much, he thought, but a hot meal beat jerky all hollow every time. Swinging down, he tied reins to the hitching rack and slid his long gun from its deerhide case. Time he got to the porch, the tavern wench was already at the door, smiling wide at him. She looked a mite grimy, but she was put together right well, and if Caroline hadn't been so much on his mind, Jubal might have been interested in the rolling of her hips and the milky white breasts near tip-exposed by the lowcut blouse.

"Howdy, stranger," she said. "Come on in and set. You meanin' to stay the night?"

Inside, the place was shadowy and smelled of old grease. A plank laid across two whiskey kegs was the bar, and there was a table at the far end of the room. Ragged blankets hung behind it from the ceiling, cutting off the kitchen and sleeping rooms from the tavern. Dreary and cobwebbed, it was uninviting and made more so by the gap-toothed grin of the straggly-haired old woman who stuck her head through the blankets.

The tavern wench laid her rounded hip against Jubal's leg. "We got catfish stew and rabbit stew and cornbread. Got us some right good popskull whiskey, too. Dollar'n a half for all you kin eat and drink; half dollar more, you want to heist my dress. Now, do you mean to stay the night—"

"Ain't stayin'," Jubal said, "just eatin', and I'll take the rabbit. Reckon one drink of whiskey'll suit me."

One hand on her hip, the girl said, "Color of your money, mister. Some folks try to beat us out'n our due."

Jubal rattled his purse, took out silver and showed her. Smiling she ran her tongue over lush lips and took his hand, squeezing it as she led him toward the table. "You kin stand your rifle yonder and take a seat." She raised her voice: "Maw! Fetch the rabbit stew." To him again, she said, "Cup of whiskey acomin'. Right sure you don't want somethin' else? There's them that say I'm particular good."

"Expect that's so," Jubal said, patting her haunch, "but this day, I ain't got the time." He sat in the chair she indicated, propping his long gun against the table edge; the blankets were at his back and he faced the door.

Watching her move barefoot to the bar counter, he thought he'd have made time, just a while back. But after Caroline Monteleone, all women paled, even the rich and active Lisette de la Rassac and her plush New Orleans home. He blinked, just realizing he hadn't given a single thought to Lisette since seeking out Caroline on the street. She'd make out, and so would Tom Pickett, probably together.

Jubal put his hands on the table and leaned back. Seemed a shame not to tell Tom about this journey, but there'd been no time for side trips. If there was another tick of the clock to be used, it was better spent with Caroline. All that soft black hair, tumbled loose over a silken belly, with brown-tipped breasts poking up through its scented cascade; the way her eyes looked right up into his, and how she moaned while she arched and twisted, her pointed fingers raking at his naked back—

Jubal rubbed one hand over his face, as if he could somehow drain the feel and flavor of her from his blood. He saw the tavern wench approaching, and the tin cup of whiskey in her hand. He watched that elbow draw back, instead of the arm reaching out to put the cup before him. That movement, and the careful creak of a board behind him, beyond the blanket, brought him awake sharply as if a rattler had buzzed at his feet.

He threw himself aside just as the girl tilted the cup and hurled whiskey at his face, just as her other hand knocked away his rifle. Jubal hit the floor rolling, and looked up to see something long and heavy billow the ragged blanket and smash against the table.

"Paw!" the girl yelped. "You missed the bastard— help—"

She was scuttling for the rifle when Jubal wheeled around on the floor and kicked her feet out from under her. The wench slammed down hard, but his long gun went sliding across the room. On his knees, he snatched the pistol from his belt and cocked it.

Club in hand, a grizzled man lunged through the blankets, with the gap-toothed woman right behind him. Jubal pulled the trigger and the ball jerked the man to one side; his club clattered against the wall. The old woman cursed and brought a double-barreled short gun down in line with Jubal's head. He hurled his pistol at her and went to ground again, rolling across the girl as she tried to get up, flattening her again.

She screamed, "Son of a bitch!" and hit at him with his own rifle barrel. The old woman cut loose with one barrel, and Jubal felt the hot kiss of the ball at his cheek. Skinning knife out now, he went in low and fast. The flash from the other barrel blinded him, seared his face, and his reaching blade went into something soft.

Behind him, the girl screeched again, and Jubal tried to see as he whirled and backhanded the wet blade around, picturing in his mind's eye the muzzle of the rifle yawning at him. He missed with the blade but hit with his knuckles, hit a mighty lick and fought for his balance while the green spots faded and his eyes cleared.

They were all down, he saw—the man centered in the chest, lying on his back and staring up sightless, lips peeled back from yellowed teeth; the old woman sat on the floor, empty pistol in her lap as she held both hands pressed to the widening red stain of her belly and glared hate at Jubal. The girl lay still, her neck kind of bent to one side, Jubal's rifle clutched in both hands. He took a step and bent to lift it from her, easing down the hammer.

Wheezing, the old woman said, "Bastard, bastard," repeating it over and over, weaker each time, until the last curse hung in her wattled throat and she fell over to one side to kick a time or two.

Rifle at his hip, Jubal stepped over her and parted the blankets with the gun barrel. Nobody else there in the kitchen, nobody in the big sleeping room with cornshuck mattresses on the floor, dusty and long unused. One more room—and Jubal's jaw tightened when he saw the booty piled there: clothing and boots; weapons and saddles and bridles.

Backing away, he moved into the tavern and prodded the girl with the toe of a moccasin, but she didn't stir. To be certain she wasn't playing possum, Jubal knelt and put his ear to her mouth. He didn't feel breath, and looked again at the way her head sat angled on her slim neck. She either broke her neck when she got knocked to the floor, or his backhand blow had done it, backed by the weight of the heavy knife.

Before he went around back of the house, Jubal reloaded his own pistol and the fancy, two-bore one the old woman near about got him with. Both in his belt and rifle easy across his arm, he made his way to the corral where a dozen horses milled around, beyond sight of the road.

Jubal looked around and saw where one beatdown path led to the outhouse, another to the sagging, broke-back barn, and one more winding off through the trees. He followed that one, seeing where high grass was bent off to one side or the other, turned down by something being dragged.

Farther on, surrounded by pine saplings, stood an old mud chimney, and fire-blackened foundations where there'd once been a house. Off to one side stood the well, with shovels stuck upright in a hole close by. Jubal leaned over the well housing and peered down. When his eyes got used to the shadows, he could see something white poking from fresh dirt— a man's stiff hand.

"Knock 'em in the head from ahint that blanket, strip 'em, haul the bodies here and throw 'em down the well, then shovel enough dirt on top to keep down the stink. Ready-made grave for the lord knows how many men was grinnin' at that tail-switchin' gal when she throwed whiskey into their eyes, just afore the old man come down with that club. Jesus; was I horny and followed her in the back, I'da' been hit time I ducked through the blankets, or got steel between my ribs."

And as he turned away from where many men were piled atop each other, Jubal knew it was also his inattention that had almost put him among those corpses. All day, he'd been thinking so hard on Caroline he was barely conscious of his surroundings; any renegade Indian could have taken him out of the saddle, any slinking brigand ambush him. Befuddled as he was, he'd be no good to himself, his men or Andy Jackson.

The sound of horses brought him trotting to the inn, rifle at the ready, but they were his own men pulling up at the hitching rack.

"Well now," Barton Roberts said, "we figured maybe you got lost."

"Damned near did," Jubal said. "You want a meal and whiskey, you got to serve yourself."

When he showed them why, Cody Youngblood pushed back his cap and whistled. "That's a waste of woman flesh, cap'n; you might of kept the gal alive."

"She had other ideas," Jubal said, and led them to the storeroom.

"Ain't that somethin'," Daniel Smith grunted. "I heard tell of things like this along the Natchez Trace; but never thought to run up on one. Say they got a well full of dead men out back?"

"By the looks of all this plunder," Barton Roberts said, "they killed more'n their share. What you mean to do with it, Jubal?"

"See anything you fancy, take it," he answered. "Real owners won't care. Goddamn—this could of been goin' on for years, with that lot in yonder sellin' off a pile every once in a while."

"Must be gold around somewheres then," Cody Youngblood said.

"Or put away safe in New Orleans," Daniel Smith commented.

Mason McGee stood gawking. "Reckon there's a softer saddle amongst it?"

Jubal didn't grin with the others. He said, "Stew on the stove, and what plunder you can't haul, I'd be obliged was you all to stack it aside the road."

"For them as finds it," Barton Roberts nodded. "Fair enough. I take it you mean to set you a fire?"

"Had it in mind," Jubal said. "This goddamn slaughterhouse fair itches the back of my neck, and I reckon to fix it so nobody else gets killed here."

"Know somethin'?" Cody Youngblood said. "It appears I done lost any hankerin' for stew, but I wouldn't leave *all* that whiskey to the fire."

To strip the place, they had to keep stepping over bodies, and it got so that Jubal turned his head away from the girl, but then he'd see the surprised look on the man's stiffening face, and the pure hatred frozen into the snarl of the old woman.

After they turned the stolen horses loose, Jubal was glad to put a torch to the house, and stood awhile to see that it caught good. Mounting his horse, he rode after his men, swearing to keep Caroline in the back of his mind until the job was done and they were heading downriver.

Chapter 26

It was too early and Caroline knew it, but she made it a habit to pass the castiron gate every day, just in case a message was there for her. Sometimes she paused to look in at the garden, losing its blooms now in autumn chill, and often she stared at the doorway through which they'd passed together. When she closed her eyes, she could see the bed she had shared with Jubal Blaze, and the ache of that went deep, so that she would have to hurry to her own small house and busy herself at something, anything.

Shopping the markets took as much time as she could give the chore, and often Turpo came by for coffee, and to gossip of the sales taking place at the old Alcantari mansion, even with Felipe gone. For the sake of company, she put up with his slyly probing questions, parrying them as a matter of course.

Narcisse Marigny didn't visit often; she was tired after washing for others all day, but some nights not too weary to slip out down the Ramparts with a man at her side.

And Catherine Villars—the elfin girl seemed to have vanished, although her older sister did not fret over her absence. When Caroline could stand the loneliness no longer, she went next door to ask the loan of books, any kind of books that might keep her mind from dwelling upon Jubal Blaze.

Pierre Lafitte looked up from his table in surprise. "Madame, do you read?"

"A bit better in English than French," she said. "My—I was sent to school, where I once lived."

"You hear that, Marie? Madame, I have attempted to send young Catherine to school, but what does she do? The fencing school alone interests her, no fit exercise for a lady, *hein?* If she and my brother—well, it is to one's advantage to read directions upon a map, missives from other ships, necessities such as those; and there is always the *billet doux*." Winking his bad eye, Pierre got up and clumped to a shelf upon the wall. "Search these titles, madame; you are welcome to any and all. If you would interest Catherine in reading—"

"Merci," Caroline said. "I will try, but I have not seen her for some time."

From the kitchen, Marie Villars said, "She is— away."

"As Felipe," she said, looking closely at the books. Most were on navigation or armament, but she found a history of France.

"Ah, that one," Pierre said. "Catherine mentioned he spoke of traveling with the Lafittes. He did not do so. It is said he journeyed north alone; his saddlebags were packed for a long trip."

"His body servant is still here," Caroline said, holding the history book in both hands.

"To keep the house open for the selling of certain goods. The Lafittes retain Alcantari's share of the money, proving he trusts us more than we would trust him."

"Thank you," Caroline said, "for this book and all else."

Gallantly, Pierre bowed. *"Mon plaisir,* madame. One might wish your fortune had been different. If you ever have need of our services—"

"I shall remember your kindness, m'sieu."

At home, she could not concentrate long upon the book; kings and queens and faroff battlefields were not real to her, but Caroline forced herself to continue reading. Before dusk, she stoked the stove and began to prepare food she was not interested in. Someday she would cook for him, and she would make each meal a banquet, a feast. She stared at the pot she stirred, realizing she didn't even know his likes and dislikes. Did Kaintucks eat the same sort of things Creoles enjoyed?

When a carriage pulled up next door, she moved to the window and looked out. Twilight was gathering along the Ramparts and a wraithlike ground mist was beginning to rise, but she was certain of three figures descending from the carriage. Who could not know the bounding joy of Catherine Villars as the girl rushed into the house, or not recognize the tall, almost stately form of Jean Lafitte? The other man turned his face her way for just a moment, and Caroline thought she'd seen him before, but he followed quickly into the house before she could be sure.

Happy that Catherine had returned, she was eating her *court-bouillon* with some relish when the girl burst in the back door. "Caroline, oh Caroline! I must tell you."

She saw the happiness upon Catherine's face, the shining glow and subtle changes that could mean only one thing. "He loves you."

Catherine's cloak swirled as she kneeled at Caroline's knees and caught her hands. "It is true, *chérie.* Oh, I knew it! In my heart I knew it all the time. Now I am no longer a girl, but a woman—*his* woman."

"I'm so glad for you," Caroline said, not envious but wishing her own romance could be so simple, that Jubal Blaze might take her away as Jean Lafitte would claim and protect his young lover.

Catherine put her head upon her friend's knee. "He was very tired from travel, from dealing with those *cochons* who would put a price upon his head. The little house; it was there he met with men to be bribed, men to be reminded of past favors, and I was his hostess. Not a servant, you understand, although some leered at me as such. *Mais non,* I was his lady, and so he treated me. I was so proud."

Nodding, Caroline pictured the lovely front room,

the girl moving graceful and erect as she served Lafitte's guests. Crystal, candlelight and beauty.

Catherine said softly, "When they were at last
gone, I turned down his bed and helped him off with
his coat. Quiet, he was, thinking. I turned away to
leave him, sad in my heart that I could not comfort
him. When I reached the door, he said but one word,
my name. Ah! It was enough, and I flew to him with
a happy cry. Carrie, he was so gentle, and there was
no pain, only love."

Stroking her friend's glossy hair, she felt a little
twinge. How different all might have been for her, had
she first lain with Jubal, had it been he who had taken
her maidenhead. To know only love, and not revulsion, not to feel hate and despair.

Head lifted, Catherine said then, "Oh; I have been
selfish, but I just had to tell you. Your own man, the
true one—there has been no word?"

"Not even from Felipe," she answered. "Catherine,
you are my closest, my dearest friend. I never really
had a friend before, so forgive me for not knowing
how to trust. Sit here, *chérie,* and let me get you
coffee. Then I will tell you how I plan to be with
Jubal, to get away from Felipe."

The girl's eyes were wide as Caroline related her
story from the beginning, and they had filled with tears
by the time Catherine heard of Solah's death and
subsequent burial. She dabbed at them and said, "Carrie, I bleed for you. It is wrong for one to be so
happy while another is so sad."

"No," Caroline said, "for your happiness is mine
also. Just—it is difficult for me to trust any white,
more so for me to think I may be one of them. Yet
you and your sister found good men among them, and
perhaps I have, too."

"Not of the blood?" Catherine asked, astounded.
"You are not—"

"I do not know," Caroline said truthfully. "Jubal is
to search out evidence for me. If it is so, that I am
in no part Ashanti, then there is a chance for me, for
Jubal and me, I think. Otherwise, Felipe will never let

me go." She told the rest of it then, omitting no names, no detail she recalled.

"But of course," Catherine said, "I know of the Le-Croix plantation, who does not? If you are heir to that estate—but no; there is a brother. No again, my friend —the same father, but a different mother, *comprenez-vous?* The father, that one is dead years ago; I am sorry."

Caroline shrugged. "I cannot feel sorrow, for the only father I knew was named M'Nele, a brave, proud black man; a true Ashanti."

"Your half brother is Lucien LeCroix," Catherine said. "I know him well, because he takes instruction from the same fencing master. Nice enough, I suppose, but never fierce as a swordsman should be. What will happen to him, if you are to become mistress of the LeCroix lands? But *non;* I forget he is the man. Still, if your father named a daughter in his will—oh! What do women know of these things? I must ask Jean."

"There is little you do *not* know," Carrie said with a smile.

Returning the smile, Catherine said, "I learn to help him; I learn the foil, the rapier to help him. If these dogs try to pull him down, I will fight at his side. When they attempt to trick him, they must first fool me." She cocked her head and looked over one shoulder. "I hear the horses stirring, so I must leave you now. Jean has a Kaintuck with him, one who laughs too often and easily, and I ride with them back to the little house. But tomorrow, Carrie—you come with me, and we will see what we may discover."

She stood up, then threw her arms about Caroline. "I do not care if you are of the blood, or white as *le Bos* himself. I love you, Carrie."

"And I you," Caroline said through her tight throat. Then she was alone but no longer lonely, and when she went to bed, it was to dream of a gentle giant. He stood between her and slavers, guarding her from whips and irons, blocking out the dark threat of Felipe de Alcantari.

She was awakened early by Catherine, who hurried

her through breakfast and led her outside into a cart drawn by a small, shaggy horse. "My Jean would have me driven in a carriage, but I do not wish to make trouble for him, *hein?* The white ladies—pardon, *chérie* —will frown to see an octoroon in a fancy carriage. *Alors;* we depart for the LeCroix plantation. It is not so far, but I have brought lunch for us, and excellent wine. For celebration, you understand—my love and your love to be."

The city was already beginning to teem with life as Catherine maneuvered the cart along the road toward Chalmette, and the blanket around Caroline's shoulders warmed her until the sun was stronger. They passed a string of Kaintucks trooping sullenly for the river and training, and coming the other way, farmers bringing their produce to market, black children skipping along behind goats and milk cows, copper women balancing woven baskets upon their heads.

Then they turned north along a road whose surface had been hardened by crushed oyster shells, made white and dusty smooth. "Just to see," Catherine said, clucking to the horse. "To show you what may be yours. Last night, I spoke to Jean about you, and someone will look into the records." She eased the reins and looked at Caroline. "There are many pots upon the stove, these days, a *potage* cooking that I do not like; too many ingredients. That Kaintuck—if he *is*—had me sent from the room before he spoke more with Jean. I know there was a discussion with Pierre earlier, and I have this feeling that someone may be putting *le Bos* in danger. No matter, now; look, there is the boundary post for the LeCroix lands. The house is much farther along."

In this part of Louisiana all land was flat, Caroline thought, with always the threat of the great river poised close by. But this land was carefully tended, well cleared. She saw where sugarcane leaves had been left to enrich the soil after the stalks had been taken, and the brown skeletons of cotton plants that would fall before next planting. The fields stretched on and on, broken by treelines left as buffers against storm winds, carpeted by green pastures where cattle grazed behind split cypress fences. White herons prowled for crayfish in backwater inlets, and occasionally a river gull wheeled overhead, crying harshly against the pale sky.

"Rich land," Catherine said, "a very large plantation; I do not know how many thousand of acres. Ah —see off there through the lane of the oak trees? A great house, *non?* So far, Lucien LeCroix has not brought a wife home for it."

Caroline peered at the building, tall and wide, bordered by a well-tended lawn. "It is raised on stilts," she said.

"For the water, when it comes," Catherine explained. "High brick foundations, but as you see, none for the slave quarters beyond. It would not be wise to go closer, Caroline."

"I have seen enough," she said. "It makes me think my mother might have lied. Could such as I be born to a manor so grand?"

"Birth is but an accident; sometimes good, sometimes bad. *Certainement,* you could belong here. But as for me, I would not change my life for all of that; I am too happy."

Partway back to town, Catherine drew the cart off the road and beneath moss-hung trees, so they might picnic upon the grass. They had almost finished the fried chicken when another cart rattled to a stop beyond them and a lanky, threadbare man grinned his way to them. He spoke to Caroline; *"Bonjour, madame.* Could you spare a bite, a drink of wine?"

She gestured to the remains of lunch. "Help yourself."

Catherine moved slightly to one side and pulled her cloak closer. The man wolfed chicken and washed it down with gulps of wine, mumbling about the weather between bites and swallows; his eyes followed Catherine, clung to her every move. Caroline began to feel uneasy as Catherine said, "Keep the bottle, m'sieu; we must be on our way."

He wiped his mouth. "What is this, the yellow wench speaking for her mistress? Or perhaps you are both yellow wenches, out for a lark with each other? I have heard of such things between quadroons, and when I hear them, you know what I say? I say that what such women need is a man."

"Carrie," Catherine said calmly, "climb into the cart."

The man drained the bottle and flung it aside. Narrow eyes glinted and his feet moved to block Caroline off. *"Oui;* I thought it strange that a white woman would ride in such a poor cart, and now I know you are not white. I am a poor farmer who does not own fancy women like yourself, but I know what to do with you—oh yes, I know." He stroked his crotch.

Catherine Villars glided toward him, eyes big and dark, a damp smile upon her face. "Are you sure you can please us both?"

His unshaven leer widened. "In turn, little whore, or at the same time. Come here."

"Catherine," Caroline said, "please do not—"

She saw only the quick gleam of sunlight from polished steel, and the man yelped as he staggered back, tightly gripping his slashed arm.

"Bitch! You cut—"

Catherine's sharp blade swung in hungry arcs. "Only a nick, *cochon.* I could as easily open your dirty throat. Run, run, damn you, before I change my mind!"

He edged away from the long knife, bulging eyes watching it, right arm dripping crimson. "I—I did not mean—"

She lunged in, right arm extended, her body a smoothly flowing line behind the blade, and a great piece of the man's shirt fell away. He fled then, leaping down the road for his cart and clumsily scrambling into it. When he yelled hoarsely, his horse bolted, and the cart bounced wildly behind.

Catherine said, "The fool; I should have gutted him on the spot."

Caroline's heart was still racing and her mouth had gone suddenly dry. "He—just because he thought we were not white—oh, I hate them so."

The girl lifted into the cart and gathered the reins.

"Not all of them, *chérie;* there are Jean and Pierre; there is your Jubal; maybe even yourself."

"Yes," Caroline murmured. "Maybe even myself." Her hands were trembling, and she hid them in the folds of her dress.

Chapter 27

She saw the jaded horse before Catherine stopped the cart; it was hitched to the post before Caroline's house, sweated and dust-covered, with its head hanging. She swung down and touched Catherine's hand. "Thank you, *chérie*. It seems Felipe has returned. And thank you for showing me that a woman can stand up to a man."

"Provided she knows how to use a blade," Catherine said. "I will teach you, Carrie. Tomorrow, perhaps we can visit the fencing master, so you can see Lucien LeCroix."

Nodding toward the house, Caroline said, "If he permits." As she approached her own door, her stomach began to tremble.

Felipe had thrown aside boots and coat; there was several days' growth of beard upon his face, and he was travel-stained. But although he appeared weary, his eyes gleamed as he looked at her. "So; where have you been?"

"With Catherine Villars," she answered. "Are you hungry?"

"Not for food," he said. "I stopped by the house, where Turpo made me a meal. You remember Turpo, *non?*"

"Of course." The warning tingle in her belly grew stronger.

Felipe drank wine from the bottle neck. "A faithful servant, Turpo; because he knows if he does not attend to his duties, I will peel his back. Fear commands obedience; would you agree?"

"But not loyalty." Caroline took the blanket she had been using as a cloak, and brought it into the bedroom.

"A mustee philosopher," he said, stretching out his legs. "Heat bathwater, philosopher, and we will discuss loyalty."

He knows something, she thought. But how could he? She had been so careful, and there had only been that one time—that single, wondrous night with Jubal. Adding fresh wood to the stove, she placed a metal tub on top, and filled it with water from the cistern. Glancing at him now and then, she saw him sprawled and rumpled, so unlike his usual self.

"You had a liaison," Felipe said then, after another pull at the bottle. "Turpo reported this to me, that you arrived here just past sunup one morning." He drained the bottle and flung it across the room with a crash. "Who was it, wench? Who is the man dares to trifle with the mistress of de Alcantari? I'll have his blood."

"Turpo is a fool," Caroline said, keeping her voice calm, "and a lazy one, at that. Else he might have told you I often take early morning walks—while your spy is fast asleep. I am alone; what would you have me do?"

The wizened little black only suspected, she thought; he did not know for certain, and had not followed her to the meeting with Jubal.

"For now," Felipe said deceptively, "I would have you bring another bottle. Then you may undress your master and bathe him. Perhaps Turpo was overeager to find evidence for me; perhaps not. On the other hand, I might beat a confession from you."

Caroline steadied herself. "And you would hear only what you wished to hear, whether truth or not." She went to the cupboard and opened another bottle of wine.

At the table, he took it from her, his lips curling. "Your brain is nimble for a woman; too much so for

252

a black woman. All right; I shall let pass your small indiscretion, for now."

He was playing with her, Caroline felt, cruelly teasing her. Threats were there, spoken and unspoken, and for some reason of his own, Felipe meant to keep her teetering uncertainly on the edge of his anger. Standing behind him, she lifted his shirt over his head and raised arms. She could not allow him to beat her. Catherine stood up to a man who would have raped them both, and Felipe had his back turned; there was the keen fish knife in the cabinet—

But what then, even if she could bring herself to cut his throat? Felipe de Alcantari was well known, and could not vanish as easily as her mother, could not be interred in the back yard. There would be questions, a search, and his mistress would be the first suspect. Putting the shirt to one side, she came around before him to kneel and slide off his trousers. She did not want to see the bulge in his undergarments, and her hand shook as she reached to loosen them.

She stood up. "I—I think the water is hot." She hadn't thought this far ahead, to this intimacy of flesh. Before, it hadn't mattered, but now there was Jubal.

Felipe didn't offer to help with the heavy tub; she struggled it from stove to floor and found soap and towels. Naked, he stood in the water while she soaped his hard body, avoiding his swollen staff until he caught her wrist and forced her hand to it.

"Here is where your loyalty lies," he hissed. "This is your master, and never forget it, wench. If ever I am certain you spread your legs for someone else, I will turn you over to a herd of stinking, sweating blacks to be their plaything."

Gnawing at her lips, Caroline rinsed and rubbed him down with damp cloths, not bypassing his crotch this time. So long as she was owned body and soul by this man, there was no other response but acceptance. She could kill him, or she could run away, or she could obey. With the third alternative, there was a chance she would see Jubal again, that he would bring evidence from the North, documents to free her forever from domination by this or any other man.

When Felipe stepped from the tub, she toweled him dry as he smiled thinly at her. "Bathe yourself before coming to me," he said, "but do not tarry."

No softness, no word of kindness, only the gift of his used bathwater; she removed her dress and bathed quickly, dreading his hands upon her body, his weight between her thighs, and the deep penetration that would make her feel as if she was betraying Jubal. Towel about her hips, she took yet more wine from the cupboard and drank deeply, drank again, but there was no time to numb herself. Already he stirred restlessly upon the bed.

Lying flat upon his back, Felipe held the wine bottle upon his belly, close to his erect manhood. His eyes roamed her body. "You are a beauteous wench for certain, and well I know the flames that sleep inside that silken flesh. It would be a shame to waste them upon savage blacks, but if there is a lesson to be taught—"

"As you please," Caroline said. "Perhaps I would enjoy it."

"Bitch!" he said, and caught her arm roughly to pull her down. "You would mock me—*me?*" His hand slashed her face and Caroline caught her breath, determined not to cry. He slapped her again and again, but only when Felipe clamped viciously upon her breast did he wring a gasp of pain from her.

She was limp when he rolled her over and mounted her, driving his hardness brutally into her flinching body, burrowing into her depths with driving, slamming power. Caroline rocked with the creaking bed, her eyes closed as she battled to separate mind from body. She had done it with Kleppner; could she manage the same retreat from Felipe?

"Respond, you bitch," he grunted, digging fingers into her buttocks. "Damn you, damn you."

Though he rocked her from side to side, though he bit her throat and sledged against her belly, he could not reach her now. She concentrated upon what might have been, what the future might yet be when Jubal Blaze returned.

"Very well." Felipe rolled from her and came up to kneel astride her chest, to grip her hair and force himself upon her in another way. There was no denying him, because he then used one hand to pry open her jaws, cursing her for a yellow bitch.

But at last it was over and she hid her shamed face in a pillow when he lay sated beside her. In a while, she heard the click of the wine bottle against his teeth, and he said calmly, "I believe Turpo now; I think you have found yourself another man. But I forgive you, since I will not leave you again, and you will never have a chance to see your lover. If somehow you manage an assignation, I will kill him."

Clenching a handful of sheet, Caroline said, "Once I thought you were wonderful. I would have done anything for you, and willingly. Now you might as well put me in chains, or sell me."

Felipe's laugh was brittle. "Sell you? No, my dear. I have plans for you. While I was away—"

"Not with the Lafittes," she said.

"*Eh bien,* so you know that. True, I did not travel with brigands; the story was useful, as they are useful to me in replenishing the Alcantari coffers. I had other business, a thing that has nothing to do with pirates and their loot."

"You went to the Lafittes," Caroline said. "They did not come to you."

Felipe sat up, propping his back against the iron of the bed. "A gentleman is sometimes forced to low companions, but I suspect my run of bad luck is over. Before much longer, the name of Alcantari will regain its splendor. A toast to that time. Bring glasses, Caroline; I would have you share this bottle with me."

She walked nude into the other room. Though she had resisted him, even dared to bait him, there was no anger in Felipe now. It had burned out of him with the first loosing of his passions, to be replaced by a smirking kind of satisfaction. She brought glasses, puzzled by Felipe's change of moods.

Thin cigar clenched in his white, sharp teeth, he acted the cavalier, pouring wine for her, inclining his head in a mocking bow. "To the Alcantaris, then; *santé.*"

She drank to rinse the taste of him from her mouth. He refilled the glasses. "You were left alone, so you took walks at dawn, *hein?* If you had known where I was, how far I traveled, the gold that changed hands, perhaps you would have stayed close to the hearth. All you have seen is this miserable hut; you do not know the house of Alcantari. Once it was glorious, a show-place for all the city. It can be so again. Tomorrow, I will take you to the house."

He stopped talking to drink, and in the silence, a joyous tinkle of laughter floated from the house next door; Catherine Villars, sounding the happiness of her love.

"Why?" Caroline asked. "If your fortunes have taken a turn for the better, you do not have to display me again, in hopes of provoking creditors to a duel."

Felipe's laughter was nothing like Catherine's. "You have a quick wit and a quicker tongue, wench. Oh, no doubt there will be challenges, but after the first few idiots are laid to rest, others will accept things as they are." He put a hand upon her bare shoulder. "Do you wish to know where I have been, what I have done?"

"If you want me to know, you will tell me," Caroline said.

For a moment, his fingers tightened upon her shoulder, but Felipe laughed again and released her. "There will be much to learn, Caroline, but you are intelligent. You will adapt to the new life." A droplet of purple wine escaped his lips and moved down his chin. "There are no records, only the bill of sale, which can be explained. Officials have been well paid to document your true lineage, and soon all New Orleans will sympathize with you for your travails. Creoles are such romantics they will believe anything."

Caroline frowned. "What are you talking about? I—I do not understand. My true lineage? What does that mean?" The night Solah died in her arms, the tale her mother choked out; had Felipe overheard? Narcisse Marigny said he had come home twice that evening.

Felipe blew smoke and flicked ashes upon the floor. "Of course you are surprised. The very thought came upon me by surprise, also."

Caroline held back a shiver. Had Felipe followed Jubal out of the city and—and killed him? No, no! He had no idea Jubal Blaze was her lover; Felipe was gone *before* that night—or was he?

Stroking her arm, Felipe said, "Understand, my *chérie,* there has been much misfortune for me of late, and if I am not always cheerful, ever the tender lover, I ask your pardon."

Voice low and smooth, he went on: "From the very first, I realized you were a grand prize, that I had done nothing more significant in my life than buying you from that slaver. You said once you would have willingly done anything for me, and yes—I for you. I was angry when I heard Turpo, shocked. I did not mean to mistreat you, but I was blinded with jealousy. Especially when I planned so much, maneuvered and intrigued—then to know you were unfaithful—it was too much, Caroline. I will make it up to you, every day of our lives together."

The change was too sudden, too complete, and she did not believe him. This was not proud, arrogant and cruel Felipe talking, but a suspicious stranger. She said nothing; she waited, her mind racing with possibilities discarded as quickly as they surfaced. She could see no logical reason for Felipe to be good to her, no use he might have for her in furthering his ambitions.

"There," he said, and drank more wine. "I have humbled myself to you."

Wetting her lips, she said, "There is no need, between master and slave."

"Ah, *mon bichette,* but there is the point. Soon we will no longer be master and slave, but equals. That startles you, *hein?* And well it should, that Felipe de Alcantari would go to such great lengths to marry his mistress."

Caroline gasped. *"M-marry?"*

He swayed as he patted her cheek. *"Magnifique,* eh? Only I would dare such a thing. White cannot marry black, according to the law, but ah—what if the black is proved to be white, if she was orphaned and stolen and sold into slavery, against all laws of society and humanity? Hearts must bleed for such an unfortunate, and must rejoice when she regains her rightful place. Will not most Creoles applaud me for being so forgiving? The others, those who would mumble in their beards about stained merchandise—those will face me beneath the Dueling Oaks."

Caroline could only swallow dryly and stare at him.

Felipe drank again, and spilled wine onto his chest. Blinking at her, he said, "Stunned, eh? Well you might be, to know an Alcantari would go so far to prove his love. Officials have been bribed, documents forged, and all is in readiness. I tell you, the city will rock upon its foundations; it will forget the British threat and the intolerable Kaintucks that roam our streets. There will be consternation and outrage; a hue and cry will be raised to find the villains responsible for your abduction. And I—the tragic figure who unwittingly bought a white woman and took her to his bed as mistress. But when I acknowledge my error and announce that I am taking the only honorable solution by making her my wife, New Orleans will salute me."

Why, *why?* The wine was having its effect upon Felipe, but when he was in his cups, he was never crazed. He meant what he was saying, every impossible word. Caroline put a hand to her throat and felt the pulse beating wildly there. Felipe wanted to *marry* her, to change her status from mustee mistress to honored wife, and had gone to a great deal of trouble to arrange it. There had to be a reason, some dark compulsion she could not fathom.

That shadow in the night when Solah was dying; that half-felt presence beyond the window. It could have been Felipe, *must* have been Felipe, spying, taking in each agonized whisper her mother made. He saw an advantage for himself; there could be no other reason.

He didn't love her. Only a little while back, he'd slapped her and forced her to do something that should only be done in love. Jealous, Felipe claimed—but why then curse her for a mustee, a yellow bitch? Knowing she was of the blood, what possible cause could he have for taking her to wife and—and possibly bearing his sons, his name?

What a terrible man he was, so cunning, so basically evil. She meant nothing to him, no more than a piece of meat bought at the butcher's block. If her mother was right, if there was the possibility she was *not* Caroline Monteleone, Felipe meant to take every advantage of that, strip her of any fortune, and discard her, as he would if she was truly a mustee.

She said, "Why are you doing this, Felipe?"

Drunkenly, he grinned at her. "Out of my great love. But why ask the reasons, *ma petite?* Accept your great fortune. Think what it means to be white, legally white. To say nothing of the honor of becoming an Alcantari. Tomorrow, I will see that the story gets out, and a few days after, I will be the consummate gentleman and have the marriage banns posted."

"You do not love me, Felipe—nor do I love you."

His smile vanished. *"Merde!* All that matters is what I say. Do you hesitate, wench? Do you realize the signal honor I do you?" Felipe's eyes glittered dangerously. "If you think—"

"I think I will wait," Caroline said, and had no time to duck the explosion of his fist.

259

Chapter 28

Several times during the journey, they made out ragged Indians flitting through the woods beyond rifle range, but none came close to Jubal's little band. He guessed word of the Creek punishment in Alabama had broken the spirit of the tribes, but that didn't stop renegades from hitting and running, so he put out a sentry every night, and the rest slept well back from the circle of campfires.

One night while embers burned low, he rose from behind the fallen tree that covered him and hammered a shot at a noise in the brush. Before the echoes died, his men were out of their blankets, locks eared back on their long guns and waiting. The horses snorted nervously.

In a while, Jubal said, "Might of been a bear."

Nearby, Barton Roberts muttered, "Might of been a woods runner with an empty belly and a sharp knife."

"Whichever," Jubal said, "I don't aim to get slipped up on again." Reloading by feel and experience in the dark, he said, "You all go on back to sleep. Scared him off, I expect."

And Cody Youngblood said, "Don't know how in hell a man can sleep, what with folks loosin' off guns ever whichaway."

Mason McGee's slow voice drifted through the night. "You won't have no trouble. You and a mule is the onliest critters I ever seen kin sleep standin' up."

There was muffled laughter and a stirring around as

they sought their beds again. Jubal pulled the blanket around his shoulders and hunkered behind the tree trunk. He'd been touchy ever since he damned near got his head knocked off at that tavern back down the Trace. And though he kept telling himself that family was deserving of hanging a hundred times over for the murders they had committed, it still went against the grain to kill women. Whenever he thought of that bar wench lying with her neck broke and skirts hiked up over plump thighs, the picture kind of drifted over and got mixed up with memories of Caroline Monteleone. God knows why; they were nothing alike. Maybe it was because they were both women, or because Caroline was so much woman she represented every other female.

Jubal hunched deeper into his blanket and listened to the night, and when the forest turned slow, drippy grey, rose to stretch and kick up the fire. Time the others rolled out, he had coffee boiling and side meat sizzling in lard.

That day was no different; no little bunch of cabins calling itself a town could supply flints to make a worthwhile load for a flatboat. Jubal pushed men and horses hard, reaching farther north as the road got better and the country more settled. It was just like New Orleans, he thought; not in looks, but in the attitude of men surprised that Andy Jackson was still piddling around down yonder, while most everybody knew the Redcoats had given up.

At last they came into Paducah, their mounts gaunted and saddlesore. Jubal led them up the main street to a combination general store and tavern, and climbed wearily down to tether his horse. His men followed him inside, trailing their rifles, scraggly and unkempt in stained buckskins, looking wild and ornery. Two barmaids shrank from them, and the pot-bellied landlord came trotting from the store, rubbing hands on his apron.

"Ale," Jubal said, spinning silver upon the bar, "and whatever you got to eat, then beds. We come a far piece."

"Yessir," the man said, jerking his balding pate at the girls. "Might you have news from the south?"

Jubal buried his face in a tankard of ale, lowered it and sighed, "Aye; Andy Jackson's still waitin' for the British fleet to come on in—if they ain't moved already."

The man had small, bright eyes set in a chubby face. They moved to Jubal's men rared back at a table, to their weapons, and back to Jubal. He said, "General got all the men he needs?"

Jubal wiped his mouth. "We ain't runnin' off; I'm Cap'n Blaze, and Jackson sent us clear up here lookin' for flint he needs right bad."

The landlord's face brightened. "Come to the right place, then. Man named Watson has got him a ledge of first-class flint on his land, about three miles out. Totes some in ever once to a while and trades for flour and the like. Ain't much call for it hereabouts, since most folks finds their own, but I take it off'n his hands and swap it downriver."

Jubal nodded. "Figure he's got enough for Jackson's whole army? And a way of us gettin' it out'n here? I can pay for diggin' and haulin' help, and for a flatboat."

The man wiped his hand on his apron and extended it across the bar. "Name's Mixon; I was proud to serve under Andy afore I got too fat and old. Bigod, if'n the general needs flint, he'll get it, if'n it takes every man in town to dig and haul it. And we'll be glad for the chance."

At the table, Barton Roberts held up his tankard. "Most sounds like we're home, cap'n."

Jubal shook Mixon's hand. "Damned if it don't. We been thinkin' nobody give a damn, that they figured the Redcoats was whipped and it's all over. Andy don't see it thataway."

"Anything you want," Mixon said.

Rubbing his face, Jubal said, "Be obliged was you to feed and rest us a spell. Then I'd be willin' to swap five wore-out horses and tack for the best horse in

262

town. I got one more chore to do, but I mean to be back time the boat's loaded."

. "Spread your blankets by the fire there," Mixon said. "Susie—Delma—stir your shanks and git meat on the table; fill up them tankards again. Cap'n, you got no worries here. While you all rest, I'll see to all else." He shook his head. "Bigod; ol' Andy's fixin' to light into the Redcoats again, and I ain't there."

"I'll bear him word of what you done," Jubal promised, and fell to when the barmaids, giggling and rolling their eyes now, brought a leg of beef and a platter of steaming peas and potatoes.

"Barton," he said when the bones were picked clean, "I got to ride up into Illinois. You see to the flint." He weighed his purse in one big hand, and took out two gold pieces, then shoved the hide sack across the table. "Mixon'll help get the boat and wagons. If I ain't back, don't wait on me."

Barton Roberts said, "Sure you don't need company?"

"Best I go alone. Don't expect Indian trouble, and I'll stay in the saddle. This ain't got nothin' to do with the army; it's personal-like." Jubal brought in his blankets and spread them, noticing that Mixon had closed the tavern and was standing in the store part, talking fast and low to other men.

Lying on his back, toasted by the fire and lulled by a full belly, Jubal closed his eyes but kept one hand upon the two-barreled pistol in his belt. He was stretching it some, shirking responsibility for gathering the flint while he took off north on an errand for Caroline Monteleone, but he'd given his bounden word. With any luck, he'd be back before the stuff was mined and hauled and packed into a flatboat, before a crew was arranged for. It was easy enough to go floating downriver, but something else to know where sandbars and snags waited to rip out a craft's bottom.

He hadn't forgotten the treachery aboard another flatboat, nor tales of river pirates that might wait in ambush around any bend of the river. But this time he had four good men with him, and they'd get the boat through, come what might. Dozing, he thought of better things, of midnight hair long and silken, of body and hands and mouth that could be gentle and fierce together. Jubal went to sleep smiling.

True to his word, Mixon had a fine horse waiting for Jubal when he woke, a deep-chested stallion with solid bone and a damn-you eye. "Take you to hell and back," the man said, "long as you kind of respect him. Saddlebags is packed and the gals will see to your bedroll." Mixon fingered the sparse grey hair around his shiny head. "Was you men with Jackson for the Creek fight?"

"Come down from the Carolinas and Tennessee with him," Jubal answered. "He purely put it to the Creeks, and if'n them New Orleans Creoles gets off their gentleman asses, he'll do the same to the British."

"Susie's bringin' breakfast," Mixon said, motioning Jubal back inside. "Wisht I could be with you when the hooraw starts, but time comes to set back. This here tavern and store does right good most years, and Susie and Delma—most like my own blood, but a heap more comfort of cold nights. Just like my featherbed beats cold, hard ground. Long as a man don't make a practice of it, goin' to war learns him things. Now that don't say I won't fight, does somebody come stompin' on *my* ground, and I reckon was Andy Jackson to ask me, I'd take down my musket again. But a man ought to think on tomorrow, onct to a while."

Riding out of Paducah on the fractious stallion, Jubal kept him on the bit until he settled down and thought about Mixon. It was true that a man should think on tomorrow. Pa said so, too. Jubal wondered what Pa would say, was he to ride up to the house with Caroline next to him in a carriage. Time you settled down, Pa would say, and Jubal would be lucky to pry him loose from Caroline, once he saw what a beauty she was, how much a lady she was, to grace the womanless halls of Tarboro.

"Pay attention, fool!" Jubal said, as the stud horse skittered from a falling leaf, and said it to himself, also. *Follow the wagon road all the way,* Mixon had said,

264

and it'll take you clear to Marion, which ain't all that much of a town.

Enough for a lawyer who had something very important to Caroline Monteleone, and therefore damned important to Jubal Blaze. Maybe the papers had something to do with the situation she was in, somehow beholden to a man she didn't love and wasn't married to.

He hadn't asked what the documents were, and Caroline hadn't gone into detail, but there was the ring of hope in her voice, and a hint of promise that still lingered in his blood. Get to Marion and find the lawyer, get the papers, hurry back down to Paducah and bring the flint downriver. If he hadn't gone off on that fruitless hunt with Tom Pickett, Jackson would now have the army's muskets ready—but then, Jubal might not have seen Caroline on the street that day. There'd be no pretty little house to go back to, no note to leave in the iron gate, no straight, slim woman with all that honeyed fire to her.

Shaking himself, Jubal eased the reins and the stallion went into a lope, shaking his head for the sheer joy of running. Cold wind whistled in Jubal's ears and cleared his head, so after a spell he pulled in the big horse and patted the muscled neck. Two farmers in a wagon put guns across their knees when Jubal approached, but nodded howdy to him while watching him close. Up the road, a pigtailed youngun waved to him, and he waved back. Piney woods smelled good, and the air was crisp. Back home, his brother would see plenty of rations put by for winter, and firewood laid in. The slaves would grow fat and lazy, and there'd be good times in town, good times at Tarboro when folks came calling; logs crackling in the fireplace and mulled wine to hand; ladies with pink cheeks and roguish eyes, men hollering like fools as they rode out to hunt.

Caroline would fit in there; she'd stand out anywhere in the world. There'd be green spite in ladies' eyes when they saw her, and men would shake their heads and say what a fool for luck old Jubal was, riding to war and coming home with a lady so fine as to shame all the Tidewater highnoses.

Settling into the journey, he allowed the stud to jog some, then lope, and follow by a walk. The horse worked willingly, and Jubal thought Mixon had done him proud by furnishing it for the trip. They covered the road together, swinging wide once and waiting out a body of horsemen that might have been anything, including trouble. By nightfall, when Jubal grained the horse and rubbed him down before staking him to pasture in a little glen hidden from the road, they were in Massac County.

Jubal supped cold, not sure of the country, and he slept with his long gun beside him and the fancy pistol in his hand, the one taken from the old woman who'd near killed him with it. Up at dawn and shaking some with cold, he dared a small fire and fried bacon to go with skillet cornbread and coffee. Cleaning up after, he led the stallion to water and gave him his fill, then saddled and headed north.

At a bridge, a querulous old man said yes, that was the way to Marion, and anybody'd know they was in Williamson County. "Fine horse," the old man said. "Trade you a musket and one of my gals for him."

"Don't believe so," Jubal said. "Much obliged, but I need to get on into Marion afore sundown, and I expect your gal couldn't pack me."

"Hee-hee!" the old man chortled, throwing back his head and exposing a toothless mouth. "My gal'd give you a ride you won't forget, youngun. Musket, axe and *both* my gals, then. I'd throw in their ma, but she ain't worth much."

"Old man," Jubal laughed, "you wouldn't know what to do with this here stud horse, no more'n I could handle two high-ridin' gals."

"Could hire him out to stud," the old man said, leaning on a twisted walking stick. "Old woman won't let the gals collect nothin', so they just gives it away. But I kin see you ain't in a dickerin' mood, nor a diddlin' one, neither. You git old as me, you'll look back and understand there ain't nothin' more important than them two things. So I'll say good day to a young fool."

Still grinning, Jubal galloped the horse a way and rounded a curve before slowing him. Up ahead, a man slouched in a saddle, shotgun across the pommel and a pair of lean hounds ranging ahead. There was a shaggy, wolfish look to the man, too. Jubal eased his long gun from its scabbard and halted the stud.

The man lifted one hand. "No call for alarm, stranger. Just goin' about my business. You see any niggers down the road?"

Slave hunter, Jubal thought. "No, nor sign of any." Nigger chasers were necessary, but so were buzzards.

"Must of took to the woods," the hunter said, not taking his eyes off Jubal, even when the lead hound darted into the brush and started to bell.

"Dog says so," Jubal said.

The man legged his horse to the side, head twisted to watch Jubal until he was under cover. Jubal heard the quickened slam of hooves then, and the excited trailing of the hounds. Runaway niggers had to be run down like any other stock busted the fence, but Jubal didn't have much use for them as made it their life's work.

The stallion was heaving some, but they made it into the town of Marion two hours before sundown. Jubal looked out of place among the city folk and dirt farmers, and he was stared at by shopkeepers and women in bonnets. Jubal saw there was one central street, and rode slowly past a smithy, a white church, and a river off to his left. Feed store, saloon, and there—a painted sign: Artis Barker, Attorney at Law. Swinging down, Jubal hitched the horse and carried his rifle up stairs hung to the side of a building with a general store below.

The door swung back just as Jubal was ready to knock on it. The little man looked like a lawyer, frock coat and string tie and eyeglasses. He had his hat on, ready to leave. His hands danced nervously at his coat lapels. "Yes, yes? I meant to have an early supper, but if your business can't wait—"

Jubal filled the doorway, eyes taking in the piled-up desk, drawered cabinets and brass spittoon, oil lamps, a musty smell. He eased forward, rifle across his arms until the lawyer backed up. Jubal put a moccasin against the door and shut it. "You lawyer Barker?"

"That—that I am," the man said, retreating behind his desk and taking off his hat. "People up here don't carry weapons around, sir. We're civilized here, civilized."

"Hope so," Jubal said. "I come for some papers belongin' to Miss Caroline Monteleone."

Barker's face went loose, then tight. He sat down, removed his spectacles and polished them against his coat. "Monteleone—Monteleone—there was once a family here by that name; the smith, I believe. But there was an ugly killing, yes, a killing; son of an illustrious citizen, yes. The smith had to flee, but papers —papers belonging to his daughter; no."

Jubal watched the man put his glasses back on, watched him tug out a square of linen and pat his chin. He said, "Think some more, lawyer. The lady said she has papers here, and I take the lady's word."

Barker jittered. "Lady—*lady?* Why, she—" he saw something in Jubal's face that stopped him. But he pushed out his scrawny chest and shook his head. "No documents here concerning the Monteleones."

"Set quiet," Jubal said. "I come too far to be turned aside. Reckon I'll see for myself."

"You—" Barker said, starting up from his chair, then closing his mouth and sinking down again.

Nodding, Jubal placed his long gun against the wall and opened one drawer after another, scanning the papers there, looking for the name. He heard the lawyer shifting, the chair squeaking, and stilled the little man by dropping a drawer on the floor.

Nothing in this cabinet, nor that one. The desk, then. Up close, he could smell Barker's fear and knew something was wrong, knew the squinchy bastard was hiding something. With his skinning knife, he flipped papers off the desk one by one, making them sail.

268

Caroline said her documents were here. He moved around the desk and yanked open another drawer.

He'd miscalculated the little man. With a yelp, Barker broke for the door, quick as a field mouse. Jubal balanced his knife, shrugged, and let the lawyer pound on down the stairs.

There was a to-do in the street below, but Jubal kept searching, and in the bottom drawer, came across a faded flyer that crinkled with browned age in his fingers. Smoothing it open on the desk, he stared down at the bold lettering. A thousand dollars in gold, it said, for information leading to the discovery and return of one girl child, age two years, thought to have been stolen by runaway slaves . . . Justina LeCroix, beloved daughter of Mrs. Xavier Rigaut LeCroix of Louisiana, parish of Orleans . . . any information deeply appreciated. . . .

Justina LeCroix—that was the name. Caroline had given him. This must be what he was looking for. He continued reading the document and straightened with an oath when his eye fell on the missing child's description. One line stood out with stunning clarity . . . "a small birthmark upon her left buttock, somewhat in the shape of a scorpion. . . ."

"Bigod!" Jubal said. "I know that mark; I sure as hell do!"

Voices shouted in the street as he folded the poster and placed it carefully inside his shirt. Two girls couldn't wear the same kind of mark, and if Caroline was this Justina, and seeking proof, why, here it was. He picked up his rifle and opened the door a crack, listening. Then he crossed the room swiftly and raised the window on the other side of the office, stepping through and hanging by one hand before dropping lightly into the alley below.

Men were gathered at the foot of the outside stairs, one with a shotgun. The lawyer kept pushing him and pointing up. Jubal eased from the alley and mounted his horse. Two steps from the hitching rack, and he cocked his long gun, eared back both hammers of the pistol and laid it across his thighs.

"Evenin', gentlemen," he said. "You with the shot-gun—don't turn around, less'n you mean to lose the top of your head. Lay it down gentle and back off. *Back off, goddamnit!*"

The lawyer squeaked and the fat man with the gun put it down quickly, then backed into two other men in his haste. Hands shoulder high, he turned and said, "Now lookee here, I'm the legal appointed sheriff of this town and—"

"A right smart un," Jubal said, edging the big stallion into them. "Reckon you're too smart to follow me out in the dark. Does anybody come after, they sure as hell better come soft and mean as Injuns, and just as ready to lose their hair."

"A—a savage, savage," Barker whispered. "He looted my office, sheriff. Do something."

"Like what?" the fat man asked.

Heeling the stud sharply, Jubal jumped the horse at them, knocking men spinning, reins dangling as he cut loose into the air with the rifle and one barrel of the pistol. A squall wild as any bloodthirsty Creek burst from his throat as men rolled and scampered away from flying hooves.

They bolted down the street, roared past the smithy and by the church, on along the riverbank and into twilight, thundering on and on as the stallion put his heart into the flight. The town was far behind them when Jubal slowed the horse, reined him in and walked him so he could catch his wind.

"Damn," Jubal said, "but wouldn't Barton Roberts and the boys give a pretty to be in on that? Civilized people, horse—yessir, downright *civilized*."

He laughed into the trees, into gathering night, the paper warm against his skin and the scent of horse sweat sweet in his nostrils.

Chapter 29

Head aching and jaw swollen, Caroline clamped her teeth against the pain. She sat erect against the far door of the carriage as Turpo drove them through the city, as passing torches threw harsh light upon the coldly furious face of Felipe. She would not ask where he was taking her, would not speak to him unless he forced her.

It had been a mistake to deny him, to enrage him so by not leaping at the chance to marry him. Felipe would never forgive her for that blow to his pride, and she wondered why she'd taken such a chance. Something, some warning that sounded in the back of her mind; a distrust of his turnabout—and the bright memory of Jubal Blaze—whatever the cause, by turning down Felipe, she'd placed herself against her master, her owner, and that could never be allowed.

The carriage lurched, and Caroline braced herself. She was frightened, but that was something else she would not give him the satisfaction of knowing. Had he actually bribed officials to declare her white, and was it too late for him to backtrack? Felipe could do anything that suited him, she thought; irate as he was, he'd accept his losses to keep her helplessly in bondage and wreak vengeance upon her.

Turning off the street, the carriage stopped before a massive iron gate that barred the way to a brooding house set well back from Rue Dauphine. Turpo bellowed Felipe's name, and she watched a crippled slave bear a torch to the gate, dragging one foot. Slowly, the gate creaked back, to close again behind the carriage.

Felipe looked at her. "Now you will learn, you bitch. You will discover how fortunate you have been with me. And when you know that in the marrow of your bones, when you are ready to crawl to me and beg forgiveness, a message will be sent."

Climbing down from the seat, he reached in to catch her wrist, to jerk her from the carriage. Caroline fought to keep her balance, so she wouldn't fall at his feet. Felipe pushed her toward the door of the shadowed house. In a moment, it swung open, held by a mulatto in livery, a huge, grinning man with protruding lips and small, beady eyes.

"Ah, Pitot," Felipe said, "I see you are healthy as ever."

"*Entrez*," the servant said. "M'sieu and madame, they will be happy to see you, sir." His muddy eyes reached out to Caroline.

Felipe pushed her into a waiting room where a fire glowed without cheering the drab room. "I have brought the LaLauries a little gift."

"I see," the mulatto said, licking at his heavy mouth. "Please to help yourself to refreshments, sir. I will call them from the attic."

"The attic?" Felipe said. "They begin early this evening."

Pitot's grin stretched itself. "They will be most happy to postpone their pleasures, and inspect m'sieu's —gift." Soundlessly, the man's feet moved across dark carpeting, his thick shoulders rolling away from them.

Pouring a glass of brandy, Felipe drank it off. "Louis and Delphine LaLaurie have exotic tastes, as you will soon discover." He refilled his glass. "Stupid wench, did you think to upset my plans? They will proceed while you are in—seclusion; first the rumors, then authentication of the tragic story. By then, I assure you, you will be most docile and ready to come to terms."

They came hurrying from a side door, a thin man with a short beard, a woman whose dark red hair

272

spilled over bared shoulders, a woman whose startling, lush beauty did not quite reach her green eyes. She moved to Felipe with a swirling of skirts, and put the length of her ripe body against him, rounded arms going about his neck as she kissed him hungrily, lingeringly. Caroline stared as Felipe brazenly stroked the woman's haunches while her husband stood by smiling.

Breaking from his mouth with a sigh, the woman said, "It has been too long, Felipe; we have missed you."

"Oui," the thin man said, stepping forward to extend his hand. "Delphine has often spoken of our good times together, *mon ami."*

"Louis," Felipe said, "Delphine—I bring you my new mistress, this mustee wench who needs certain disciplines."

Delphine turned. "Ah yes; a lovely child. I understand why you have stayed away from us for so long. But you will stay and join us, *non?* We have acquired two very young girls who will please you, and of course, you have long been a favorite of mine."

"I regret I cannot remain," Felipe said. "There is no couple like you in all Louisiana. But I must attend to pressing business, and I ask that you treat Caroline as if she is your own. Indeed, she will be yours, until she begs to see me."

Delphine swayed closer to her, green eyes sliding over her body, rich lips touched by the tip of a darting tongue. Caroline smelled a musky perfume and recoiled. "But of course," Delphine purred, "one hopes she will not be too fragile, that she will last awhile."

"I prefer her not marked," Felipe said, "but if you must, you must."

"Louis," the woman said, "come here and inspect this wench. Intriguing, is she not? Almost white, one would say. Tall and slim, but such darling breasts. *Cher* Felipe, we cannot thank you enough."

"I am in your debt," Felipe answered. "In utmost secrecy, *non?"*

"Naturellement," Louis LaLaurie said, stroking his beard and eyeing Caroline closely. "A prize, Felipe.

Are you certain you cannot remain, even for a short while?" The man's voice was as thin as his body, and his eyes were fevered, his skin sallow.

"My carriage waits," Felipe said. "Perhaps I can arrange a visit soon."

"Please do," Delphine said, stroking his arm and pressing her breast into him. "It is so much more delightful with you present."

Felipe looked at Caroline as he kissed Delphine again. "Learn well, wench."

She stood stiffly, arms at her sides and hands clenched, despising Felipe de Alcantari with every fiber of her being, hating him with her eyes as he strode from the room and left her with two strangers—*three;* Pitot the servant lurked near the fireplace, rubbing big paws together and chuckling.

Delphine ran one hand through her flowing red hair and said to the mulatto, "The chains; this one will fight. It is in her eyes."

"Just for a while," Pitot said, moving from the room.

Louis said, "Caroline; a pretty name, a pretty body."

Swallowing, she said, "What—what manner of people are you? I am not a beast, to be chained and beaten. I will not—"

"Oh, but you will," Delphine hissed, and caught her arms. Louis was with his wife then, helping to hold her down as she struggled against them, against cruel hands and pressing bodies, as she fought to keep her dress from being ripped away.

Caroline got a hand into the woman's hair and yanked hard, but the man's slap made bright spots dance behind her eyes, and when she jerked a knee upward at his groin, he took it on his hip. Then her breath caught sharply in her throat as Delphine clamped a brutal hand upon one breast and twisted.

The big mulatto was weighty upon her then, spreading her feet. Caroline shuddered at the bite of cold iron manacles upon her ankles, and writhed frantically when others were fastened to her wrists, pulling her arms painfully behind her back.

Naked, she lay panting upon the carpet, spitting at

them as her chains rattled and manacles dug into her flesh. Delphine LaLaurie laughed as she stood back and worked her dress down to step out of its clinging folds. Creamy legs flashed bare, and the lush body glistened, heavy but firm breasts rolled, and firelight found sparkling kinship in the crimson fluff of her pubic hair.

Caroline lay stunned. This woman was stripped to the buff before a mulatto servant, posed nude before her husband and another woman. And Louis La-Laurie was peeling off his own clothing, lean frame trembling with eagerness. In shocked disbelief, she stared at the giant mulatto, his livery falling like leaves, his distended manhood impossibly big. Was she to be raped by Pitot, while the LaLauries sported themselves shamelessly nearby? It was insane, filthy, and Caroline began to realize what Felipe meant about punishment. This was more cruel than the bite of a blacksnake lash, more degrading than being sold on the block or marched in a cavvy, for the horror of it would remain with her always.

But Pitot didn't approach her first, nor did Louis lower himself to the floor beside her. Hair hanging loose, breasts swaying, Delphine LaLaurie came to her with knowing hands and a searing mouth. Rolling, try-ing to keep her knees locked, Caroline found herself pinned down, her chained arms in agony behind her back. Closing her eyes, biting her lower lip until she tasted blood, there was nothing more she could do to resist them.

She tried very hard to put herself into that empty place she'd reached with the slaver who first violated her flesh; she concentrated upon freeing her body of her spirit and blocking her mind so that nothing they did to her mattered. But it did, it *did,* and when the mulatto took his turn upon her, Caroline could not hold back the scream that died whimpering in their hellish laughter.

It was the only cry she allowed herself, for she realized that these animals fattened upon pain and reveled in agony. She hated them. God, how she hated them, even when they left her alone while the servant shared his mistress with his leering master.

But it went on and on, endless eternities following one another as the debauchery continued. The woman and two men, breaking apart only to drink strengthening brandy and rest for a short while; the woman and herself; the grunting men and herself. It could not be, should never happen, and Caroline could not imagine any decent man—oh Jubal, Jubal!—ever desiring her body after these terrible things had been done to it.

Sweated and bruised and forever stained, she was at last pulled to her feet and shoved up the stairs by Pitot, that yellow and hulking apeman. Chains slid and clattered about her feet, and she staggered. At the attic door, he did something with a great key, and used another one behind her back, so that one hand came free, but she was too used up to try and fight him.

Holding a candle high, he pushed her into the long, low room, stood grinning above her while he fastened a manacle into a wall hook. "Mustee woman," he said, "I am leaving the candle this night, so you may look about you and see what happens to those who even think of resisting. Think on them, slut, and remember what I have here between my legs for you."

Then he was gone and the candle flickered across the floor, firm in its shallow holder, as Caroline began to see and hear them. They groaned softly; they stirred with metallic rattlings and uncurled themselves to blink staring eyes at her. "Please," the whispers came, "oh lady, please, for the sake of God—"

Shaking, she drew herself into a tight, defensive ball. They were deformed shapes upon nests of rags, each of them chained, some of them whimpering for mercy. Caroline saw a scarred face, an arm that had been twisted from its socket and broken; she saw a girl little more than a child, with bloody furrows across her thin buttocks. She saw other things too horrible to contemplate, bodies that had been subjected to awful tortures, eyes that had gone vacuous and blank in a form of escape. The attic was filled with LaLaurie slaves, collected here in mutual, animal pain. They were all objects of torture for those darkly convoluted minds below, helpless and hopeless subjects of insane master and mistress. And now she was one with them.

Her throat was dry, her mouth filled with evil tastes. She hugged her knees and spat, hawked to clear her throat. "How—how many are here? How long have they used you?"

A moan answered her; inane babbling answered her; the two children begged, but only one bent and twisted man made sense. "When we die," he mumbled, "they replace us. I have been here forever."

Jerking at the chain, Caroline only hurt her wrist. She said then in the old language, "Is there an Ashanti here?"

The same cripple answered: "Once I was."

"Still," Caroline said. "We are still Ashanti, and an Ashanti does not surrender to enemies."

A girl sobbed; a woman crooned to herself. The man said, "I fought them. See what they have done to me. You are new; they have not used hot irons upon you yet, nor chained you so long one way that you can never stand straight again. But they will, woman —they will. Before they do, use a knife upon yourself. Hear me well, Ashanti. Death is better."

Caroline buried her face upon her knees. Death or abject surrender to Felipe de Alcantari. *He* had done this to her, given her over to the LaLauries to break, to defile. Could she hold out against them? Was there any logic in holding out, in not sending a message to Felipe that she was ready to accede to his demands and marry him? She pulled in a deep, shuddering breath. Who besides Felipe would ever want to be with her now? That bastard; that vile, strutting, arrogant bastard; for secret reasons of his own, he would take her to wife and even lie with her, knowing full well what the LaLauries had done to her.

Felipe had been in this charnel house before; he was friends with Louis and Delphine; he was familiar with the bitch-woman's wet kisses and the curves of her body. No doubt, he had also shared her with her husband and that slavering mulatto stud.

The other slaves had turned from her now, curling like so many tethered mongrels upon their heaps of rags. Only the toothless Ashanti sat watching her from his clear eye; the other was milky. As the candle burned low and sweat dried upon her flesh, she began to tremble with chill, in utter shame. But she would not cry; she locked her teeth into soft flesh just above her knee and swore she would not give way to tears. In three languages, she swore another oath: that somehow she would find a way out of this house of terror; that someday, she would stand and smile down upon Felipe de Alcantari's dead face.

The candle went out. The night dragged on and on as winter wind shook the slate roof and fingered cold down into the attic. Sometime after dawn, shaking and hurting, Caroline dozed fitfully, snapping awake at the sound of moans, at the creaking of the house. Pitot came for her then, laughing at the poor wretches who shrank from him, at Caroline for moving stiffly and slow.

"Like leading a white bitch on a leash," he said behind her as she reeled down the stairs. "Delphine and Louis, they think it is a great joke that you cook for them and me. They enjoy you, mustee woman; they say they hope you will not call for Felipe, but me—I tell them you are already broken."

Head down, Caroline watched where she placed her feet, careful not to stumble and give him an opportunity to jerk her upright with the chains. She was dust-streaked and her hair was tangled; the imprint of other bodies clung to her and she was afraid. *Death is better,* the crippled Ashanti said, but Caroline knew her spirit could never rest until it had seen blood—LaLaurie blood, Alcantari blood, and red oozing from the belly of this mulatto swine.

He shoved her into the kitchen. "Wash yourself there, bitch. If your hands are not clean, I take a whip to your ass."

Raising her head, she said, "I want to speak with M'sieu Alcantari."

Pitot chuckled. "I am correct, *hein?* One night, and you are ready to go on your knees. But listen, mustee —the LaLauries have not had their fill of you yet, nor have I. The message will go out when *we* are ready." He locked an end of her chain into a hook near the wash sink, near the stove. "Prepare a breakfast for us, and then we will prepare a long day of *amour* for you."

In the other room, Caroline heard the woman laugh, the deep tones of the man's voice. She picked up a long knife and held it close, testing point and edge with her thumb. The chains, she thought; the damned chains. She could move only so far, and Pitot would be watchful. She wouldn't get the steel in his belly and there was no way to get to the LaLauries.

Washing in the sink, ignoring the cold water, Caroline dragged her fetters to the cupboard and back to the chopping block. A fire in the stove fanned welcome heat across her naked back as she began to prepare breakfast. Each slice of smoked bacon was a stroke into the flesh of *them,* and she cut savagely. Eggshells became their heads, and she broke them joyously.

She ate in quick bites, pouring strength back into her tired body with each hot swallow of coffee, each gulp of bread and meat. But when Pitot came into the kitchen, she was meekly at the stove, turning the omelettes. She saw his muddy eyes rest upon the knife, then upon her slumped shoulders. He grunted and carried platters into the other room, came back for the coffee.

Favorite of his mistress, the mulatto ate at table with the LaLauries, his whinnying laugh coming back to Caroline. She pried at the heavy lock with the knife blade and failed to scratch it. She muffled the chain with a rag and tried to drag its bolt from the wall, without success. Panting, she rested and listened to the clink of cups, the rattle of silverware upon china. They would soon be at her again, as Pitot promised. Even though she was ready to surrender to Felipe, they did not mean to free her until they had slaked their animal lusts upon her cringing flesh again and again.

She thought of the wretches in the attic, the broken bodies and the minds driven mad. *Death is better,* the old Ashanti said. Caroline dragged the lard crock from the cupboard and scooped out masses of the stuff to spread it upon the walls, the floor. She spread stove kindling upon it, linens, anything that might burst quickly into flame.

Opening the stove door, she used a ladle to scoop out redhot coals, and spread them upon the grease, the cloth. Smoke began to spiral up, and Caroline hurried before they would smell it. Stretching, she barely reached a whale oil lamp, and emptied it upon the gathering flames. Heat struck fiercely up at her, and she backed to the chopping block, to catch up the knife again. Shielding her face with one arm, she crouched there while the fire leaped higher, as it turned swiftly into an inferno.

The door crashed back and Pitot lunged into the kitchen, shouting. She flung the skillet at him and the mulatto staggered, roaring in surprise and rage. Caroline darted the length of her chain and cut viciously at him, the knifepoint only gashing his sleeve as he rocked back.

"Fire! *Fire!* The wench has set the house aflame!"

She had to back away from tendrils of flame that bit at her legs, and coughed in swirling, acrid smoke, but the fire had a good hold now. Caroline caught up a heavy pot and smashed it through a window and the flames fed ravenously upon fresh air. Back she went, and back, reveling in the shrieks of Delphine LaLaurie, in the curses of her husband and the baying of Pitot.

Maybe people outside would see the smoke in time; perhaps the horses and fire fighters would come racing in time; perhaps not. The house was in the heart of the city, and New Orleans was awake; neighbors would fear the spreading of the fire and cry alarm.

Squatting behind the chopping block, Caroline

worked at her chains while flames roared and heat gathered thickly around her. She had difficulty breathing now, and something crashed in the smoke.

Death is better, the Ashanti said, and he was right.

Chapter 30

Cold water splashed over Caroline, an icy shock that made her gasp and cough.

"Damn!" a man yelled. "White woman here, all chained up—hurry, damnit, *hurry!*"

Several of them then, throwing buckets of water, prying at the wall hook, smoke thick and swirling about them. Caroline panted: "The—the attic! Slaves chained in the attic—get them—oh please, get them out!"

Somebody battered the wall with an axe, and she felt herself being lifted in strong arms, choking as she was carried from the blazing kitchen. Men shouted everywhere, running men, others working at a bucket line, hurling water and passing back empty containers for more. Eyes smarting, shivering, she felt a blanket passed around her shoulders and huddled gratefully within its shielding warmth.

"Lady, what the hell—"

"Miss, miss—why did they have you chained? Where are they, the LaLauries?"

Her face hurt; her lips ached. "The attic—did you get them out? Oh God, so many poor, tortured blacks up there—"

"Comin' out now. Damn—look at that! Some of 'em can't walk."

"Water! More water over here!"

Hands propped her erect, moved her back from the leaping flames, maneuvered her through a curious

282

crowd to the street. Her knees were weak, and the chains still rattled about her ankles.

"Carrie! Oh *mon Dieu*—Carrie!" Catherine Villars was hugging her close now, stroking her wet hair. "We searched for you everywhere, but we did not think he would take you to *them;* the pig, the unspeakable bastard! Are you all right, *chérie?*"

"Animals," Caroline said into the girl's shoulder. "Wild beasts—they kill their slaves slowly, torture them—oh God, oh God—"

"Look out!" a man bellowed, and she lifted her singed face to see a pair of harnessed horses plunging wild-eyed at the crowd, scattering it right and left. Pitot rode the driver's seat, his reins slashing the horses' rumps, and in the carriage Louis and Delphine LaLaurie were clinging to each other.

"Stop them! Kill them!" The crowd gathered itself, surged after the carriage, but it was thundering swiftly down the street, and men could only run after it, shouting, throwing stones.

A thin woman kneeled before a small black girl, trying to soothe the child, wrapping her in a cloak. Two men supported the broken Ashanti, their faces pale and strained; others carried the ravaged bodies of more slaves, and Caroline saw that their eyes were ugly.

"Merde! To do this to blacks—fiends, *cochons!* Where is the constable? Who is going after that carriage? *Ma foi*—look at this one; her breasts have been cut—"

Caroline mumbled, "They care; they actually care."

And Catherine said, "The LaLauries, they are fleeing for their lives. Oh, I wish Jean were here on a fast horse. He would run them down, bring them to justice. Come, *chérie;* come, Carrie; I have Pierre's carriage, and I will take you away, carry you to safety."

"I—I want to tell them about—"

"Non!" Catherine was firm, her guiding hands strong. "There will be too many questions. They think you are white, and if they mark you as a LeCroix, you

will forever wear the shame. They will pity you, to be sure, but also, they will scorn you. *Vite,* now."

She was one vast bruise, glad to slump in the girl's protective arms, to be cared for, guarded. The carriage rocked and bounced through the city, a city seething like a hive of angry bees.

"Those brutes," Catherine said. "I would wager there is a boat on the lake, ready to take them across. They must have known their infamy would someday be discovered, and prepared. I pray a storm arises, that they drown. I only wish that Felipe de Alcantari was with them, to be eaten by crabs."

Caroline stirred. "He—wanted to punish me. I would not marry him, so he took me to them. Oh, Catherine, I had given up, after only one night, but they would not send for him. They wanted to keep me awhile, to do—to make me—"

"Shh," the girl murmured. "Shh, my friend. They cannot reach you now; no one can. Alcantari—demanding you marry him? But how, why—unless he is certain you are wholly white. Ah yes; the LeCroix lands, the Delacroix plantation. He wants to get his hands on it and become rich. If you *are* Justina LeCroix, and wed to him, your property is his, of course."

"But there is Lucien LeCroix," Caroline said.

Catherine squeezed her shoulders. "Lucien is a man, and one of honor. How easy it will be for Alcantari to force a challenge upon him, to kill him in a duel. Then he would be master of Delacroix, the swine."

"I—I am afraid of him," Caroline said. "He told me of bribed officials, forged records to prove me white. Felipe will not let go easily, and if he recovers the forgeries, then he still owns me and I am still black."

"That one knows something," Catherine said. "He would not go to such lengths, if he did not. Yes, he will be after you, but he will not find you. This I guarantee. We will stop at a certain home for clothing, then travel to the end of the road. Can you sit a horse, *chérie?*"

"I think so. Catherine, I was ready to die, *wanted* to die, rather than be used by them again, and I—I set the fire. That mulatto—that monstrous Pitot—and the woman; she was worse than the others. All those poor, tortured blacks—but when the crowd saw them, a crowd of *whites,* they were furious. They wanted to kill the LaLauries."

Catherine said, "The people would act the same, if they found so many dogs mistreated; a passion of the moment."

Very tired, Caroline leaned her head onto Catherine's lap, drowsing until the carriage halted. She sat up until her friend returned with water and brandy and clothing, boots and jacket and pantaloons of a sea rover.

"Drink this, Carrie. I will help you dress—oh, those bite marks, those bruises. If only I could have that yellow man and his owners at the point of my sword."

The brandy burned a welcome warmth into Caroline. "Where are we going? And the driver—will Felipe be able to bribe him?"

"Our Lyons? He would gladly cut Alcantari's throat. Lyons is Pierre's lieutenant, a corsair who has bloodied the seas from Barataria to Bordeaux, come to manhood despising the Spanish dons—and anyone who acts like them. Sit up, Caroline—keep this blanket about you. Where do we go? Where Alcantari and the authorities dare not, to Barataria itself, stronghold of *le Bos.* You will be under the protection of Jean Lafitte."

More brandy numbed Caroline, calmed her into a restless sleep where she dreamt of black men and women writhing upon rag piles, mewling their pain and terror. She would have been their executioner, if help had not arrived quickly, and she would have died with them. Whimpering in her dreams, she clung to the comfort of the girl, and when the carriage stopped, came blinking awake to stare at the night and smell salt wind off black marshes.

A campfire glowed beside the road, and Catherine called out to armed men about it as she helped Caroline down. *"Holà*—Luis, Gino, Nez Coupé! I bring *le capitaine* a friend."

A squat and hairy man who'd lost part of his nose to a sword stroke peered at Caroline, "A very small one."

"We shall need the courier horses," Catherine explained, "and if our coach has been followed—"

Nez Coupé tugged at his beard. "Then we will no longer be bored. Go with care, *ma petite;* the wind rises and the *pirogue* will be unsteady."

Catherine smiled. "I am one with the water, old friend, but I thank you. The horses?"

A dark, slim man with a golden ring in one ear led them to the campfire. "The mare leads and the gelding stumbles, Catherine, but they know the trail well."

"Carrie?" Catherine said, and Caroline lifted a booted foot to the stirrup, pulled herself atop the horse.

Nez Coupé looked up. "A quiet one. She will be a change for *le Bos.*"

"You great fool," Catherine laughed, "this one is only a friend. Would *I* bring Jean another woman?"

The dark man flashed bright teeth up at them. "When the great shark only kisses his dinner, the redfish. *Bonne chance*, Catherine."

Catherine rode ahead slowly in the night, and Caroline's horse followed docilely, as if he had made the journey many times before. To the right, a swamp bird cried high and keen, and something splashed heavy in unseen depths. Wind rustled tall reeds that clacked softly in a winding sheet of lifting fog. She pulled her head deeper into the heavy jacket collar and snugged her legs to the horse.

The excitement and fury had drained from Caroline, leaving her limp and very tired. She nodded with the motion of the plodding horse, drifting in and out of vivid dreams—the manacles upon her wrists and ankles, the sweating bodies interchanging; pain and fear and disgust. It would never happen to her again, she swore; never again would she wear chains and be made whore for anyone's twisted lusts. She would die first, or kill first.

Forcing open her eyes, she tried to peer through the night and find Catherine Villars, but could only hear the sound of the horse ahead, the softer, more careful noises of the swamp. Catherine knew how to fence, to use sword and knife, and was probably handy with a pistol. Caroline would learn from the girl, from Catherine's pirate friends, and if Felipe ever came near her again—

She was a fugitive slave now, an escaped black. Felipe could send hunters after her, have her dragged back to serve him, or more likely, to be beaten. And forced into marriage with him? Caroline didn't know; that union would have to be far more important to Felipe de Alcantari than his severely wounded pride. But she would neither marry him nor be his mistress again. Catherine was taking her to the buccaneer's lair, where no man dared come after her. But would the Lafittes accept her? They were in business with Felipe, using his family mansion as a clearinghouse for smuggled goods. Profit could mean more to them than giving refuge to a runaway slave.

Her horse stopped suddenly, and Caroline blinked awake. Catherine had tethered her own mount and was kneeling to strike flint to a whale oil lantern. Lowering herself, she looped reins over a sturdy pine branch and stared at darkly lapping water so near, at narrow, shallow boats drawn to the reedy shore.

"It is not far from here," Catherine said, dropping the shield upon the lamp, "but you must not be frightened, and sit very still in the *pirogue*. These small boats tip easily, but they can go where large ones cannot, through the hummocks and across mud bars. Trust me, Carrie; I have poled a *pirogue* through these waters many times."

"I trust you," Caroline said. "I owe my life to you."

"*Mais non*," Catherine answered, "but to your courage in setting fire to the LaLaurie house. By doing so, you freed not only yourself, but all those miserable creatures. Oh, I hope the police catch up with the La-Lauries and put them in jail for life."

"Would they?" Caroline asked. "After all, they are aristocratic whites, and we others only blacks."

"*If* you are black," Catherine said. "That is yet to be resolved, but whether you are of the blood or not, Carrie, you will always be my friend."

"And you mine, Catherine."

"*Eh bien;* let us be off then. Sit up front, *chérie*—carefully, now. Hold to the sides and do not panic if an alligator should rise close by. They hunt at night, but will not bother us. Take the lantern and hold it in the bow. The light will guide me."

Gingerly, Caroline felt her way into the hollowed cypress log, kneeling near the front and placing the lantern before her. When Catherine picked up a long pole and pushed the *pirogue* from the muddy shore, water was only inches below Caroline's hands and the tiny craft rocked alarmingly, but settled into a smooth glide.

"The water is shallow here," Catherine said, "and dotted with many marsh islands. It turns and twists into many false channels, so that only Jean Lafitte's people can find their way; others will be lost in the great swamp."

Damp air was chill upon Caroline's face, and she flinched when a great owl shrieked close by, when huge, luminous eyes reflected the glow of the lantern.

"*Un caiman,*" Catherine said as the swish of a heavy tail swirled water and the long head vanished beneath the surface. "M'sieu alligator will not attack anything as large as himself, and he fears the light." She worked the long pole deftly, turning the nose of the *pirogue* into this channel between hummocks, then into that one.

Clinging to the lantern, to the sides, Caroline felt water wash over her fingers, and felt the ghostly caress of moss brushing her face. A giant bullfrog strummed its bass voice at them, and once she saw the swift, looping ripple of a swimming snake.

Then there were lights ahead, springing into view

when their craft nosed around a flat island, lights and voices raised in rollicking song, and the scent of woodsmoke, of spiced food. Caroline's heart lifted, and when the boat grounded its flat nose upon sand, she moved cautiously forward and climbed out to hold the *pirogue* stable for Catherine.

Holding her hand, Catherine guided Caroline from the beach, past a bonfire where men laughed with women of many colors, along a path of broken shells. Catherine answered greetings but did not stop, and they climbed a slight incline beyond shacks scattered haphazardly, other, smaller fires, a beached and overturned ship's gig, long racks for drying fish and meats.

"There is the big house," Catherine said. "Is it not grand? Ah, they call him pirate and assassin, but my Jean is more the gentleman than any in New Orleans. Wait until you see the furnishings, *chérie,* gold plate and carved woods and silks—the best taken from galleons of the cursed dons. Those who have visited here know that *le Bos* is a gracious host, and now—now he has someone to stand at his elbow, to serve his guests." The girl stopped, looking up at the veranda that ran the length of the house set high upon posts to protect it from furious seas. "My Jean, he does not deny me, nor hide me from visitors."

"Nor should he," Caroline whispered. "He has every right to be proud of you."

Squeezing her hand, Catherine led her up the steps and onto the porch. From there, Catherine could see lights bobbing far out on the water, lights that could only be ship lanterns, and there were many of them, Jean Lafitte's pirate fleet riding at anchor.

Inside, the main salon blazed with candles, and the corsair himself turned from a table laden with maps. "Catherine."

"Chéri, chéri!" The girl ran to him and flung herself into his arms, lifting her mouth for his kiss. "Oh, how I missed you."

Lafitte laughed. "In just two days?"

"Two hours is too long," Catherine said, "or two minutes." She clung to his arm when she turned and said, "I have brought a guest. You remember Caroline Monteleone, who lives next door to Pierre and my sister?"

"But of course," Lafitte said, dark eyes crinkling at the corners. "Who could forget? Alcantari is not with her."

"I would not bring anyone else without your permission," Catherine said, and launched into the tale of how Caroline had been turned over to the LaLauries, how she had been rescued from a blazing house, Catherine's voice showing her anger, Lafitte's darkening face reflecting it. "And if I had not been searching for her, that *cochon* might have taken her back. There was nothing else I could do, but bring Carrie here."

Jean Lafitte moved to a carafe of golden wine and poured some into a silver goblet. He brought it to Caroline and looked down into her face. "Welcome to Grand Isle, madame, to Barataria. Here we are all outcasts, most of us hunted and scorned. But here we are also strong and protected. Sea wolves we may be, but a pack with rules and honor. You are my guest and Catherine's friend; you will not be molested by anyone."

Caroline lifted the goblet. "My gratitude, m'sieu."

A quick smile broke the somber face; he nodded and strode back to his table as Catherine came to take her arm. "Come, I will show you to a room and share my clothing with you, although you will find breeches and boots more comfortable here." Down a hallway, she whispered, "Jean may seem abrupt, but he has much on his mind. There are emissaries coming to him from the city, and from the British fleet in the Gulf. If his own people do not realize Jean's worth, there are others anxious to do so. Here is your room, Carrie, and now I will bring you something to eat."

"Please," she said, "no. I—I couldn't eat, right now."

"Wine, then," Catherine said, "or the Spaniards' brandy. You must not blame yourself, *chérie*. All was beyond your control. I know, I know—now you think of the great red bear, this Jubal, and wonder what he would feel if he hears. No one in the crowd knew who you were, but if word does somehow reach his ears, he must feel only sympathy for you, for what you have gone through. It would be so with my Jean—except that he would seek out and kill those who harmed me."

Caroline sat upon the bed, hands fisted in her lap. "Jubal Blaze might do the same, if he loves me. Except for one thing."

Puzzled, Catherine stared at her. "And what thing is that?"

"Jubal does not know I am of the blood," she answered. "I never told him."

"But surely," Catherine said, "that may not be so. You may be this LeCroix woman, and if you are not —Felipe de Alcantari has gone to great trouble to make it seem so."

Caroline looked up. "I cannot lie to him. I will not."

Sadly, Catherine murmured, "Sometimes a small lie is better than a great loss."

Chapter 31

Although the boatmen's names were Markham and Trist, they might have been thrust from the same womb, they seemed that much alike to Jubal. Short and chunky and bearded, they wore dark stocking caps and grew heavy slabs of muscle along their shoulders; their hands were heavily callused from using poles and manning stern sweeps. Although they'd grumbled at taking down a flatboat so lightly loaded, gold pieces soothed their business sense and they admitted the craft would travel faster.

One man stood in the bow, the other posted himself aft at the sweep, and Jubal's men jumped in once the grounded end was shoved loose from the bank. Jubal moved midships and checked lashings on the barrels there, sturdy oaken barrels packed to the brim with shaped flints, enough for Jackson's army, enough to go against the Floridas, did old Andy put his mind to another war there.

Barton Roberts and Daniel Smith lounged along gunwales nearest the bank, deceptively casual but with their long guns primed and powder horns and shot bag near to hand. Across the craft, Cody Youngblood and Mason McGee sat on deck with rifles between their knees, backwoodsmen uneasy on deep water but already watching the far shore.

Settling down at the cargo barrels, Jubal stretched his legs and horned fresh powder into the pan of his rifle. He'd nigh ridden his tail off, getting back down from Illinois, damned glad for a good horse beneath him, gladder yet he had been able to do Caroline Monteleone a service. He didn't know if the reward flyer he'd found in the lawyer's office—that lying little pipsqueak—would do what she wanted, but it was all he could come up with, and he had the feeling it was important.

The description of the scorpion-like birthmark on her silken haunch—Jubal sighed and leaned his head back. You couldn't rightly call that mark a blemish, but more like a design, a small target, like. It was set just right to center a man's palm when his hand cupped that shapely, tender flesh.

How come the lawyer denied having any papers? Time Jubal first mentioned the Monteleone name, Artis Barker had been jumpy as a widow woman who'd swallowed a physic just before a suitor came courting. Just that one faded old poster hidden away in a bottom drawer, when Caroline acted like she expected a heap more. Well, when the set-to with the lobsterbacks at New Orleans was over and done with, if Caroline needed anything else to get turned loose from whatever bind she was in with that lace-cuffed Creole, Jubal would journey on back and see to lawyer Barker. If he had to reach down and take hold of his innards and jerk the little bastard inside out, that's what it would come to.

Sliding down some on the deck, Jubal propped his head against a cask and closed his eyes, drowsing in the weak sunlight. He could see her plain, the proud, shining look of her eyes; the soft but firm set of her mouth, skin creamy as magnolia blossoms. Jubal turned, realizing he didn't even know how old she was. Young, surely, but wise and experienced beyond her years.

Funny thing; he'd always figured to settle down someday, if for no other reason than Pa expected it of him, to raise a passel of younguns and keep the plantation up to snuff. When Jubal got around to it, there'd been the idea in back of his head that he'd pick him some untried filly that had her a handsome dowry and a chance at inheriting some land, maybe; a gal with wide hips to make for easy childbearing, and enough sense to run Tarboro house.

Now, all he could think about was Caroline Monteleone, and she was no shy filly saving of her maidenhead. She knew more tricks than a well-used whore, and performed every one like she enjoyed it better than all else. To listen to his friends back home, they for certain sure wanted them a wife hadn't ever been bedded; pure and unsullied is what they said. Jubal turned again on the deck, thinking that they who talked so about pure wives went wenching in the slave quarters most every night, getting their pleasure with blacks and leaving their wives to be used like brood mares.

It was a pure waste to leave a passionate woman to her own empty bed. Thing was, white women wasn't supposed to be passionate, but Jubal damned well knew better, and before meeting up with Caroline, too.

And with a woman like her, a man would be too busy for his eye to rove, maybe too wore down to even think on diddling strange quim. Be a pleasant kind of wearing down, too; the sort to make a man warm to the marrow of his bones, content as a tomcat afore a blazing hearth. Clear up to the Carolinas, there wouldn't anybody know Caroline once had some arrangement with a fancy Creole, and wouldn't anybody ask. Tarboro neighbors would come to pay respects just like she was the finest lady around anywheres—and bigod, Caroline Monteleone was that and more.

She dressed better than any Tidewater highnose, and talked better, too—and in two languages to boot. Just looking at her was enough to make your blood sing, but she didn't put on airs. She was straight out honest as any man. She had a serving girl, a saucy yellow piece that she didn't make hop every time she snapped fingers. That was a good sign, also; Jubal could never cotton to folks that put spurs to a horse just to make it sashay around, nor kept niggers scared of the whip.

It was a puzzlement to Jubal why she hadn't been snapped up by some biggity plantation owner, why she had this "arrangement" with the strutting Creole;

mean-eyed son of a bitch, for all his lace and geegaws. Did he have a wife stuck off somewheres, and worked him up some kind of hold on Caroline, through her family or some other way? Could be her daddy was hard up and owed money; could be she didn't have a daddy and her mama was down sick and needed taking care of. Maybe the serving wench was the only slave she owned.

From the stern, Markham hollered out: "Watch that snag, Trist!"

"Done poled it off," Trist called back.

Come down to it, Jubal thought, pillowing his head on one curled arm, he didn't know doodly squat about Miss Caroline Monteleone. Except she was so damned beautiful she made his groin ache to see her, and made him choke up when he smelled her. He knew she was a golden-white fire in the bed, a fire in his blood no other woman could put out, that she held him deeper and slicker and more velvety than any woman had.

"Sandbar thataway!" Trist sang out, and Markham grunted as he laid his weight into the sweep and moved the bow into deeper water.

The boat didn't rock like an ocean-going vessel, but skidded downriver smoothly, and the gurgle of water against its gunwales lulled Jubal. He'd stayed a long time in the saddle and got back in time to see to buying the boat, hiring its crew. The old innkeeper Mixon had most of the work done when Jubal returned, and folks nearby pitching in to help. Keep a sharp eye out for river pirates, Mixon warned; ain't so much up this far, but down below they kin be busy as seed ticks in a hound's ear.

Jubal slept then, dreaming candlelight celebrating along fine, sleek legs, dreaming the stormy look in her black eyes when she gasped his name in her cresting, dreaming and wishing for another long night like that one in the special little house behind the iron gate.

He popped awake as a ranging fox when a hand touched his shoulder. Barton Roberts grinned down at him. "Way you was carryin' on, figured you might's well take a spell at watchin', whilst I whomp us up some stew."

Stretching, Jubal sat up, yawned and climbed to his feet, long gun cradled in his arms. "Reckon how far we come?"

"Further'n a fast horse relay," Cody Youngblood said at the rail. "Damn if'n this ain't the way to travel."

"Seen anything?"

Cody scratched his stubbled chin. "Biggest ol' mudcat in the world, I expect; two Injuns on the bank, two more fishin'."

"No river pirates?" Jubal asked.

"What do a pirate look like?" Cody Youngblood grinned back.

Jubal eyed the bank slipping rapidly past. "Reckon we'll know when we see one. How's old Barton goin' to fix a stew, without he burns a hole in the boat?"

"These flatboaters is right slick; got 'em a regular stove that don't get too hot underneath, do they keep the deck sloshed down with water. Learned us a heap of things like that, whilst you was off lollygaggin'. Missed you a fine time with them Kentucky gals, cap'n."

Jubal watched the treacherous grey of an underwater sandbar off to one side. "You all must of stayed to the loose uns, since nobody got knocked in the head."

Cody spat over the side. "All patriotic gals, givin' their all for Andy Jackson's soljer boys, and damned if'n two of 'em didn't have more to give than we could take. No wonder ol' man Mixon can't hardly stir his stumps, what with them two jumpin' around atwixt his blankets."

Nodding, Jubal saw a speckledy crane lift clumsily from a bog and flap off through the woods, and a big loggerhead turtle heave off a log into muddy water. The river was getting wider along here, sort of pushing out against its banks, and when he looked beyond them, he could see driftwood and trash hung far up in the limbs of tall cypress trees, showing where the river reached when it went on a highwater rampage.

Glad enough when Cody stopped talking about the

women back in Paducah, Jubal leaned on his elbows and glanced downriver. There were plenty of hidden coves where canoes could lie waiting, fast long craft ready to be paddled hard by bunches of cutthroats. Most likely, though, any attack would come when the flatboat tied up for the night, and Jubal wondered if there was some way they could stay to the middle of the river.

"Not less'n you aim to run head-on into a big ol' stump, or meet a log comin' hard," Markham said. "Anyways, with us ridin' so high in the water, them pirates'd have to be damned fools to figure we got a good cargo."

Jubal said, "Could be they'll figure we're totin' a real light one, but real rich. Daytimes, they could take a good look at these woods runners and not bite off more'n they can swallow, but at night—"

"Expect you folks are right easy in the woods," Markham said, leaning on his sweep. "Wouldn't be too hard for a couple of boys to lay out yonder and catch 'em comin' in."

"Might set up somethin' like that," Jubal agreed, "us takin' turns on ambush every night we stop."

"Won't stop that many times, cap'n. Tonight, tomorrow night—maybe one more, do we get hung up somewheres. The river's a sight quicker'n goin' by land."

That soon to see Caroline again, Jubal thought, and his blood quickened in anticipation. Would she be as anxious to see him, as excited? Maybe she wouldn't be able to come to the little house right away; and suppose that her Creole sent her off beyond reach. Bigod, he'd find her, was she hid anywhere in Louisiana or beyond, if it meant taking hold of that Frenchie by the heels and shaking him loose from his teeth.

Touching the folded reward circular tucked beneath his shirt, Jubal walked back along the low rail, woodsman's instinct making him scan the trees and each point of land along the bank. It wasn't long to sundown; already there was a red stain to the river, and soon they'd have to pull in for the night.

The landing place the helmsman picked was a good one, a brown sand beach back in a little eddy, where the trees didn't march clear down to the water. There was brush and driftwood handy for the fire, and it took only a few minutes to land river catfish enough for all. They were damned good, Jubal thought, fried crisp in lard after being rolled in cornmeal, and he had a bait of them washed down by coffee and a dollop of corn whiskey.

"Barton," he said, "reckon it's you and me for the bushes tonight. We'll go in there a piece, spread apart and lie quiet. Can't let no pirates get ahold of Andy Jackson's flint."

Turning to the others, he assigned the boatmen to stay on board, and if worse came to worst, they were to cast off and take their chances with the nighttime river. "Now," he said, "Mason McGee'll camp in the bow with his long gun ready, kind of keepin' an eye on the fire and Daniel Smith and Cody Youngblood there. Daniel, Cody—best you fellas make up bedrolls appears like you're in 'em, only you'll be out beyond the firelight. And I'd appreciate it, was everybody to sleep light as a hungry bobcat. Come daylight, we'll be on our way again."

And just before dawn turned the tops of the trees grey, while shadows were still thick and dark below, Jubal's senses alerted him. Bringing his rifle from beneath the blanket, he eared back the hammer and listened, staring hard into greyblack cover that might hide anything.

A twig crackled, and Jubal could just make out the hulking shape of a man held motionless by the sound. Easing the long gun out, he centered it upon the figure and began a slow squeeze of the trigger. Barton Roberts would have better sense than to be meandering around the woods this time of night, and no honest man would come slipping up on a camp thataway. Had to be others with him, Jubal figured, but it wouldn't cut it to let the man get too close.

Still, he held back until the man moved again, came sneaking on near good as any Indian, and there came another one ahint, moving low to the ground. Jubal stroked the trigger and fire thundered the shadows. The big one jerked around and fell over backwards. The other fellow let out a holler like he was snakebit and went crashing off through the brush.

Must be some more, Jubal thought, because just about then Barton Roberts' gun went off, its echo followed by that *yip-yip-yip* old Barton made when he was following hounds on a hot trail. Skinning knife out, Jubal leaped forward, yelping like a Creek warrior. The big one didn't wiggle when Jubal stomped down on his belly, so he passed on after the other he'd hit, following him by the noise of snapping limbs and the like.

Another gun busted loose, but the man ahint it was firing blind and the ball *whupped!* off through the trees. Time he caught up with the staggering man, Barton Roberts rose up out of the ground and laid his rifle barrel across the pirate's head. Made a pretty, hollow-melon thump, Jubal thought, but reached out and put his steel into the man's back anyhow.

Barrel propped against his thigh, Barton Roberts poured powder from his horn and dusted more into the pan. Slick and fast, he used patch and ball and ramrod to reload. "More of 'em," he grunted, "but they takin' off like a passel of turpentined cats."

"Might's well let 'em run," Jubal said. "It ain't the best time of day to be trackin', and I expect they got a bellyful right now." Reloading his pistol, he moved back to where he'd nested for the night and readied another ball in his long gun. "Won't do to just walk up on the fire," he said. "Them woke-up woods runners are just achin' to punch a hole through anything movin'."

"I'll halloo 'em," Barton said, and threw back his head to call out like a turkey gobbler.

They came into camp slowly, so they'd be recognized, and the Tennessee men stood up to meet them, guns at the ready. First sunlight glinted off Mason McGee's rifle barrel where he crouched in the boat, and the rivermen were under cover.

"Pack came snakin' up," Jubal explained, "and we dropped two. Might be them others'll hightail it for good, not knowin' just exactly what they run into."

"Might's well fill our bellies then," Barton Roberts said, "and git to gittin' afore they change their minds."

"Pirates, was it?" Cody Youngblood asked.

And Barton answered, "Must of been; hollered too easy for Injuns. You want to haul out that fatback and meal, Tennessee man?"

Tensed, Jubal eyed the forest until they'd breakfasted and shoved off from the sandy beach. The pirates had come down on them fast, almost like they knew about when the boat would tie up for the night. The attack had been cut off before it got started good, but the pack might return. It wouldn't be all that hard to follow the flatboat downriver and wait until it came aground again. Did somebody know what they were carrying and mean to stop the cargo from reaching New Orleans? With all the hullaballoo going on back in Paducah, it would be easy enough for some Tory to get wind of the shipment and pass word to more traitors. He'd have to keep a sharp eye out from here on.

Glad when they pushed the flatboat off and climbed aboard, Jubal helped Markham at the sweep, battling the powerful current until it was safely out in midriver and pointing its blunt nose south. They were riding down to the city, to where Andy Jackson and his men waited for the attack of the British, which was bound to come off soon.

If it hadn't already, Jubal thought; if the general's troops weren't facing highly trained and stubborn Redcoats with not enough flints to keep their rifles going. It just might be too late, what with that run up to Natchez with Tom Pickett, the search that hadn't paid off and had damned near got them both done in.

Was it too late for Caroline Monteleone, too? All manner of things might have happened to her by now —she might have been spirited away, or fled the city if it came under bombardment by British men-of-war. Caroline might have been hurt by a siege mortar, or one of those new-fangled rockets it was said the lobsterbacks used. He refused to think of her lying dead.

But, hands tight upon the flatboat's rail, Jubal Blaze urged the craft to hurry, hurry, as if by brute strength he could push it faster down the Mississippi.

quickly so that I may show you to Le and la Roy.
Père ... Père Antoine blesses all who come. "Jean"
Lafitte's rich wine cellars and good there ...
could forgive him even the ... four death
... could forget, from the ... fountaine ...

Chapter 32

Caroline awoke to song, a rollicking sea chanty rising
from the beach below Lafitte's house, and for a moment she did not know where she was. Then it all came
back to her—the fire and escape from that house of
torture and the flight south with Catherine Villars. Now
she was safe in the stronghold of the awesome Gulf
buccaneer.

Sitting up and stretching, she winced at bruises and
scratches inflicted by the LaLauries and their mulatto
Pitot. Shamed memories flooded her, and she clenched
her teeth, but forced a smile of greeting when Catherine rapped lightly upon the door and skipped gaily
inside.

"Cocoa and *brioche*," she announced, placing a
silver tray upon the bedside table, "and hot bathwater
awaits down the hall. Then, *chérie,* a choice of clothing
—anything you wish, silks, satins and brocades; fine
linens. The Spaniards had no further use for them."

The cocoa was sweet and strong; gratefully, Caroline
sipped it as she munched the flaky roll. "Does your
Jean attack only the Spaniards, then?"

Catherine dimpled. "Others in his command are not
so particular, but the Baratarians swear they have never
molested an American ship. I would not put it beyond
some of his captains, especially that evil Gambi, but
le Bos had better not find out. My Jean is proud and
happy to be called *Américain.* Come, Carrie—eat

quickly, so that I may show you to your bath and help you choose clothing."

Caroline looked at the outfit the girl wore, short pantaloons and high boots, a brilliant red sash, a silken blouse and a knitted shawl draped over her shoulders, a scarlet ribbon holding back the wealth of tumbled dark curls. "You do not wear fancy dresses."

Shrugging, Catherine said, "Only when my Jean entertains; then I act the perfect lady. To move about among these corsairs, to fence with my friend Dominique You, it is easier to dress as a man."

"Then it will be better for me, also," Caroline decided and swung long, slim legs from beneath the coverlets. There were the marks of manacles upon her ankles, an angry blister flaming along one shin.

Wrapped in a quilt, she followed Catherine down the hallway and into the bathroom. There she stopped, staring hard at a pair of mulatto girls who waited with soap and towels.

"The chubby one is Blanche," Catherine announced, "and the tall one is Pauline. Do not look shocked, my friend; there is no slavery here, no color line. Any servants are paid for what they do, as they should be. When the men of Blanche and Pauline gamble away their share of plunder, the girls work."

"Which is often," Blanche muttered. "That swine cannot stay away from gaming. There will always be another ship, he says, and does not listen when I tell him that between ships there can be hunger. I cannot eat the fine dresses he brings home."

"Nor I," Pauline said, testing the water in a huge copper tub and adding cold water from a pitcher. "Besides, my drunken man steals back my finery and wagers it. He *says* he does, anyway. If ever I catch him giving presents to that slithering bitch Josefina—"

Laughing, Catherine helped Caroline into the tub. "A good soak will do you good, *chérie*. Afterward, some herbs and salves to heal your wounds. Ah, how I wish the LaLauries had burned to a crisp in their house."

"And Pitot," Caroline said. "Do not forget the butler; he was worse."

Catherine stepped back from the tub. "If his mistress did not take him with them, M'sieu Pitot will be found somewhere in the city. He has nowhere to hide, for whites and blacks both seek him."

"And the LaLauries," Caroline asked, "what will happen to them, if they are caught?"

"Who knows? If they had been stopped at the fire, when the temper of the crowd was high—but they got away. As time passes, the outrage will seem less, and perhaps a heavy fine, perhaps a ban upon them ever owning slaves again."

"But no more," Caroline said, sinking deep into hot water. "All those crippled men and women; those poor, tortured souls; money in the city coffers will not help them."

Catherine sighed and perched upon a stool, crossing her booted feet. "It is the way of the world; whites rule and blacks suffer."

Pressing a washcloth against her sore face, Caroline said, "I swear, if ever I am proved to be white, I will not rule but share, as you do here."

"One race will love you for that," Catherine said, "but the other will not. Pauline—do you have medicines for our friend?"

Thin-faced and bony, Pauline nodded. "Those that heal and those that kill. We have heard of your torture, Madame Caroline; if you are again taken, I will teach you the use of herbs to stop the heart and burn out the belly."

"And gladly will I learn them," Caroline said, "for I will not be chained again."

"*Voilà!*" Blanche cried. "And I will instruct you in the use of daggers and pistols. I also had a brutal master, one who beat me and tied me down. That bastard smeared the juices of a mare upon my crotch, so his stallion would attempt to mount me. It would not fit, but the snorting beast almost killed me. One day, I sat and watched a baby mockingbird trapped in a cage. It was hung in the courtyard, and that day, I saw the mother bird fly food to her baby, a bright berry. When she left, the little one fell over and died quickly, for the berry was poison. It was a great lesson to me, to know a mother would poison her own child, rather than see it prisoner."

Blanche handed Caroline a thick towel. "So that very night, when my master came to me, I cut his throat and escaped into the swamps. It took a very long time and much trouble, but at last I was picked up by a *pirogue* near Barataria. I have been on Grand Isle ever since, but I may leave when I decide and no man beds me unless *I* wish it."

Pauline bobbed her head in assent. "Here a woman may choose her own man. It is always a surprise to the new men. Stand quietly, madame, so I may oil these cuts." Feeling worlds better after her bath and such gentle treatment, Caroline followed Catherine on a tour, first of the great house, then of the island's main part. The house was magnificent, surrounded by a long, wide porch that kept off summer sun and held sea winds at bay during the winter. It sprawled, but not haphazardly, for Jean Lafitte had planned it for comfort and entertaining, and as a defense against man and nature. Heavy oaken shutters could be swung to guard its screened windows, shutters whose gun slots could command every inch of the land about.

"There has never been an attack here," Catherine explained, "but *le volet* is useful against storms. There are times when the Gulf roars up over the island and tears at the foundations of this house. Yet it stands strong, just as my darling stands."

To the unknowing, the house presented a picture of indolent opulence, its richness perhaps overdone with tapestries and silver, carved furniture and gold, statuary and priceless carpets. There was a bountifully supplied kitchen and a wine cellar dug below, dark and cool for the storage of brandies and wines labeled by manufacturers of a dozen nations. And there were weapon cabinets always quietly at hand.

Dressed in the fresh but simple clothing of a seaman, Caroline paid due respect to Catherine's pride in

305

her home, and before they stepped out upon the veranda, the girl handed her two things—a small, efficient-looking pistol and a sharp dirk.

"Not that you will need them on Grand Isle, understand. But without weapons, one is naked here. We will practice with them, and with the rapier. It is good not to be helpless, *hein?*"

"Very good," Caroline agreed, and walked down the steps to become the object of attention for a thousand curious eyes.

She sought Catherine's hand and the girl smiled. "A pretty lot, are they not? Fierce as they seem, I assure you, but not one is fool enough to lay a hand upon the lover, or the guest, of *le Bos*. So many races, so many tongues, but each man and woman loyal to Jean Lafitte. See over there, the dark ones of mixed blood—Maltese and Catalans; that broad-shouldered man with but one eye: a Portuguese. Even Spaniards are among us, but they were once *peons* and have no love for the cruel dons."

Caroline heard English spoken, and French, and languages she could not recognize. As Catherine pointed out the low log fort and its cannons, she saw men who seemed to have been scissored from dark bronze, men forever marked by the harsh sea. Some were young and swaggering, some going grey and bearing many scars, but all had the same look of an eagle. Swords rattled at their sides, pistols were thrust into their belts.

"And there," Catherine said, "a Kaintuck. Several such young men have come to join *le capitaine,* for gold and adventure."

This one stood tall and slim, his shirt open despite the cold; his hair was shaggy gold and his eyes matched the bright sky overhead. He stared at them, and touched his forelock at Catherine, but his bold and eager gaze clung to Caroline.

"Miz Catherine," he said, putting himself in their path. "This a new recruit? Kind of spindly, I'd say, but I'd be glad to take—him—in my crew."

Laughing up at the man, Catherine said, "I'd wager

you would, Robert Gray, but Caroline is special guest to *le Bos*."

His voice was husky-silken, and there were laugh crinkles around his eyes, a flashing of square, white teeth. "Caroline; a fine name, a special name for a special guest."

"Robert Gray," Caroline said, "a strange name for a corsair."

His laugh was hearty, and there was a certain appeal to the way he threw his head back and loosed it so freely. "Not all privateers have been French, Caroline. Blackbeard, Morgan—there's plenty of solid English examples."

"Pirates," Catherine said, "not privateers with letters of marque. Robert, you know how sensitive *le Bos* is about that."

He made a sweeping bow, one hand upon the hilt of his cutlass. "Your pardon, mam. Sometimes I can't seem to get the difference straight in my head. Maybe you can help me, whilst I walk around with you."

Catherine pressed Caroline's hand. "A spring colt, this one," she said, dropping back into French. "A young stallion who must jump every fence simply because it is there. But he leads his own crew and Jean trusts him. I think his youth will someday get him killed."

"Not fair," Robert Gray said. "Been so busy learning the sea, I had no time for twisting my tongue around foreign speech."

Surprising herself, Caroline said, "You should have paid more attention in school—or was it a tutor you ignored?"

For a moment, his face tightened; then the laugh rang out again and he said, "Tutors; I used to drive them mad. But you have had better education."

Dropping her face, Caroline moved closer to Catherine, becoming more interested in the palmetto-thatched houses scattered between Lafitte's mansion and the beaches. They were almost hidden in heavy undergrowth and shadowed by wind-twisted oaks that had been dwarfed and leaned all one way, away from the sea. Each one- or two-room house gathered a thicket of shrubs and oleanders about itself to break the almost constant wind, and beyond them Caroline could see orange groves, only dull remains of their golden fruit left to winter now. And there, banana trees with ribboned leaves going brown; a drifting odor of smoke, a quickly passing scent of oil; and always, always the salt breath of the restless Gulf.

Conscious of the man beside her, Caroline saw many vessels at anchor in the safe harbor behind the island, bobbing and swaying with the motion of greygreen water. They gave some idea of Jean Lafitte's power, for all were armed, cannon nestling behind gunports, swivel guns fore and aft.

"Will you stay with us long?" Robert asked.

Not who are you or where did you come from, Caroline thought; not are you black or white. "I do not know," she said.

"I hope you will," he said, and pointed to a small ship. "That one is mine."

Catherine Villars also pointed, but at the horizon. "And what is that? Is it Gambi come back from the Caribbean? I had hoped he would meet his match out there."

"Just talk," Robert said, peering at the dark speck so far out. "Gambi's talk. He knows full well that Lafitte is the chief and never have Baratarians been so well off."

Catherine made a face. "He will be trouble, that one. He mistakes courtesy for weakness." She turned and looked back at the big house and Caroline turned with her.

There was Lafitte, a telescope raised to his eye, watching the ship in the distance. Lowering the glass, he slowly paced the veranda and turned suddenly into the house.

"We should return," Catherine said, and started up the slope. Men and women were coming out of the shacks, alerted by word of the incoming vessel. Caroline walked stiff-backed, noticing the motley clothes the women wore, grimed and tattered finery looted from some luckless ship. They noticed her, and whispered among themselves.

"Hola, Roberto!" one of them called. "Is that your new woman? She dresses like a man."

Whirling, Catherine spat it: "And so do I, Lupe. Does that make me less a woman?"

"I—I did not mean you, senora," the woman said. Her black hair was matted, and huge golden rings winked at her ears. The ripped damask gown she wore looked out of place, dragging just above sand and bare feet.

"This one is guest of *le Bos,* my good friend. Any who troubles her will answer to me, *comprenez-vous?"*

The woman muttered, "She should speak for herself," but when Catherine said, "What?" she answered, "Nothing, senora; *nada."*

When they reached the steps, Robert Gray said, "I hope to see you again, Caroline. I will show you my ship."

"Perhaps," she answered, and smiled back at the bronzed, handsome face. He seemed such a boy, but had evidently made his mark among these rough men, to captain his own crew. Caroline could feel his eyes upon her back as she mounted the steps and crossed the perch behind Catherine.

Inside, Lafitte was putting on his coat, and Catherine said, "Not Gambi, then?"

"Anglais," Lafitte answered. "The Gulf is filled with them. I have been expecting their emissary. *Chérie,* will you see to the preparations?"

"But of course; the English will discover that Lafitte the corsair is also Lafitte the gentleman and gracious host. Come, Caroline."

In the kitchen, Catherine gave orders to Blanche and Pauline, and scurried about checking food and drink. Caroline stood aside, wondering why the British should approach the smuggler base, and why Lafitte prepared to receive them as guests. She thought of

Jubal Blaze, captain in Jackson's force of riflemen sent to defend New Orleans. That approaching ship contained Jubal's enemies, and perhaps he even now awaited their onslaught, returned from his journey with a supply of flint.

And with the legal papers that might prove her identity, her claim to a position on Plantation Delacroix?

"Quickly, *chérie,*" Catherine said breathlessly. "We must dress. You can help me with them. We serve and smile and stay in the background; when they begin to speak of business, we will leave them."

At a large *armoire,* Caroline selected dresses for them both, and brushed Catherine's hair. Outside, a signal cannon boomed, and through a window she could see oarsmen casting off a small boat. The British ship was at anchor, bright flag snapping in the breeze, and on shore, the Baratarians gathered in uneasy clusters, some of them standing ready at the breastwork cannon. On the corsair ships, all gunports were open and agile seamen swarmed monkeylike into the riggings.

Caroline wanted to ask Catherine if her man meant to deal with the English, if his force would side with them against the city, the country itself. But she said nothing; she owed her very life to Catherine Villars, and had been accepted here, given safe refuge where Felipe de Alcantari's vengeance could not reach her.

"Do I look like a lady?" Catherine asked, pirouetting in a blue dress of watered silk that set off her flashing eyes and golden skin.

"Every inch," Caroline said. "Are you certain you want me with you?"

Mischievously, the girl winked. "It will confuse them, the stuffy English. They will not know which of us is Lafitte's mistress, or if both of us are."

And in the main room, Jean Lafitte saluted them both. He wore a fresh white shirt and his captain's coat with the brass buttons; his glossy hair was combed back and his moustache waxed. Here in his own home, he had put aside rapier and pistols.

"How beautiful you are, ladies. *Les Anglais* will be impressed and envious. Ah—I hear a signal from the beach. They are coming."

"Food will be ready in a moment," Catherine said. "I will see to brandy and wines."

Caroline found crystal goblets in a cabinet and took them down. She smelled fragrant smoke as Lafitte lighted a cigar, and heard the tramp of boots upon veranda steps. When they came into the room, preceded by one of Lafitte's lieutenants, Catherine stood at Caroline's side, poised as if she were greeting a rich plantation visitor, as if she were landed gentry and not mistress to a feared privateer.

The first Englishman was in dark blue with white breeches and a cocked hat bordered by gold braid. "Allow me to present myself, Mister Lafitte: Captain Nicholas Lockyer, His Britannic Majesty's navy. My aide, Lieutenant Johns; and Captain McWilliams of the army; Mister—ah—Smithers, a royal representative. I bring you missives from my commander."

Stiffly, Captain Lockyer held out a packet wrapped in oilskins. Lafitte accepted it, but tossed it upon a table without breaking the seals. "In Louisiana," he said, "business must wait its turn after hospitality. Please take seats."

Catherine nudged Caroline, and they marched forward to serve wine and brandy. Caroline knew all the visitors were watching them, but one stared harder than the rest, the man in dark civilian clothes. When they hurried to the kitchen and returned with platters of steaming food, when they distributed the embossed silver dishes and stood back, ready to refill any glass, the man was still eyeing Caroline. When she looked directly into his eyes, he dropped them and became interested in his plate.

Searching her memory, she came up with where she had seen him before—at a cafe table across Rue Royale, sitting beside a huge, intent man in buckskins: sitting beside Jubal Blaze.

Another image nudged her mind, that of a man

much like him who had gone into Pierre Lafitte's house on the Ramparts one evening, a man who was also familiar with Felipe de Alcantari.

And she was certain that he had recognized her.

[faint mirrored text bleeding through from previous page]

Chapter 33

Each of them had something special to show her, a certain trick developed through experience with the blade. Dominique You, small and quick despite his little paunch and huge moustache, used a backhand stroke when he was in trouble, dropping low and hacking at an opponent's legs.

"Cut him off at the legs, and where can he go? *Non, non:* not like that—this way, madame; put your shoulder into it. Ah, *c'est bien!*"

Nez Coupé, he of the chopped nose, preferred a two-handed slash that came whistling down from overhead. "If he avoids this, drop to one knee as the blow passes, then lunge out and up, *comme ça!* By Saint Elmo, madame; you learn very quickly."

Beluche watched for a while, swarthy and sullen, shaking his leonine head at the idea of a woman using cutlass or rapier. But after seeing Catherine and Caroline parrying with cased blades, he rose at last to impart his knowledge.

"Very pretty, that. But when he is close to you, when his hilt locks with your own, what then? A strong man will hurl you over the rail and into the sea. Do not hesitate; jerk your knee into his groin, then smash his face with the hilt. When he staggers back, split his brisket."

Robert Gray had this to offer: "A whirling attack, Caroline. Feint with your feet to draw him off and use your point. Don't try to match strength when quickness will do better. Pretend you're tiring, let your point sag like this as you pant hard; show him that your knees are weak, then—but I hope you never have to fight."

He remained with her while she rested, passing her a kerchief to wipe away the sweat. Blanche, the black house servant, sat close by, wrapped against the cold, as Catherine and Lafitte's chief captains talked away together, each claiming his trick was best.

"They are all good," Robert said quietly, "but a beautiful woman—"

Blanche stood up then. "A pretty woman needs to help herself more than a man. Look, child—see how I lift my hands to my face and plead with him not to touch me, not to rape me. But of course, this only inflames him, *hein?* I move one hand from my face to the back of my neck, so. And then—"

The knife glittered from nowhere, leaped out and across an imaginary throat in a swift, deadly arc. A chill smile upon her lips, Blanche said, "It was so I killed my master. The bastard could not believe his throat was cut and tried to stop the blood with his hands. Him and his stallion! I would have killed the horse, also, but he was a slave like me."

Striding to them, Blanche turned to exhibit the cunning sheath that held a two-edged dirk between her shoulder blades, its small handle screened by her hair and the red scarf, the *chignon*. "With a little change, it can be carried behind the thigh," she said. "Lift your skirt for him, flip it into his face while you go for his belly and gut him good. When you have learned all these things, I will show you the use of pistols."

Erectly, she walked away over the sand, skirt rippling in the wind, and Robert said, "She fights like a man. I guess it's because she hates men, most of them, anyway."

"She has reason," Caroline said, pulling on a heavy jacket. "Many of us have cause to hate."

Robert's strong hand helped her rise from the dune, early winter sun playing across his cheekbones and touching a sensitive mouth. "On Grand Isle, no one asks questions of the past. Sometimes we speak of it;

often little pieces come together one by one. Captain Lafitte now—they say he once had a wife and child, that Spaniards killed them both and that's why no prisoners are ever brought in from Spanish ships he takes. He'll make war against them forever, I reckon."

It was nice, having her arm in his, to feel protected by his slim body. "And you?"

"No great mystery about me," Robert said. "The youngest son and a black sheep, a ne'er-do-well bored with clerking in the family warehouses, bored with foolscap and ink and a business that would never be mine. I guess I was bored with myself, too. So here I am."

Near the beach, they stood in the shelter of a wind-tortured oak and she felt the warmth of his breath sweet upon her cheek. Caroline took a step back from him. "And you've become captain like Dominique You."

Ruefully, Robert smiled and dropped his hand from her arm. "Dominique was once a master cannoneer for Napoleon himself, it's said. You avoid me, Caroline."

She looked out to sea where clouds were gathering. "I—I like you, Robert Gray. I enjoy being with you and hearing you laugh. But please don't press me; not now; not yet."

"Answer me just this, then: are you promised?"

"There—there were no promises made," Caroline answered. "But he—oh, I have no right! I may never see him again, and I am—there's another with a hold upon me. Ask me no more, Robert. I am n-not what I seem."

His hand was leaf-gentle upon her cheek, his skyblue eyes held hers. "Consider this, Caroline: many of us, *most* of us can never leave Grand Isle. We're wanted; there are rewards out. If you've done something to bring you here, here you might remain. I'll wait, my lady."

She pressed his hand against her cheek, wanting to cry, to explain, but she could not. Sea rover, pirate, whatever Robert Gray was called, he was a good and true man. Could she admit to having a lover while

315

being owned by another man, confess that after all, she might be just another runaway slave?

And there was Jubal Blaze, a slow and steady fire in her blood, Jubal Blaze, who might this moment be racing back to New Orleans with documents to prove that Caroline Monteleone was in truth Justina Le-Croix, white woman and possible heir to a great plantation. Those papers would allow her to return to the city and spit in Felipe's face. Could she speak to Robert of Jubal's great, tender body, of the enchanted blending they had achieved that long and lovely night?

"I appreciate your being my friend," she said at last. "I very much need friends, Robert."

"I'll wait," he repeated. "The world changes and we must all change with it."

She moved away from him, down the beach, and kneeled to pick up a pinkwhite shell. "Will Lafitte fight with the British?"

Robert scuffed sand with the toe of his boot and looked out to sea. "Not him; he is first a Louisianian, next a Frenchman. And the British want his pledged word he will not attack any Spanish ships. He will never give them that."

"But he didn't deny them."

"He's playing for time, I think, while he sends letters to Governor Claiborne. They promised him thirty thousand dollars and a captaincy in the Royal Navy—ha! Lafitte is already rich, and commands his own fleet. But there was another letter, a direct threat: help them fight the Americans, or English ships will come down upon Barataria and destroy it. *Le Bos* has another problem: Pierre is jailed in the Cabildo on charges of piracy."

Caroline came to her feet. "I didn't know that."

Gesturing, Robert said, "Three English brigs out there, waiting; Pierre waiting in a cell; the city itself holding its breath for attack, and the governor doesn't even answer Lafitte's messages. He's under a terrible strain."

She said, "He seems such a gentleman, so polite and kind; not at all the sort to command this fierce group."

Lifting an eyebrow at her, Robert said, "He commands; don't doubt it. But there *is* trouble with Gambi and his men. He's the only one among us who would not give his word not to take American ships. As if Lafitte didn't have enough problems."

Caroline walked faster along the sands. "I must speak with Catherine about Pierre; perhaps I can help."

Robert beside her, she hurried toward the big house, but as they neared it, he put a hand upon her arm and stopped her. "Gambi's men," he said softly. "It appears they're gathering for trouble. I don't see Gambi himself, but you can be sure he's behind this."

Perhaps twenty corsairs were spread across the path to the house, led by a swarthy giant with a green kerchief about his head and a pistol in his hand. He moved out in front of the others, roaring for *Capitaine* Lafitte to come out.

Caroline saw Lafitte stroll out upon the veranda, where he stood silently, arms crossed upon his chest. He wore no coat, and his ruffled white shirt made a fine target.

The ringleader called out: "We are Gambi's men, and by our eyes, we will take orders from no one else! Understand that, Frenchman? All this nonsense about honoring the American flag—so much shit. Gambi says—"

Caroline didn't see Lafitte's hand move, but there was a flash and a sharp explosion. The swarthy giant staggered, pistol spinning from nerveless fingers; he reeled around to face his men, and she saw the gout of blood leaping from his throat. He spread his arms and fell like a storm-blown tree, crashing face down into the sand.

Lafitte stood upon the veranda, a curl of smoke drifting from the muzzle of a pistol, an unfired weapon in his other steady hand. He had not spoken a word.

Gambi's men shuffled and muttered; cautiously, two of them stooped to grasp the wrists of their dead comrade, and slowly they dragged him limply behind them as they retreated.

317

Quietly, Robert Gray said, "He commands. Will I see you for supper, Caroline?"

She glanced at the now-empty porch, and down at a dark stain soaked into the sand. "I—I will let you know." Then she went up the path and climbed steps, hesitating a moment at the door before entering it. The lesson had been stark: Jean Lafitte would brook no challenge to his authority, and now all Grand Isle knew it.

Sitting before his desk with quill pen in hand, Lafitte nodded to Caroline as she passed through, his smile warm and welcoming as if he had not just killed a man. She couldn't speak to him, but hurried down the hallway to find Catherine.

The girl was furious, stalking like a caged jungle cat. "I would have killed more of them, but Jean made me remain inside. Wretches, *cochons!* To dare face him that way, *him* who has made them rich and kept them from slaughtering each other."

Caroline poured wine. "I did not know Pierre was in prison."

Catherine drained her glass. "That cowardly governor; Claiborne seeks revenge against Jean, and because he cannot face *le Bos* himself, takes Pierre hostage instead. My sister is beside herself."

"But Jean has offered to help defend the city."

"That pig does not believe him," Catherine said, "does not trust him." The girl stopped pacing and stood close to Caroline. "I have a plan. The governor's militia watches for Baratarians entering New Orleans, but who would suspect women? If no one holds you here—"

"I would like to look for a message from Jubal," she answered, "a note left upon an iron gate. No one holds me here."

"Bon! Prepare for the trip, then. We ride as men, and will change into women's clothes at my sister's. I go now to tell Jean."

There was little for Caroline to do, beyond donning a heavy cloak and filling saddlebags with bread and meat. Heart lifting at the thought of Jubal's message, of actually seeing Jubal, she waited impatiently for Catherine. There was danger in the city for her, where vengeance lurked in the form of Felipe de Alcantari; he would never forgive her for spiting him, for exposing his friends as criminals and running away. But there was Jubal Blaze, and the debt she owed Catherine Villars; they were more than worth any risk.

Bouncing into the room, Catherine handed her a pair of small pistols from the armory. "Two barrels each and easy to hide. I carry the same. Oh, Jean was uneasy about allowing us to try this, but I convinced him. We leave the rapiers but keep our knives, and I carry a purse of gold. Are you ready, *chérie?* Are you certain you wish this?"

"I wish it," Caroline said, and kissed the girl's cheek. *"Alors;* let us go."

This time, the *pirogue* moved across marsh waters in daylight, not half so frightening as the previous trip, and Catherine handled the shallow craft expertly. Horses jittered in a pole corral on the far bank, and they had some trouble calming them and cinching the saddles. Catherine let out her mount when they hit the solid trail, and Caroline was forced to hang on, ducking low branches and rocking with the motion of her horse until the edge was off its nervousness and they settled into a canter.

At the corsair guard post, they changed mounts and plunged on, anxious to reach the city before dark. Both horses were blowing when they jogged them into town and turned toward the Ramparts, and Caroline felt as though her ribs had been jolted loose. A tremble shook her as they approached Pierre's house, and the dark, empty one just beyond, the house where Felipe de Alcantari kept his mistresses.

Catherine led the horses around back and tethered them. Seeing Caroline's apprehension, she said, "Do not fear. There are more important things than him, and if he puts himself in our path, we will run over him."

Inside, Marie Villars swept them both into her arms, crying. Comforting her sister, Catherine swiftly ex-

319

plained what they meant to do, release Pierre Lafitte. "Arrange for a carriage, *ma soeur;* fast horses and a driver from Barataria. We will need dark clothing, Marie, as befits a grieving mistress and her sister."

The older woman put a hand to her mouth. "Catherine—you are putting yourself and Caroline in great danger."

"No," Catherine said. "I am lifting some of the load from Jean's shoulders, and Carrie has her own reasons."

Marie Villars looked at Caroline. "That Alcantari, he has been at the little house many times, and in between, his black man. We have heard what he did to you and nobody speaks to him. But he is still a threat to you, madame. There is word he searches the city and has offered a reward, but not officially, of course. He would not admit to the authorities that you have run away, nor that he placed you in that house of torture."

Catherine moved to the *armoire* and went quickly through it for clothing. "Did they catch them, the LaLauries?"

"Mais non; they were sly ones. It is said that they are on the way to France, but the mulatto butler, *une grande bête,* he drove himself directly back to the house after taking his owners to the boat. The crowd, *ma foi!* but they were angry. They dragged him from the carriage and tore him apart. His body lay in the street a long time before police took it away."

"Good," Caroline said. "If any man deserved death, it was Pitot. Catherine, would it be better to put a dress over these breeches and boots? If we have to ride fast—"

"I think yes," Catherine said. "There will be time, *chérie;* we will pass by Jean's house and seek a message from your great red bear. If there is none, perhaps you wish to leave a note for him."

"Yes," Caroline said, "we can stop there on the way to the Cabildo."

"Prends garde," Marie Villars said. "Take great care. I will see to the horses and carriage. Tell my Pierre—I would tell him myself, but he has ordered

me and the children to remain here—tell him I await him, and *bonne chance.*"

Catherine looked in a mirror. "There; am I not a mourner? But one who may assuage her grief with gold and dry her tears upon a rapier's blade, if need be." She turned to take her older sister in her arms. "Do not fret, Marie; we will release him."

Cold twilight was beginning to settle upon the city when they walked quickly from the Ramparts, faces hidden in the hoods of their cloaks. "A fog is coming in from the river," Catherine whispered. "Wonderful; it will help us."

There was no message in the gate of the house where Caroline had spent the magic night with Jubal. They went into the courtyard and looked at the door; nothing there, either. Inside, by the light of a taper, Caroline wrote a quick letter saying that her circumstances had changed, that she would reach him as soon as possible. Hesitating a moment then, her fingers gripping the quill pen, she added: "I love you." She did not address or sign the note; he would know who it was from, and in case Felipe had somehow gotten word of their rendezvous, there would be nothing to lead him to Jubal Blaze. Wrapping her letter in oiled paper, she brought it back out to the gate and placed it snugly between iron pickets.

"Now," she said to Catherine, her voice breaking just a bit, "I am ready."

"He will come," Catherine said. "Have faith, *chérie.* See, the city is filled with soldiers and sailors, like bees swarming everywhere. Your *capitaine* will be among them when his journey is done."

There was excitement in the streets, torches flaring everywhere, knots of men gathered in cafes heatedly discussing the upcoming fight, the battle sure to take place soon. Were not a fleet of six gunboats and the schooner *Josephine* following three barges of armed men down the river? Perhaps Commodore Patterson meant to face the British at the mouth of the Mississippi and drive them back into the Gulf.

Caroline pieced together a general picture from

snatches of conversation from groups they passed. New Orleans was in turmoil; General Jackson had convinced most people that it was to their benefit to repel the invaders, but others still felt the Kaintucks were the enemy, that England now would help return Louisiana to France, where she rightfully belonged. It had not been so long since the tricolor flew here.

Head close to Caroline's, Catherine whispered, "This is good; everyone is so excited they will not concentrate upon watching the Cabildo, and the Place d'Armes."

Across from the massive cathedral, a closed carriage was parked, its horses stamping nervously, the coachman adjusting harness. "As if awaiting a late worshipper," Catherine said. "It is ours."

Before the church and the Cabildo, the *banquette* was made of great sheets of slate, neatly fitted together, slippery from beading fog. The heavy mist swirled like a winding sheet before the forbidding gates of the old Spanish prison, trying to smother the entrance torches. Catherine murmured, "I see only one guard here, another at the courtyard cell door where they must be holding Pierre. Some silver here, for a gold piece would be suspicious. For the other one, doubloons to keep him busy counting. If you will keep this sentry occupied, *chérie*—"

Then to the guard: *"Bon soir,* m'sieu. Is it permitted for Pierre's family to visit?" Catherine's hand slipped between the grillwork and the sentry's hand met it.

"But of course, madame. Only for a little while, you understand."

"Certainement: I will be quick."

When the gate swung back, Caroline said, "I—I cannot bear to see him confined, cousin. I will wait here."

The gate guard was a rotund man in a leather jacket, cutlass by his side and a musket over his shoulder. "I shall be glad for the company, mam'selle; it grows lonely with no one to talk to."

Caroline dropped her hood, so that he could see her face in the dancing torchlight, and watched him smile with pleasure. Coyly, she flattered him in a soft voice, speaking of bravery and how a woman could also be lonely. And when he put aside his musket and stroked her breast, she did not flinch, but sighed and placed her head upon his shoulder, her hip against him. "And you are so bold, *mon capitaine.*"

"But no fool, *bichette.*" His hand wandered beneath her cloak, around her waist and stroked her thighs. "Ah; no weapons but those a beautiful woman normally uses."

Caroline burrowed her face into the base of his throat, thankful he had not found the sharp blade hanging sheathed between her shoulders, nor the pistol tucked into a boot top beneath her dress. When he cupped both her breasts, she pressed against him and looked over his shoulder. The cell sentry had vanished, and she saw Catherine, saw Pierre Lafitte leaving his dungeon.

Reaching to stroke the man's head as she kissed him, Caroline slid her fingers down beneath her hair and flicked out the dirk. She laid it cold against the sentry's throat, cold and hard and strongly there as he stiffened.

"Careful, m'sieu," she whispered. "You said you are no fool, and only a great idiot would risk losing his head. Your comrade is intelligent; already he is paid and gone. It would be wise for you to follow his example. Gold or blood, m'sieu; the choice is yours."

Pierre Lafitte held Catherine's pistol in his hand, and light winked from Catherine's blade. Quietly, the gate guard said, "I repeat, I am no fool. With gold, a man can disappear into the Kaintuck army."

"Here then," Catherine said, putting a purse into his hand, "the same as the other received."

Caroline waited until Pierre removed flint from the man's musket before lowering her knife. The guard wavered, then stepped back. In a second, they were through the gates and racing across the fog-blanketed street to the carriage.

"What women!" Pierre said. "Climb inside, *vite, vite!*"

"I think it is best you go alone, Pierre," Catherine said. "Tell Jean of the American flotilla going downriver, for it may not be meant for the English. We will follow on horseback, when Marie knows you are safely gone."

"My love to her," Pierre said, and vaulted to the front seat beside the driver. *"Alors!* We will see you at Grand Isle."

Caroline and Catherine moved swiftly up Rue Royale, avoiding knots of roistering soldiers, turning off into darker streets where they both kept daggers in their hands. Caroline's heart was thumping, but she was filled with a certain wild gladness. She had in some part repaid her friend and the Lafittes for their kindnesses.

And she had stood up to a man, an armed man, and put the fear of death into him. She breathed deeply of the wet night air and thought of what she might have done, had the sentry tried to give the alarm.

She would have sliced his throat.

Chapter 34

Next day, they were well out into the river and Jubal felt better, safer. River pirates had made their strike against the flatboat and failed; there'd probably be no more attacks, and soon the vital flint would be unloaded at New Orleans.

The city meant Caroline Monteleone, meant the house with the garden in front and so much glory inside. It was cold enough now for the fireplace to be going, Jubal thought, and pictured redgold light playing over her bare skin. The image was so vivid it stirred his loins and tightened his hands upon the rail.

No cause for one woman to reach down into a man's belly like that; lord knows there'd been plenty of other women, and some near about as good-looking, some near about as eager to get with it. But with Caroline, it wasn't only what she did, but how she went about it. Now, the beautiful Lisette de la Rassac was better than a fair to middling bed partner, and had done the same things with her hot, tantalizing mouth, wildly stimulating things that girls in the Carolinas wouldn't even think about. But somehow, when Caroline got going on a man, there was a heap of difference, like she wasn't just doing him a favor, but as if she enjoyed herself just as much.

The candle flickering beside the soft bed, the rhythm of her hips and the surprisingly strong grip of her long, tapered legs; that searing depth of her, so alive and giving. It had made him do something he'd done to no other woman, kiss all the way down from the tautly pulsing breasts, down her flat and trembling belly to the sultry beckoning of her furry mound.

Jubal knew the true taste of her now, could never forget it. Taking a deep breath, he shook his head to clear it and forced himself to watch the wooded banks of the river slipping by. Would she be there, waiting for him? Caroline had promised a message, but he hated to delay a minute longer for her to come running to meet him. He had to prove that marvelous night wasn't just something conjured up by an inflamed memory.

Drifting in toward the right bank of the river, the flatboat hesitated and wobbled in a great eddy. It was then that the long canoes shot out from beyond a point of heavily forested land, coming fast in the echo of a shot. In the bow, Daniel Smith clapped a hand to his suddenly bloody head, tottered, and fell overboard, still hanging on to his long gun.

On the sweep, Markham shouted and angled the flatboat out into swifter current, but the canoes were fast, and almost upon them. Jubal leveled down on the front paddler in one boat, a big Indian in buckskins and wearing a long feather in his greasy hair. The ball smashed him sideways and his dripping paddle spun away. That canoe slewed off and the next Indian loosed a shot at Jubal, wide by a foot or so. Jubal put a bullet into his chest with one barrel of the handgun and broke the arm of another with the next barrel.

Around him, he heard other guns going off as Barton Roberts and Cody Youngblood found targets. In the stern, Mason McGee was methodically firing and reloading. Cody was cursing something fierce, because he'd come a long way from Tennessee with Daniel Smith, only to have his friend hit the river with a ball through the head.

The closest canoe was in trouble, spinning around in the current, two dead men sprawled in it and another hanging partway over the side with his head underwater. Reloading, Jubal got off a shot as the last man dived into the river, centering upon the bobbing head and grunting with satisfaction when the buck yelped and sank in a spurt of red swiftly washed away.

"Look yonder!" Barton Roberts cried. "There on shore—a white man, bigod! The son of a bitch put 'em up to it." He braced his rifle barrel on the railing and fired, but the movement of the boat threw him off and the man on shore was untouched. The forward boatman choked out something in a strangled voice; his knees folded and he hit the deck with his face. In back, Markham called his friend's name.

"Cut up that other goddamn canoe!" Jubal yelled, and emptied his pistol at it.

A rifle ball chipped a long splinter from the deck-house beside Jubal's head, and he pulled it in to use powder, patch and ball, to work the ramrod smoothly. When he looked around again, the canoe was gone. Then the boatman hollered, and Jubal saw two half-naked bucks coming over the stern, one of them chopping at Markham with a short axe.

Jubal dropped that one, hurled him backward with a thunderclap from his rifle, then darted forward to knock the other one in the head with the barrel. The flatboat yawed, nobody at the sweep, and Jubal caught hold of the swinging tiller to steady it. He saw Mason McGee trot back and near take off an Indian's head with one swing of his skinning knife. Cody Young-blood was still cursing, firing and reloading, and now Jubal couldn't see the white man on the bank. The fight had gone too far downstream.

Smoke-blackened, Barton Roberts' face pushed close to Jubal. "All over; they're hightailin' it—what's left."

"That bastard on the bank," Jubal said, "reckon who he is?"

"Never find out," Barton answered. "Got him a horse back in the trees, I expect. Paid them Injuns to hit us, then lit out when he seen it didn't work."

"Markham!" Jubal roared. "You ain't hurt all that bad; get on over here and point us into the bank."

The boatman patted a kerchief at a cut on his head. "Fella'll be long gone, time you get there."

"Gone south," Jubal said. "Ain't nothin' north of us for a long piece. Any luck, and I can cut off the son of a bitch, get 'tween him and the city. If'n I don't have to kill him right off, I mean to find howcome these flint kegs are so important to him."

With Mason McGee's help, the helmsman wrestled the boat into shore. "Want some help?" Cody Youngblood asked.

"Best you all stay with the boat," Jubal said, leaping lightly to land. "In case somebody else has got ideas. Tie up here for a spell and wait on me. If'n I ain't back afore dark, well—get them flints on down to Andy."

He loped up the bank and took to the woods, moving inland where the trail ought to be. Jubal moved quickly and easily, in his element, moved with very little sound, conscious of leaf and bush and tree bole. He'd grown up with a rifle in hand, first because of Indian trouble, later on when big Tidewater planters took to sending horsemen to burn out new settlers, and still later when it meant meat on the table or going without.

Sliding past a big sycamore tree, he circled a patch of briars and found the trail. Jubal squatted to look closely at it, to study tracks. He rose and eased up the road a ways, then back down. Far as he could tell, no horse had left fresh tracks along here; all had crumbled a little around the edges from night dew or wind. So the mysterious white man hadn't made it this far yet —if he was coming south. If he'd lit a shuck back upriver, Jubal was plain out of luck.

Finding a nest back of some young loblolly saplings, Jubal hunkered down and checked the priming on his weapons. Natchez or Choctaw, maybe Chickasaw; they'd been used for the attack, and a good thing they couldn't shoot worth a fiddler's damn from a moving canoe, else all the flatboat crew would be dead. As it was, two men lost, and somebody was going to pay dearly for them.

Jubal made himself one with his background, unmoving, breathing slowly and shallowly, his eyes raking the road, the underbrush, his ears tuned for the slightest sound out of the ordinary.

Sitting quietly like this, he had a difficult time forcing Caroline Monteleone to the rear of his mind; she insisted on floating right back up. He couldn't help wonder how Tarboro neighbors would take to her, her being so beautiful and all. Husbands would be envious and wives kind of spiteful, especially certain wives he'd dallied with. But Pa would take to her right off, glad that Jubal was at last showing some sign of settling down.

Caroline would purely be a picture to delight the eye, all dressed up in a ballgown, coming slowly down the winding stairs of Tarboro and all eyes searching her out, everybody weighing her as the new mistress of the plantation. She'd stand the test, all right; it wasn't as if she hadn't handled niggers before, wasn't as if she was brought down fresh from up north. The household would run smoothly at her hands, for he could sense she had steel to her, a strength that maybe even she didn't suspect.

Damn; how long would it be before a whole passel of little Jubals and Carolines were running around the place? It'd be something, teaching a youngun to ride and shoot, and when he got old enough, what and when to plant, and how to oversee the niggers. And Caroline could show the gals about keeping house and setting table, doing needlework and whatever else girl children did.

Jubal watched the trail and listened for the dirt-muffled clopping of a horse. His brother Abel wouldn't much care for the whole thing; since Jubal hadn't shown all that much interest in running the place, Abel had kind of took over. He was always closer to the land. But come down to it, Abel could take half the plantation and half the slaves, too. By law, the younger brother was left out in the cold, but that never seemed right to Jubal.

Hell; there was plenty for both, and Abel could put himself up a house grand as Tarboro, did he want to. And that river bottom land not yet cleared; it wouldn't take all that long to get it ready for planting, to move on across the river and lay claim to more forest. Two Tarboro plantations would be stronger and more productive than one.

He heard it coming fast, a pounding of hooves upon the beaten trail, a horse being pushed. Jubal braced the muzzle of his rifle upon a pine branch and sighted along the barrel. He didn't want to kill the man right off, and it always went against the grain to put a ball through a horse, so his shot had to be just so. It ought to knock the man out of the saddle without tearing him up completely. Jubal wanted to talk with this fellow, and find out why he'd been after the flint, find who put him up to the raid, maybe. It seemed like more than one person didn't want Andy getting the army's muskets in working order.

Fancied-up fellow, Jubal thought as the horse loped into sight, plume in his hat and a velvet suit, even a sword banging against his thigh. Taking a deep breath and holding it, Jubal squeezed down on the trigger, leading the man and horse like he'd lead a running deer. The rifle went off and the man kind of jumped up before falling backward out of his saddle.

"Damn," Jubal said, automatically reloading before stepping out onto the road, "sure hope he didn't break his neck when he hit."

The horse dropped to a trot, then a walk, and stopped to look back. Jubal kept the rifle steady as he approached the man on the ground. Moustachioed and with a little pointy beard, his pretty suit was dirty and he held his right hand tightly to a leaking wound in his left shoulder.

"Well now," Jubal said, "seems like you was in an almighty hurry."

In heavily accented English, the man said through set teeth: "You ambushed me, shot me for my purse."

"Oh," Jubal said, "I reckon settin' them Injuns on us is cause enough, and I ain't interested in your purse. Am interested in howcome you killed off two of my men when there ain't anything worth havin' on that flatboat."

330

"I will say nothing to a highwayman," the man gritted. "Nothing."

Leaning his cocked rifle against a sapling within easy reach, Jubal took out his skinning knife and went to one knee. He ran his thumb along the keen blade. "Feller got shot through the head come all the way down from Tennessee," he said. "And the boatman, he hired on to give a hand, more'n for money. Since you got cozy with them redskins, mayhap you know somethin' about their ways. Course, Choctaws and the like can't hold a candle to Creeks and Cherokees, when it comes to downright mischief. One time I seen 'em keep a captive alive and kickin' for nigh onto a whole week, and him screamin' and beggin' to be killed all the while. Wouldn't done him a lick of good to get turned loose, you see; near about all the hide was peeled off'n him by then."

The man's eyes widened and he licked his lips. "But you—you are a white man; you would not use Indian methods—"

"Way I see it," Jubal said, *"you* used Injuns on my men, so I figure first thing, I'll pry that rifle ball out'n your shoulder, and if'n that don't loosen your tongue, I'll take your scalp. Ever hear the sloshy noise a scalp makes when it gets snatched loose from the headbone?"

"Mon Dieu," the man muttered. "It should not have come to this. It appeared so simple—"

Stropping the big knife over his buckskinned thigh, Jubal said, "Expect it was you ahint that first raid, too?"

"May—may I sit up? My shoulder, it pains very much. *Oui;* there was word of your flint, but I made the mistake of hiring fools who allowed themselves to be trapped." The man's face was pale through its smearing of dust.

"But you're a Frenchie," Jubal said. "Way I hear it, the French are always makin' war with the English. You ought to be plumb delighted for them flints to get to New Orleans where they can help kill Redcoats."

"The—French and English are at peace now. There —you would not be carrying water? *Non?* Ah well—

331

there have been offers made by the British to turn Louisiana back to us, once the Kaintucks are beaten and forced out."

Sitting back on his heels, Jubal said, "So a bunch of New Orleans Creoles are workin' against us. But what I want to know is, how you get onto what I was doin'? Who put you up to it, told you where I'd be headin'?"

Licking his dry lips, the man said, "Water; my throat is very dry, m'sieu. I can speak better if I have water. There is—is a bottle in my saddlebags. For the love of God, m'sieu—I am badly wounded and in great pain."

Climbing to his moccasined feet, Jubal picked up his rifle and lowered the hammer gently against the pan. Half-turning, he balanced the skinning knife in one hand and took two long paces down the road toward the calmly grazing horse. Turning suddenly back, his eye caught the wink of metal in the Frenchman's hand. Jubal flipped the knife with a sweeping, overhand motion. It went *chunk!* into the man's chest and his mouth fell open; a little hideout pistol dropped from his fingers. He reached both pawing hands up to the hilt of the blade buried in his body and tugged weakly at it. Then blood gushed out of his mouth and he dropped over onto one side.

"Goddamnit," Jubal said, "now looka there what you made me do."

He went back and put a foot on the man's chest to retrieve his knife, and wiped it on the velvet coat. There was some gold in the purse, but not all that much, and a few pieces of silver. Jubal took the little gun and walked up slowly on the horse, clucking to it. The saddlebags were near empty, too, and he figured the Frenchie had been traveling hard. There was a packet of letters, and he opened them, holding them turned to the light.

They only named one name, the bearer's, and that hit Jubal low down in the belly: Sieur Michel de la Rassac. *Rassac!* Lovely, sensuous Lisette's husband was always out of town on business. Yes, Jubal thought; business for the lobsterbacks and rebellious Creoles

332

who wanted the United States out of New Orleans, out of the Louisiana Purchase.

But Lisette hadn't known where he was going or when. Somebody else might have, though, the man who'd introduced him to Lisette de la Rassac, the same man who had led him on a wild goose chase up to Natchez and delayed the flint that much longer— Tom Pickett.

Loosening the girth, Jubal let the saddle drop to the road. He slipped the bridle from the sweated horse's head and spanked its rump smartly. It cantered off through the trees.

"Might be what you call a coincidence," Jubal said. "But time I get back to the city, I mean to ask friend Tom to explain it all to me."

He left the body in the road, turned into the woods and began the long, ground-eating lope that would take him back to the river and his flatboat, his waiting crew.

Jubal thought that Tom Pickett better have the right answers. He was such a cheerful, accommodating fellow, it'd be a damned shame to tear his head off.

Chapter 35

When the signal gun boomed across the island, Caroline was walking back from fencing practice with Robert Gray. He stopped and stared out at a fog bank masking the bay. "Probably the British coming for Lafitte's answer. They won't like it, and if they've come in force, we may have to fight. He's already moved all shallow draft ships to the other side of the island, just in case, my felucca among them. I must hurry to it."

"Robert," she said, "please be careful. You—I would hate to lose so good a friend."

He made a face. "I never thought I'd dislike that word—friend. I want to be much more than that to you, Caroline."

"I know," she said, "and I still ask you to wait, Robert. Or to forget me altogether."

There was pain in his skyblue eyes. "I can't forget you. A kiss for luck, then?"

Holding up her mouth to him, she felt the soft hunger of his lips, the quick caress of his hands along her body. Then Robert Gray was gone, trotting across the island to duty with his ship. She looked after him, thinking what a kind man, a good man, he was. If it wasn't for Jubal—

The thing screamed in from the sea with a vicious splitting of the air, and Caroline flinched at a leaping furrow plowed in the sand. The *boom!* reached her then, and she saw a plume of smoke leap from the side of the brig that broke from the fog. A ship firing on Grand Isle, and not British! She saw the American flag fluttering from its mast as she turned to run for the main house.

Men were jumping to the cannon, running for gigs to take them to their ships, and from the clutter of shacks, a woman shrieked, a corsair roared curses. A broadside from the ship raked the island, a thundering blast of iron shot ripping a hole in the parapet and leveling shacks. More ships loomed from the fog bank, all with the same brilliant flag showing, all with the stars and stripes gleaming from masthead and bow and stern.

The Baratarians hesitated; one flung aside the match about to touch off a cannon. "Damned if I fire on that flag! It's my own!"

And as she reached the steps of the big house, the Lafittes came leaping down them, yelling commands to take to the bayous, not to resist. Dazed, Caroline staggered when a cannonball tore a great chunk from the roof of Jean Lafitte's house, and stood uncertainly.

Catherine Villars leaped past her, pistol in one hand, cutlass in the other, following her lover. "He will not fight them!" she shouted back. "Run, Carrie—to the bayous, the *pirogues!*"

Caroline turned and saw a corsair ship catching wind in its sails, saw it moving out into the bay, heading for the American schooner. Gambi, she thought; only Gambi would defy Lafitte and attack. But even as she watched, the dark ship lost its mast, and a gout of flame mushroomed from its deck as hot shot ignited gunpowder there. The schooner and brigs continued to hammer the stricken vessel, and corsairs went over the side as fire roared higher and the rigging caught.

Another shell whistled across the porch and ripped a gaping hole through the house. A great splinter whipped by Caroline's head, and she jumped down from the steps to run blindly through smoke and scattering, yelling men, while guns continued to spit thundering fire from the sea.

Smoke was thick about her as she stumbled for the

far side of the island, a bitter taste in her throat and a smarting in her eyes. All was confusion about her: fighting men who were not fighting, but running; smoking cabins and screaming women. Over there, the large warehouse where Jean Lafitte kept his smuggled goods, as yet untouched by cannon fire; and when Caroline topped the rise in ground, she could see corsair ships moving away along inland bayous, navigating those little-known routes that would bring them back to the Gulf and safety in flight to the open seas. Small boats were hurrying from the shore, and she stood uncertainly for a moment, looking for Catherine Villars, for Robert Gray, for any familiar face.

Something rapped her sharply along the head, and Caroline's eyes glazed as she fell. Dimly, she could hear the yelling around her, the explosions rocking the island; faintly, she was conscious of booted feet slamming past her and gritty sand against her cheek. She fought against the darkness, but it came to wrap its black blanket about her, and she slid into its smothering folds.

"This un ain't dead," a faraway voice said, and she was jerked to her feet. Swaying there, knees threatening to buckle, her head throbbing, Caroline tried to clear her eyes.

"Git over there with them other goddamn pirates," the man rasped, and shoved her roughly.

Her sword was gone, and her pistols, but she felt the slight weight of the dirk in its sheath hidden between her shoulder blades and knew she wasn't completely unprotected. They thought she was a man, Caroline realized, because she wore the head kerchief and pantaloons and jackboots that were practically uniform for Baratarians.

Gingerly, she touched the side of her head and felt the lump there, knew that her face was smeared and was glad for it. Working her way to the center of stunned and muttering men, she hid herself among the prisoners. A hand touched her shoulder and she looked around.

Puffing out his moustache, Dominique You said,

"Do not fear, *chérie*. No one here will give away your secret."

"The Lafittes, Catherine, Robert Gray?" she asked.

"Clean away, it seems. I am the only big fish in the net!"

Caroline pressed fingertips against her bruise. "But *why?* Why did they attack us?"

Lafitte's second in command shrugged. "Who can say? *Le Gouverneur* Claiborne has long been our enemy, especially since the time he offered a reward of five hundred dollars for Jean Lafitte's capture. Imagine, only five hundred. *Le Bos* posted his own reward notice then, putting a price of *fifteen* hundred upon Claiborne's head. I can tell you, all New Orleans was laughing."

Guards with ready weapons encircled the huddle of prisoners; other men were busy looting the storehouse and putting the torch to Jean Lafitte's home. "What— what will they do with us?" she asked.

Off to one side, a woman screamed, but another laughed drunkenly. Dominique You rolled his shoulders again. "If they discover you are a woman—that. If not, perhaps you will be lucky, and be hanged with the rest of us."

"Jean Lafitte will never allow that to happen," Caroline said.

Smiling at her, Dominique You said, "Perhaps you are right. Perhaps he can make them see he never meant to fight with the British, that he is first a Louisianian, an American. Let us hope so, *chérie*."

Caroline sank to earth and propped her aching head upon her knees. The American navy was no better than pirates, looting and burning, taking any woman they could find. Some of the women didn't mind, she knew, but a coldness grew within her belly. No part of her body could ever forget Kleppner's brutality, the slaver's cruel possession of her flesh. And Felipe; at times, there was rape with him also. She could not be ravished again, passed from hand to hand, could not lie beneath one sweating, grunting body after another while her secret places were penetrated. Black blood or totally white, Caroline Monteleone was her own woman now, and by all that was holy, she meant to stay that way.

She stayed close to Dominique You when the prisoners were herded by groups into small boats and rowed out to the schooner *Maryland,* keeping her head down and being inconspicuous. She climbed the boarding ladder like a man, and slouched below with corsairs now mumbling angrily that they should have given battle. It wasn't in them to surrender without a fight, when about all they could expect was a noose. Dominique You slapped one malcontent into silence when the man cursed Jean Lafitte for running away.

The hold of the schooner was dark and dank, packed with eighty prisoners. For two days and nights they clung together for warmth and ate of the slop lowered in buckets, sleeping when they could and whispering of escape, of the fate awaiting them if convicted of piracy. Caroline recalled the Cabildo and the cell she'd helped Pierre Lafitte to flee, but the gallows wouldn't be erected there, Dominique You said; it would be built in the Place d'Armes, so all the city's curious could gather to watch them swing.

"That fool Gambi," Dominique You growled. "One wishes that he burned with his ship. It was his raids that turned the Kaintucks upon us. *Le Bos* insisted only Spanish ships be taken, but did Gambi listen? *Mais non;* that one sailed against any flag, and it may be that the warehouse held articles looted from American vessels, things that can be identified. *Merde!* We are done, if that is so."

And Caroline said, "They need him. If the British offered Jean so much, why should he be worth less to the Americans?"

"Ah," he sighed, chewing one end of his moustache, "if all was only so simple."

On the third day, the *Maryland* sailed, and that afternoon, Caroline got into trouble. In small groups, the Baratarians had been allowed on deck for air and exercise, and since she had gotten by so far and needed a clean breath of air, she climbed to the deck with

Dominique You, Beluche and another. She might have been all right if a guard hadn't been anxious to show his authority, and pushed her when she lagged, eyes uncertain in the setting sun, salt and wind after so long below decks. When the man lifted his hand from her shoulder, it caught her head kerchief, and suddenly all her hair went tumbling down her back.

"Damme!" the sailor grunted. "Looks like we got us a wench here."

"Quick," another said, "hide her afore the officers see. They get a peep at her, *we'll* never see hide nor hair."

Dominique You stepped forward. "M'sieu, if you will but—"

A gun butt in the belly drove him gasping back, and the sailor who wielded it hissed, "Get 'em all back below, 'ceptin' her. Hurry this bitch over ahint the stern gun, so they can't see from the bridge."

Caroline opened her mouth to scream, but a callused palm clamped across her chin, and she was jerked from the deck, kicking and twisting. Sparks rainbowed behind her eyes when someone struck her, and another fist drove the breath from her belly. When she could gulp air, when she could see, they had her spread on the deck behind a canvas gun covering.

A seaman, burly and bearded, crammed her kerchief into her mouth; a lean, ferretlike man crouched at her head, drawing her feet, tugging down her man's breeches. Caroline arched her back and squirmed, but they only laughed as they held her.

Across time and half a continent, her mother's words came back, Solah's wisdom: *Survive, child; live.*

They would only hurt her more if she fought them. But she was not a slave now, perhaps not even black, and she'd sworn never to allow herself to be mauled again. Teeth grinding into the balled gag, Caroline forced herself to stop resisting them, for they would take her anyway. And because they were in a hurry, they hadn't stripped her, and the dirk pressed itself

339

between the deck and her spine, snug in its sheath. Maybe, just maybe—

Shuddering, she felt hands pawing beneath her shirt, rough hands that kneaded her breasts and pained the nipples. At her thighs, other fingers prodded and raked. The sailor holding her wrists whinnied softly through slack lips, watching his friends fondle her, his muddy eyes eager and gloating.

Pockmark grinned brown-toothed as he cupped her mound, her haunch. "Pure silk, her cunny hair be— but look to her ass; got somethin' scarred on it."

Beard crushed her breasts and made her writhe. "You be more used to them has the French pox; take your turn quick, for afeelin' on her tits makes me randy."

"Pure silk," Pockmark muttered, using his fingers to part her, "them pirates hid out their best piece."

Caroline stiffened as he poked at her mound, as he set himself and thrust strongly up into her hating body. He sheathed his hard length in her, and rode her up and down, keeping her legs veed apart with the bracing of his own.

Ferretface snickered. "Got her skewered better'n beef on a spit, and she sizzles about the same, I'd say."

"Just you hold to her hands," Pockmark panted, pushing and pulling. "Don't want her clawin' at me none. Fine—fine and juicy—"

"Hurry on it, you bastard," Beard said, twisting at Caroline's breasts until she sobbed against her gag. "If'n I don't get my go at her afore the officers see, I'll break your goddamn back."

"No need for officers to catch on," Ferretface said, licking at his lips. "Got a fair wind in the tops'l and they're still countin' off their plunder. We kin fuck her clear into the night and over the side with her when we're done."

Caroline rode the impact of Pockmark, relaxed her arms and legs as he groaned and soiled her deep within. The knife, she thought; the double-edged sharpness of the secret dirk, and somehow these faces overlapped Kleppner and Felipe and became one hateful visage.

She closed her eyes against the intrusion of Beard when he took his place at her thighs, forcing his thickness, his ugliness, upon her, weighting himself against her belly.

"I got a mind to shove mine into her mouth," Ferretface whinnied, "if'n somebody'll hold to her arms."

Pockmark grunted. "That scrawny pizzle of your'n wouldn't do for a gag, and she'd lief as not snap it right off."

"Not her," Ferretface said. "Lookit how she's aturnin' and shakin' it on John's big rod. Fair eatin' it up with her quim, she is. She's gettin' hotted up for certain."

Beard hammered at her, sledged at her, and it was true Caroline was responding, but not out of passion. She had nothing but scorn for these pigs, and nursed a whitehot hate as she pretended, as she lifted so she could wrap her legs about the thick waist of the sailor raping her. Surging and moaning behind her wadded gag, she rolled up on her shoulders, so no wandering hand would discover her hidden blade.

"Turn—turn loose her arms," Beard gasped. "The wench needs to hold to me."

One hand free, and she tucked it behind his head, bringing it down to her breasts as he began to stiffen out in the throes of completion; the other hand—and hunching to Beard, with him, she rolled partially onto one side. Close at her shoulder, she could see Ferretface slavering down at their joining. Hilt of the dirk solid in her right hand, she snapped the knife out and backarmed its needle point deep into Ferretface's groin.

He wheezed, and she pulled out the steel to drive it strongly into Pockmark's upper belly, just below the ribs, where she twisted it. His mouth fell open and his eyes popped wide; he made a strangled noise, but Beard was jerking in a blind cresting and heard nothing but his own heart.

Spitting out her gag, Caroline held the last sailor's bearded face to her heaving breasts with both hands. He

341

had stopped thrusting, and she dropped her legs from around his body.

The mockingbird, she thought; the mother bird that brought a poison berry to its captured young, seeing it dead rather than a prisoner. The slave woman Blanche had cut her master's throat because of that bird.

Almost gently, Caroline reached around the man's throat and drew the honed blade from ear to ear in a single motion. Hotness gushed down her body when Beard tried to speak, when his big hands spasmed upon her hips. Then she threw him off, rolled from beneath him as he kicked like a beheaded chicken.

On her knees, shirt clinging wet and red to her body, she drew up her breeches and pulled off her boots. Wiping the dirk upon the kerchief they'd used to silence her, she put it back into its sheath and shook her hair over it.

They were sprawled about her, grotesque in their puddles of crimson, and Caroline knew only a coldness, only a slight surprise that it had been so easy. She looked to her left, where night was falling swiftly upon the shoreline, upon trees black and shaggy. Water gurgled about the stern of the *Maryland* as she lowered herself over the side, took a deep breath and let go.

Icy and black, the river closed over her head, tried to pull her far down into its bubbling maw, but she fought it and broke surface with a gasp to strike out for the near shore, swimming strongly and smoothly with the current.

She might never make land, and didn't know where she was going if she did. But at least now she would die clean, and die free.

Chapter 36

She was chilled through and still damp, but the river was behind her now, and the long, cold night spent huddled shivering upon a bed of pine boughs, with more of them piled atop in hopes for warmth. The *Maryland* was gone, too, the ship bearing Baratarian prisoners and dead men; *her* dead men and be damned to them.

Walking quickly along the road and rubbing her hands together, Caroline tried to warm up, but the chill was difficult to shake, for it seemed to have gotten into the marrow of her bones. Weak winter sun slanted through tall pines and sprawling liveoaks, but didn't help. A bluejay called harsh alarm at her approach and a fox squirrel chittered from a high branch. In its echo she heard the creak of wheels and the slow rhythm of hooves. Instinct moved her into shielding brush, where she waited crouched until she could see the wagon.

A black man handled the reins for two horses and there seemed to be no outriders for the loaded wagon. Stiffly, Caroline moved into the road, holding up one hand. Quick for all his bulk, the driver brought up a shotgun.

"Please," she called, "I'm alone and mean you no harm."

He hissed the horses to a stop, but the shotgun didn't waver. There was something familiar about him, something known in the set of wide shoulders, the sullen curve of mouth. In startled Ashanti, she said: "Tchaka—the Mandingo!"

It was him, the slave in Kleppner's cavvy who'd risked his life to save her that fearful night when she was about to be mauled by Kleppner's riders.

Lowering the gun muzzle, he sucked in a sharp breath. "You! Where your mother? How you—"

His Ashanti was accented and broken as ever, but never had Caroline been so glad to see someone. She trembled with cold as she walked to the wagon and lifted a hand to the big black. "Help me, brother; I am frozen and hungry."

Effortlessly, he lifted her onto the seat, muddy eyes intent. Tchaka reached behind him and brought out blankets to bundle her, and from between his feet, offered a jar of clear white whiskey. Its hot bite was welcome, and Caroline thanked him for it, burrowing deep into warming blankets.

"Some dried meat and cornbread a week old," he said.

"I am grateful, brother. How is it you drive alone, with no white man watching?"

Tchaka rolled thick shoulders, glancing at the walking horses, then back at her as she wolfed down the food. "Man trusts me, but I be gone soon as I find where to go and money to get there. You run off, too?"

Between bites, Caroline told the man almost everything that had happened to her since Kleppner had taken her and Solah. She spoke rapidly, pouring it out in painful spurts while the wagon rocked and horses plodded on toward New Orleans.

"Good you killed them," Tchaka said. "Come close to wringing some white necks like chickens, myself. But I learn to wait, to think how to get away safe. Not like you, running with nowhere to go and no gold to keep me."

Stomach filled, snuggled into warmth, Caroline said drowsily, "You were the fighter. I thought you would escape at first chance, but you are right, Mandingo; one must wait and think it through. This is a different land."

"Got me a fair master," Tchaka said, "but it does not change his color. Learned horses good; learned some Choctaw from old Indian stable hand; found out I could learn white talk quick, too. This Ashanti does not lie easy on my tongue."

"Then speak English," Caroline said. Being with him brought it all back, the cavvy, the raping of Solah, her own loss of virginity; degradation, pain and death. She was very tired and needing sleep; it was difficult to think, to go beyond a vague plan to reach the Villars house and see if Catherine's sister could help. But that would bring her close to Felipe, and she didn't want that.

"Where you go?" Tchaka asked. "You a mess, woman, muddied up thataway. They take one look at you, they know for sure you run off. Us comes up on another wagon, best you hides in back anyhow. Look too white to be ridin' with a nigger." He clucked to the horses and made them move a little faster. "Take you far's I go, near about. Has to put you off ahint the barn, I reckon, find you warm clothes. Don't want nobody on Delacroix plantation to know you been there."

Caroline sat up straight. "Delacroix—owned by Lucien LeCroix?"

Head swiveling to her, Tchaka grunted assent. "Know him?"

"Not yet," she said, "but it's a good time to introduce myself."

"Long's you don't cause no big trouble, woman. I been workin' too hard at putting money by, swappin' with the Choctaws and such."

"No trouble," Caroline promised, pulling the blanket tighter about her body. "You know, Tchaka, you're a good man—Mandingo or not."

He shook his head. "And I ain't figured you out yet. Not Ashanti, not black, not white, but with a dab of everything throwed together and maybe too much gumption for a woman."

Drowsily, Caroline said, "I haven't sorted myself out, either, but I think I'm starting."

345

When she opened her eyes, the wagon was turning up a crushed shell road beneath magnificently spreading liveoaks. Clouds had gone from a pale sky and sunlight tried hard to warm the land. She smelled pungent woodsmoke from cooking fires and heard laughter from one of the whitewashed slave cabins. The big house waited, tall columns and mellowed bricks and a quiet air of antiquity.

"Can't put you off in them clothes," Tchaka grumbled. "My woman'll give you somethin' fit to wear; not fancy, but clean."

"I'm much obliged to you," Caroline said, "and in your debt for saving my life, before. I won't forget, Tchaka."

Back of the big house at the barn, he pulled up the horses and helped her down, hurrying her between hay bales and stalls to his quarters. A black woman blinked open-mouthed at them, a proud-looking woman, strong and tall. Her eyes stretched wider when Caroline removed the blanket.

"Molly," Tchaka said, "this here is the Ashanti I told you about. Run onto her on the river road, comin' back from the Choctaws."

Molly said, "You don't look like no Ashanti I ever seen."

"Don't get your back up," Tchaka said. "Put out some water and borry her your good dress; she's goin' to see Mist' Lucien."

Molly softened. "Come ahead, girl. My dress be too big for you, but I kin take it up some. You eat today? Tchaka, chunk some wood on the stove; stir yourself, man."

"Now yonder," Tchaka said, "is a woman pure-D Ashanti—startin' with her mouth."

Molly hustled him from the room then, and put down warm water, homemade soap and a washrag. Sponging herself off, Caroline swung the sheathed blade back into place, and felt Molly's eyes following it.

"I knows that trick," Molly said. "Keeps that leather string at your throat and it don't look like nothin', but what it holds in back can come in mighty handy."

"It did," Caroline said. "Will I need it with Lucien LeCroix?"

"Uh-uh, child. Mist' Lucien, he a gentleman don't mess with a girl less'n she wants it. Had him a wife oncet and never got over losin' her to swamp fever." Handing her a towel, Molly said then, "My man told me about you and him in that cavvy; you and your mama, too. Tchaka, he feels right bad about mouthin' off back then, but he was right off'n the boat and didn't understand nothin'."

"He's a fine man," Caroline said, "strong and courageous and smart. He won't always be a slave."

"No," Molly agreed, "he sure God won't. Scares me some, he does, always plottin' and plannin' on freedom. What *I* goin' to do in Africky? Don't talk Ashanti and don't talk Mandingo; gets by in French some, but that won't help none."

Taking the plain linsey-woolsey dress the woman offered, Caroline drew it over her head, then stared ruefully down at her bare feet. Her seaman boots were somewhere in the Mississippi river, but she might have been there herself, and she wondered if her escape and the slaying of her rapists would bring trouble down upon Dominique You and the other Baratarians. By now, the ship was in port and its cargo of sea rovers disgorged to whatever fate awaited them. She was glad the Lafittes and Catherine Villars had not been taken, happy that Robert Gray was yet free—if free they all were, and not dead.

"Ain't got but one pair of go-to-meetin' shoes myself," Molly said, "and they'd flop right off'n your feet. Howcome you wants to see Mist' Lucien?"

The door opened and Tchaka came back in. "Her business, woman. I seen Mist' Lucien, and he's waitin'." He looked at Caroline. "Told him I picked you up on the road, and that's all."

She put a hand on Molly's arm. "I'll return your dress soon as I can, and thank you. Tchaka—"

"Thisaway," he said, "and best you walks in front. Didn't tell him you black or white. Don't know my ownself."

347

He led her to the back door of the big house, and in the kitchen, two black women stared sullenly at them, but glanced hurriedly away at Tchaka's frown. Through a hallway he whispered, " 'Cause you ain't all gussied up and barefoot, they thinks you trash. Whatever you is, it ain't trash. Yonder the library. Reckon I waits here."

Raising her chin, Caroline opened the tall, carved door and walked into the bright, open room as if she belonged there, and perhaps she did. Lucien LeCroix rose from behind a teakwood desk, a slim young man with dark hair and high cheekbones. His smile was welcoming, curious.

"My wagon man said you had a misfortune, Miss—"

Walking up close to him, Caroline said in French, "I am called Caroline Monteleone, but that may not be my proper name. I have been told I may be Justina LeCroix."

Lucien's face went slack, then tightened and his brown eyes sought her own. *"Sacre!* Forgive me, mam'selle, but it is a great shock, you understand. Please be seated—some wine, perhaps? A touch of brandy?"

"A little sherry, *s'il vous plaît.* I did not mean to shock you, m'sieu. My—misfortune causes me to be inopportune."

Hands shaking visibly, Lucien LeCroix poured wine for her and a large dollop of brandy for himself. She took the fragile, long-stemmed glass and watched him. "I ask for nothing, m'sieu—only protection for the moment."

She sat upon a brocade couch and he took a chair opposite. *"Pour le bon Dieu,"* he said, his face flushed now, "if you are indeed my long lost sister, call me Lucien. Ah, if only my father—our father—was alive. He searched; oh, how he searched, and went unsatisfied to his grave. Those runaways—but you know the tale?"

Sipping wine, Caroline said, "They were M'Nele and Solah. It is said they took a hostage north."

Lucien rubbed his cheek with long, narrow fingers.

"It has been so very long, and although he did not want to admit it, *mon père* himself believed all were dead. The posters, the reward, the detectives, years of regret and mourning, all for nothing."

In a steady voice, Caroline told him how M'Nele and Solah died, and he got up to refill his glass. From the table he said, "They were carried on the rolls as Manuel and Sarah. Not everyone knew their savage names."

She said, "I am not here to prove a claim, Lucien. I am not certain. A man—there is a possibility of papers being found and delivered to me, but I dare not go into New Orleans just yet. I—I am afraid for my very life. There is another man, Felipe de Alcantari—"

He put down his glass with a bang and slapped his forehead. *"Certainement!* That is where I have seen you before—the Quadroon Ball, and Alcantari strutting with you. *Ma foi!* That arrogant, bloody—" Breaking off suddenly, Lucien stared at her. "But you are not a quadroon; you cannot be."

"Perhaps I am, Lucien. I was so certain I was Solah's daughter, but then my mother—then she swore I was not, when she was dying." Caroline placed her bare feet under the couch. She looked directly at the man who could be her half brother. "I have been treated as a mustee, in all manners. For that, I have shame but no guilt."

Clenching his hands, Lucien said through his teeth, "That *cochon.* My name is old as his, and he dares to sully it—"

"I do not think he knows," Caroline said. "There were others, also. It is what one with black blood must suffer."

"Not on Delacroix plantation, by all that is holy! You—" Caroline could see him struggle to gain control. He went on, more calmly, "We will talk much, you and I. But first, more suitable clothing and if you do not mind temporarily wearing something of my poor wife's—and a good meal, and I will show you letters from my father—"

349

Again, Lucien paused and touched a fingertip to his silken moustache. "I recall there was a mark of a certain shape."

"Like a scorpion," Caroline said. "I bear such a mark."

His smile was bright, relieved; Lucien strode to take her hand in his. "Then I believe you, and am happy for it. This house has been too long without a mistress, and I welcome you, *Justina*."

"You are kind, Lucien, but impulsive. If the papers come from the North, perhaps then we can celebrate becoming a family, my becoming legally white, through and through."

Leaning over her hand, he kissed its back gently. "I celebrate now. I would like to give a grand ball, invite aristocracy from miles around, but you are right; I am impulsive, and you mentioned danger—"

"It would be better no one knows I am here," she murmured, "not just yet. As you say, we have much to discuss."

He left her side to tug at a bellpull, and she thought how good he was, a handsome man only a few years older than herself and sensitive. Were they truly sired by the same father from different mothers? Caroline wanted desperately to think so, but she would not claim blood kinship to him until she was certain.

"Escort mademoiselle to the guest rooms," he said to the mulatto maid who appeared. "Not Gabrielle's room, you understand, the one beside it. I will bring dresses for her to choose from."

The woman's liquid eyes touched hers only briefly. "Yessuh."

"And a bath," Lucien said. "Soaps, perfumes, all that a lady requires." To Caroline he said, "Until later, then, Justina."

The maid glanced up and away, and Caroline knew the name meant something, realized that keeping her presence here secret might be difficult. Black gossip passed among them swiftly, leaping from servant to servant across fields and into the city. She would have to find a way to block its passage, else Lucien LeCroix

350

might be endangered, also. The arm of Felipe de Alcantari's vengeance stretched far.

Following the girl up a flight of carpeted, curving stairs, she paused to stare at the life-sized portrait of a beautiful young girl. She was golden and glowing, and the artist had caught the light dancing in her seagreen eyes, the love that softened a rosebud mouth. Gabrielle, she thought, the wife yet mourned by Lucien. She moved on into a long hall and turned behind the maid into a suite of rooms that surprised her with opulence and taste.

"What's your name?" she asked.

"Netty—mam'selle." The pause was just long enough.

"For Toinette? A pretty name. Have you never been without shoes, Netty?"

The girl's lips poked out. "Not for me to say, for I know my place. I go to draw your bath now, as the master says."

"*Un moment.* Who was Justina?"

Netty's mouth turned more sullen. "Master's sister, it is said. But it is not right for him to call *you* by her name."

"If it pleases him," Caroline said, "it is therefore right. Or shall I tell him you disapprove?"

"*Non,*" the girl said, "*non.* He is not cruel, that one, but stubborn. He would send me away."

"Then keep it to yourself," Caroline said. "Not one word to anyone else, understand? If I hear a single whisper—and I am wise in the ways of blacks—I will ask Lucien to sell you. I am not cruel, either, but I fight for my life." To add strength to her threat, she slipped into rapid Ashanti: "Being sold is better than having your tongue ripped out or being staked on an anthill."

Netty's eyes expanded until they seemed to fill her face. Moistening her lips with a quick tongue, she whispered, "I do not understand that *sauvage* talk, but I have heard it often; never by a woman white as you. Perhaps it is conjure."

"Think on that and seal your lips." Wondering at

351

herself, Caroline marched past the maid and readied for her bath. As she sank into the luxurious hot water and lathered herself with scented soap, she realized her personality change must have been taking place slowly, and became complete when she repaid her rapists with the dirk, that snug, deadly little weapon that rested now beside the tub, so that Netty stepped gingerly around it.

Survive, Solah said; *stay alive.*

There was more than one path to survival, not always through letting men do what they wanted to her body. There was also the way of strength, that of the blade.

Great, powerful Jubal Blaze already knew that, and it did not spoil his gentleness. Maybe even now he was waiting for her, had left his note in the garden gate of the Lafitte house. Caroline thrilled to the thought, her warmed flesh tingling.

Jubal again, taking her in his arms, his big, hard body so tenderly against her own, not taking, but giving, giving—and there was the difference. It made a woman need to give back.

She would not tell him what had happened aboard the *Maryland*, for it would only hurt him. Neither would she allow Felipe's path to cross his, for that might kill him, and she would kill Felipe herself to save Jubal Blaze from harm.

Rinsing her body with new water, Caroline stood up, fingers straying to the mark of the scorpion upon her buttock. *A bad sign,* the conjure woman had said, as had the voodoo doctor. Well, the scorpion could also sting its enemies.

She stepped from the tub and the maid reached to fold her in a huge, fluffy towel. Caroline knew then she'd won, that the girl was terrified, and there'd be no gossip to race into New Orleans and Felipe de Alcantari. Not just yet, anyhow.

A knock came at the door, and Caroline nodded Netty to open it. Feeling girlish and spritely, she stepped forward to smile at Lucien LeCroix, who stood upon the threshold with a mighty pile of women's clothing overflowing his arms.

When he smiled in return, for one startled and uneasy moment, he was not a man who might possibly be her half brother, but simply a charming man.

Chapter 37

The docks were busy, but there was an air of tension about the river and hanging over the city, a nervousness apparent in sweating stevedores, an eagerness that showed in Jackson's prowling troops. Jubal Blaze saw to the unloading of the flint kegs and found a wagon to haul them out to camp.

He was anxious to be done with military foofaraw until the actual battle was to hand, because *she* was somewhere in this bustling town, deepsoft eyes and redripe mouth and the enchantment of that pale golden body. Jubal had to get to her, see her, talk with Caroline of his plans for their future.

Barton Roberts stood on the dock and spat his chaw into the hurrying river. "Reckon ol' Major Benton'll be put out that we made it back, totin' what we went after. I swony, I don't know how Andy puts up with that uppity bastard, after he had a hand gettin' the gen'l shot like that. We goin' straight to him?"

"Straight to camp," Jubal said, "and get them flints to the men. From all this stirrin' around I see, the fight must be gettin' pretty close."

Peering downriver, Barton Roberts said, "Ain't nothin' sailin' upstream, looks like. Means the Redcoats got a stopper in the river mouth."

"Most like," Jubal said as the last keg was loaded into the wagon. "And was it me runnin' the war for the lobsterbacks, I'd already have men put on shore down yonder, ready to march on the city."

Cody Youngblood sauntered over to join them, saying, "Expect the gen'l got him any help from these Frenchies yet?"

"If'n he ain't," Jubal said, "we can handle it ourselves."

"That there Frenchie you busted up on the bank," Barton Roberts said. "You mean to do somethin' about his friends?"

"Soon's we get unloaded and I see Andy," Jubal said, fretting because that too would keep him from seeing Caroline Monteleone. But not for long, he told himself; he'd slip a note into the castiron gate of that special house where they'd spent the night, and be back with his shirttail flying. Would she be ready for him? That dandy with a hold on her—could she cut loose from the man in a hurry, or would there be some kind of complication? Jubal wasn't about to put up with too much delay, was it the lacecuff Frenchie's fault.

"I'm in an almighty hurry," Jubal announced. "You all get that wagon out to the quartermaster at camp, and mind you keep a sharp eye along the way. Some folks was damned anxious for that flint not to get home, and might be they'll try again atwixt here and yonder."

Cody Youngblood grunted. "Purely hope so; I ain't forgot ol' Daniel Smith head-shot and knocked in the river. Whole damned tribe of Injuns don't pay back for Daniel."

"Them tied to that de la Rassac feller might," Jubal answered. "I mean to see to 'em right off."

Climbing onto the wagon, Youngblood said, "Was you to have trouble gettin' answers out'n 'em, I'd be obliged did you call on me. Good as ary Injun with a skinnin' knife, I reckon."

"I'll do that," Jubal promised, and turned to trot away from the river, shouldering his way through what seemed to be an aimlessly eddying crowd. Used to Tennessee and Carolina men by now, nobody gave his long gun and smoke-blackened buckskins a second glance, so he made good time to Rue Bourbon and down it to the Absinthe House where Andy Jackson had his sometime headquarters.

This time of day, only a few brightly dressed Creoles sat at the bar and gaming tables, but a careful whisper followed Jubal into the back. Some of them must have been here, he thought, when that little bantam rooster pointed a sword cane at Jubal's throat and got thrown across the room for it.

The general wasn't in, the sentry said, but Colonel Coffee and the major were. Naturally, Benton would be hanging around a warm dry place, Jubal thought, while Andy was out checking defense positions and the like.

Reporting to Colonel Coffee, he said, "Got the flint, enough for two, three armies, I reckon."

From the corner, Major Benton said, "It took you long enough, Captain. We were about to give you up as lost."

"And hopin' so," Jubal said.

Benton stood up. "What do you mean by that, sir?"

Colonel Coffee made a conciliatory move, but Jubal said, "Just about anything you want to read into it, Major. I been led on a fox chase, jumped on, shot at and damned near sunk a time or two. I just ain't in no mood to diddle around with you."

Benton bristled. "Sir, if you were a gentleman—"

"Whatever the hell that might be," Jubal said. "Can't be land nor money, account of Tarboro plantation's got enough of both to put the Bentons in the shade twice over. But if it's actin' prissy and dressin' pretty, I expect I ain't much of a gentleman, and best you take that to heart, mister. Any kind of duelin' foolishness like you mixed up with on the gen'l, and *I'm* purely bound to act like any other ol' woods runner. Which means I'll just jerk your head clean off'n your shoulders and kick it across the pasture."

Red in the face, wheezing with rage, Benton choked out: "Colonel, you—you are my witness. I demand satisfaction."

Coffee said, "Now, gentlemen, the general has

specifically forbidden affairs of honor until this campaign is finished."

"Honor, shit," Jubal snorted. "You challenge me, and I'll choose pine saplings so long you can't even pick yours up, much less swing it—or mayhap I'll choose flat-out ass kickin' or head-buttin'. Whichever, when it's done with, there'll be a dead man on the field. Nobody walks away with his arm in a sling and talkin' about first blood."

Gone ashen now, Major Benton steadied himself by gripping the table edge. "I—I should have known a piney woods farmer would have no conception of gentlemanly honor."

"Got a conception to pitch you out through the window, you don't keep your mouth off me." When Benton spluttered into venomous silence, Jubal said to Coffee: "Got a stopover or two to make afore gettin' to camp."

"Go ahead," the colonel said. "You've earned it. But see that your company is ready; we expect word of the British land march any day."

Stopping at the bar, Jubal bought a drink, then another. They didn't add to the racing of his blood, for the image of Caroline had already done that. Borrowing pen and paper from the publican, he scratched out a letter, clumsy at it and wishing he could tell her how he felt, say it pretty as men who wrote books.

He found the little house with the garden behind its gate, disconsolate because there was no message there for him. Tucking his letter safely into a little iron curlicue where the wind couldn't steal it, Jubal stood awhile, hoping hard that somebody might move around in the house. But its windows were deserted, the house silent; no smoke curled from its chimney. Shoulders drooping, he moved away and headed for Rue Royale.

Jubal could pass a certain tree in the woods, mark it in his mind, and come back to it months later, straight as a bee with a load of pollen. He cruised the crowded street until the place looked right, felt right, and entered the building where Madame Lisette de la Rassac lived.

Brushing aside a black doorman, he stalked into the luxurious house and headed for the bedroom where he'd spent some delightful hours with a beautiful, eager wife. Ready wife and a home designed to lull an unsuspecting, stupid farmer; he'd come to both with the assistance of one Tom Pickett. Pickett knew about the flint shortage in Jackson's army, and the woman—God knew what he'd rattled on to her about while he was in his cups and befuddled by the deftly sinuous attention she paid him.

She turned from the dressing table as he crashed back the door, lovely and lush as ever, all creamy skin and downcurling hair, those melon breasts full and firm. "Why—*Capitaine* Blaze! How nice to see you again, but I didn't hear you announced, and to just break into a lady's boudoir—"

"Where's Tom Pickett?" Jubal still carried his rifle, and brought the smell of forest and campfire into her room, overpowering those delicate, musky perfumes.

A smoothly arched brow lifted at him. "M'sieu Pickett? I have no idea, *chéri.*"

"No more'n you know where your husband is, I 'spect."

She stroked a brush over her shining hair, shrugged nearly bare and shining shoulders. "Michel travels here and there. I do not concern myself too much with his whereabouts."

Watching her, Jubal listened behind him and sat upon the edge of her bed, that exciting bed he'd shared with her. Before Caroline, he reminded himself. "Don't reckon you have to fret about your husband travelin' no more," he said, seeing no reason to soften the news. Spies, all of them, or at best English sympathizers who'd made a fool of him and endangered the defense of the city—*their* city.

"Your man is dead," Jubal said. "He set Injuns on us comin' down the river. I caught him on land and killed him. Don't seem right, puttin' horns on a man by diddlin' his wife, then havin' to let daylight through him. Most times, it's the other way around."

She sat unmoving upon the stool before her mirrored table, hairbrush in midstroke. It seemed a long time before her lips moved. "M-Michel? Michel is d-dead—and you killed him? *Cochon—bâtard!* My husband, my Michel—you *chien lit!* You would shit your own bed—*chiottes!*—whelp of a mangy bitch—"

Lisette came at him with hair flying, long nails clawing and eyes aflame. Jubal slapped her hands aside and tumbled her across the bed. When she tried furiously to kick him, he put a big hand on her stomach and pressed until she stopped.

"Sure don't act like a lady makes a game out of cuckoldin' her husband," he said. "More like a woman workin' with him, using herself with his knowin' of it, and might be, enjoyin' all hell out of screwin' just the same."

She hissed at him and struggled helplessly, like a snake with its back broken.

Jubal said, "I ain't told Gen'l Jackson or the Provost about you and your husband—yet. I advise you to light a shuck out of Louisiana, fast as you can; was I you, wouldn't even stop to collect a whole lot of fancy clothes and the like. You won't look near so pretty in a jail cell."

Lisette went quiet, went kind of flat as emotion ran out of her. Pale, silent, she fought no more when Jubal took his hand from her.

"Won't be nigh so easy on Pickett," he said, "soon as I find him."

He left her like that, and moved swiftly from the room, from the scent and softness and hate of her. Outside, he eased into an alley and waited, keeping his eyes on the front door. It wasn't long before the black hurried onto the *banquette,* still dressed in the de la Rassac livery. He turned right, and right again at the next corner, as Jubal drifted behind him, keeping close to the walls and shielding his bulk with passersby whenever possible. But the man, intent upon his mission, never looked back.

Two more squares, then around a cart piled high with dried Spanish moss and past a fishcart, into a narrow alley where the black rapped at a door set into mildewed brick. Before he could lift his hand to knock again, Jubal was upon him like a mountain panther, stifling the yelp of surprise and cartwheeling him down the alley.

The door opened and Jubal hurtled through it, shoulder low and bringing up the butt of his rifle. Somebody stumbled back and smashed a wooden chair as he fell. Another man shouted before Jubal axed the heavy barrel around and cut the cry off short.

"Well now, Tom," Jubal said to the man in the wreckage of the splintered chair, "looks like you got your tail in a crack, don't it?"

Shaking his head, Pickett said, "Damn! Is that how you come into a house, like a wild bear on the loose?"

"Every time a man calls himself friend gets a real friend killed off on me. Michel de la Rassac now, he's paid his part of the score for tryin' to make off with Jackson's flint and shootin' ol' Daniel Smith through the head. Daniel now, he come all the way from Tennessee to make war for this town, and didn't figure folks in it to get him killed."

Pickett wasn't smiling now, and his eyes were wary. "Jubal—I suppose Rassac talked?"

"Just afore he died."

"No sense in my attempting to talk you out of this, making an offer in good, hard gold for you to forget everything you saw and heard? Jackson has his flint, so what's the harm?"

"Daniel Smith's the harm," Jubal said, conscious that the man he'd chopped with the gun barrel was stirring on the floor.

Carefully, Pickett kept his hands away from his body. "You'll never prove anything in court."

"What court? Andy Jackson's got New Orleans under military law, and that means he's judge and jury. Too high up to be his own executioner, though; expect he'll get somebody else to haul on the rope."

Pickett glanced at the man on the floor, then back at Jubal. "I'm not a traitor, Jubal. I'm an Englishman doing his duty for the crown. I could have had you shot in Natchez, or anywhere along the way, but I only led you on a chase, because I like you, man."

"Took a likin' to you, too," Jubal said, " 'specially since you might of saved my life on the street that night."

"Then let me go," Pickett said. "A drumhead court-martial, a hangman's noose—that's no way for a man to die, Jubal."

"Been a heap of folks died if'n I hadn't found that flint."

Pickett kept his hands high, and got one knee beneath his body. "You can't win against Packenham, anyhow. You can't beat trained British troops in a head-on battle. We would have had the pirates with us, may still get them on our side, since the American navy was stupid enough to smash their stronghold at Barataria. There will be a dozen routes open into New Orleans and—why should you care, anyway? The Creoles don't."

Easing his gun butt to the floor, Jubal said, "Stand up, if you've a mind to, but gentle like."

When Pickett came erect, he said, *"Franklin!"* sharply, and the man on the floor made a lunge for Jubal's legs.

Close up, the rifle ball almost tore off one side of the man's head, and the blast was thunderous in the little room.

Tom Pickett was quick; his head slammed into Jubal's chest and one hand dipped beneath his coat, all in one blurred movement. Jubal fisted him hard in the neck and pivoted to one side. Pickett went down again, but light from the alley winked on the dull metal in his hand.

"Give it up, Tom," Jubal said.

Pickett swung around on his knees, the pistol coming up. Jubal shot him in the chest with the short gun he'd taken off the murdering woman on the Natchez Trace, then triggered the other barrel when Pickett only jerked and didn't let go his pistol.

On his back then, eyes peeled wide and distorted mouth pulling raspily for air, Tom Pickett kept trying

361

to say something. Jubal stepped over and put a moccasined foot upon the hand still clenching the pistol butt.

"Trouble with you all," Jubal said down to him, "is you don't understand us atall. Was you to take the city, we'd just come on down and take it back, account of we *have* to. We don't much care a damn about politics and what the rest of the world's doin', long as you all leave us alone."

"J-Jubal," Pickett managed to gasp, "Jubal—I did like you."

"Me, too," Jubal said, "and that's the pure-D hell of it."

While Pickett died, Jubal loaded his weapons again, settled the little gun in place beneath his buckskins and hung the rifle over a crooked elbow.

"Reckon it's better'n hangin', anyways," he said softly, and walked out into the alley, where a curious crowd dissolved at sight of his set face.

"I will say nothing to a highwayman," the man gritted. "Nothing."

Chapter 38

Caroline looked and felt like a lady as Lucien helped her into the coach with its emblazoned coat of arms, its liveried driver and footmen. His former wife's clothing fit her well, perhaps a little too snugly, but the high shoes were perfect, and she luxuriated in the warm woolen cloak, the fur lap robe Lucien tucked solicitously about her knees. The maid Netty, suspicions allayed or at least quelled by Caroline's threats, had done an excellent job on her hair. It was piled in shining coils and ringleted around the jeweled earrings Lucien insisted she wear.

Her bruises didn't show, and she felt beautiful, cared for; she felt free. If Caroline knew a nagging of guilt, she put that aside, for it could wait until she was proved either Monteleone or LeCroix. Today belonged to her, from the crisp bright sunlight and the lift of excitement in the air, to the deference with which she was treated by Lucien LeCroix. For now she would be taken to the house with the iron gate, and surely, surely, there would be a letter from Jubal there. At the thought of it, her heart leaped and she could feel her face go hot.

Between them, there should be no secrets, but an open and honest sharing. Still, how could she tell him of her past without hurting him? No man could picture his woman being repeatedly soiled by rapists, and would he look at her differently if she confessed to killing other men? The softness, the tenderness might be gone from her in his eyes.

She could explain Felipe, she thought; Jubal would understand that much, feel her helplessness in the matter of being bought. And he would exult with her in the documents he'd found for her, be glad she could free herself forever of the Felipes of the world and take her rightful place in society. If there was no proof she was a LeCroix, then she would have to talk it out with Jubal and take his advice, for he was all that meant anything to her now. And God, how glad she was for him.

Beside her, Lucien said quietly, "This entire city should be at your feet, Justina; never has such loveliness been celebrated. Once this business with the British is done, I shall give you the grandest ball New Orleans has ever seen, and all will come to pay their respects to my sister, at long last returned to the arms of her family."

"Will they, Lucien?" she asked. "It will be difficult for them to forget another ball, where *gens de couleur* were sold to the highest bidder, myself among them. Felipe de Alcantari will not allow them to forget."

He frowned. "That one; he should have been removed from society long ago."

She put a hand upon his. "Please, do not even think of challenging him, Lucien. He is a dangerous, a deadly man. He *enjoys* being an angel of death. I fear even to be seen with you, for that reason; he will seek vengeance, and—and—" At the thought of being dragged back to the house on the Ramparts by Felipe, at the idea of this fine man beside her being forced to meet the hungry steel of Felipe's rapier, Caroline's voice faltered. "Besides," she continued, "I may always remain a mustee, with no claim to your name."

Turning his hand so that their fingers laced, Lucien said, "I will not believe that, *chérie*. There is this— feeling I have, although I find myself wishing it were not so." Lucien looked into her eyes as the carriage slowed. "I sincerely believe you are my sister Justina, but I carry treachery in my heart, a hope that you are not. You are—you are the first woman since the death of my wife—but enough. We are at the address you wished. Shall I place the letter for you?"

"Non," Caroline said, "but *merci;* it is a thing I should do for myself."

The gate was the same, but the garden beyond seemed untended, its flowers gone in the chill of winter. The iron panels were empty, and Caroline swallowed disappointment. Perhaps Jubal was not yet returned from his trip north. She stared at the house; it was a beautiful place, a place of magic. Carefully, she wedged her letter to Jubal into a cleft in the castiron design of the gate, so no vagrant wind could steal it, and hoped nothing else would.

Keeping her face shielded by the hood of her cloak, Caroline reached for Lucien's hand and was helped back into her seat. She felt his thigh tremble and recoil as her leg brushed it, and sorrowed for him. Turning away his face, he said something to his coachman, and the carriage started up again.

"The governor has called for volunteers," he said then. "He sits in his house on Rue Toulouse and writes dispatches for help. Edward Livingston does little better; he reads resolutions to citizens at Tremoulet's coffee house, but we Creoles do not believe a thing until we have seen it for ourselves. In this case, when the Redcoats are before our eyes, it will be too late."

Caroline sensed his reluctance to discuss anything personal, the battle he was fighting against his attraction to her. She said, "If Governor Claiborne had not attacked the Lafittes at Barataria—"

"A foolish, prideful move," Lucien agreed. "You know them well, these pirates?"

"Passing well, I think. Perhaps they are pirates, perhaps not, but in any case, faithful Americans. I saw them refuse to fire upon the flag, and flee. Those men are not prone to panic, and had it been the English flag, Barataria's stronghold would still be theirs."

She wondered if Catherine Villars and her Jean were safe, and remembered the *pirogues,* the shallow marsh waters beyond Grand Terre and Grand Isle, where heavier vessels could not reach. And Robert Gray; had he gotten away with his chief, or was that bright smile crushed by some heedless cannonball?

Dominique You was imprisoned, crowded with other sea rovers in dank cells of the Cabildo. What of Beluche, Nez Coupé? Caroline put her hands into her lap and clenched them. The Baratarians had made her one of them, and she felt as if she were somehow deserting them.

"Perhaps they can still be brought to our side," Lucien said. "Is it possible?"

"Some of Jean Lafitte's ships were burned, his warehouse looted, men killed," she said. "I do not know. This much I am sure of: if he accepts the British offer, Redcoats will enter the back door of New Orleans."

"So different," Lucien sighed, "such a change from those candle moths who can only flutter helplessly and chatter incessantly of fashions and gossip. You are a constant source of amazement, Justina. Delacroix plantation will be indeed fortunate to have such a mistress, one with brains as well as beauty. As regards the Baratarians—I will speak with General Jackson myself; he can certainly use their ships to blockade the river, their experienced cannoneers in his artillery. If he agrees to pardon them, is it possible you may know a way to contact Lafitte?"

Caroline thought of the little house where Marie Villars waited for Pierre. "It is possible." There was also the house with the iron gate and drawn curtains; someone might be inside, some daring person acting as liaison, as spy for Jean Lafitte. Who better than young Catherine? A pulse began to hammer in her throat; maybe Catherine Villars had found a note from Jubal, and was hidden waiting for her.

She said, "May I borrow the carriage for a while, Lucien?"

"Anything of Delacroix is yours," he said gallantly, wistfully. "Do you need money, anything?"

"No," she said. "But I remembered something."

"I will probably be busy for hours with the general and these Creoles who have to be talked into defending their own city. I had hoped to take you to dinner, but perhaps it may still be arranged. Cabal is our driver, and knows I may be found at Tremoulet's or the Absinthe House. You can trust Cabal—especially since Tchaka charged him to watch closely over you. The Mandingo seems to have a spell put upon him, but then, so do I."

When he alighted upon the *banquette* of Rue Royale, Caroline said to him, "I will tell you about the Mandingo, Lucien. He and I have protected each other, but were never lovers."

Lucien flushed and rubbed at his silken moustache. "I—I did not mean that, *chérie*. You owe me no secrets."

"We will talk," she said. "If I am to be a member of your family, you should know everything about me."

He doffed his hat and bowed. "Only if you wish to tell me. Cabal, drive the lady where she wishes to go."

Caroline watched him plunge into the Rue Royale crowd, tall and slim and wide-shouldered, a gentleman to the bone. She was proud to call him brother, and uneasy about the emotions shown raw when she was close to him. She didn't mean to stir him, and tried to avoid it, but his eyes clung to her every movement. She lifted her chin and sank back against the cushions. It would all work out when she was legally declared Justina LeCroix; Lucien would accept the inevitable then, and they would be a family.

A family; there'd been no such closeness since Solah died, and M'Nele before her. As Justina LeCroix, she would have blood ties, a home and roots. Perhaps there would never be respect, not here where wagging tongues would speak of her days as a mustee mistress, of her time as a pirate wench. But under the protection of Lucien LeCroix, the cutting words would not be hissed in her presence.

And there was Jubal. Oh yes, Jubal. She reached to tap upon the carriage roof. A slot opened and a blue-black face peered down. "The same house," she said, "the one we just left."

"Oui, mam'selle," Cabal said.

She saw them along the streets—Kaintucks lean and wolfish, sailors from many nations, mulattoes and *griffes libres,* satin-clad Creoles whose swords were part of their dress; windburned bayou men, raffish flatboat men—but nowhere walked the great red bear she longed to see.

"Wait here, please," she said to Cabal, and trotted to the iron gate. Her letter was gone! She looked up and down the street and saw only a sooty chimney-sweep and a brown washerwoman balancing a basket upon her kerchiefed head.

Still well oiled, the gate swung easily to her hand, and Caroline hurried through the sad winter stubble. She lifted the doorlatch, and it gave also. Inside lurked shadows, but she knew a lift such as the first woman might have felt had she been allowed to return to her garden.

"Catherine," she whispered. "Catherine—it's Carrie, and I'm alone."

A softly muscled body flung itself against her, staggered her, and they held each other, laughing, almost crying. "I—I thought you dead," Catherine Villars said, stepping back and wiping at her eyes. "But word came of your capture, and then you were thought dead once more. *Sacre!* You must have taught them a lesson aboard that ship."

"Thanks to a story about a mockingbird, and a sharp dagger."

"But the river—"

"Better leap into it than be thrown in with my throat cut."

Catherine shook her gently. "Ah, yes—I knew you had courage."

"Jean and Pierre?"

"All right, waiting in new palmetto houses upon Last Island. Jean means to come into the city."

"And Robert Gray?"

"With them yet," Catherine said. "Your great bear?"

Caroline stared at her. "You have not seen him, or the letter I placed in the gate?"

"*Mais non, chérie.* There is a place where I slip over the fence—"

Putting a hand to her throat, Caroline said, "Then he must have found it. He's in the city, Catherine; Jubal is here, looking for me. But—but why did he not leave a message for me, in turn? I—I asked him to meet me here, in this house. Do you think he will come? Oh, Catherine—he must, he must."

"He will; *certainement,* he will. Let us go into the kitchen where it is warmer. I must say, you do not look like a river rat, nor a Barataria wench, but a *grande dame.* You are not back with Felipe?"

"Never!" Rapidly, Caroline told her friend of Lucien, of his acceptance of her. "Lucien means to enlist, I think; to raise a company. But where is Jubal? The British are so near, and—"

"Drink this," Catherine said, pressing a glass into her hand. "There is much coming and going in the city; perhaps he had no time when he found your message."

The brandy was fiery, and Caroline gasped at its shock. "How many know of this house, Catherine?"

The girl cocked her head. "Only Jean and of course Pierre; and Marie; no more, I think. Oh—your red bear. There may be others, men with whom Jean has had dealings. But as many think he is to be contacted at the house on the Ramparts, through Pierre. Now of course, since Pierre is an escaped pirate—" Catherine laughed, and Caroline recalled that stark, tense night when they had helped free Pierre Lafitte from the Cabildo.

She said, "Lucien LeCroix is a friend; he may even now be speaking with General Jackson, urging him to pardon the Baratarians and use them to defend the city. *If* Jean has not turned his back upon the United States."

"He sulks," Catherine said. "He is hurt and angry, but not a traitor, my Jean."

Caroline held out her glass. "My heart is bursting, and I prattle of wars, when all I wish is Jubal Blaze. But I cannot wait here forever for him; Lucien's coach is on the street, and he will be anxious. Yet I *must* wait. Oh Catherine, what am I to do?"

The girl poured more brandy and kissed her cheek. "Go back to the carriage. I will be here all day and night, watching. If your man brings a letter, I will call him in, tell him where you are, how childishly eager you are. *Ma foi*—is this the queen of the Quadroon Ball? Is this the corsair wench who used a knife so well and swam the great river? I would not know her."

"You were as terrible," Caroline said, "before Jean saw you as a woman."

"That I was, but I was always certain he would. If this giant Kaintuck loves you one part as much as you care for him, all will be well, *chérie.*"

Caroline rubbed her temples. "I will return with word for Jean from Lucien, from the general."

"Perhaps your man will be waiting."

Holding the girl close, Caroline said, "Oh, I hope so. There is so much I must talk over with him, explain to him, ask of him."

"And do with him." Catherine smothered a giggle. "Hurry back, Carrie, but with more care, *hein?* It would not do for all the world to know of this meeting place."

Lifting the hood about her head, brandy racing in her blood, but not nearly so intoxicating as the thought that Jubal had her letter and would surely come to her soon, soon, Caroline paused for a moment in the grey-brown garden. Even if he had found no papers in Illinois, even if Solah had lied with her dying breath in order to protect a girl she'd come to love, Jubal would come to her. Jubal would understand. She rolled the honeyed taste of his name upon her lips, savoring it as she brought the iron gate to her and walked through it.

"Mam'selle!" the coachman called sharply from his seat.

But the hand already closed hard about her elbow, and she was whirled about to face Felipe de Alcantari. His face was dark with anger, his eyes like black icicles.

"Bitch!" he said, and no more, because she reached

under her hood for the dirk and chopped at him with it.

Clapping a hand to his face, Felipe staggered back, and she darted into the carriage, crying out to Cabal to hurry, hurry.

The horses flung forward, and behind the carriage, she heard the snarling cry: "There is nowhere you can hide from me! Hear me, wench—I will find you and drag you back!"

Chapter 39

Jubal couldn't get loose for a spell, there was so much to do, preparing his company for the fight. The men were fat and lazy, dulled by good food and wine and women, but they were in better condition than the companies of play soldiers he'd seen marching up and down in the Place d'Armes. Colorful Creoles at last come to the colors, laughing and carrying on as if they wouldn't have to face three or four times their number of hardened British regulars; dark Acadians fresh from the swamps, but with the look of men who'd handled weapons all their lives; flaxen-haired farmers from the German Coast of the Mississippi, their hands more used to plow and axe, and units of blacks, free men of color. That last bunch puzzled Jubal; it didn't seem to make sense they'd do battle for white men, unless it was just to get in some killing against other whites.

Hell, he thought, there was even a raggle-taggle band of Choctaw Indians going along, hoping for a chance to loot. When English artillery got to bellowing along the line, there'd be damned few sometime soldiers wouldn't be running for the rear holding their asses in both hands.

Horseback, Jubal glanced longingly toward the main part of town, where Caroline Monteleone was waiting to hear from him. Before long, he swore; first there'd been the settlement with Tom Pickett and Lisette de la Rassac, then old Andy so damned sick he could hardly stand, but firmly in charge anyhow.

And all the hullaballoo with the Redcoats already marching on the city.

Andy Jackson had him an idea, though; he meant to throw the British off balance with a quick attack, before they could get themselves set. So he was sitting his saddle now, shaken by fever and chills, his arm wound slow to heal, poised out yonder by Fort St. Charles and watching his troops straggle past, all twenty-one hundred mixed-up men, knowing full well about twelve thousand Redcoats were on the road.

One good thing, though; Old Hickory had unbent enough to accept a goodly bunch of pirates, and the corsairs brought their own field guns, their own ships to throw a blockade across the river so the English had to land far below the city. Bunch of them got turned out of prison for the fight, the way Jubal heard it. Seasoned fighters, those, used to cannon and cutlass and blood; precious little booty they'd cull from fallen Redcoats, and mayhap they were better at sea than on land.

Damn; it seemed like everything in the world was conspiring to keep him from Caroline. Here it was just two days before Christmastide, and he wanted to buy something for her, some golden bauble to match her flawless skin. And here he couldn't even get to their trysting place. Maybe, he thought, if the attack threw the Redcoats back on their heels for a while, he could ride over and see if there was any contact to be made at the house.

There was so much he wanted to know about Caroline, everything about her, from the time she was a pigtailed youngun until she'd bloomed into the ravishing beauty she was today. He wanted to hear all her joys, all her sorrows, to kiss her in the middle of a reminiscing smile and tell her she'd never again shed a tear.

And she was the only woman he'd ever wanted to tell his own story to, to expose his soul for. One night, he thought, a single incredible, fantastic night was all it had taken for Jubal Blaze to fall in love.

"Damned whistlin'," he said aloud, and Barton

Roberts marching beside him looked up in puzzlement, making Jubal roar with unreasonable laughter.

"Ain't *that* damned funny," Barton Roberts said, "account of them lobsterbacks might have dragged cannon off'n them boats already."

"Ain't laughin' at the fight," Jubal said, "just at how lucky a man can get."

Barton Roberts shifted his long gun to the other shoulder and spat brown tobacco juice. "You about the god*damnedest* feller I ever seen. Here it's colder'n a witch's tit, and us about to light into a whole passel of downright mean Redcoats, and you call it lucky. Your daddy must of busted you in the head with a lighterd knot when you was a weanlin'."

"Whatever he did," Jubal said, "he flat give me more'n my share of luck. Hell, *can't* no Redcoat stop me now."

Shaking his head, Barton Roberts said, "Hear tell Injuns listen to a medicine man tells 'em no ball can stop 'em. Seen me a whole lot of dead Injuns anyhow."

"Got some kind of spell on me, all right," Jubal grinned, "and soon's I can, I'm goin' back for another dose." Squeezing his horse, he rode up the column, howdying the men he knew, feeling warm in the weak sun, feeling good.

About nine miles, Jackson had figured, to where the British had landed troops, and if they had artillery with them, the attack might run into heavy going. But the spirits of the men were high, and they swung along in good order, eager for action after so long sitting around camp. No Creoles, these men, but woodsmen long used to trotting silently through the trees, their rifles a part of themselves. Jubal looked proudly upon them as they turned off the road and filtered over marshy ground and through cypress trees. He left his horse tethered there by the road and legged it after his troops, catching up just as they began to deploy.

"Colonel Coffee's yonder," Cody Youngblood said, "and if'n you poke your head through the brush, you kin see them damn fools unloadin' boats from acrost the river. Nary a picket out."

Jubal saw British sailors and a handful of men in skirts. Blinking, he realized the skirts were kilts, that the soldiers were Highlanders.

"Sure pretty," Cody whispered, sighting along his gun barrel. "Seems most a shame to cut down on 'em."

Over near the colonel's position, somebody loosed a shot, and immediately a ragged volley broke from the covering woods. At the riverbank, men staggered and fell; a few tried to run, but there was no escape from the sharpshooters.

"Lookit that fool," Barton Roberts said. "Runnin' head on for us! Damned if'n he ain't attackin'."

The Highlander came doggedly on, rifle at his hip and long bayonet flashing in the sun. Rifle balls plucked at him, spurted muddy sand at his feet, but he kept coming until a hail of lead cut him down only a few yards from the treeline.

Cody Youngblood grunted as he reloaded. "They got many more like that un, the big fight ain't goin' to be no Sunday social."

Following Colonel Coffee's signal, Jubal moved his men onto the shore to use their tomahawks in demolishing the boats. Methodically, the bodies were looted and everything usable carted off. Jackson's troops were used to making do or going without, and they wasted nothing. But nobody touched the big Scot who'd so gallantly attacked, except to cross his arms over his chest and lay his rifle beside him.

"Howcome they wear them skirts?" Mason McGee asked. "Sure don't act like no women."

Jubal said, "Tradition, I reckon." Looking across the river, he saw other British, a pair of gunboats. "Won't be long afore we're meetin' more of 'em. This'll make 'em worry some, though, maybe give Andy time to get his defenses set."

Smoke from the shattered boats began to lift into the sky, and Colonel Coffee waved the men back into the trees. Jubal moved silently, thoughtfully, memory of the brave Highlander still with him. Why the hell didn't the English stay on their own side of the water? It was a damned shame to ship men like that four thousand miles from home, to die needlessly.

He concentrated upon Caroline Monteleone, and the black mood left him by the time he was back in his saddle. Now he wanted to hurry back to town, to find some Christmas present worthy of her beauty. When he saw her this time, they'd talk about what was needed to free her of any obligation to that fancied-up Creole, and he'd get to give her the reward poster hauled clear back from Illinois. Jubal wished there'd been more for her, documents he was certain the weasely lawyer had made off with, but maybe the flyer would do as well. It described her birthmark perfectly, and thinking of that little spot on her satin haunch made Jubal's fingers itch.

When the column was back on the road, somebody started singing, and other men took up the tune. Jubal rocked along on his horse, wondering how Caroline had two names, and what had happened to her since the old poster. No matter; she was a whole lot more woman than any he knew or ever hoped to run onto, and he'd help her get her life all straightened out. Would she like Carolina and Tarboro plantation? If she didn't, he could turn it all over to his brother and come back down here. Anywhere was all right, so long as Caroline was there with him. And it would be good to stop playing soldier, to be done with war, so he could spend all his time with her.

They moved into the city and were met by cheering civilians; women applauded from balconies and mulatto women passed out bottles of wine. The men took to strutting some, like it had been a sure enough battle, but first chance Jubal got to leave the column, he took it, pushing the horse through the crowd and onto a side street.

He felt like a youngun sneaking out for his first doings with a girl, kind of shaky inside and trying not to tremble on the outside. Back then, he hadn't been sure what to do, or how well he'd come off, set against a girl who'd been to the hayloft a heap of times before. Though he'd been in more than his rightful share of warm beds now, Caroline still gave him that uncertain feeling which made him look forward to it with more excitement.

Turning up the wrong street, he was frustrated and angry with himself for not finding the house right away. The next one over, that was it—and there sat the special house behind its high walls, behind the castiron gate. Jubal dismounted and tied the horse to a hitching post, his heart sinking when he saw no letter.

But somebody moved against the house, a small girl he stared at hard. Sure it was Caroline's serving maid, Jubal pushed on the gate and walked into the garden. The quadroon girl spun to look at him, one hand on the doorlatch, the other out of sight behind her slender body.

"I'm lookin' for your mistress," Jubal said, "Miss Caroline. Is she about?"

The girl said something in rapid French and Jubal shook his head. "Sorry; I don't understand."

In halting but musical English she said, "Please come inside."

He knew a drumbeat in his blood as he followed her, a tenseness spreading throughout his body. Caroline, he thought; she was here.

"We—I don't care to be seen outside much, me," the girl said. "So; you are Carrie's bear."

"Bear?"

Her laugh was musical, too, and Jubal saw she was very young, but also very sure of herself. It was a shame she carried black blood; she'd be a raving beauty, otherwise. She said, "Me, I am Catherine Villars, and my—Carrie, she is not here, *hein?* There was a letter for you, but—someone took it."

"Took her letter?" Jubal took a long stride and towered over the girl.

"Easy, m'sieu—perhaps you do not know—"

"About that lace shirt Creole? I know. Was it him took my letter, and where *is* she?"

Catherine nodded. "Please to sit and I will pour

377

you wine. *Oui,* it was Felipe de Alcantari took the letter, and almost took Carrie, but she got away." The hidden hand came from behind her back to ease down the cocked hammers of a derringer and place it upon the mantel. "I thought maybe he came back, or sent somebody. I was ready for him."

Twisting his coonskin hat in both hands, Jubal forced himself to squeeze into a chair, glancing toward the open door of the bedroom where he'd spent that long and loving night with the loveliest woman ever to grace the sheets. "Is he her husband?"

A dark eyebrow lifted as Catherine poured wine for him. *"Mais non;* no. But there is a, how you say, arrangement. She don't wish it no more, her, but Felipe—"

"Damnit," Jubal said, "he don't *own* her. What the hell right's he got to grab a letter meant for me? And you said he tried to force her to go with him? I'll break that bastard's neck."

Catherine smiled. "I think maybe you could. But she is safe, our Carrie; she is protected by Lucien LeCroix. He may be her brother. She's been waiting for you, to find out for sure."

Jubal held out his glass. "Ain't got much for her, but I'm carryin' somethin' might do for proof." After swallowing more wine he said, "Mind tellin' me where she is, how I go about findin' her?"

"Delacroix plantation, out on the Bayou LaFourche road. But take care, you; Felipe knows who you are now, and he is a dangerous man."

"He scares the plumb hell out'n me," Jubal said. "But I reckon I better walk wide of him till Caroline says not to. Damn; wish I understood half of what's goin' on atwixt her and him."

"She had told you nothing, then?"

When Jubal shifted his weight in the chair, it creaked. He said, "Not much."

"Then me, I won't tell you any more. That is up to her, *hein?* But I wonder— Ah, m'sieu; life has its tangles."

"This ain't her house?"

"*Non*, nor mine. It belongs to Jean Lafitte."

Jubal knew that name; it had been spoken often around Jackson's headquarters, and not too kindly. "That pirate? What's she got to do with him?"

Catherine's eyes flashed. "Some call him pirate, some a patriot. But remember this, great bear—Jean Lafitte gave Caroline protection when she fled from her—from Felipe de Alcantari. If you care for her, you owe him for that."

A spunky one, this; Jubal glanced at the belly gun she'd put atop the mantel and wondered at a servant who'd have the courage to use it on a white man. "Didn't mean to rile you none," he said. "Reckon you're right faithful to your mistress, and that's fine. I been needin' to see her for so long, and to have that Felipe feller steal her note to me—you wouldn't have any idea what was in it?" After he asked, Jubal felt silly, because blacks didn't read.

Catherine Villars shrugged. "It was a privacy, *non?* I know she wishes to meet you here, but not when, not how."

Climbing from the chair, Jubal handed his wine glass to the girl. "I'm obliged, and expect I'll go find out for myself."

"On Bayou LaFourche road," Catherine repeated. "And m'sieu—remain armed and watchful."

The company could do without him, Jubal thought, back out on the street and untying his horse. There oughtn't be much stirring until Jackson got everybody out to the edge of the city and building a defense. Might have to put troops across the river, too, and Jubal hoped his company wouldn't be among them. He'd just as lief stay this side of the Mississippi, where Caroline was. Major Benton might get his back up when he found that Jubal was missing, but the hell with him. Right now, there was more on Jubal's mind than the British.

He rode out of town, asking around until the bayou road was pointed out to him, then put the horse into a long lope. That damned Creole, trying to force Caroline back into their arrangement—how bitter that

379

word lay on his mind—when she wanted no part of it. There'd come a time, Jubal knew, when he'd plain have to face up to this Felipe, and the day couldn't come too soon to suit him.

Letting the horse drop into a jog to breathe, Jubal touched his jacket where the reward poster lay folded next to his hide. Caroline would be happy to see it, and maybe it would settle everything for her. He meant to speak his mind right out to her, and she ought to do the same.

But what if she didn't love him, if she'd been just playing at love? Jubal hunched his shoulders, not liking to think about that possibility. Caroline couldn't pretend that well, he figured; nobody could. When he told her his true feelings and asked her to be his wife, he'd be able to read the answer in her eyes.

"Come on, horse," he said, "you're totin' a man in one hell of a big hurry."

Chapter 40

Still shaken from her encounter with Felipe, Caroline went directly to her room when the carriage arrived at Delacroix plantation. Behind her as she fled up the steps to the porch, she heard the horses being readied for the return trip to the city. She was glad Lucien had not been with her at the little house; he would have been forced to challenge Felipe, and that would have meant his death.

Upstairs, she poured brandy with a shaking hand and knew she'd marked Felipe de Alcantari's cheek with her blade, that she'd cut him deeply. The wound would heal, but his savage pride would not, and he'd threatened to come after her. The first sip of brandy tasted bitter, so she left the rest untouched. Sitting on the side of the bed, she tried to still her fears and take stock of the situation.

In Felipe's eyes and those of city officials, she was still his property, a slave. She had committed the unforgivable sin of slashing her master, a crime compounded by her running away to live with the corsairs. And if the authorities ever discovered she had stabbed three white men aboard the ship, she'd most certainly be hanged. Blacks were not allowed to defend themselves so forcefully.

Jubal—what if Jubal didn't bring back evidence that she was Justina LeCroix? She would still be legally a black, and Lucien would be forced by law to turn her over to her rightful owner. She wouldn't go, she thought. Catherine had said many Baratarians got away. They could be found and rejoined, and at least one of them could look out for her welfare—Robert Gray, if he still cared to.

This time the brandy lay better upon her tongue, and stilled her trembling. For a while, she watched the lonely flicker of the fireplace, but its warmth wasn't enough; she needed more, the secure feeling Jubal's arms gave. Maybe he wouldn't come looking for her until after this battle the whole city was awaiting with bated breath. But she could not deal with that, the chance of something happening to Jubal Blaze, so he'd never return. No; he was too alive, too vital, and his going would tear the bottom out of whatever world she had left, whatever kind of life she might hope to have.

Rising from the bed, she went to the vanity mirror and pushed impatiently at her hair. The woman in the mirror looked rich and safe and not frightened, but that woman was a lie. Would it be better for her to return to the Lafittes now, before she made fatal trouble for Lucien LeCroix? That was the logical thing to do, for Felipe would be on her trail even now. But what she felt for Jubal Blaze had nothing to do with logic, and perhaps a few more days at Delacroix wouldn't be too selfish.

Someone knocked at the door, and when she said *entrez,* the maid sidled inside. Netty said, "One waits below and asks for you." Lifting her eyes, she added: "A man."

Putting a hand to her throat, Caroline said, "What does he look like?" Not Felipe, she hoped; please, not Felipe.

Netty wrinkled her nose. "A Kaintuck who smells of horse and smoke. I—your pardon, mam'selle, for my conduct before. Mast' Lucien is so—is such a fine man, and—"

Caroline couldn't hold back the smile that grew when she heard Kaintuck. "And," she said, "you have hopes of his taking you into his bed. He could do worse, Toinette. I have no designs upon Lucien, so you have my blessing."

The maid's face lost its tension and Netty's eyes sparkled. "The one below—he is your man?"

"He is one I have waited for. If another man should call, a Creole who wears a sword and a fresh cut upon his cheek, and Lucien is not here, please tell him I have gone."

"Mais oui," Netty said, evidently delighted to be part of a romantic conspiracy.

Caroline didn't even look in the mirror again; she darted through the hall and down the stairs in bounds. In the waiting room, Jubal Blaze lifted from his chair with arms spread wide, and she ran joyfully into them. He felt so big and solid and *right;* she loved the scent of woodsmoke and horse sweat in his buckskins, the tangy scent of man.

When she lifted her mouth, Jubal's came down to it, gently at first, spiced with longing. But as they held the kiss, as she flattened her breasts against his wide chest and her flicking tongue met his, Jubal's mouth turned more demanding, more bold, and Caroline's entire body threatened to go limp. With an effort, she untangled from him as her eyes blurred with happy tears.

"Jubal, oh my Jubal! How wonderful it is to see you, touch you, kiss you."

He kept his hands upon her slim waist, his chest heaving. "Been too long a time, Caroline. I'll never stay away from you that long again, war or no. I—Wait." Letting go her hips, he burrowed into his jacket and brought out a folded paper. "This is the reward poster sent out by your daddy, describing his stolen baby—right down to the birthmark on her haunch, shaped like a little scorpion. Guess I'll have to get used to callin' you Justina."

Stepping back and unfolding the flyer, Caroline read it swiftly. "There—there was no more?"

Jubal said, "I figure there was, or used to be. Turned that feller's office inside out, but he must have hid out

383

any other documents—or turned 'em over to somebody else afore me."

She moved to a desk and placed the flyer inside. Turning, she said, "Perhaps this is enough. I thank you, Jubal."

"Was you to ask, I'd bring back the whole state of Illinois, or anything else you might need. I want to do things for you, Caroline."

She sensed his eagerness, responded to the hungry maleness that tensed his big body. His very nearness, his simple touch could rouse her as Felipe never had. Perhaps it was Jubal's honesty, she thought, the tenderness underlying his incredible strength; whatever his appeal to her might be, she was not going to question it. She'd as soon question the sun.

"Jubal—this isn't my home; not yet, anyhow. But I—I need you so, want you so much—" Caroline reached for his hand. "I think Lucien will understand. Come with me, my darling."

Moving up the stairs, his big thigh brushed hers and she trembled. At her door, he whispered huskily, "I been on the road and at war in the woods. I ain't fitten to—"

Inside, with the door pushed shut behind them, Caroline fitted herself to him, standing tippytoe to feel the power of him, the solid bulk of him. Her mouth raced over his corded throat, and her hands searched his chest, his muscular back, lingered at his hips.

A wordless groan burst from Jubal, and she felt herself being lifted, swept up and carried to the bed. His lips crushed hers; his tongue coiled as hers welcomed it, and Caroline was finding it difficult to breathe, shaken by the runaway hammering of her heart.

"Let me undress you," he murmured. "Just lie still, darlin'. Migod—you're so beautiful you hurt a man's eyes."

His hands were gentle, careful, as she arched her back, lifted her arms so he could remove her dress and petticoat. His warm, tingling breath washed her skin and moved at her throat. Shuddering, she reached for his shoulders and found them bare, his skin sleek and smooth beneath her ranging fingertips.

Knowing the caress of his lips upon her throat, Caroline stroked his hair, her body moving in voluptuous tick-tockings without conscious volition. Her breasts ached with the need to give, and Jubal soothed them one by one, loved them sweetly as his hands fondled her trembling body and found her thighs.

Back at her ear, her cheek, her lips, he murmured, "I love you, Caroline—I love you so damned much I can't think of anything else, anybody else."

Joyfully, she opened for him, and Jubal entered her slowly, slowly, and oh so deeply. She locked him into her body, made him prisoner there with satin clingings and silken surgings, holding fast to his maleness, digging her fingers into his hips and her teeth into his chest. Never had she felt so serenely beautiful, so wonderfully needed.

Moving with him, to him, over him, Caroline released all her pent-up emotions, and the bubbling tidal wash of them cleansed away the hurt other men had given her. She felt purified and adored, for while Jubal was taking, he was also giving, and tiny flames raced the length and breadth of her body, tendriling hotly along her every nerve end. Caroline absorbed him, inhaled him, became him in that final ecstatic upheaval that shook them both to the very core. Then she drifted in a warmsweet river among water lilies, limp and floating, until she was gently cast up upon a fairy beach whose soft sands were silvered by an understanding moon.

When the world came back around her, it was better, and she snuggled to Jubal, caressing him with all her body and her mind, with her very soul. For a little while, she was content, but far inside her, the little spark of renewed arousal began to glow, fanning itself until it spread leaping again.

So quickly, she thought, and knew she could never have enough of this wondrous man, never do enough for him in any way. In total abandon, Caroline made love to Jubal, meeting his every desire and lifting him to dizzier and wilder heights of passion. Each time was another marvel, another impossibly perfect blending, until, replete at last, they lay drowsily in each other's arms, while outside, the wind murmured approval at the window, and inside crackling wood made soft, small noises of applause in the fireplace.

At her ear, his voice was gentle. "Caroline—Caroline, you're a fairytale come alive, the princess who walked in my dreams since I was a youngun. You're the golden woman all men seek, and *I've* been lucky enough to find you."

"Princesses have golden hair," Caroline whispered.

"Not any more. Mine has hair like spilled midnight, but the rest of her is pure gold."

She was content to lie against him and listen to Jubal tell of his home in Carolina, of Tarboro wrested from the wilderness by ancestors and grown lush through the years. She would like it there, he said, even though all other women would at first hate her for being so beautiful, and all other men envy him.

There was Abel Blaze, he said, younger and closer to the land than Jubal had been, working with the slaves and the soil to produce tobacco and cotton, cane and food crops. He'd have to lean on Abel for a spell after he got home, paying close attention to running the plantation, as he should have years back.

"Kind of fiddled around too much," he said. "Daddy put up with me account of I never got in too deep trouble, but I sure didn't do enough on the place. Be different, time I get back."

He gave her a running description of the big house, a man's description which covered many things she didn't care to know and omitted a lot of things she did. "Not pretty as this place," he went on, "but reckon that's because no woman's been in it for so long. Abel's been waitin' for me to get married first, as the older brother, but I ain't put my mind to that, till now."

One arm across his bare chest, Caroline said, "Jubal."

"You ain't already married, are you?"

"No," she said. "Jubal, there are things you don't know—"

"And things I don't mean to hear, 'cept do you like hound puppies and fuzzy kittens; can't stand collard greens myself, but if you like 'em—"

She laughed and he patted her haunch, caressed the small mark there. "Have you the finest house niggers around; we mostly breed our own and hand-pick 'em. Won't be as many light ones, though; my Pa wasn't ever much for messin' around the slave cabins, and I reckon Abel's no great hand at it. As for me, I never went near 'em; always figured it'd be too much like mountin' other stock, calves and the like."

Caroline felt a little chill, and burrowed closer to him. Ear pressed to his furry chest, she could hear the slow, strong beating of his heart backgrounding the deep resonance of his voice. In the fireplace, wood burned low, flickering fitfully. Wind rattled the windows of the room and mourned under the eaves.

"Course," Jubal said, "you can carry your maid along; spunky and pretty as she is, she'll drive all the bucks slap crazy."

"Catherine," she murmured, "Catherine Villars, and she's not—"

"Won't have any breed her, less'n you so say." Gently, he lifted her chin. "Reckon I'm going about this hindside to, but I love you, Caroline Monteleone —or Justina LeCroix—and soon's this set-to with the British is done, I mean to marry you, if'n you'll have me."

Caroline pulled back from him and sat up. "Jubal, I have to tell you—"

The knock on the door was discreet but firm, and repeated itself immediately. Netty's voice came through the panel: "Mam'selle—I would not disturb you, but he insists, and I fear him. The master is not yet home and I—I fear him."

"Run her off," Jubal suggested.

In French, Caroline asked, "Is it the man with the cut face?"

"*Oui,* and the cold eyes."

Swinging her legs off the bed, Caroline said, "I am coming." And to Jubal: "There is someone—"

"The Frenchie," he said, "and you sure as hell don't have to face him alone; not anymore."

She slid the dress over her head and reached for the thin golden chain that had replaced the leather thong. Jubal had his back to her, and didn't see her settle the sheathed dagger into place. "I don't know how he found me here," she said. "Jubal, he's a dangerous man, and furious at me. He—I wish Lucien were here, but then I'm glad he isn't."

"Seen some bad uns in my time," Jubal grunted, legging into his fringed pants and pulling them up.

Before he could protest, she had opened the door and was down the hall. Hurrying downstairs, trying to think of some way Jubal would not be endangered, she saw Felipe de Alcantari standing stiff and ominous in the waiting room. Her throat went tight, but she forced herself to keep walking.

"A bit rumpled," he said, "but wearing finery to suit the lady of the house."

There was a big patch on the cheek she had wounded. Caroline said, "How did you find me? What do you want?"

His eyes chopped at her. "So saucy. Finding you was simple, since the coach bore the LeCroix arms. What do I wish? If it were vengeance, you would have already felt my steel."

"You trespass," she said with more firmness than she felt. "Leave Delacroix, m'sieu."

"Before speaking with its master? Ah, but I have some interesting facts to tell M'sieu LeCroix."

Behind her, Jubal said, "This feller botherin' you, Caroline?"

Felipe put a hand upon his sword hilt and lifted a mocking eyebrow. "So—the Kaintuck." His English was spitefully accented. "The Kaintuck you wasted all those passionate words upon, *chérie*. Are you certain he can read?"

Moving to her side, Jubal said lazily, "And you're the thief stole my letter, I reckon."

Caroline saw Felipe's face go dark. He said between set teeth, "Take care, m'sieu. I see you wear no sword, but that may not keep you from being spitted upon mine."

"If'n you can do your spittin' with a pistol ball in your teeth," Jubal said, "why, go right on and try."

She put a hand upon his arm and felt the tenseness in him, the coiled readiness that belied his casual manner. Felipe stared coldly at them together and said, "To be expected, from a Kaintuck. I will give you a chance to shoot at me, m'sieu—when I also carry a pistol. But later, when I have settled things with my mistress."

"That don't rattle me none," Jubal said. "She told me about you."

She knew well the cruel twist of Felipe's mouth as he said, "Ah, but did she also tell you she is my *slave?*"

The shock of it rippled Jubal's arm beneath her hand. Caroline tried to say something, to find words, but could only stand mutely appealing as Felipe chuckled and reached carefully into his satin coat.

"No derringer, m'sieu. I would not miss the pleasure of meeting you upon the field of honor. This is only a paper, you see? If you *can* read, here—see for yourself."

Breath gusted from Jubal as he took the document and his face was pale; a muscle twitched at his set jaw. "Says here—says here you bought Caroline Monteleone." Jubal might have been pushing the words painfully through gravel.

"At the Quadroon Ball," Felipe purred, "although she is much paler than the belles usually there. One might almost mistake her for white, *hein?*"

Jubal swayed at her side, and there was agony in the eyes he turned upon her. "Caroline—"

Felipe said, "She did not inform you?"

Jubal said, "Damnit, Caroline—"

"I—I tried," she said desperately. "I swear I tried, but the time never seemed right. Jubal, oh Jubal— would it make so much difference? If I'm Caroline

389

Monteleone or Justina LeCroix, would it change me so?"

"Ah," Felipe said, *"that* story, the missing heiress returns to the bosom of her family—her white family. I do not think even simple Lucien LeCroix has swallowed that imaginative tale. Has she informed you of the reward poster she saw in Illinois? What was the town—ah, no matter. If you will return my bill of sale, m'sieu?"

Jubal dropped the paper as if it scorched his fingers. His mouth was thin, and there seemed to be a shield over his eyes. Caroline could no longer look deeply into them. She said, "Jubal, whatever my name is, I'm the same woman."

From his great height, he stood looking down silently upon her, and Felipe said, "That might do with a Creole, *chérie;* Orleanians are more *sympathique,* but the Kaintucks have a word for such as you—nigger."

Jubal's lips worked and his head swiveled toward Felipe. "Mister," he said, "I don't thank you for tellin' me. I'm Captain Jubal Blaze of General Jackson's army, and I ain't hard to find, do you want to work up a duel over your—property." He looked at her again. "And I don't thank you none for *not* tellin' me."

Caroline could only stand sickened and helpless as he turned and padded swiftly from the house without glancing back, without another word to her. Her eyes blurred and she put one hand to her hot face.

Paper rustled as Felipe recovered the bill of sale and thrust it back into his coat. *"Eh bien;* today I shall down two birds with the single stone. The Kaintuck is disgusted with you, but there is still some business with Lucien LeCroix."

She brushed at her eyes. "You—you bastard!"

"Not so, *ma petite.* I am legitimate—no!—do not reach over your shoulder. I would hesitate to kill you, but perhaps the slicing off of one breast—"

Dropping her hand, she fisted it. "I would have told him."

Felipe sighed dramatically. "With the same result. These *sauvages;* they will bed a black, but never kiss

390

one. A provincial attitude, *non?*" He chose a chair and deftly maneuvered his sword so he could sit comfortably. "Now, wench—I think I prefer brandy, to cut the taste of that one from my throat. How you could choose such a primitive, I cannot understand. If you used your body and bed to ingratiate yourself with your—ah—brother Lucien, I might see." His voice changed, lashed out at her: "Brandy, you bitch!"

Caroline moved an inch, then another, choking back a bitter flavor in her mouth, fighting the need to scream.

Chapter 41

Was it only a few minutes, or had time stretched out long and thin? Felipe de Alcantari sat there smirking, legs out to display new hose and polished silver buckles on his shoes, sat telling her with great delight of the things he meant to do to her, once she was back in the house on Ramparts.

Time didn't mean much to Caroline now; she was trapped in that horrible moment when Jubal looked at her as if taken suddenly ill, as if the very possibility of black blood in her veins made her a pariah. Her own stomach turned as she continued to relive Jubal's shocked stare, his face gone ashen and set. She barely heard the detailed obscenities Felipe was mouthing.

Oh God, did Jubal hate her so? She had done nothing but love him.

"Justina and—M'sieu de Alcantari." Lucien LeCroix came into the room, and she couldn't remember hearing the carriage arrive. "Justina, are you ill?"

He was beside her, taking her cold hand in his. She said something inaudible, and Lucien turned on Felipe. "M'sieu, if you have somehow upset my sister—"

She watched Felipe rise and bow as he answered, "My apologies if I have, m'sieu. I came to meet with you, and if the sight of me has startled her, I am saddened."

"Come, Justina," Lucien soothed. "Sit here, take some brandy; it will bring the color back to your cheeks. Now, sir—you are a guest in my home by your own invitation. I must ask that you explain your presence."

There was an edge to Felipe's words when he replied, "If the name of de Alcantari is not welcome here, I might consider that a grievous insult. But welcome or not, I have a right to be here, LeCroix. I have come to speak with my wife."

She raised her eyes, no less shocked than Lucien.

"Wife," Felipe repeated, and brought other documents from his coat, approaching to lay them upon the small table. "Here—the banns, as they were published by the Church of St. Anne; the signature of Father Antonio Perez attesting to the date and manner of ceremony performed. The names stand out, do they not? Felipe de Alcantari and Justina LeCroix. You will also note the signatures of witnesses."

Coming up so abruptly that her chair crashed backward, Caroline said, "Liar, liar! I have never been in St. Anne's, nor ever seen Father Perez! Never have I spoken marriage vows with you, and never would I!"

Perplexed, Lucien looked from one to the other. "But the records—"

"Falsified, forged!" Caroline stormed. "Oh, you cunning, miserable man—all this while, you knew and were plotting. When I refused you—*cochon!*—serpent! —you changed your plans. Lucien, Lucien; please believe me. I do not know how he discovered I am not the mustee he bought, but in some fashion, he did. I am *not* his wife, and would go on the block again before becoming his wife, even in name."

Coldly, Felipe said, "Father Perez and the others will testify, if they must. But as a gentleman, LeCroix, I trust you will not sully your honorable name in common court. It will be difficult as it is, silencing whispers about your sister's past."

"Le grand menteur," Caroline spat. "What a great liar you are!"

"Madame," Felipe said, "there are limits beyond which even a wife may not trespass. Were a man to say that to me, I would spill his blood beneath Dueling Oaks the next dawn."

393

Through her hurt and anger, she saw the half smile play about his cruel mouth and realized what he was about. Lucien; he had come here to taunt Lucien LeCroix into a duel, so he could kill him and become master of Delacroix plantation. That's why he first asked her to marry him, why he had gone to such trouble falsifying records. Long ago, Felipe had boasted he could do just that, and none in the city would dare speak aloud. A wife's property belonged to her husband, and with Lucien entombed, Felipe would strut this land, and gamble its riches at the tables.

He was speaking again: "Even your brother must realize the necessity for discipline, madame. You will learn that a woman does not speak to her husband in such a manner, even before family. I think you will learn quickly enough, with a taste of the whip."

Lucien LeCroix shuddered. "Sir! You will not threaten Justina in my home. A gentleman would not—"

"*Oui?*" Felipe said silkily.

"No!" Caroline blurted. "No, Lucien—please. He is trying to taunt you. I—I will accept."

Perplexed, Lucien's face turned to her. "But if these are forgeries—"

"I will go with him," she said, her mouth gone dry and her throat aching. "It does not matter, my brother."

"But I insist—"

Caroline moved to lay a chilled hand against his face. "Please."

Lucien hesitated. "For you, then; for your desires only. I will have my attorney look into this affair, you may be certain, and I shall see to it that all officials concerned are questioned."

She was dizzy upon the stairs, and steadied herself with a hand upon the railing. How sly Felipe was, how thoroughly evil. All this time, he knew about Solah's dying statement and her burial in the back yard. The bastard had even forced her to make love that very night, and God only knew what lay in store for her, once Felipe got her back in the little house.

It might be worse than the pain and degradation inflicted upon her by the crazed LaLauries and their mulatto butler.

Inside her room, she stood uncertainly for a moment, praying that Lucien wouldn't allow himself to be led into a challenge. But how long could he, a man of tradition and honor, put up with taunts and deliberate provocation? Sooner or later, Felipe would have his way, and there would be another death under the Oaks; no duel, but murder.

Stripping off her dress, she eased back into her cleaned clothing from Barataria, and covered breeches and shirt with a simple, warm woolen dress. Riding boots looked incongruous with it, but they were necessary, as was the heavy, hooded cape and gloves.

Right now, Caroline didn't know which man she despised more, Felipe or Jubal, but at least Jubal Blaze wasn't a danger to anyone else, and he certainly wouldn't be planning outrages upon her body. No, for Jubal Blaze was just too damned good to sleep with her. Even if some way she was proven to be Justina LeCroix, there would always be that lingering doubt in his mind. He said her hair was spilled midnight; now it would be Negro black. *I love you,* he said; now he wanted to hawk the words from his throat.

Well, he could go to hell, and she hoped he'd sizzle beside Felipe de Alcantari; they richly deserved each other. Touching her ears, Caroline decided she would keep the jeweled earrings. She might need them, and Lucien wouldn't mind. She went to the window and lifted it; the kitchen roof lay below, and was only a short drop when she hung by her hands. Crouching there, she listened for an uproar within the house, in case her fall had been noted.

Another drop, and she was on the ground, bending low to dart for the carriage house and Tchaka the Mandingo. He was alone in the stables, and she rushed to him. "Tchaka, I must have a horse, and quickly!"

He stared. "What you up to, gal? Mist' Lucien, he know——"

"It's not Lucien I'm running from, but the man who calls himself my master. I'm trying to save Lucien from being killed in a duel. Damn it, Tchaka—"

But he was already leading out a horse and throwing a saddle upon it, big hands agile and swift with bit and bridle. "They asks, what I tell 'em?"

"That I rode *away* from the city. Can I cut across the fields without being seen?"

"Straight on ahint the barn, you headin' for town. What I tell Mist' Lucien?"

"I'll get in touch with him, somehow." She had a foot in the stirrup then, and lifted to the horse's back. "Thank you, Tchaka."

He said, "Look like you born to trouble, gal."

"Perhaps I was," she answered, and legged the horse around the barn, walking it until its hoofbeats wouldn't be heard in the house, then put it to a gallop. Caroline had trouble hanging on, but she meant to go far and fast, to get a good start before Felipe realized she wasn't coming back down the stairs. Cold wind whipped the hood from her head and flung her hair free. Wind teared her eyes and numbed her cheeks, but she didn't slow the horse until it was blowing hard.

Keeping to the woods as long as she could, she was forced to cut onto the wagon road by swamp ground, and looked often over her shoulder to see if Felipe was coming. She was into the edge of the city without seeing him, and thought he might have been thrown off track by Tchaka's misdirection.

Jubal had come this way, she thought, with his mouth set hard and frowning, putting behind him his dalliance with a black woman. She allowed the horse to walk, then put him into a trot that shook her backbone, hating Jubal with every awkward bounce. She had only one place to go, for certainly Felipe would head straight for the house with the iron gate. But he would not suspect her of going exactly where he meant to drag her—to the Ramparts.

Pulling the horse up before Pierre Lafitte's house and glancing at what had been her place next door, Caroline dismounted. Aching and heartsick, she led the horse right through the small gate and across the yard, to circle the house and hide him behind it.

"Who's there?" Marie Villars called out.

"*C'est moi,*" she answered, "Caroline Monteleone." The door flew open. "Come in, child."

"I may bring danger."

"We are used to that here. Come in."

Warming numbed hands at the stove, Caroline accepted a glass of wine. "Pierre and Jean, they are safe?"

"At Last Island," Marie said, "but they will not stay there for long. Good news, child; the Kaintuck general has accepted their offer to help his army. If the foreign ones do not take the city, the Lafittes will not be hunted men, but pardoned and in respect once more."

Caroline drank wine. "Dominique You, Beluche— others in the Cabildo?"

"Already freed. Is it not wonderful?" Marie looked closely at her. "But you are in trouble, and I speak of other things."

"I have nowhere to go," she answered, sinking into a cane-bottom chair and holding booted feet to the stove. Quickly, she explained the situation while Marie listened intently. "I thought first of Catherine, but so will Felipe, and he knows that house. So next I thought of finding the Baratarians and joining them again. Is it now possible?"

Marie said, "I have heard *un petit peu* of this Kaintuck. With him, *c'est fini—non?*"

"He hates me for the chance of black blood. That chance changed me from a woman he loved to—to an animal, transformed my touch to that of a beast he must cleanse himself of. *Mais oui,* my friend, *c'est fini.*"

Marie's face was sad. "It is often so, with us, of the blood. Catherine and I, we are most fortunate."

"So am I, to see him for what he is. Enough of such men, such pure *white* men. How may I find Catherine, for certainly she has gone to Jean?"

"They are below the city, five, six miles, near the Rodriguez Canal. Not far from Villère plantation, I think. Baratarian ships are blocking the river, but *les Anglais,* their soldiers are already ashore."

Caroline rose. "Then I go to them. Here, I will bring danger upon you, and if I belong anywhere in this world, it is with them."

"A moment," Marie said. "It is a far way on horseback, and soldiers travel the road. Rest awhile, have some wine, and I will see to a carriage. Besides, a dress like that at the cannons of Dominique You—"

Showing her canvas breeches, Caroline said, "I have these."

"First, the carriage, then I shall find some of Pierre's things for you. They will be too large, but warm—and a hat, a kerchief to cover your hair. One learns to be wary, *n'est-ce pas?* Such is the matter of the horse, for Alcantari will seek you that way."

"Marie," she said, "only a few whites have treated me decently, but the bloods—"

"Have bad ones, also. But we help each other because we must; there is no other way. Drink your wine and rest."

The stove threw good, crackling heat. Standing close, Caroline stripped herself, knowing the wisdom of Marie's advice. Felipe would be looking for a woman on horseback; if he saw her at all, it would be as a man in a coach. She drew the cloak about her body and stood with head bowed, trying to wash Jubal Blaze from her mind.

"Voilà!" Marie said. "Now there is a method of stopping wars. One so lovely appears upon the field dressed so, and all men stop shooting each other to stare."

Rummaging in a sea chest, Marie found woolen breeches, a heavy shirt and coat. "Keep the cloak," she said. "And you will need a belt to hold up the breeches. Ah—a wide one; this hat, worn but serviceable, a Baratarian kerchief."

"A sword," Caroline said, "and pistols, if you have them."

"I have seen the small knife between your shoulders. Is it not enough?"

"No. I will not allow him to make me a slave again. No man will do that to me."

Marie Villars pursed her lips and went to an *armoire* to withdraw cutlass and scabbard; from a mantel, she took a pair of pistols. "Primed and ready, these. There are others in the house, so do not fear. The coachman is Louis, a black who served Dominique You until an unfortunate encounter cost him a foot. He is to be trusted."

Dressed in rough, concealing clothes, weighted by sword and pistols, Caroline adjusted the kerchief around her hair, pressed the cocked hat upon it. Then she took Marie in her arms. "A thousand thanks. Oh, the horse outside—"

"Already hidden in a stall. Caroline—please tell my Pierre I am fine, that I await him."

"Certainement."

"I would be beside him," Marie said, "but he does not wish it, for the children." Her eyes dampened. "Take care, child; *avec le bon Dieu.*"

With a kiss, she was outside, hurrying to the coach, nodding to the hunched black driver. She peeped through a curtain and saw no movement in the house next door, Felipe's house where he kept slave mistresses, where he would never hold her again. There was no horse before it, and she smiled grimly; no doubt he was raging about the empty house in the city.

The coach jerked forward and she settled back upon the seat. Houses; she'd been happy in the small, clean one up north, but then she was a child with parents, or people who seemed to be. Then the shack at Kleppner's slave compound, grimy as the man himself, where she had to smile and pretend. And the house on the Ramparts, at first kind and warmly enveloping because at first Felipe had been the same; that one turned into a brutal prison.

The LaLaurie home—oh God; it would have been far better to die there in the fire she'd set, rather than to go on being used as a mindless piece of meat by them all.

Then the house with the iron gate, where she waited

for a stranger, a man both overpowering and somehow beautiful, and where the night had been one of
utter beauty. And Delacroix, another glorious time
with Jubal Blaze, until it all changed. Must it always
change, turn painful? Caroline rubbed knuckles at her
eyes, determined not to cry.

They were passing a group of cavorting Creoles,
young men shouting and laughing as they made their
way to war. General Jackson must have gotten volunteers from the city, she thought, and immediately
wondered where his Captain Blaze would be. Pushing
that thought aside, or trying to, she looked farther
along the road to where a long column of Kaintucks
moved at an easy, silent slouch, long guns slanted
back over their shoulders. Among them rolled cannon
drawn by straining horses, artillery served by men in
Continental blue.

Afraid she might see a giant of a man on horseback,
she drew the curtains and settled back again, wrapping
the cloak tightly about her. Where would she find
Catherine Villars? Possibly on land, probably upon
the river, surely standing beside her lover, who knew
her for what she was and happily accepted it. Some
men were such blind fools, and a few were not.

The artillery; she remembered that was Dominique
You's forte, the big cannon and the tales he told of
acting as chief to General Bonaparte. Perhaps he had,
but he was lieutenant to Lafitte now. It should be easier
to find Baratarian cannon, those guns they had not
turned on an American fleet which punished them so
severely.

The coach rocked ahead, slowed often by men and
horses, but never stopped. The air was damp and cold,
a match for her spirits. It mattered little now if she
was proved to be Justina LeCroix, for Felipe's manipu-
lations had taken that into account, and she didn't
want to be the cause of Lucien's death. Even now,
Lucien was gathering a company of his own and
preparing to march against the British. Not Felipe, of
course; he would swill brandy in a cafe and sneer at

fools who risked themselves for peasant Kaintucks. And he would pay spies to search for her, bribe police, hire hunters. She shuddered; her only safety lay with the corsairs, for they didn't fear Felipe de Alcantari or crave his silver.

Jouncing harder, the coach turned off the road and drove partway into a field. Louis opened the door, lined black face showing nothing. "We be here," he announced. "Got to walk it, here on in."

When she alighted, Caroline saw the stump of the man's foot, the crutch and said, "Thank you, Louis."

He bobbed his head. "Was you to catch up one of them sacks in the boot, I kin take t'other."

"Aren't you going back?"

"Uh-uh; figures to bring ol' Dominique drink, case they run out."

"But—your foot."

"I manages, missy. I kin stand by a gun good's anybody, I reckon. Ol' Dominique now, he set me up in business after a cannonball downed me, got my name changed and all, so's nobody'd know me for a runaway. Fight comin' up, and I mean to pay him back some."

Caroline smiled. "Perhaps I can handle both sacks."

Louis shook his head. "Much man as anybody."

She went to the back and unstrapped the luggage cover, lifted out a pair of burlaps that clanked heavy with bottles. Caroline gave him one, and Louis shouldered it, as she said, "I believe you. Which way?"

"Stay clost," Louis warned. "Them sojers liable to see you a woman and act up. I 'spect ol' Dominique's got his guns a piece down the line, yonder where them fires is jumpin'."

They went slowly because of his crutch, passing men who were busy scooping more dirt from a wide, dry ditch, others who were off-loading bales of cotton from mule-drawn wagons. Beyond the ditch spread a treeless field, rimmed with liveoaks, and farther off lay the river.

Cutlass banging clumsily at her side, pistols digging

into her stomach, Caroline began to pant under the weight of her sack, but she felt better anyway. She was nearing her own kind, men who didn't give a damn about another's color or origin.

Chapter 42

It had been days since that Frenchified son of a bitch had hit him in the face with Caroline's blackness and backed it up with a bill of sale. It had been days since Jubal had slept worth a damn, either, and thinking back on it, he figured he ought to have busted up Alcantari some, anyhow. But it was like getting kicked in the belly by a walleyed mule; knowing Caroline had black blood in her plumb knocked all the wind out of him.

How could any man reconcile thinking he was in love with a nigger? Only another nigger, maybe. God-damnit, she should have told him straight out, instead of letting him make such a fool of himself. And there he was, talking about marrying her and carrying her home to Tarboro. Jesus—what if their first youngun had come out black and kinky-headed? Word would have jumped all across the county and he'd probably have had to kill three or four men before leaving home. Jubal thought about standing to the men who'd put a bad mouth on his wife and son—oh, goddamnit, a son! He just wouldn't be able to do it, because how could a man stand to truth?

Sitting on his blanket roll, Barton Roberts said, "You been actin' like a cat just had his ass corncobbed and turpentined. I swony, was you to bite yourself, you'd fall out of your own pizen."

Jubal glared at him. "Ain't in no mood for funnin', mister."

"Whatever's got you by the short hairs, don't be atakin' it out on me and the rest of the boys. Take it out on them lobsterbacks; lord knows there's a passel of 'em waitin' out yonder for us."

By concentrating, Jubal was able to see to his shot and powder, a bait of cornbread and half a smoked ham for his plunder sack. Barton Roberts lounged back and went on like Jubal was paying attention to him: "Got us a whole bunch of new gen'rals, too. Be more like it, did they send us more rifles and less gen'rals. Hear tell the lobsterbacks got twelve, fifteen thousand sojers acomin'. Scrapin' the bottom of the barrel, I reckon we put together about two, three thousand—if'n you count them Creoles, pirates and two nigger companies. Goddamn; don't seem right for niggers—freeborn or not—to be layin' gunsights on white folks."

"Long's they sight on British," Jubal said. "You got nothin' more to do than lollygag around here?"

Unperturbed, Barton Roberts said, "Company's ready to go; boys is chompin' at the bit, figurin' won't be no Redcoats left, time we get there. Take me, now —I ain't all that eager to get shot at. You need help with that blanket roll?"

"Goddamnit!" Jubal said. "When I'd ever need help with anything?"

"Comes a time," Barton Roberts answered, "and a man's a fool for not takin' help when it's held out to him."

"Go on," Jubal said. "Go on and holler up the company. Ain't takin' my horse today, since it's only about six miles, so I'll be headin' the column."

Slinging his powder horn and bullet pouch to his belt, Jubal hung blanket roll and plunder sack over one shoulder, long gun across the other. Ready as he'd ever be, he stalked outside to head up his company. Moving them out, he stretched long legs to a fast pace, meaning to beat the reserve force of Kentuckians to where Jackson had his main defense line set up. Hadn't been for Major Benton's hemming and hawing, his unit would have been long gone before now. Benton

404

still had his back up about Jubal facing him down in front of Colonel Coffee.

Piss on Benton, Jubal thought, warming to the steady, ground-eating pace, and on the nigger companies sent out to kill white men, and piss on every goddamn shade of black and brown and that special shade of light golden skin that was nothing but a lie.

Cody Youngblood pulled up beside him. "Hey now, cap'n—you mean to run us slap to death afore we get there?"

"Boys want a fight, don't they? Bigod, they'll get there in time to make one."

"Way I hear it," Cody Youngblood said, "won't be a whole lot agoin' on till the mornin'. Maybe t'other side of the river, but not over here."

"Hear a heap of damned things," Jubal said savagely. "You hear one of them Creole lieutenants deserted to the British? He'll be givin' *them* an earful about our positions, the weak points and such."

Cody Youngblood spat tobacco juice and grinned. "That's howcome them Kentucky boys is suckin' hind tit; they're the reserve. But hell, I don't see there'll be no weak points."

"Get a better look, do we get there in daylight," Jubal said. "Tell the boys to keep comin'. Hell, they can't dogtrot a little ol' piddlin' distance, they been on their asses too long, drinkin' up fancy whiskies and whorin' with—with half-breed wenches."

"Black, white or mixed, atween their legs, them women look plumb alike," Cody said, and dropped back to the column.

Hell they do, Jubal thought. All this time, while other planters crossed their own blood on wenches, while they lay up in the slave cabins and passed out black wenches like cigars to visitors, Jubal couldn't stomach it. But along comes a woman looks so damned beautiful, looks so white, and he took to rutting with her like she was the best in the world.

She was, damnit. There'd never been better, but that didn't change the blood in her veins, didn't balance out with her lies about being a white LeCroix, and sending him on that fool's errand in Illinois. That prissy Creole laughed at it, that old story, laughed at Jubal, too. Could be Caroline was snickering up her sleeve at how she'd near put one over on a country boy.

Then he remembered her eyes, and how they looked at him. No, she wasn't laughing; she wanted right bad to get out of what she was, bust away from Alcantari and the brand of mustee. But she couldn't do that; no matter how hard she tried, the blood in her would not be denied. She couldn't slough off that nigger stain like a snake shed his skin.

He kept walking fast, heated body not feeling the cold now, wishing he could walk on until he dropped. Maybe he'd sleep the night through, then. Maybe he wouldn't dream of golden skin and a ripened mouth—all honeyed, of hotblack eyes turning soft as thistledown.

Up ahead, Jubal saw Major Benton's chill, petulant face, and slowed for directions. Benton pointed left off the road. "Center of the line, captain. It's the thinnest spot; see that you hold it. If you can't, General Adair's Kentuckians will come up to support."

"We'll hold," Jubal said. "Why don't you come along and see to it?"

Without waiting for reply, Jubal turned his column off and circled them behind the beehive of activity going on along a barricade of close-packed cotton bales. Good idea, those bales; they'd turn any rifle ball made, but cannon shot might knock them every whichaway, and the men behind them.

Barton Roberts was at his shoulder again. "Ever see so much to-do, cap'n? Wish it didn't mind me so of them Creek Injuns gettin' set to face us back in Alabama."

"Creeks didn't have that big ditch out front," Jubal answered. It looked good to him, that old millrace revetted with boards and some places twenty feet wide and five deep. It stretched for about a mile, anchoring one end to the river. The British would have to come across that, after moving through the big open field out yonder. Jubal felt a little sorry for them already, but only a little. Was they to leave folks alone, wouldn't be no call to shoot them. Might not be all that easy, he admitted; a bunch of cannon hauled off ships in the Gulf could make things a mite hot for defenders over here.

Heading his company into an empty place along the line, Jubal put them to scooping out the ditch more, and they got cook fires going behind the cotton bales. He looked off to the right and made out artillery pieces there; all along the barricade, shaggy frontiersmen were settling in, laying shot and powder close to hand, burrowing in like old he-coons facing out from a hollow log. They'd be as hard to pry out, too. Jubal was just as glad he was this side of the ditch, because coming across that field would be some like walking into a giant scythe.

He picked his own spot, with a good field of fire between two bales, and put down his blanket roll. Behind him one of the boys was cooking up stew, and it smelled pretty good. But there was nothing like the woman odor of Caroline's flesh, the clean smell of her hair, and the honeysuckle scent that rose from her parted lips.

Damn! Jubal snatched at his plunder sack and used his skinning knife to chop off a slab of ham. He munched it as if he was poison mad at all meat, and interspersed his attack with grinding bites of cornpone. Hadn't been for this war with the British, by now he'd be tearing up half the town, drunker than a skunk in a hen coop. That might help wipe her from his mind. As it was, he had to sit here and play all kinds of tricks on himself to keep from dwelling on what she looked like, how she talked, the way she moved, that special softness of her thighs and belly—

He was doing it again. A man had to be slap-dab out of his head to think so much on a mustee wench, and one doing her damnedest to pass off as white, at that. That "arrangement" she kept harping on—some arrangement; bought like any other slave up for auction, and used by that strutting Frenchie as his personal whore.

Rewrapping ham and cornbread, Jubal wiped his knife blade on his buckskinned thigh. And what he'd come to think of as Caroline's body servant, that sprightly little quadroon, why, that was her *friend*, and somebody else's slut. Seemed like the whole town of New Orleans had played him for a fool—Tom Pickett making up to be a friend and turning out a British spy; Lisette de la Rassac, bedding down with him just to keep watch on him for Pickett and her husband.

Cody Youngblood came up and offered a tin cup of coffee. Jubal thanked him and sipped at the hot, bitter brew, thinking it matched the feelings inside him. Cody said, "Never seen you so down at the mouth, Jubal. This here fight look that bad to you?"

"Ain't the damned fight," Jubal said. "I'm welcomin' that. When it's done, I'm for home."

Squatting beside him, Cody said, "Feel sommat the same; been draggin' ass through the woods after ol' Andy for a long spell. My old woman might be took up with somebody else, thinkin' I'm buzzard bait."

"Women are like that," Jubal said. "Smilin' and swishin' their skirts and apt to lie as not."

Cody Youngblood rubbed a hand over stubbled cheeks. "So that's the burr under your tail. Some New Orleans woman you took up with, she split the blankets. Now me, I never heard about you over in Tennessee, but them Carolina boys talk you up as a sure enough stud horse that don't mind whose barn he visits. Mean to tell, one of them Creole ladies put hobbles on you?"

"Mean to tell nothin'," Jubal said. "Beholden for the coffee."

Standing up, Cody looked down the line toward the cannon. "They say them pirates got women with 'em. You figure that's so?"

"I figure anybody messes with these women down here has got him a head rattles like a dry gourd."

Cody grunted. "Might be another woman can heist your tail and pull out that sandburr afore it works clear up your ass."

Jubal stared after him as he left, sensing some truth

in the advice. There'd be time for that after he got home and settled down to helping run the plantation, time to quit helling around and find him a wife, a good and solid woman to bear him sons. She wouldn't have to have any shiny black hair and a mouth flavored with honeysuckle; she wouldn't even have to diddle a man so wild and so tender in turn that his innards turned over. Just a woman to wife.

Jubal said, "Hell," and unkinked his legs by walking up and down the company position. Sure enough, this was the thinnest-held part of the line, and it was for certain that turncoat Creole would tell the British that. Thing was, this part of the defense was manned by the best and coolest shots in the country, bar none. Men who could head-shoot a running squirrel at a hundred yards wouldn't miss a Redcoat out to himself, much less come marching shoulder to shoulder. And with the Kentuckians hunkered down in the rear, ready to come running in case the British did get close to the ditch, attacking this part of the line would be worse than stirring a yellow-jacket nest with a stick.

Night was coming on and mist fingering grey through mossy oaks when Jubal posted sentries and turned in. Wrapped in his blanket near the coals of a cook fire, he made himself sleep, and muttered at dreams into the cold, damp night. The dreams were always the same, about a fine-boned woman with flowing black hair and golden skin, who kept laughing at him.

He awoke to the rattle of gear and a stirring throughout camp. Fog hung thick along the ground and like dirty sheets in the liveoaks, but beyond it could be heard the vast murmuring and shifting of the enemy. Jubal went at his ham and pone again, not knowing when there'd next be time to eat, not knowing if there'd be call to. On his left, the colorful bunch of Creoles and niggers were hollering and laughing; on his right, some pirates were singing French songs around their cannon. Jubal wished to hell that only mountain men were on his flanks, but there was no changing now, and Andy Jackson was mighty lucky to get those extra pirate guns.

Mason McGee squinted along his rifle barrel. "Can't see for that fog, cap'n. But listen at them drums."

At his right elbow, Barton Roberts said to Jubal, "Ain't drums that makes my asshole pucker, it's athinkin' about them rockets. How you reckon they fire 'em off?"

"Expect we'll find out afore long," Jubal answered, propping his ramrod against a cotton bale. The bale was handy to hold patches, powder horn and balls, too.

"Now," Mason McGee said, "there's a caterwaulin' out yonder."

"Bagpipes," Jubal said. "Heard 'em afore; squeal like stuck hogs."

"Sure take a heap of gettin' ready, them fellers," Mason McGee said.

"Just as soon they took all day," Barton Roberts put in, "and then changed their minds. Them fellers blowin' pipes and beatin' drums is the ones wears skirts, hear tell. Thing is, they got no better sense than to keep acomin'."

"Fog's breakin'," Jubal said, and something big and mean *whooshed!* overhead to explode behind them. Immediately, the pirate cannon replied, and from somewhere beyond Jubal's sight, big English guns sassed right back.

"Goddamn," Barton Roberts said, "yonder they come, and ain't they pretty?"

They were that, Jubal thought, a long line of men in red coats and black skirts, their bayonets shining where morning sun glanced off them, marching straight up and close packed into the open field. Officers strode before the line, swords up and glittering; battle flags fluttered. Along the cotton bales there was quiet, a stillness that pulled itself out thin and tight as a fiddle string.

Then a rifle cracked, and all along the barricade, little spurts of flame and smoke jumped out. Great gaps appeared in the line of marching Scots, but they closed ranks and came steadily onward.

Cannon were making such a racket, Jubal was hard put to hear his own long gun go off. He sighted and pulled trigger, reloading with quick and practiced skill to sight again. The taste of powder smoke was heavy on his tongue, and his skin prickled, his ears rang. The Scots came on, and now he could see red faces under bearskin hats, but not a whole lot of them. The ground shook with the roaring of pirate artillery, and suddenly the marching line wavered, tried to gather itself, then broke. Only a handful made it back to the cover of the trees; the rest of the proud regiment was down, most of them lying still, a few kicking and twisting.

"Mighty nigh a shame," Barton Roberts hollered, mouth close to Jubal's ear.

Jubal yelled back, "They ain't done. Yonder comes another bunch, carryin' ladders and such to span the ditch."

It was fire and load, fire and load, until the barrel of Jubal's rifle was almost too hot to touch. While it cooled, he used the pistol on a fool officer who somehow got across the ditch and up to the barricade.

Every once in a while, a British cannonball *whumped!* into cotton bales, or squalled off through the trees. The rockets Barton Roberts worried about weren't so much; they made a power of noise and scattered some iron about, but mostly far off the mark. Behind Jubal's men, the Kentuckians kept pressing forward, eager to get in some licks of their own, and at the parapet things got confused, some men falling back to reload, and others cramming into their places to fire.

Jubal elbowed some over-anxious Kentuckian and laid his sights on a man riding a horse, a man waving his hat and hollering. Horse and man went down, but damned if the officer didn't climb up and take another fellow's horse, left arm dangling. Aimed a mite too wide, Jubal thought and when the officer showed again through rolling smoke, knocked him sideways.

Off to the right, another line of red trotted forward over the bodies of those who'd gone before. A single pirate cannon went off, and the whole middle of the

411

skirmishers were smashed down. Must have loaded that thing to the muzzle with rifle balls, Jubal thought, and dropped back to give his place to a Kentuckian, near sick to his stomach of the killing.

Finding a water gourd, he drank deeply and splashed some on his powder-grimed face. There was a heap of brave men dying out yonder; this wasn't a battle, but slaughter, and maybe the British would take the lesson to heart. Maybe what was left of them would sail home and leave folks be, leave men to their hunting and planting and spreading ever westward.

Sighing, he took up his rifle and moved back to the barricade.

Chapter 43

They had hugged and kissed and were seated on a log beside the fire when Catherine Villars asked why she looked so drawn. Caroline glanced at crippled black Louis, being pummeled lovingly by Dominique You, at the extra supply of wine they had brought to the cannons. The fire was cheery and the corsairs cheery and Catherine's eyes sympathetic, so the story —the two stories—broke from her in a rushing tumble of words. She poured it all out, the cunning of Felipe, Jubal's betrayal, her flight from Delacroix plantation, the heartbreak that was hers.

"So I—I came to you," she finished, eyes blurred, "to my only friends."

Catherine took her hands and warmed them between her own. "And rightfully so, _chérie_. But with a battle coming very soon?"

"One also fights beside friends, _non?_"

"That _chenille_ Felipe, that trouble maker, and your great red bear no better, I say. To hell with them both, and as for Felipe's marriage claim upon you—I will speak to Jean about it, and something will be done. When _c'est fini_, this battle, _Capitaine_ Lafitte will be respected once more, adored by all New Orleans, and there is little they will deny him." Catherine stood up, hands upon her hips, looking boyish in her men's clothing, but very determined. She also wore weapons.

"Look you, _mon amie_, I must soon leave, must take

413

a boat to Jean's ship. Will you come with me, perhaps to the vessel of Robert Gray?"

Caroline looked into the fire and shook her head. "I do not think I am ready for Robert yet, for any man. I will stay here with Dominique You, Beluche and the others."

"Here there will be more peril, I think."

Lifting her head, Caroline said, "I welcome it."

Swiftly, Catherine stooped to kiss her cheek, "Other women from Grand Isle are here, to cook and carry water—"

"I will serve the guns," she said, "if Dominique You permits."

"*Bonne chance,* then," Catherine said. "We shall meet after the fight."

Caroline only nodded and looked after the girl as she walked lithely away. After a moment, she got up and approached Dominique You. He twirled his moustaches and stared at her. "So, you wish to serve the gun, *hein?* I will not ask why, little one; I will only explain what must be done. This rammer, it is to be used after each shot, to cleanse and cool the bore, to tamp the cannonball. It must be dipped in that bucket of water often." He hesitated. "Up there, you will be exposed to fire from *les Anglais;* does that bother you?"

"Nothing bothers me," she said.

"Ah, so it is that way. *Eh bien,* then: take out your hurt upon the British. But not tonight, *ma petite;* tonight we drink wine and eat; for some, it will be a last supper. *Les Anglais* will come at dawn, I think."

Court bouillon and hard bread were ashes in her mouth, but she forced them down. All the wine did was make her moodier, and she sat for hours just looking into the embers of the dying fire. But wine caught up with her at last, and she crawled into blankets to dream of a man with a single body, a man whose face changed from Felipe's to Jubal's and back again, for they no longer seemed so different.

Sounds during the night startled her, brought her up to stare about, and she had to keep telling herself

414

she was with people who could be trusted. Someone had kept the fire going low, and she was grateful for its warmth, for the guardian barricade, for blanketed men between her and the rest of the world.

It was almost dawn when Caroline jerked awake at a hand upon her shoulder, to see Nez Coupé's grotesque face grinning down at her. *"Café royale, mam'selle;* no other breakfast this morning, for those *Anglais,* they do not respect proper hours for battle. What civilized army would attack at dawn?"

She cradled the tin cup in her hands, sipping a hot and heady brew that cleared away the painful residue of leftover dreams. Keeping the blanket about her shoulders, she stood up and peered along the barrel of Dominique You's cannon, to see only cold wet mist shrouding the specters of oak trees. She had just finished her brandied coffee when a high explosion echoed against the earth; she dropped her cup.

"Hold fire!" Dominique You called. "It is only a rocket. Wait until I see flashes from their real guns." He squinted through a ship's glass at the writhing fog. Something large and heavy rushed overhead, and he said with satisfaction, "Ah, there!" and leaned to make adjustments with the gunscrew before kissing the touchhole with a smoldering match.

The cannon bellowed and jumped back, leaped up. When it came to rest, Caroline was through the cotton bales to swab its throat, to wait until powder and shot had been fed it, so she could seat the ball firmly with her rammer.

Once later, she caught a glimpse of English soldiers marching toward them, but she was kept too busy for staring. Musket balls plucked at the barricade, and heavier iron slashed at mounded earth near the ditch, came thundering overhead to snatch limbs from liveoaks or claw a giant hand at cotton bales.

She had never heard such noise. At first each was distinct: men yelling, cannon slamming, the lighter crack of busy rifles, but soon it blended into a continuous, painful roar that stormed around her, grinding right through her sweating, tiring body. It became hard work, scampering from the barricade, dipping the swab, passing it into the barrel, waiting until the gun was loaded, leaning her weight into tamping the ball, then jumping back to cover until the gun had hurled another defiance at the enemy.

Powder smoke blackened her face and arms; its acrid taste was thick in her mouth, and she began to feel bruises from bumping into things, to know a dragging of tired arms and weary legs. But Caroline kept going until blessedly, for a while at least, the guns fell silent. Dominique You handed her a cup of wine which she drank greedily.

"You are a good cannoneer," he said. "Rest while you may, little one. *Les Anglais* have not given up the fight yet."

Caroline used the time to refill her water bucket, to mop at her streaked face. A tall, thin man rode up on a prancing horse, followed by lesser men in blue coats. He looked ill and drawn, but his face, beneath a shock of white hair, was glowing.

"Captain Dominique, is it? Why have you ceased firing?"

Dominique You turned up dirty palms. "The powder, *mon général;* it is good to shoot blackbirds, perhaps, but not Redcoats."

She watched General Andrew Jackson turn in his saddle and snarl at an aide: "Bigod, tell the ordnance officer he'll be shot as a traitor if Dominique complains again of his powder."

As the man cantered his horse away, Caroline heard him say, "I wish I had fifty such guns on this line, with five hundred such devils behind them."

Tugging at his moustache and grinning, Dominique You said, "That one, he could be a Baratarian; a few generals like him, and we might be marching on London. But who would want such a dreary city? *Alors, mes amis*—it seems new powder has arrived."

"And new British," Caroline sighed, crawling to her feet and propping erect with her rammer. The battlefield was cluttered with tangled piles of dead and moaning wounded, yet when she looked up and down the line behind the barricade, she could see no injured. Stupidly, impossibly, fresh English troops were advancing across the littered field, jaunty and confident as if most of their comrades hadn't been killed.

"Fire!" called Dominique You, to his guns of Battery Three, and "Fire!" echoed Beluche to his cannons of Battery Four. The slaughter began anew.

Caroline was unaware that rifles had stopped firing, or that the attack was destroyed. She knew only that the gun barrel was elevated, so she had to go tippytoe to use her swab, that enemy cannonballs kept striking around them. When she at last reeled away from the sizzling gun, her legs gave way and she sat down hard. Her ears rang and she coughed in the eddying smoke. In a moment, she realized that a great stillness hung upon the field, a heavy quiet broken only by the crying of the wounded.

"Is—is it over?" she asked. "Will they come again?"

Dominique You placed a hand upon her shoulder. "I hope not, *chérie*. It does not please me, to shoot down such brave men. For our Kaintuck riflemen, it was done an hour past. We have been at work silencing a stubborn English battery. Yes, I think the battle for *Nouvelle Orléans,* it is over, such a short time after it began."

Sagging, Caroline rested her head upon a cotton bale and closed her eyes. Someone gave her a wet rag, and she passed it over her face; somebody else presented a bottle of red wine, and she gulped at it. Maybe she fell asleep, but perhaps she only rested, blocking out sound and sight and pity. When next she blinked around, Baratarians were squatted around new fires, eating and laughing and drinking in celebration. But then, these men were used to walking with sudden death, and she was not. Somehow, it seemed much worse to destroy men who had done nothing personal to her.

Beluche brought her another bottle, leaving it at her feet when she only stared owlishly at him. *"Eh bien*, little cannoneer, put it from your mind. It is always thus, the need for a fête after battle."

"To celebrate what?" she asked.

"Being alive," he said, and walked away.

She murmured after him, "If that is so precious."

This time, she did sleep a little, curled into a ball on the ground, warmed more by wine than by a slow sun that penetrated the fog and chased its last wisps from the field. Someone put blankets over her, and another man made a roll for her head; she never felt him slide it beneath her.

Coming awake all at once, she felt as if she were smothering, and fought free of blankets to dare a look beyond the ditch. Lean Kaintucks were out there, doing what they could for British wounded; Creoles and *griffes libres* bound hurts and brought water. She thought she even recognized some Baratarians out there, but knew she wasn't going to join them. Instead, she dipped a bucket of fresh water from a barrel and made a better job of washing, using her head kerchief for a towel.

"You are still upset, *chérie?*" Dominique You balanced a wine bottle upon his knee after sitting on a bale. "Wars are foolish, *hein?* There is little either side could do with that field, yet so many men bled upon it. It is more reasonable to fight for gold."

"Or freedom," said Caroline.

He drank wine and wiped his moustache with the back of his hand. "In all wars, one side or the other claims they fight for freedom." Dominique You drank again. "But nobody is free."

"I will be," she said.

"To *liberté,* then." He pointed a fat thumb at the battlefield. *"Egalité, fraternité;* all the dead are equal and free."

She patted the kerchief over her arms. "Catherine Villars?"

"Safe, as are Jean and Pierre. There was little fighting from the ships, but Kaintucks on the other side of the river found *les Anglais* more fierce. Defenses were overrun there, or run from; the reports are unclear."

Caroline put her jacket back on. "I must become a Baratarian, you know."

"You already have," Dominique You said. "Before this cannoneering, you became a corsair when those pigs aboard the *Maryland* were found dead and you were gone. We had no wine, we prisoners, but you were toasted anyhow. And I for one recalled just how Pierre Lafitte escaped the Cabildo. For whatever good it will do you, *chérie*, you are one with us."

He upended the bottle and tossed it aside. "In time, mules and men will come for these guns. For a time, we will be darlings of the city, but how long before we are called pirates again?"

"It does not matter," she said.

Dominique You shook his leonine head, that shaggy head too big for his small body. "Ah, it matters; it matters."

She put on her hat and walked a little way. Black Louis was not at his coach, but celebrating with his old comrades. She stroked a horse's neck, thinking she would wait for Catherine Villars, or return with the men; with them close by, Felipe de Alcantari would not come for her. Baratarians defended their own.

Lucien LeCroix would be disappointed, she thought; he had so wanted her to be his family—or something else. But it was better to stay away from him, for his life was doomed if she didn't. She frowned; Felipe might get Lucien on the field of honor, anyway, under some trumped-up excuse. Would he dare assassinate a man, then move onto his property, claiming his right as husband to Lucien's missing sister? Felipe would dare anything. How furious he must have been, to discover she'd fled, that he couldn't immediately wreak sadistic vengeance upon her.

Perhaps he'd flown into a rage at Delacroix and blamed Lucien for her escape; maybe Lucien had never returned to the company of Creoles he'd raised to do battle with the British here. Caroline lifted her chin and marched toward the Creole unit beyond; perhaps they would know Lucien's whereabouts.

A drunken nobleman laughed at her, recognized

her for a woman and tried to put his arm about her waist, but she slipped away and asked other, more sober men. No, there was no LeCroix in this company; perhaps across the river. The drunk trailed her and used his paws again. Caroline tripped him up and legged back to her corsairs, laughter following in her wake.

She stopped walking. Across the river; had Jubal Blaze also been over there, in a group battered by the English? Perhaps he was dead or wounded, even taken prisoner. Caroline commanded her legs and they took her reluctantly forward. It would be better if Jubal fell; she could not hate a dead man.

Did she *hate* him? When she thought of Jubal, she felt weakened and ill, not so much angry as sickened. Damn him, anyway! Why should thoughts of him intrude, when Lucien was so much more important? Even Robert Gray was more important, and she had not thought to inquire about his ship.

At her own fires, she asked Beluche what he'd heard. He was pulling on a pair of handsome boots certain to have been looted from a dead Britisher. *"Capitaine* Gray? *Le Bos* sent him for casualties across the river. Since every doctor in the city is out here, one supposes the wounded will be ferried to our Chalmette field."

Going back to the carriage, which crippled Louis had tucked behind a group of oaks for protection, Caroline climbed into the driver's seat so she could watch the river. In a while, she saw a familiar barque pull in next to a makeshift wharf of tied logs thrust out into the muddy water. As it rocked there, she caught sight of a bare, bronze head: Robert Gray.

She climbed down and hurried along the parapet, ignoring milling Kaintucks and jubilant Creoles. When she neared the floating dock, she saw them being carried gently ashore, the bloody wounded, the waxen faces of dead men and those about to die.

"Imagine," a Continental officer said, "we estimate three thousand British dead, with more to fall retreating in the swamps. The count here is not complete yet, but we believe we suffered less than a score killed. What a smashing victory!"

A doctor, his smock already soaked and spattered, moved to new patients. "Smashing," he said.

Caroline was moving toward the ship, toward a widely smiling Robert Gray, when she saw—"Lucien! Oh my God, *Lucien!*" she cried.

He lay upon the bank, eyes fluttering and cheeks drained of color, a dark splotch across his blanket. She kneeled beside him and cradled his head. "Lucien, hold on. The surgeon will come—"

Lucien's eyes had trouble fixing her. "J-Justina? I— I thought you ran—ran away."

"Don't talk," she begged. "Wine, *pour le bon Dieu!* —wine for this man!"

His pale lips sagged, struggled to form words. "But I must speak, my—my sister." He tried to lift his hand and could not. She stroked his hair. Lucien whispered, "You are the last—the last LeCroix. See—see that I am entombed on my land—our land, beside our father."

The weak and wavering hand rose with great effort, to touch her cheek. "A—a witness."

The doctor kneeled beside them and lifted the blanket; his jaw tightened and he put back the covering.

"Witness," Lucien husked, "for the sake of God, a witness."

"Oui," the man said, "I am Doctor Lejeune. How may I—"

"This—is—my—sister," Lucien whispered. "I claim —this woman—as—Justina LeCroix, heir—heir to Delacroix plantation—and—all—upon—it."

"Yes," the doctor said, "yes, m'sieu; I understand. If there were a priest—"

"Justina," Lucien said. Then the dark ribbon of his life flowed over his chin and he was gone.

Unashamed, she cried, held him close while the rain of her sorrow washed at his face. Lucien, poor, poor Lucien who had so long mourned a wife named Gabrielle, who had been so ready to welcome a sister. She held him and wept.

A hand stroked her hair and she lifted her face. Robert Gray said, "Your lover?"

"My brother," she said.

"I will see to him," Robert said. "Caroline, I will see to him."

"Justina," she corrected. "Call me Justina LeCroix."

A hand stroked her hair and she lifted her face.

Chapter 44

Dry-eyed, she listened to the priest's incantations, to his friends who stared questions at her as they said Sorry, sorry. Caroline heard wailing from the slave quarters, heard the death song and knew they worried over what would happen to them.

Long after the others had departed in their coaches, wearing black dress or black ribbons, she stood by while Tchaka the Mandingo sealed the niche with mortar. Lucien LeCroix lay in his family tomb, one of the few—oh, very few—Americans killed in the battle. Now she was the last LeCroix. Lucien had said it, claimed her with his dying breath. She would accept the part.

Moving from the cemetery and its gnarled watchman oaks, she went to the big house, holding her long skirts from contact with the damp ground. On the veranda, two corsairs looked cold, so she invited them inside. They were Robert Gray's men, and more of them were about the place. She was grateful to Robert for seeing to details, for bringing Lucien home and arranging the funeral.

She crossed the waiting room and turned into the library, feeling pale and solemn in another dress from Gabrielle LeCroix's *armoire*. With few alterations, all the clothing would fit, and from now on, she would look like the mistress of Delacroix; no more breeches and kerchiefs. She would be all Lucien hoped for.

"It's cold out there," Robert said from beside the

423

fireplace, where flames danced red-orange, skipped yellow and cheery, ignoring death. "You didn't have to stay; the big black knows his work, I'd say."

Caroline held her hands before the fire, rubbed them. "I didn't know Lucien long, but I was all the family he had left."

"If you are," Robert said.

Bit by confused bit, she'd told Robert Gray the whole story, including her worries about Felipe. She said, "He believed I am; Felipe has filed documents saying I am. Lucien *wanted* me to be his sister."

"This Alcantari man," Robert said, "he wasn't among the mourners today?"

"No, but he'll be close by. He wants this land and house, wants the blacks. I can't prove I didn't really marry him, and under the law, everything belonging to his wife is his. It's what he wanted all the time, Robert. He's going to win, and I don't see how I can stop him."

A golden man, he leaned against the mantel, woolen shirt open at the throat, pistol in a bright sash, soft boots that reached above his knees. "I can stop him."

She backed away. "No, Robert; he's so deadly, so—"

His laugh brightened the room for a moment. "Duel him? I'm no gentleman bound to fancy rules. You want him out of the way; *le Bos* and Catherine Villars ask that he not bother you. As for me—" His eyes told her the rest, greygreen eyes that searched her own for an answer.

"Perhaps he won't come here," she said quickly.

Robert moved from the fire. "My men have food and drink and the run of the cabins out back. They're content to stay here while the city lionizes General Jackson and the Lafittes."

"So long as they don't force themselves upon the black women."

He smiled, the even white smile she remembered from the island where they'd walked the beach and listened to the sea wind. "They don't have to; they've plenty of silver. But with all their talk of Barataria, they might put ideas in slave heads."

Too close; he was too near, so Caroline slid away to the sideboard and searched for brandy. "They don't need ideas of freedom. I mean to free them all."

"What?"

Defiantly, she faced him. "That's right. I've been a slave and I know what it's like."

"But the plantation, girl; how can you work it without slaves?"

"Pay them," she said. "The older ones may want to go back to Africa, and they can earn passage. Those who want to leave may do so."

Robert's eyes crinkled. "You'll set other planters on their ears. *Pay* blacks? They'll think you mad, or worse —that you're one of them, that you carry black blood. That could ruin you, too."

She poured brandy and offered him a glass. He took it, face gone serious. "Caroline—damnit, I can't stop calling you that—the first move you make toward manumission for your blacks, Alcantari will be down upon you with police and writs. You don't even know how many slaves you own, yet."

"I don't *own* anybody," she said. "Nobody *owns* anyone else."

"Most of the world thinks differently. Alcantari certainly does. It would be easier to kill him."

Caroline quickly swallowed her own brandy. It took some of the graveyard chill from her. "I—maybe you can just frighten him, make him stay away from Delacroix."

Twirling his glass between strong fingers, Robert said, "This is a large, rich plantation. If he's left alive, nothing will stop him from trying to claim it—and you. But I suppose there is another way; those papers he has, the marriage documents. I wonder, will he have them on file with the authorities, or keep them himself?"

"I don't know," she said. "There's the little house on the Ramparts, but he wouldn't keep them there. The Alcantari mansion is more likely, but if Felipe has already put them in the city files, it's too late.

Oh—and Robert—he still has the bill of sale for me, if he wants to use that."

He'd used it once, she thought, on Jubal Blaze, and with good effect.

"You don't personally know my men," he said, "and I'd as soon keep it that way. But among them are some of the best thieves in the world, cutpurses, pickpockets, highwaymen who could steal the ball from a loaded cannon before the gunner could use his match. If I find where the documents are kept, they'll have to take the entire file, because most of them cannot read."

"It's a thought," she said. "Robert, I so appreciate all you've done, all you're doing to help me."

He put his glass upon the mantel and took her hand. "It's not only because Lafitte wants you protected."

"I know," she said, "but—"

"You've been hurt," he said. "I know that. Let me heal you, Caroline; allow me to try."

Robert knew she might have black blood, knew she could very well be Caroline Monteleone, mustee slave, and not the highborn Justina LeCroix, but he didn't care. He was interested in her as a woman, only as a woman. She didn't take her hand from his. His eyes seemed to grow bigger, expanding until they were all she could see. Leaning to her, he slid his free hand around her waist and drew her gently to him.

He smelled of the sea, of open, clean air, and the tender seeking of his lips was flavored with kindness. Needing someone, she clung to him and felt the shaping of his hard, young body, so strong and dependable. Robert held the kiss a long time, only slowly parting her lips for the exploration of his tongue.

With a gasp, she pulled free of him. "Oh please! Robert, it's so soon, and there are so many things—"

"But you haven't run away," he murmured, "as you did on Barataria. There's such a wonder to you, so much beauty and giving, Caroline. No man can be satisfied with just a touch of it."

Shaken, she walked to Lucien's desk. "Just a little time, Robert; I ask for only a bit of time. The legali-

426

ties, Lucien's attorney, Doctor Lejeune's deposition, bankers to be seen—there is so much to do." Lifting her chin, she looked at him. "But I am not running away. I will never run again."

His smile was pure sunshine. "Good; I will wait."

She sat at the desk, sorting through papers and ledgers, trying to make sense of it all, but she was acutely conscious of Robert Gray. When he came to sit beside her and help, Caroline could feel the warmth of his skin so near, and her nostrils flared at the man smell of him, the barely contained excitement. Could she, dared she love again?

She might always see Jubal Blaze's face, always hear his voice, know his caress, even when she was in the arms of another man. That wouldn't be fair to Robert, so she would try very hard to drain Jubal from her blood, because Jubal didn't want her, had never wanted her as she had wanted him. Caroline stared down at the blurred pages of a ledger and bit her lip. Jubal Blaze could have been anything—pirate, slave, Indian —and she would have given him her love without doubt, without question.

Robert whistled softly. "It seems, madame, that you have come into a very large inheritance. Delacroix plantation has been well managed. There are more than a hundred slaves here, and except for a few staples, the place is self-supporting. Look—masons, carpenters, blacksmiths, stable hands, house and field workers."

She shook her head to clear it. "And a white overseer. He will have to leave."

"Why? Blacks always work better under a—oh, yes; you mean to free all your slaves. I hope enough remain to plant the crops."

"I think they will. Oh Robert, if Felipe gets his hands on Delacroix, he'll lose it at the gaming tables— slaves, land, house, and all."

Robert opened another account book. "We'll just have to see that doesn't happen. Mister Alcantari should be steering his way here now, perhaps with lawyers and constables to set his sails. If so, it will make our task only a bit more difficult. I'll leave you to your counting house for now, my dear, and explain the situation to my eager band of thieves."

Caroline understood most entries in the books, the day-by-day costs and complexities of running a vast plantation. Here was Lucien LeCroix, and his father before him, and his father before that. Our father? she wondered, and saw that Delacroix had never been run by a woman, but now there was no one else. She could do it; she was good at figures, and if she had to, could strike a bargain with any haggler. If only the blacks would work for her, with her. She knew a moment of doubt, but clung to her decision: there'd be no slaves on Delacroix.

There was a cough, and Caroline looked up to see the maid standing in the doorway. "Yes, Toinette?"

The girl's eyes were puffed from crying. She said, "Already they come, circling like vultures. M'sieu—" Netty dabbed at her eyes, "—m'sieu Lucien's attorney, his banker, the overseer. You—you will not let them sell us, madame?"

"Do not worry," she said. "M'sieu Gray is where?"

Netty's eyes flickered. "The pirates? They remain hidden, but they watch."

"Send in the gentlemen," Caroline said.

Attorney Gilbert Rochemore was balding, wore a broadcloth suit, and smiled readily. Henri Perritt's eyes darted behind thick spectacles and he carried a banker's comfortable belly, a trick of cocking his head to be certain he caught every word. Tom Mackey was uneasy near them, shifting his boots and sometimes scratching at his sun-faded hair or his ragged moustache.

"Toinette," Caroline said, without rising from behind the desk, "brandy for the gentlemen."

"Sorry to intrude at such a time," the lawyer said, "but Lucien's estate, his heirs—"

"There is one heir," she said firmly, "me. If you have not spoken with Doctor Lejeune, his deposition will soon be here."

Rochemore sipped his drink and nodded. "Lucien said you have strength. He spoke about you, madame,

428

certain you are his sister, that you wear the family appearance and pride."

The banker stirred in his chair. "Perhaps all are not so certain."

Caroline looked hard at the fat man. "Perhaps one *should* be, *hein?* The LeCroix have dealt with your bank for generations, but that can be changed."

"Madame," Perritt said, "I meant only to justify——"

"M'sieu Rochemore," Caroline said, "I assume there will be papers for me to sign? I would like them brought quickly, please. Delacroix must be seen to, without delay. I have been going over the account books, and I know where Delacroix stands and what must be done to prepare for spring." She glanced at the banker again. "And my brother kept clear records of deposits and withdrawals. You will find me no less attentive."

The overseer made a noise when he gulped his brandy, and licked his moustache. To him, Caroline said, "Mister Mackey, you may stop by M'sieu Rochemore's office tomorrow and be paid to the end of the month, but I expect you to leave Delacroix today."

Mackey's mouth fell open. "You—you *what?* Looka here, I been overseer for—hell; you bringin' in somebody else?"

"No," she said. "I will see to the blacks myself."

He grunted. "That so? Be some kind of fool if'n you try, but might be you kin git along with niggers better, account of——"

"Go ahead," Caroline said. "Speak up."

Mackey clamped his mouth and stood up. "Not me, missy. Not whilst you got them cutthroats hangin' around. Them goddamn pirates'd soon gut a man as not."

"Good day, Mister Mackey," she said.

The banker held both hands over his stomach. "Ah, madame—did he mean——"

"Baratarians, m'sieu," Caroline said. "Delacroix is not without protectors, and neither am I."

The lawyer laughed. *"Sacre bleu!* Now I believe the tales I heard of a wild woman serving a cannon against the British, and how you came to be with Lucien

429

when he died. Madame, if you will allow me to help myself to brandy? Ah, *merci.* Madame LeCroix, I am not so sure you *need* protectors, but please count me among them."

The banker blinked behind his spectacles. "And me, madame. M'sieu Rochemore knows me for an honest man."

"I do not doubt this," said Caroline, "but for the sake of appearances, he will look into Delacroix accounts. *C'est juste,* M'sieu Rochemore?"

"Correct, madame." Rochemore saluted her with his glass. "Henri, Henri—we came here expecting to find a helpless girl and found a lady firmly in charge. Madame LeCroix, tomorrow I shall call upon you to clear all legalities, if I may."

"Merci," she said and stood up. The banker shrugged and grunted his weight from the chair to make an awkward bow. Eyes dancing, Rochemore bent over Caroline's hand, and only she heard his whisper: "A timely stroke, the Baratarians; who would face them?"

When they were gone, Netty skipped into the room. "Madame, you have discharged the overseer! That is good, for when M'sieu Lucien did not know, he was cruel, and each year the girls ordered to his bed were younger."

"It does not mean work ceases," Caroline said. "Tomorrow, I will explain to all, every black on this land. There will be changes."

"Oui, madame." Netty hesitated, then said, "Before, when I thought you of the blood, I was rude; please forgive me."

And behind her, Felipe de Alcantari said, "Wench, remove yourself."

With a gasp, Netty fled and Caroline put both hands atop the desk. "I expected you."

He sauntered into the room, his finery not quite so fine now, marked by too much celebrating. Felipe's eyes were red and his hand shook as he poured brandy and drank it off. *"Ma chérie,* I thought it best to arrive unannounced. Henri Perritt and Gilbert Rochemore, were they not? Ink-stained lawyer, greedy banker, but you faced them down, *non?*"

"With the truth," she said, glancing beyond him at the doorway, "as Justina LeCroix."

Felipe poured more brandy. "And not as Madame de Alcantari? No matter; I will adjust that oversight when it suits me."

"No!" she said.

He wheeled on her, the fresh scar of her knife still on his cheek. "Do not deceive yourself, wench; you only *play* the role of a lady, and that only so long as I allow it."

"Until you gamble away Delacroix as you did the Alcantari fortune," she said. "What then, Felipe? Will you arrange to turn me black once more, and sell me? Or will I simply disappear, as other girls did from your house on the Ramparts?"

Lips peeled back from his teeth, Felipe said, "Bitch, you have never known the flat of a blade, and it is past time." He drew his sword as he strode toward her.

"Now what," Robert Gray said, "do you mean to do with that thing?"

Spinning on his heel, Felipe faced the doorway, sword pointed up, balanced and ready.

"Very pretty," Robert said from behind a steady pistol, and the two burly corsairs with him grinned and nodded, "but if you mean to show us more, do hurry. I'm about to blow off your head."

The other Baratarians snaked into the room along both walls, pistols dangling casually from their hands. Robert said, "Shall I kill him here, Caroline? The carpet can be replaced."

Felipe quivered. "You—this is a coward's way!"

Voice low and ominous, Robert said, "And what way is yours, Creole? Such a heroic sword to be used upon a woman. Drop it!"

Arm shaking, Felipe lowered his point, but clung to the hilt. "This—it is of my family, this sword; it has served the Alcantari honor—"

"You son of a bitch," Robert said, "I can gut-shoot you."

The sword fell clattering from nerveless fingers and a dark, grinning corsair scooped it up. With a quick, powerful movement, the man broke Felipe's sword across a lifted knee. The other one, a shambling giant, exposed gapped teeth as he asked, "Want me to do the same to his back, cap'n?"

Robert said, "Search him, his clothing, his purse."

Felipe spat it: "If you *cochons* dare touch me—"

"Now, now," said the big pirate, and knocked him down to sit upon his supine body and rifle through Felipe's clothes.

"Caroline," Robert said, "my advice is to kill him here and now, and be done with it. Outside, if you wish."

She looked down upon Felipe and saw the big corsair hand a packet up to Robert Gray. "It—it's too callous, Robert. Those papers—"

"A bill of sale," he said, "for one mustee wench; no marriage records."

"Just make him go away," she said.

They jerked him up, propped him between them, and Robert said, "You live for now, Alcantari. But only as the fox lives ahead of the pack. Understand me, Creole—you will be hunted in the city, the parish, all of Louisiana; we cutthroats, we pirates, are good at man-hunting. Still, you may be lucky—if you run far and fast."

She watched Felipe's face, gone deathly pale and stricken, a trickle of blood at the corner of his mouth. His eyes were glassy, staring ahead at something only he could see. They walked him from the room, and Robert came to her as a horse clattered away outside.

He held out his arms and Caroline went into them, her head upon his chest.

and robes is stocked the Colony bound for the Spice
Islands and any humans destination, that should

Chapter 45

Home looked good with springtime just down the
road and trees threatening to bud up soon, but none
of it brightened Jubal's black mood. He'd been riding
with a load on his back and a knot in his belly ever
since he left the army in New Orleans, and not a
damned thing happened on the road to let his spite
out on; no road agents, no Indians on the prowl or
desperate runaway slaves. Hell, he thought, he hadn't
even been able to make Major Benton work up a good
mad and say something ornery so Jubal could hammer
him.

The army was heading back, but its pace was far
too slow for him, so Andy Jackson took his resigna-
tion back in the city and turned him loose. *Maybe,*
he'd said, when Andy asked would he be ready in
case he was needed again, and maybe he'd had a
bellyful of soldiering for a spell. Gets thataway sometimes, the general said, and my thanks to you, Cap'n
Blaze.

Sitting a tired horse, Jubal looked out across early
greening fields of Tarboro, over black and fallow
fields waiting the plow. There was more cleared ground
than when he left home, more raw-topped stumps to
be grubbed out by sweating field hands. His brother
had been busy as usual, never content to let be or
make do. Abel would spread the plantation over half
the state, given time. Jubal had never seen the sense
of it, working from can't-see to can't-see just to pile

gold atop silver. Man had his house and horses, had clothes and money to spend, that ought to be aplenty.

But could be he was wrong; his hoorawing around the country had only brought him full circle, back home with a hurt in his belly whiskey couldn't dull.

Hounds came baying from around the barns when Jubal turned his horse into the yard, and he hollered them off before old George came limping after. In a face like wrinkled-up black velvet, George's eyes rolled white. "Afore God, if'n it ain't Marse Jubal!"

"Kick them dogs back, George," Jubal said. "Howcome you look at me like I'm a haunt?"

The dogs scampered off when George waved his stick. He said, "Marse Jubal, folks said you was most likely killed dead down yonder."

Jubal took down his long gun from the saddle and passed the reins to the old man. "Only the righteous die young, George."

George cackled. "You ain't all that young no more."

"Damned if'n you ain't right," Jubal said. "See to the horse and carry my plunder on into the house after. Where's my pa?"

The smile wiped itself away. "No way to send word, Marse Jubal. Your daddy, he took a spell and went quick."

Jubal's hands tightened on the rifle. "And Abel?"

"Out to the new ground," George answered, "but Mistress Purity, she to the house."

"Purity? My brother got himself wedded?"

Nodding, George began to lead off the horse. "You been gone a mighty long time."

"A long time," Jubal agreed, and walked to the house, up the river gravel carriage road that circled between flower bushes his Ma had planted. Pa dead and in the ground; Abel married and the face of the land changing, life turning itself inside out while he was off soldiering. Only the house hadn't changed; it was no Tidewater mansion, nor fancied up like some places in New Orleans, but it was a good house, built solid to stand against the years, big enough to raise families in.

Moccasins soundless on scrubbed wood, he climbed the steps and stood on the porch, seeing how his Ma's wisteria vines had climbed clear up the house. They'd be a sight in a few months, all purple blossoms hanging like fragrant grapes. Pa liked to set in his rocker then, drinking in the smell of them along with his sugared whiskey and water.

Jubal's lips moved. "I'm right sorry, Pa. Damnit, *I* ought to been the one to stand at your bed when your time came."

A yellow-face wench peeped from the front door. He didn't know her, and her voice trembled when she said, "Yassuh?"

He walked at her and she scooted, scared off by the wildman look and smell of him, the guns and skinning knife that were part of him. Jubal went into the house, across the entry hall and the sitting room to reach up over the fireplace and hang his rifle on its old pegs. Gently, he ran his fingers along the engraved barrel of his father's favorite shotgun, turned away quickly and put his tail to bake at the fire, hands behind him. He breathed in memories that tugged at him, saw himself as a towheaded youngun in this room, Abel crawling on the floor and squalling because Jubal wouldn't give him something or the other. For a second there, he could swear he smelled Pa's old briar pipe and heard the click of Ma's knitting needles.

"Yes," she said, coming into the room, "yes?" She stopped and widened her eyes at him. "Why—you must be Jubal."

He wished she didn't have silky black hair hanging away down her straight back, nor eyes so dark and long-lashed; he could wish she didn't wear a ripe mouth like a flag. But this one wasn't Caroline; this one was white clear through. Blazes didn't marry up with anything else.

"I'm him," Jubal said, "and you're Purity—Purity Blaze. Shame I missed the weddin'."

Her hand fluttered to a pertly rounded breast. "But you—we thought—and Abel sent letters—"

435

"I been hither and yon. Did Pa have a good buryin'?"

"Of course; Abel saw to everything, and folks came from miles around—oh; I'll send a boy for Abel right away. Can I—are you hungry?"

"Some," Jubal admitted. Her voice was nothing like Caroline's; there was a sulkiness to it, and maybe it was because she wasn't all that happy to see him. Jubal remembered his coonskin hat and took it off. Unfastening his belt, he set it and its weapons along the mantelpiece next to a porcelain doll he didn't recall. "Be a mercy to have a hot bath, too, but I reckon it can wait till I've seen Abel."

He saw she was taking better hold of herself, moving from surprise and maybe a mite of fear into the confident mistress of Tarboro. "May I offer you whiskey? Belle will have to poke up the fire and heat you something."

"Belle's still the cook," Jubal said. "That's something. Believe I will take a dram of corn, mam." He moved for the cupboard where the whiskey was kept, but she beat him to it. Moves right nice, he thought; some narrow in the hips but with a good wiggle to her. Had the look of the Walters family about her, or maybe the Dixons; both were mostly black-haired and tended to throw more fillies than colts.

Purity drained clear whiskey into a glass, and when her long fingers accidentally brushed his, drew them suddenly back, color highlighting her cheekbones. "I—I'll send for Abel and see to your meal, your bath—"

Puzzling after her as she fled, Jubal wondered at her nervousness. She'd probably heard tall tales about his helling around after women, he thought, or brawling some in the taverns. Or it might be she was some spooked by the return of the older son. Jubal rolled Tarboro's good corn whiskey around inside his mouth before swallowing it. That was most likely it; Purity had already gotten used to running the house, and here came a shaggy woods runner who might take it from her, for the law of the land was the eldest son inherited. Primogeniture, the book called it, one among those shelves of volumes Pa made sure his younguns read.

Well, he sure as hell didn't mean to snatch up the land, for Abel worked on it harder than anybody else and knew more about it. What Jubal had in mind was kind of a partnership, taking on his share of the load for a change. Too bad he hadn't shouldered his part while Pa was alive to see it.

Jubal moved about the room, touching books, the old sofa, the cherrywood breakfront that held crystal glasses Ma had been proud of. He had himself another splash of corn, and catching the odor of something good wafting down the hall from the winter kitchen, let his nose guide him there.

Purity jerked her head around when he entered, the black banner of her hair flying. "I would have called you."

"Know where it is," Jubal said. "Howdy, Belle; I swony, you gettin' younger and fatter by the day."

The cook beamed at him. "You scalawag; you always was the lyingest youngun in the county. Set yourself, Marse Jubal; you appears gaunted."

"Ain't had none of your cookin' too long," he said, moving past stiff Purity to put his feet under the kitchen table. "Seems like them New Orleans victuals just don't stick to a man's ribs." Now why the hell had he brought up New Orleans, and memories of a cozy house behind an iron gate, golden wine and a whispering fire on the hearth?

"Nothin' but greens 'n fatback and ol' biscuits. Do better by you, come supper."

But there was steaming coffee and fresh churned butter and golden honey, blackstrap molasses from last season's cane crop, and Jubal set to with a will. When he looked up, Purity was watching him with a grimace of distaste quickly erased. Jubal said, " 'Scuse my manners; been hunkerin' down with a skinnin' knife for a spell, eatin' whatever didn't take a bite of me first."

Belle chuckled behind him, but Purity only lifted a darkfeather eyebrow. Caroline had eyebrows like that, only longer and with a funny little lift to their ends; maybe her eyes were kind of slanty, too, but he wasn't certain sure about that.

"You a Walters girl?" he asked.

"My father is Thomas Mixon," Purity answered, moving farther from him.

Had to be one or the other, he thought, and said, "Know your daddy; used to fox hunt with him. Don't recall seein' you around the yard, howsomever."

"I was small then," Purity said.

Belle snorted. "Musta' been in diapers, 'cause Jubal, he duty bound to notice any gal out'n 'em."

"Belle!" Purity said sharply, and Jubal figured she would have said a whole lot more to the old woman, but about then Abel came trotting into the kitchen.

Jubal's chair fell over when he jumped up to enfold his brother in a bear hug, then hold him off at arm's length and look him over. "Damned if'n you ain't the gentleman, Abel; broadcloth and a white shirt, bigod. You turnin' Tidewater?"

Abel's smile was strained but welcoming. He hadn't grown any, Jubal saw; still a head shorter and some lanky, hair darker than his own and bony in the cheeks. That could come from working so long in the fields, seeing to the niggers himself and never putting trust in an overseer.

"Welcome home, Jubal," Abel said. "You've already met Purity?"

"Got you a right pretty woman," Jubal said. "Pert and sassy, too. How—with Pa, Abel, how was it?"

Without seeming to shake loose of Jubal's big hands, Abel stepped back and accepted a cup of coffee poured by the cook. "Quick," he said, "no pain to speak of. He asked for you."

Jubal stooped for his chair and straddled its seat. "Good he had you to hand, anyhow. I couldn't of got back did I know."

Hiding his face behind a tin cup, Abel said, "At the end, he kept callin' me Jubal."

Jubal looked at the floor, scoured white by Belle for so many years. He said, "Mean to talk some with you about the place, Abel, but I'm wore down by travel. Get me a bath and some sleep, then you and me can jaw some. Any of my old clothes left?"

"You'll have to ask Purity," Abel said, interested in his coffee. "She sees to the house."

She said, "Your room is practically untouched. We —weren't sure you were coming back, but just in case—"

Back to Jubal, his brother said then, "I have to ride over to the Candless place, see about breedin' some niggers. Might take a spell, so sleep all you need to; supper'll be some late."

When Abel hurried out without a backward look, Jubal stood and stretched. It was plain to see the boy was fretting, but that would be settled, come supper time. Funny Abel never asked about the wars or the neighbors who'd toted rifles to them. Somebody had to stay to home and take in crops, but seemed like there'd be some interest in who was living and who got left on the field.

When Jubal started upstairs, the yellow wench came slipping down sideways, like she was scared he'd grab her and run off. Behind her tramped Louella, who'd been a house servant ever since Jubal could remember. She gave him a wide flash of teeth. "Marse Jubal, your tub's fixed, and sure God you kin use it. Smells like a randy goat."

"Louella," he said, patting her solid haunch, "you wore out any more bucks?"

She laughed. "Go on with you, boy; was you a black buck, I'd see how much rooster you *really* is."

Feeling more at home, Jubal went into his old room and peeled off buckskins to stand naked before the new-laid fire. The washroom was straight across, and many's the time Louella had snatched him over into the tub to scrub him down good, when he was a youngun. He grinned and rubbed his beard; still a fine figure of a wench, she could still probably give a man a good ride and some to boot. His grin faded; black and white didn't mix, no more than horse and cow. When you crossed a jack on a mare, you got a mule, but the mule wasn't either one. Like a yellow wench, or a mustee.

He stamped into the washroom and eased into the steaming tub to lather himself good with some of Belle's soap, the house kind she cooked up with rose petals mashed into it. It took some doing to get his hair unsnarled, and the hot water seeped right on into his bones to make him nod.

Figuring he'd shave and get his hair trimmed later, Jubal went still damp to his bed, the bed that Pa had made longer especially for him when he got to growing so. It was piled with quilts and he sank into the feather mattress with a sigh. Eyes closed, he began to see things against their lids—the Creeks hollering and running; British coming head-on at the defense line like so many bright-painted wooden soldiers, only toy soldiers didn't bust up and bleed; and Caroline Monteleone, goddamn her for haunting his dreams.

Turning, he thumped the pillows, but she kept walking through his mind, coming right on to the bed so the firelight could caress the silky gold of her flawless skin and tip with pink the erect nipples of her high, meloned breasts, so it could linger its diamonds into the rich ebony fur of that compelling vee between perfect thighs. So real, so real, damnit; he could smell the musk of her, feel the dipping of the bed as she eased beneath the covers with him.

It didn't help that he put his back to her image; she snuggled to him and slid one arm around his waist, so that he knew the pressure of her fine body, the points of her breasts boring into his shoulders, the throbbing of her belly, and that pulsing, demanding mound.

Struggling to break the dream, to throw off the tormenting spell of Caroline, he twisted and made noises in his throat. But even when his eyes fought open, Jubal could still feel the silk netting of her hair and smell her clinging perfume. His roaming hands found the tantalizing hills and tingling valleys of her, all soft and trembling.

"What the hell!" Jubal said, and she put a small

hand across his lips, saying a warm and breathy "Shh!" into his ear.

When he turned all the way to her, she fit well against his body, squirming like she could crawl right on through his skin, and making him achingly hard. "Goddamnit," he hissed into half-darkness of the curtained room, "what—who—"

Her voice had a catch in it. "Shh, Jubal—the nigras might hear us. Oh yes, yes—you're all they say; so big and strong, so hard—ahhh!"

"Purity," he said, "just what the hell you up to?"

Softly, she giggled. "You're the one who's *up,* sir."

When her questing fingers curled about him, Jubal said *oh, shit,* with feeling. His brother's bride, the string-tight and highnosed Miss Purity was here naked in bed with him, wanting it so bad she was shaking all over. "Abel," he said.

And she purred, "Don't worry about him; he'll be gone until after dark. Oh my; you're made like a stallion."

"You're his wife, damnit."

She wouldn't let go, and now she lifted one sleek thigh across his hip, trying to aim him up into her body. "You've bedded a heap of wives, from what they say. What's the matter, Jubal? I know I'm not ugly, so do it to me—"

Finally, he got an arm between their bodies and held her off some, but not because he wanted to. "Why, Purity—why?"

Her hot mouth was at his throat, sharp teeth nibbling. "So you'll know I'm good as any woman you ever had, so you'll enjoy doing it to me so much, you'll never want to leave. There'll be plenty of opportunities, Jubal; Abel is always out in the fields, and when he comes back, he's so tired he just falls into bed. I can be yours any time, day or night. Oh, I'll be so good to you, do things to you—damn you, Jubal Blaze, come on and put it in me!"

It took some doing, but he moved her back and came up on an elbow to stare down into her shadowed face. Her lower body writhed, and her cupped

441

hands made presents of her breasts, offered them to him. "Any way you want me—whatever you want me to do—take me, have me, *mount me!*"

He sat on the edge of the bed. "You think by sharin' yourself, I won't take over Tarboro, or if I do, you and Abel will stay on."

Her hands were at his hips, digging around into his tensed thighs. "Does it matter? I'm here now, and so are you."

Putting his back to her, Jubal said, "You're a heap of woman, enough to set any man to boilin', but you're wedded to my brother."

For a disbelieving moment, she lay silent; there was a jagged edge to her words when she said, "You— you're denying me—*me?* You whoremonger—tomcattin' all over the county, but denyin' me! Damn you, I wish you'd died at New Orleans, like you were supposed to. Damn you, damn you—this is Abel's land, *Abel's!* And I'm the mistress of Tarboro. You can't come draggin' back here and claim it all—you just can't! We won't let you."

When he moved to get out of bed, she felt the movement and reached up, raked up and around his shoulder, trying to get her sharp nails into his eyes. She left furrows down one cheek, instead. Jubal damned near backhanded her, but caught himself before he broke her neck.

In the closet he found things to fit him and heard the slither of woman clothes as Purity got dressed, heard her slam the door. The mirror over the washstand showed him mean red scratches his beard didn't hide, and he touched a wet rag to them. There was no way of keeping them from his brother. That bitch —but what if Abel thought the same, worried that Jubal meant to take Tarboro? Surely Abel wouldn't put his woman up to it.

His plunder bag sat in a corner where George had put it. He took out money after getting dressed, tired as hell and ornery, feeling scratchy and awkwardly townsman without his buckskins. When he went downstairs, nobody was in sight, so he lifted a bottle of corn from the cabinet and his pistol from the mantel. Out back, he kept the scarred side of his face from old George and picked out a horse to be saddled.

"You gittin' right on with it again," George chuckled. "Ain't to home a day, and yonder you goes. Look out, ladies."

"Reckon so," Jubal said, and swung into the saddle with a lightness he didn't feel, pointing the horse toward town.

Chapter 46

She could never have gotten so much done without him. The past week bore heavily upon her as she soaked in her tub, making her eyes heavy, making her grateful for blessed heat and a time of quiet, when she could relax.

Robert, she thought, Robert Gray; always at her call, giving quiet advice and making sensible suggestions, but never trying to deter her from the path she'd chosen. Silently, Caroline thanked him for his understanding, because nearly everyone else thought her mad—the lawyer, the banker, even some of the slaves.

And she also owed Robert for driving away Felipe, although she sensed the threat of him still lurking somewhere in the dark alleys of the city. True to his word, Robert was hunting Felipe, trailing him like some dangerous wild animal. A thousand pairs of cunning eyes watched for Felipe de Alcantari, and as many attentive ears listened closely for word of him. All of Lafitte's men, all their women and business connections throughout New Orleans, their paid informants and willing spies, all sought after the fugitive. But Felipe had gone into deep hiding somewhere, somehow, his manservant Turpo with him. The Alcantari mansion was deserted, the Ramparts house empty, and no whisper of him at the gaming tables of Rue Royale.

Dead or run away, he was gone, and that was all

444

that mattered to Caroline; she just prayed he was forever out of her life.

As was Jubal Blaze, she thought, and lifted dripping from the tub to towel her body. Jackson's army was gone, headed back for Tennessee and the Carolinas, and Jubal with it, carrying his hatred of black blood like a cross. Caroline didn't want him crucified upon his bigotry; like Felipe, she wanted him nevermore to intrude upon her life.

"Forever," she said aloud, and turbaned the towel about her damp hair, then slipped into a dressing gown. Below stairs, in kitchen and barn and slave quarters, the blacks were still like so many bees dazed by a smoke pot, not quite able to function normally. They would believe it when the lawyer arrived with his load of manumission papers, each duly recorded at the city hall.

Tchaka was the only man who took her at her word, for the Mandingo knew and respected her. And Tchaka himself seemed stunned by her move to free every slave on Delacroix plantation, house servant and field hand alike.

"I want you to be overseer," she'd told him, "for the workers who choose to stay. I'm working out a payment scale for them, so that someday those who want to return to Africa may do so. Those who don't can save and in time establish their own businesses."

"Migod," Tchaka said, and muttered something in rapid Mandingo, some incantation to his own near-forgotten gods. "A black man runnin' a whole plantation. Ain't never been done afore, missy. And them white planters, they ain't goin' to like it worth a picayune."

"I don't care what they think," Caroline said. "I do care that enough people will want to stay and make Delacroix pay. Do you think so?"

Rolling burly shoulders and scratching his woolly head, Tchaka said, "I expects they will; most got no thought where to go nor what to do. Few of the younguns might scoot off, thinkin' freedom means somebody'll fill their bellies and give 'em clothes.

445

Reckon they come acrawlin' back when they gets hungry." He put those proud, piercing eyes upon her, and for a moment she saw him as he had been long ago, shackled and defiant, cursing her for being the white man's whore, but rising in her defense though it meant his own life.

"What you gettin' from this, missy? You always been a puzzlement to me; sometimes you black, sometimes you white, and sometimes you somewheres in the middle."

"Damn it," she said, angered at him. "You know my mother was chained and used by those bastards in the cavvy, and another white man beat her so badly she died. You *know* Kleppner made me do unspeakable things and sold me when he was through. Maybe I am all white; right now, the law thinks I am. But I think Ashanti, and if I carry that ancient blood in my veins, I am proud of it. Do you want to hear how my black father stood off slave trackers so my mother and I could get away? You want to know how a good, brave man died so we could be free?"

"Missy," he said, "I just don't mean—"

"*I* mean something," she said, still furious. "I mean to prove that blacks will work without being driven and beaten and chained; I want to show all Louisiana that free men, working for their own good, their own hopes, are better than men forced to live like animals. And I'll show the other planters that hired labor is cheaper and better than slave labor. Don't you see, Tchaka? It's the only way to make them listen, make them understand, by appealing to their purses."

"Gal," he said, "you purely a stemwinder. Thing is, showin' them others so many free niggers ain't danger to 'em." Tchaka closed his eyes and clenched his massive fists. "Africa; oh lord Jesus, *Africa!* I can walk like a man, like a Mandingo warrior, 'thout no fear my younguns goin' be sold off." When he opened his eyes again, there were tears in them, and he said, "Missy, goddamnit, I break my goddamn back to make it true, and if ary nigger drags his ass, he got me to answer to."

"Not to a whip," Caroline said.

And Tchaka said, "Never no goddamn whip, jes' my hands." He started to add something else, but his heavy mouth worked and his eyes clouded up again, so he just bobbed his head at her and moved out of the house, holding his chin higher and walking strong.

Now, moving into her bedroom, she knew some of the emotions that had rioted through Tchaka. They were something she could never explain to a disgruntled banker, a bewildered lawyer, to any white poor or rich. Possibly Robert Gray understood, for he had never stood against her decisions, and there were no slaves in Barataria.

What a tremendous help he'd been, going through plantation records with her, figuring out the operation of Delacroix, what needed reform and what should be continued, totaling figures and debits and assuring that what Lucien LeCroix had placed in the bank was still there, every centime of it.

There was a lot of money on deposit, and contracts that meant more, promises for delivery of cotton and sugar cane, smoked and pickled meats for the markets. No wonder Felipe had wanted control, she thought; Delacroix would have given him more than he had wasted of his own family fortune.

She hadn't been clear in her mind just how to go about this work-freedom program, because if she simply gave one hundred and three blacks money for passage, or money to establish themselves in the city, it would drain the coffers. Besides, Caroline had an idea that a great giveaway could do the recipients more harm than good. So Robert Gray had driven her into town to meet and talk with one John McDonogh.

A crusty, Bible-spouting, opinionated old man, this McDonogh, with a reputation for being the most tight-fisted businessman in the state. He was merciless in collecting money owed, foreclosing without a thought against any excuse, but he did have a systematic slave-freeing project going. He meant to send numerous blacks to Liberia, after hiring them out on Saturdays so they could earn passage, and was loudly exhorting other

447

owners to do the same. Nobody else was listening, so he was enthusiastic in expounding his theories to Caroline.

When she left him in his counting house, she knew her plan was solid, especially since she didn't mean to limit her people to one day a week hire; they'd be working for her all the time, being paid all the time, and if they wanted to work Sundays, she and the Bible had no objection.

"You're quite the lady," Robert Gray said, coming back in the coach. "Not only beautiful, but bright and thoughtful. Listening to you all this time, seeing what you mean to do, I think you're right all the way. I think the Negro will become a larger and more burdensome problem every year, freeman or slave, and I'd like to see them all sent to this Liberia."

"But so many of them are born here," she protested. "They know nothing of Africa and don't want to go."

Robert sighed. "Look at the free ones; are they accepted by whites, made friends and partners? No, and no again; only in the brotherhood of sea rovers, where all men's blood runs red. Can a Negro buck marry a white woman, or a white man marry his quadroon mistress? Not now and not ever, I think. The races are separate and always will be, and you must admit, Caroline—ah, Justina—that many of the new slaves are little more than brutes, savages fresh out of their jungles."

"There are savage whites," Caroline said.

"But they are harder to recognize; their skin makes them like the rest of us, until experience teaches us differently. The black is suspect at first glance."

"But they will never have a chance to prove they're human, so long as they're bartered like stock, and more ill-used," she said, and he had no answer for that.

Now Caroline went to the dressing table, the one that had belonged to Lucien's wife Gabrielle. It was still stocked with unguents and lotions, rouge and perfumes and mysterious salves. What would Gabrielle have thought of releasing all Delacroix blacks? Would she have screamed into her dainty mirror? And Lucien, tender gentleman, would not have understood, either, for slaves were his way of life, unquestioned. But neither Gabrielle nor Lucien had ever worn shackles or stood on the block, exhibited like a prime filly; neither had been raped, made to act the cringing bitch on hands and knees, forced to take a man's thing into their mouths—and be scorned for it all.

Neither had seen their love spurned because there might be a single drop of black blood in their veins, which of course made them lower animals, unfit to be loved by holy, pristine whites.

Fiercely, she stroked the brush through her hair, and spitefully, she used Gabrielle's creams and powders and perfumes. She would face her neighbors' spleen when she came to it; they dared not molest her while Robert and his Baratarians were about, and once they discovered she was right, that Delacroix could produce more and better crops through the use of willing labor, perhaps there would be no need for guards.

Catherine Villars, she thought; she urgently wanted to see her good friend and talk everything out with her. Even the voodoo people could help, Madame Zozo and Doctor Dambah, those prophets of the snake who'd warned her of the mark of the scorpion— that very birthmark which had proved her right to inheritance. With the *juju* priests backing her, blacks everywhere would bring word of impending trouble. Perhaps they could even discover where Felipe de Alcantari was hiding; theirs was an underground network no white dreamed existed, unfathomable as jungle drum talk and traveling as swiftly. But did she want him killed, or just forever frightened away?

Caroline looked around at a discreet tap upon her door. *"Entrez vous."*

Robert Gray came into the room. He wore fresh white linen, and looked quite respectable, clothed nothing like the half-wild freebooter she'd known on Grand Isle. Only the man himself was the same, the

449

familiar bronze hair and clear blue eyes, those even features and the mouth always so ready to smile.

Stopping, he stared at her, and she nodded to his mirrored reflection, then turned upon the dressing-table stool to face him. "Robert—how nice; is there anything wrong?"

"Only one thing," he answered. "The plantation's beginning to stir, with Tchaka's help; my men are content with food and willing wenches and good wine. Lafitte is still being toasted in the city, although Jackson's army is gone."

"Then what can be wrong?"

Robert took a long step toward her. "You're just too damned beautiful. You shine clear across Delacroix, so that I feel you if I'm in the fields with Tchaka, or down in the wine cellar. I see you everywhere I look, even when you're not there, and you walk my dreams every night. It was bad enough in Barataria, touching you, watching you walk, knowing the music of your laugh. But here, it's too much. Day and night, it's too much."

She rose. "Robert, I—"

"Oh damn," he said, and came the rest of the way to put his arms around her. Caroline stiffened, then relaxed against him, for Robert was a friend and important to her from the time they'd met. He smelled clean and warm; there was a quiet strength about him, and it seemed quite natural to lift her mouth for his kiss.

It had been a long time since Jubal, and perhaps that's what made Robert's kiss so heady. Maybe she needed to be loved for herself, not as something handy to be raped, nor as a prize purchased, nor as someone thought to be living a lie. Caroline or Justina, she was her own woman, be she black or white. Robert Gray knew her, wanted her for what she was, not what she might be, and she opened her mouth to him, laced her arms about his neck as she pressed the length of her body against his strong flesh.

Robert's tongue was vibrant, his mouth sweet, his hands eager but gentle as they searched her back, stroked her hair, lingered at her hips. Caroline felt the swelling thrust of his manhood and knew a swift, longing response. Against his lips, she whispered, "Robert, Robert—oh yes, darling—yes—"

Lifted from her feet, she was carried to the bed and lowered. She could not wait for him, and wriggled from her dressing gown without help, then her fingers were anxious at his belt, his crisp white shirt, digging into the darkly golden hair of his chest. The thought blazed through her that she could love again, that this sweetness was honeyed as the other and she was about to savor it with gladness, without regrets.

"Lovely," he murmured deep in his throat, "so unbelievably lovely, every magnificent inch of you." He leaned to kiss the hollow of her throat, his hands caressing her aching breasts, his bare skin tingling against her own. Caroline worked her fingers into his wavy hair, allowing her body to react on its own, and it did so, her belly trembling, her hips rolling in short and pleading arcs, her thighs opening, spreading themselves for the fondling of Robert's hand, the questing of slow and careful fingers.

"I've needed you so long, Caroline," he said around a throbbing nipple, and she lifted to him, to the tantalizing movement of his mouth as it trailed ever so lovingly down her rib cage. Robert's hands were strong upon her upper thighs now, and she moaned when his hotwet tongue bored into her navel.

Through blurred eyes, she peered down at his bronze curls, at the width of his bare shoulders and the scattering of sunbaked hairs along his forearms. She quivered at the trailing of his mouth, and then—and then he was with her, hungrily, adoringly with her!

Clenching him, Caroline gave herself up to the thundering rapture of being loved ardently, deeply, completely. The cresting was violent, an overwhelming sweep of foaming madness that spun her over and over in a sea of golden, bursting bubbles.

Limply, she drifted in a wondrous tidepool, stroked by wavelets, kissed by sun and sea. The kissing, the tide, became more insistent, and she groped for something to hang onto. She found him above her, and as he tenderly penetrated, she clamped him with arms and legs and burrowed her mouth into the damp, crinkly forest of his chest.

Motion then, slow and lingering; an enchanted rhythm that exulted in each glorious stroke, so that Caroline became a metronome, her hips swinging, swinging as she enwrapped him ever deeper within her fevered body. Her teeth clashed against his, and her tongue caressed his as the movement quickened, hurried into a powerful, driving hammering.

"Ahh!" she cried out, and caught the skin of his throat between her teeth. "Ahhh!" and the world burst like British rockets, to shower her inside and out with brightly burning fragments of ecstasy.

For a long time, a lusciously dissolving time, they clung together, throbbing as one, gasping as one. When later, Caroline became herself again, when she lay beside this new and exciting body, she knew she *could* love, that it was possible for her to give joyously to a man who truly cared for her.

But even as she listened to the slowing of Robert Gray's breath, even as she felt the sweat of their love-making turn dry upon her skin, Caroline fought against the admission that a shadow had been with her every frantic moment, an unwelcome intruder in this most intimate of moments.

Jubal Blaze.

Chapter 47

He was good to be with, and his experience with women of several races had given Robert a special expertise, the knowledge of what it took to fulfill a lover. Caroline appreciated that, and would not allow herself to feel guilty when they were together, which was often. Robert would appear suddenly during the day, and she would turn to see him filling his eyes with her; within minutes, they would be in bed, bodies straining, flesh blending in tender frenzy.

It had happened in the fields, behind hay in the barn, at the river, once even in the coach on the way to the city. And though it was ever good, always—always, damnit—the specter of Jubal Blaze hung close, try as she might to forever close him out. Once, while Robert was squirming under her teasing ministrations, Caroline pretended Jubal was actually there in the room with them, and taunted him inside her mind: *See, see? I can make another man wild for me, doing this—oh, and this; you were fearful of that at first, remember? But then, whores and niggers are expected to be animals, correct? Goddamn you, Jubal Blaze— watch and see if your fine white women can pleasure you as much. . . .*

Between lovings, she could shove Jubal into a far corner of her brain, because there were more important things to think about. Eighteen blacks had left Delacroix with manumission papers in hand, looking fearfully over their shoulders as if they might be snatched up again, their sudden and unexpected freedom re-voked.

"Fool niggers," Tchaka grunted. "Some'll get they-selfs drunk and wind up in a slave cavvy, papers gone. Some'll come back when they finds out ain't nobody about to give 'em *nothin'*. Few might make do, hirin' out."

"I expected more to leave," Caroline said, standing beside Tchaka to watch field hands move out in the morning.

He grunted again. "Nowheres to go, does they think on it. Here, they get took care of, make hard money. I done told 'em, harder they works, more they makes. Does Delacroix stay rich, so does they."

"It will work for them," she said, "and for you, but I'll miss you when you go home, Tchaka."

"Prime me a boss nigger ready to take my place, missy. That ain't what frets me; it's white folks."

"Other planters?" Caroline looked over at a fruit tree breaking into rioting bloom. "I hope they'll see we're no threat to them, that they can also do better with hired labor rather than slaves."

Rubbing his broad chest with the flat of a callused hand, Tchaka said, "They don't think like you, missy. They never felt no irons on they legs, nor blacksnake acrost they backs."

"So long as the Baratarians are here—"

"Might not have 'em all that long," Tchaka said. "I been hearin' things."

Caroline stared at him. "Oh no; Robert would never —he'd certainly tell me if—"

"Carriage acomin'," Tchaka said, "and I got to git. Take care, missy."

As always, an armed corsair lounged out to show himself to visitors, this time the big gap-toothed man, the one who'd knocked down Felipe and searched him. Caroline hurried around the house to meet the coach, a rich one with liveried driver and footmen riding behind.

Footmen hurried to open the coach door, helping its riders to alight. She was suddenly conscious of her plain cotton dress and low slippers when she saw their

454

finery, brocade coats and plumed hats, sateen and velvet pantaloons, hose and buckled shoes. One man was short and rolling with fat, the other lean as a starving hawk and with much the same look about him.

"Mam'selle LeCroix?" the fat one wheezed.

"Please come into the house," Caroline said, "and do forgive my appearance. I was seeing to the workers."

"Ah yes, the workers," the hawk said. "There are still *laboreurs,* then?"

"But of course, m'sieu—"

"Gaspar, Moreau Gaspar of Greenoaks; and this is M'sieu Valsin Fozatte, who owns Maison Caresse; your —ah—neighbors, mam'selle."

She led them into the sitting room, where Netty appeared immediately with glasses and sherry chilled in the spring house. "So," Fozatte said, working his bulk into a chair, "you yet keep house servants. One would wonder."

On the defensive, Caroline sat across from her visitors, knowing why they'd come. "Delacroix continues, gentlemen, and will prosper."

Gaspar shook his narrow head. "It is well that poor Lucien did not live to see this—these blacks coming and going as they please."

Fozatte's chins bobbed. "It is a *tracasserie*—a worry —to us, understand. Negroes roaming the night, attempting to lure away others; promiscuous breeding—"

"My people remain on Delacroix," she said. "The overseer—"

"A black *sauvage,*" Gaspar said.

"My overseer," Caroline repeated, "sees that the workers know their limitations. They do not travel by night, and if they did, who is to stop them? They are free, legally so."

"So are thieves and murderers, until caught," Fozatte mumbled, draining his sherry glass. Behind the puffballs of his cheeks, small eyes squinted at Caroline. "We ask you to reconsider this foolishness; take back the manumissions. Those ignorant ones will not know—"

"*I* will know," she said.

"*Un enfant entêté,*" Gaspar commented, 'a stubborn child, *hein?* Therefore she must be warned, told with certainty that—"

Robert Gray strolled unannounced into the room, and Caroline suppressed a smile. He wore a head kerchief and earring, jackboots and open shirt, a bright sash that showed a pair of pistol butts, and he toyed with the hilt of his cutlass.

She said, "May I introduce M'sieu Gray? *Capitaine* Gray, I should say, one of Jean Lafitte's most trusted freebooters. He is here with his men to see that all goes smoothly."

Fozatte swallowed audibly. "I—we did not realize you had such a formidable—companion, mam'selle, nor such powerful friends."

"It is a thing to remember," she smiled. "Please continue with your warning, m'sieu."

"Non, non," Gaspar said quickly, unfolding his length from his chair. "A neighborly visit only, mam'-selle. Come, Valsin; the lady is busy."

When the door closed behind them, Caroline laughed. "You needed only a boarding knife clenched in your teeth, pirate. They were so frightened—"

Robert drew her close and kissed the side of her throat. "That kind is frightened of the dark, but they will spread their poison—rumors and lies, conjecture and fear. So many free blacks banded together; an army capable of anything."

"I will *not* be threatened by such maggots," she said. "Our people keep to themselves and do no harm; they work harder than any slaves."

"Perhaps so, but will your neighbors allow themselves to admit it? Ah well, so long as they think Delacroix is guarded by cutthroats—but enough of bogeymen. We found the priest who posted your wedding banns and signed the certificate."

"You did? Where, how—"

"It seems he's addicted to the wine bottle, and to dipping into the almsbox. His parishioners will sigh with relief when they hear he's been transferred, just this morning. Captain Nez Coupé has long thought there should be prayers said over the dead, so the good padre is aboard the *Céleste,* bound for the Spice Islands—and any Spanish merchantman that should cross her bows."

Caroline clapped her hands. That trick was so like Robert and his corsairs. Then she sobered. "But the papers themselves—"

"Somehow spirited from official files, but Alcantari may have duplicates."

Frowning, she moved back from him. "And Nez Coupé, that dear, ugly man—why is he sailing?"

Robert shrugged. "It's his business, remember? And mine, also. New Orleans is a fickle harlot, a city that takes back the heart she so easily gives. The great commodore who attacked Grand Isle and looted the warehouse there? Well, Jean and Pierre have tried to get back their property through the courts, and—" He walked to the buffet and poured wine into a goblet. "That damned Gambi; Lafitte should have strung him to a yardarm long ago. I'm sure the necklace came from his booty; a very special bit of jewelry, rubies and sapphires still mounted and easily identifiable. The necklace belonged to a Madame Beauregard, lost with the ship on which she was returning from France."

Robert wryly saluted her with the glass. "So in the streets it is said, 'So they were only pirates, after all.' No more fêtes, no more grand balls to honor the Lafittes; and Governor Claiborne is keeping men under arms, all those he gathered to face the British. It bodes ill for the Baratarians, beloved."

"How awful!" she said. "Catherine and Marie—Dominique You and Beluche—"

"Catherine is probably on the road to see you this minute," he said. "Marie has already left the city and Beluche makes ready to sail. Dominque You—he's had enough of seafaring. Can you imagine Dominique a staid businessman?"

"Robert." Caroline knew an uneasy feeling, a foreboding. "If Dominique You can retire, why can't—"

"Dominique is old," he said. "He has enough put aside."

"Stay with me," she said. "There's enough here for

457

all of us; the freedman plan will work, I'm certain. The plantation—"

"Is only a plantation, and yours. The ship is mine. Once, long ago, I might have become a planter, respectable by now and surrounded by children. That would have made me fat, Justina; I would already be old and afraid."

The chill crept into her belly and dug in sharp claws. "You—you mean to sail away, to leave me."

"When I must," he said, "and that time will come. When the governor's men get around to smaller fish, they'll remember me. With Lafitte gone, the city will forget, and I'll come back."

"No," she said, "you won't come back. You'll go down fighting your ship in some uncharted sea. Robert, Robert—oh God—"

His shoulder made a just-right pillow for her head. Caressing her hair, he said, "The clock hasn't struck, darling. Before I go, I'll be certain you're cared for, protected."

"That doesn't matter," she said against his shirt. "I don't want you here just for that. Robert, must you sail under the black flag again, *must* you?"

"You," he said softly. "Must you stay on Delacroix?"

Fiercely, she told herself she would not cry. "Lucien believed I would, and there are the people I'm responsible for, all these people. They need time, Robert. If I leave them, the Gaspars, the Fozattes will be upon them like vultures, picking their bones. Tchaka, the others, wouldn't have a chance. And Felipe is still out there somewhere."

"You should have let me kill him," he said. "Just as Lafitte should have made carrion of Gambi."

She held him tighter. "We're arguing over the past, when there doesn't seem to be a future for us."

"There's now for us," Robert said. "Every minute we allow to slip by, that's a minute spent without return. Justina, Justina—"

"Oh damn!" she said, as a horse clattered up before the house and boots slammed against the porch. She

458

lifted shaking hands to smooth her hair and faced the doorway.

Something whirlwinded across the room, hair flying, eyes snapping. *"Chérie!* It has been too long—" and Catherine Villars flung herself into Caroline's arms. "This one, this Robert—careful of him, *mon amie;* he will break your heart. Let me look at you; ah—the lady of the manor; a difference since the Ramparts, *hein?"*

"Catherine." She held the girl's hands. "You seem happy, even though Jean has to—"

Skipping back, Catherine tilted her head to one side. "Not because he is forced to leave, *comprenez-vous?* No one forces my Jean to do anything. It is only better that he does, that we all depart this ungrateful city. He has plans, my man; another Barataria somewhere along the Gulf, another base from which to harry the cursed dons. Jean Lafitte is no supplicant begging mercy, but a great corsair chief!"

"Come," Caroline said with a glance at Robert, "sit with me and have some wine; tell me how it is in the city, what they say, what you will do."

Bouncing upon the sofa, Catherine said, "I will go with Jean, of course, sail with him wherever the winds take us. The city—*peste!* So many geese hissing and waddling back and forth. Pirates, we are called, banditti for whom gallows wait—ha! But never to our faces, never."

When Caroline brought sherry, Catherine accepted the glass and nodded. "I see Robert is gone. A fine man, that one; a woman could do worse."

"He means to sail with the fleet," Caroline said. "I cannot hold him."

"It would be caging the hawk," Catherine said.

Or the mockingbird, thought Caroline, making a prisoner of something that ought to soar free and singing. A trapped mockingbird was poisoned by its own kind, she remembered. It was kinder than the slow corrosion of captivity.

"But *you,"* Catherine said, "your name is on almost as many tongues as Lafitte. A dangerous woman, they

459

say, a madwoman who frees her slaves without recompense and *pays* them for work. Of course, there are whispers that you are of the blood, an imposter who has somehow managed to gain control of Delacroix. There may be trouble for you, *chérie*."

"I will face it when it comes," Caroline answered. "I am doing nothing against the law, and as for being a mustee—now there is no record, Catherine. I only worry that Felipe will somehow press his claim to me, and to the plantation. Jubal—" When she said his name, Caroline paused, because it was ashes in her mouth. "Jubal thought the lawyer in Illinois was lying, that someone had been there before him. Who else could it have been but Felipe? And if he found proof that I am indeed Justina LeCroix, has he hidden or destroyed it? All I have is a reward poster, the statement of a dying man and the deposition of a doctor."

Tossing her head, Catherine said, "Felipe will be lucky to keep his skin whole, much less plot against you."

"Until the Baratarians are gone," Caroline said. "And please don't ask me to come with you. I explained to Robert that I cannot, that too many here depend upon me."

Catherine twirled her wine glass between small, capable fingers. "It is so sad, when other events get in the way of love. To me, Jean is the only importance, but I think you are unsure—Robert Gray or the big red bear?"

"The bear is gone forever," Caroline murmured. "He could not stand the thought of black blood, or even the suspicion of it. He—he saw the bill of sale and took Felipe's word. Jubal d-didn't even ask me if it was true. If he had, what would I have answered —that even I am unsure?"

Rising, Catherine came to her, held her. "One does what the heart speaks, *hein*? But listen—there will be some of us left in the city; not many, but a few who listen for news. I will name these for you, so you may find them if you have need. And do not forget, you learned much at Grand Isle, much of the rapier and cutlass, the pistol—and there is always that small knife you carry between your shoulders. I see it now hangs from a golden chain. You were a Baratarian, you *are* one yet, and we do not surrender easily."

"I mean to stay here," Caroline said. "No matter what they do, I will stay here."

"*Très bien!* With such *esprit,* how can one be defeated? My dearest friend, I must go now. Jean needs me for many things, but I could not leave without *adieu.* Perhaps someday—"

Holding the girl close, Caroline said, "Yes! Perhaps someday." And because she could not say more, because she could not see through the tears that filled her eyes, she didn't see Catherine Villars depart. She was left with the warm memory of a kiss upon her cheek.

She sat for a long time, until a gentle hand fell upon her shoulder. Turning her head, she pressed her wet cheek against Robert's palm.

Chapter 48

When he woke up with a barmaid on each side of him in Edgecombe Tavern, Jubal's head was hammering like a big drum and his mouth felt like a tribe of Creek Indians had camped there for a week. Eyes squinted against torturing light, he slid one arm beneath a naked waist, and eased another sleeping woman from his shoulder.

It took some doing to wobble out of bed without rousing either tavern wench, but he made his way to the washstand and poured a pitcher of cold water over his head. That's when he discovered the discolored lump over one eye and a set of swollen knuckles. Must have been a ring-tailed rip-snorter, Jubal thought dizzily, and rinsed his mouth from a jug of corn whiskey. Naked as a jaybird, he sat on a stool and opened the shutters to piss out on the street below.

Somebody hollered outrage up at him but the tomtom in his head hurt too much for him to cuss back. He drank a little of the corn and felt some better, near about good enough to crawl off and die. He wondered who he tangled with last night, and howcome. No good reason, he figured, just that he was touchy as a rattler shedding its skin and some poor son of a bitch got in his way.

As memory came back, he recalled regaling the drinkers with tales of Andy Jackson and the wars, telling how the Redcoats got themselves whipped worse than the Creeks. He remembered buying whiskey for everybody, and how old Buster Rogers kept showing his toothless gums and joking at him for more details. Edgecombe Tavern had missed him, that was for certain, and they sang "Yankee Doodle" and "Barb'ry Allen" and anything else come to mind. Buster kept shoving jugs at him and the others, and the new girls, neither of whom had been there when he left for the wars, warmed up to him real cozy.

Couldn't remember their names now, but it didn't matter none. They'd for sure wallowed him around in that bed, though; nigh about busted it down, jumping around so. Jubal made a face at his cigar; both of them together didn't make a patch on Caroline Monteleone's buttock. They couldn't do as much for him as that little old scorpion-shaped scar she carried there on that rounded, golden haunch.

"Goddamnit," he said, and one of the barmaids stirred on the tousled bed. It was just because they were wenches, he thought, rubbing at his temples; they put the action to diddling, but maybe their hearts weren't in it. Right off, Jubal could see they wouldn't do, nor any like them. He took to pondering over what women he knew, and which could be easy reached.

One of the barmaids had yellow hair, the other one, brown. Yellowhead sat up, big breasts hanging down, blinking smeared eyes. "You sure enough a stallion, Jubal Blaze. Heard tell you was, but feeling's believin'."

"Buster still got that big washtub?" he asked.

The brown-haired girl rolled over and groaned. Yellowhead said, "Reckon."

"Beholden was you to fill it with hot water and find me a razor. Seems like I got my pants tore last night, too; don't know where'n hell my shirt got to. Expect one of you'll have to run over to the store and get me some more clothes."

The brown-haired wench muttered, "Run, hell; be lucky can I walk. Feel like I had a piney log stuck up me."

Yellowhead grinned and got out of bed. "You be whinin' for more, come night."

Jubal found a rag and used it to dip in the washpan;

463

coolness felt good against his face. He held the rag to the bump over his eye, and felt the long scratches down his cheek—Purity Blaze's mark—and what was it somebody said about a woman scorned? Couldn't let Abel see that brand, because it looked too much like what it was. Maybe Purity could have done it for him, wiped Caroline out of his head forever more; lord knows she was made fine for bedding, and hot as a fired pine knot. Could be he was a damned fool for passing up such neglected and hungry quim, but he couldn't bring himself to stick his own brother's wife. Not right then, anyway; not with her selling herself the same as these wenches, but for a whole lot higher price. A whore was a whore, and the only difference was the charge.

The bath made him human, but he couldn't shave worth a damn account of the nail marks. Scraped around them, his face looked patchy, so he gritted his teeth and cussed as the razor took off scabs and started blood. Purity Blaze was running scared, thinking he'd do her and Abel out of the land, knowing full well he could, too. Abel ought to know better, he thought, then decided Abel never really knew him, since they never teamed in the same harness, but pulled different ways.

How the hell could a man come home to settle, when nobody believed he would? How could he get by, living under the same roof with Purity thinking up more devilment and never forgiving him? Did she lie to Abel about what happened, his brother might think on killing, and that would be his right. Rinsing lather off his face and pinking the water with blood, Jubal thought he'd do best to stay away from Tarboro a spell. Let Abel figure he'd gone straight back to his rowdy ways, until Jubal planned out how to talk to him. He didn't know yet what he meant to say.

The publican kept yammering at him all through breakfast, so when Jubal finished, he paid Buster for damage and the wenches, and wearing his new clothes, crawled up on his horse. The widow Delaney, he thought, Maggie Delaney; she was a hearty woman who needed a man in her bed and knew how to pleasure him there. It beat dodging husbands, anyhow, so Jubal reined his horse to the east and took off for Maggie's place.

Only when he got there, he discovered her name wasn't Delaney anymore. It was Arlington, and Virgil Arlington kept looking at him squinchy-eyed, so he bade her and her new husband farewell. Time he drew up at Labelle Stewart's plantation, Jubal wanted to rest and have a bite to eat more than anything else. But as luck would have it, John Stewart was off on a trip to the Tidewater, and Jubal's belly was still empty when Labelle got him between the covers.

He concentrated; he really paid attention to what he was doing with the woman. She was little and randy and carrot-topped, and when she got to her short rows, she carried on like a she-bobcat, all claws and teeth and wiggly hunchings. Jubal held her down, and turned her on top, and did all the things he learned in New Orleans, until she was wilder than a horsing mare trying to reach a stud. No tavern maid, this one, but a respectable wife who just didn't get enough of it from her husband, and she loved like Judgment Day was tomorrow and this was her last chance to get caught up.

When they'd settled some, and she held his face between her small, sassy breasts, Labelle purred, "I missed you, Jubal. You goin' to stay awhile? John won't be back for weeks."

He meant to, damnit; he'd halfway planned on it, holing up somewhere to work off the madness in his blood with some horny, free-giving woman. But he said, "Reckon not, Labelle. You know how it is, me just home and all. I came to see you right off."

"And I'm happy you did," she said, trying to stroke him erect again. "There never was a man like you, Jubal Blaze. Sure you can't stay a spell?"

"Just for supper," he said. "Then I got to light a shuck for home."

Swinging her pert little bottom out of bed, she ran her hands over a tiny waist and partway down sleek thighs. "Hear tell your brother's got him a real beauty for wife. That the cause for your hurry?"

"No such thing," he said. "Ain't no man in his right

mind would leave you for any other woman." Which was a barefaced lie, he thought, because there was more to it than just beauty and special hot diddling. There was a kind of fitting together, a kind of excitement and breathlessness that stirred in him whenever Caroline Monteleone just put her deep, black eyes on him.

Black; that was the key word—*black*. Like the color of her scented hair and the silken vee of her mound; like the nigger in her blood—nigger mammy or grandpappy; nigger somewheres, to cause her to look white but make her a goddamned mustee.

"Look like you're cloudin' up to rain," Labelle said. "It was good for you, too, wasn't it?"

"Good as ever," he said. "John's a lucky man."

John had him a white wife with no taint to her. Jubal had never faulted a woman for trying another man between her legs, did she get shorted by her wedded husband, like most men faulted her. No more than he'd back off from Caroline because she was being kept by that Creole bastard, that Alcantari son of a bitch who *bought* her. It wasn't her bedding somebody else that tied up his innards in hard knots; it was her being part black. Goddamnit, there wasn't any such things as being *part* black; one drop of nigger blood made a nigger, nothing else.

Labelle fed him good, and tried to get him heated up again, but he kissed her goodbye and took his horse out on the road in the night. There was the smell of dust, and green things growing, and once an eddy of early honeysuckle, and the road was clear enough in moonlight, lonesome as all hell. He had nowhere to go but home, unless it was back to Edgecombe Tavern, and Jubal wasn't up to hoorawing the night through again.

He remembered that other tavern, the one along the Natchez Trace, where travelers got knocked in the head and chunked down a well out back. A woman decoyed for that one, too. Off in the moonlight a mockingbird trilled its exultant nightsong, and he wanted to holler *shut up* at it. There was just no damned way he could stop thinking of Caroline at all, not unless he was too blind, falling-down drunk to think of anything. The rest of the time she pecked away inside him until he quit fighting her off. Then she came flowing in her full glory, radiantly creamy as a magnolia, that cascade of ravenwing hair tumbling across bared shoulders and clear to her hips, hips that were like no others because they belonged to Caroline. If Jubal let himself slip further, he could reach out and just about feel the rare texture of her skin, the satiny heat of it; he could nearly taste the nectar of her incredible mouth, the honeyed juices of her mound.

Shaking himself all over, like a dog come dripping from the creek, Jubal urged his horse into a faster gait, as if he could leave her ghost behind. She rode with him, sometimes behind the saddle with her arms around his waist and her softwarm breath blowing down his neck; sometimes she danced ahead of the horse, fairy dancer in the moonlight, daring him to come and play with her. At Labelle's house, he must have had more to drink than he remembered.

It was late when he reached Tarboro, and he was surprised to see a lamp shining through the sitting-room window. The hounds came belling out at him and he cussed them into slinking back. When he unsaddled the horse and put him in a stall, hayed and grained him and fumbled through the kitchen, the lamp was still on. Jubal hoped to hell it wasn't Purity waiting for him, with Abel still off somewheres. He'd a heap rather face the British rockets again.

When he came blinking into the room, Abel rose from the chair by the fireplace, Pa's old comfortable chair where he used to sit and draw on his pipe. "Evenin'," Jubal said, and headed for the whiskey cabinet.

"Nearer to mornin'," Abel said.

Jubal took a big, warming drink of corn. "Growed up a spell back, Abel. Don't need anybody waitin' up on me."

"Have you grown up?" Abel said. "Have you? Look at you, face marked by brawlin' in a tavern, smellin' of whiskey, comin' home with the tomcats, because that's what you been up to—tomcattin' around the country again, throwin' money around."

"Guilty," Jubal said. "You the judge?"

Abel's body was stiff, his hands clenched. "If you don't care how folks talk about a Blaze, I do, bigod! Pa put up with it because he was too old, and—"

Pouring more whiskey, Jubal brought glass and bottle to the fireplace where a bed of coals still glowed red. He said, "Keep Pa out'n it. You got your back up at me, speak your piece, but don't go leanin' on a dead man."

Trembling, Abel said, "Always so goddamned sure, ain't you? Sure you can run off to war and come back without a scratch; sure women will fall all over you; certain sure of Tarboro—"

Jubal said, "That's what sticks in your craw, Tarboro. You're actin' pretty damned sure of yourself, certain I mean to claim my heritage and make you beholden to me for every bite in your mouth. That—or turn you out on your own. Abel, you never asked. You looked at me like I'm supposed to be dead yonder with a British ball in me, and you glad for it. And your wife—"

"Watch your mouth," Abel said.

"I ain't faultin' Purity none. She's a whole lot of woman, maybe more'n you know, and she can't be blamed for runnin' scared account of I come home."

"You didn't come when Pa died."

"I didn't know, and couldn't come, if'n I did know. Pa'd understand; he fought against Bloody Tarleton in seventy-eight. Wars ain't somethin' you leave when you got a mind to, and they're not near the funnin' they're made out to be." Jubal looked into the bed of coals, propped his elbow on the mantelpiece. "But you didn't wait up to hear about war, nor spite me for Pa's buryin'."

Abel said, "You're right. I've been talkin' to Purity, and we—I got my head set on knowin' what you mean to do."

Jubal looked at the coals through his glass of whiskey. "Suppose I mean to just tomcat and throw

468

money around? That might be real good for you and Purity, 'cause sure as sin, some woman's husband is bound to catch me out and pop me with a load of buckshot. Can't spend enough to hurt none, neither; only drink so much corn and bed so many tavern maids."

"Is—is that the way you want it?" Abel asked. "I keep tendin' the land my way, and you won't interfere?"

"No," Jubal said, "that's how *you* want it, brother."

"You mean you won't—" Abel's face went all tight and strained.

"Man comes home when he's got nowhere else to go, or when he means to hide from somethin'. A man like me, anyway. I never been a planter, nor took interest in the land, like I ought. The burden's always been on you, Abel, and I expect that's where it stays. Don't know what in hell I figured to find here—peace, maybe. Could be I been runnin' from myself, but here I am, face to face with ol' Jubal, anyhow."

"You're talkin' a lot, but you're not saying much," Abel muttered, reaching for the jug of corn.

"I'm sayin' Tarboro's yours, every inch of land, the house, every nigger save one, all the stock save horses I'll choose. I want a letter of credit to any bank in—in New Orleans, credit for say—thirty thousand dollars. That won't hurt you none, nor will about ten thousand in gold to tote with me. If'n that sets right with you and Purity, we'll ride into Edgecombe tomorrow and see to the lawyer."

Abel drank, blinked rapidly and drank again. "Is—is that all you want, and you'll sign over all claim in Tarboro to me?"

"One nigger for a body servant on the trip; three of the best horses, 'cause I mean to ride fast, and the money. Oh—one more thing; Pa's old shotgun here, for remembrance."

"Damn!" Abel said, gone bright-eyed. "Good goddamn, Jubal! I kept tellin' Purity, but you know how it is with a woman. They just got to fret over somethin'. Come down to it, you ain't askin' much, Jubal. There's ten thousand acres, and nigh three hundred niggers, and I been close with hard money, you know that, closer'n Pa, even. You sure that's all you want?"

"Reckon so," Jubal said. "You can go tell your wife she's true mistress of Tarboro now."

Purity Blaze, not Caroline Blaze. Now she would never come down the staircase in a ballgown, so beautiful that every man below would gape up at her and the women hiss behind their fans. Tarboro wasn't for her, nor for him. She couldn't help being what she was, and Jubal had been loose-footed too long to put down roots now.

He heard his brother clatter up the stairs, and sat down in his pa's chair to hold the whiskey jug and look into the smoldering coals. The moon was down, and outside the wind whispered among the eaves of Tarboro.

No mockingbird sang.

Chapter 49

During the long and lonely mornings, she learned about planting; afternoons Caroline often spent with Gilbert Rochemore, as the lawyer patiently taught her the ins and outs of trading, with little side lessons on what she might expect from the bank, and from other planters.

He seemed younger to her now, even with his balding pate and lined face, for Gilbert was a friend, and she desperately needed someone to fill the emptiness left by Robert Gray's going, by the departure of Catherine Villars.

"The city yet seethes with rumors about the Lafittes," Gilbert said, toying with his watch chain. "Are they about, are they not? Have they left for good, or is it a tactical ruse to throw off enemies? *Qu'est-ce que c'est?* No one is certain."

She had not told him of Felipe, and would not. Perhaps he was far away by now, or kept underground by fear. She said to Gilbert, "The others worry me— Gaspar, Fozatte; city merchants. All are against my freed workers, and if they become certain none protects us here—"

He reached for her hand and held it. *"Mon enfant,* I am with you, and M'sieu Perritt thinks too much of his bank to choose sides. *Chère* Justina, if I could only—"

She withdrew her hand, but gently. "Perhaps in time, Gilbert. I am much troubled now."

He smiled. "You do not think me too old?"

"Mais non," she said, "for I have myself lived a thousand years. Someday I will tell you of them. For now, remain my friend and advisor."

"But of course, Justina."

"If none will buy our crops, if the blacks are attacked and not allowed to defend themselves, how long can Delacroix last?"

Rochemore rubbed his chin. "Years, my child—financially. But if you have no workers—"

"They will stay with me," she said firmly.

He shook his head. "I cannot understand you, Justina. You are young and beautiful and educated. Yet you persist in defying law and tradition to make such an—an experiment with freed slaves. You bring gossip upon yourself by allowing pirates to remain under your roof—" Rochemore held up his hand. *"Non, non;* I do not deny your right, but such talk feeds the flames."

"Fanned by such as Gaspar and Fozatte."

"They are traditionalists, as are we all. What we do not know, we fear, *n'est-ce pas?"*

Caroline said, "I fear more what I do know."

"Ah," he said, "but you are a different kind of woman; *oui,* totally so. It is one of the things that makes you so intriguing."

Gilbert Rochemore didn't press his suit, if indeed that's what it was, although more likely an arrangement, she thought. She wondered how he would react if he knew of her possible black blood—as Jubal Blaze had, with shock and disgust?

She continued to sleep by herself, and when she wasn't wornout, used the lonely nights to practice in the big sitting room before a full-length mirror with rapier and cutlass. Over and over, she repeated every cunning trick the corsairs had shown her, each fighting specialty developed through long and bloody experience by such as Dominique You, Beluche and Nez Coupé. Yes, and also those learned from Robert Gray. Her wrists became stronger, her balance more assured, and often she was tired enough to sleep without dreaming.

In time and with Tchaka's help, she learned to load

her own pistols and to put a ball within a circle ten paces away, more often than not.

"Long's nobody sees me holdin' no gun," Tchaka said. "Them planters spooked as 'tis, without word that a nigger army buildin' up over here. Law come down on any black totes a gun, less'n the town needs him to fight them English, and that ain't likely for a spell."

She asked if he was being bothered when he took wagons to the city, and Tchaka said not much, because the merchants knew they could buy cheaper from him and he had no say in it.

But there were no visitors to Delacroix, no strange white face since Lucien's funeral, and no invitations came for Caroline. When she had to go to the bank, curious eyes and whispers followed her; men stared and women pretended not to. Some blacks gave her quick smiles, while others hurried fearfully from her presence. In the carriage or on the street, Caroline quickly checked each passing face, but never saw the one she most dreaded, that of Felipe de Alcantari.

And how many men, she wondered, had seen her at the Quadroon Ball? How many were spreading the story that the mistress of Delacroix, that wholesale freer of blacks, was black herself? Without proof—and that ominous bill of sale had been destroyed—nothing could legally be done to Caroline. But it wasn't legalities that bothered her.

At the moment, the city was still reveling in the British defeat, taking more glory and credit to itself after Jackson's army marched away. The companies of Creole volunteers were yet being fêted at balls, and the freedmen who'd fought beside them celebrated themselves. But when the carnival atmosphere waned, when all the stories of valor became worn with the telling, the city would turn to new gossip, and certainly Delacroix would be high upon the rumor list.

If only she could show them, thought Caroline; if they gave her a chance to prove that willing labor was superior to slave labor, more productive and less expensive. Would the hearts of planters be ruled by tradition or by their purses?

She felt so *alone*. Robert Gray was gone, his ship and adventuring more important to him; her Baratarian friends had all left, and Jubal Blaze—she wouldn't think about him. If she didn't have Gilbert Rochemore to talk with, Caroline might consider giving it up, selling out and going someplace where none had even heard her name. If a man named M'Nele hadn't died so she and her mother might be free; if Solah didn't lie in an unmarked grave behind a house on the Ramparts; if so many happy, planning, hopeful blacks didn't depend on her. The burden was heavy upon her, but there was no one else to bear it, so she would carry it as long as she could.

Gilbert Rochemore? Did the lawyer care enough for her to marry her, to take on the responsibilities she'd created? She didn't know, and the problem was certainly not his. Gilbert was a Creole; what he thought about her might not extend to the former slaves, perhaps not to Delacroix. There was a debt to be paid to Lucien LeCroix. Lucien would not like to see his ancestral lands ruled by a stranger. He'd died believing Caroline was his sister.

This evening, rising from dinner in the kitchen where she was routinely served now, she thanked the cantankerous old cook, a round, busy woman named Hattie. When she stood by the sitting-room fireplace, grey and still now that the weather was warmer, she could wish for winter again; a popping, leaping fire might be cheery. The candles and lamps were not; their flames were too pale and lean.

Sighing, she took her rapier from the mantel, whipped its blade back and forth, and walked over to face the mirror. Tonight sleep would not come, unless she was weary to the bone.

Outside, one of the old hounds barked; a horse rattled hooves upon the crushed oyster shell drive, and Caroline lowered her point. She wasn't expecting Gilbert Rochemore, but sometimes he dropped in without

474

warning, just to visit, to watch her responses to his unspoken courting.

Toinette appeared from the kitchen and was at the door when its knocker first fell. Caroline thought how she hadn't seen a frown or sullen look on the maid's face since Toinette had been freed, how quickly and thoroughly the girl did her work.

"Back up, nigger," the man said from the doorway, "and do it goddamn fast."

Unable to speak, Caroline only stared as Kleppner pushed his way in and strode toward her. He carried a pistol in his belt and that terrifying blacksnake whip coiled in one hand. *Kleppner!* Brutish slave trader, first man to take her body; the man who'd sold Solah to a cruel planter—*Kleppner.*

There was the smell of gut-wrenching fear about him, the ghostly clanking of chains, and he moved in an aura of savagery, with death leering over his shoulder.

Oh God—it all came roaring back over her; the shame and hurt, the degradation she'd known and fought when her flesh awakened to his, the things he'd used to make her less than human, to turn her into his animal.

His grin was confident, lascivious. "That how you greet callers, wench—your mouth hung open that-away? Nothin' but niggers here, reckon you forgot your manners to a white man."

Caroline's hand was suddenly damp upon the hilt of the sword. Kleppner's hungry smile made itself wider and sharper. "You want your ass peeled, just make a move with that sticker. I'll jerk it out'n your hand so goddamn quick—"

Leather hissed softly as the lash uncoiled and readied itself to strike.

Finding her voice, Caroline said, "Wh-what do you want? No—never mind; get out—get *out!*"

"Or what?" Kleppner asked, watching the rapier. "You goin' to call one of your free niggers? I know damned well I'm the onliest white on the place, and that for certain sure includes *you,* missy. Never seen a nigger could stand to a white man."

"My l-lawyer—"

He moved a pace nearer, muddy eyes glittering, whip slithering behind him. "What's your lawyer man goin' to say, when he sees this here piece of paper I'm totin'? What's all them free niggers goin' to do, when they find out they ain't free atall? Two things you oughta know, wench—that ol' Kleppner don't never make out a bill of sale, less'n he makes his ownself a copy all legal like; next, that can't no mustee wench turn loose slaves when she don't lawful own 'em. Now —drop that goddamn blade afore you get my back up!"

Her pistols, she thought; if she only had her pistols. The rapier slipped from her sweaty fingers and she stood facing him, her mind fluttering helplessly, as a mockingbird might beat its wings against a cage.

"Better," Kleppner said, so close now she could smell the grime and sweat of him. "A whole lot better, wench; knowed you to be smart enough not to bow your neck at your master. Less'n you been screwin' some black buck, I figure you to be good and horny by now, too. Hot bitch like you, she can't go long 'thout a man atween her legs."

Backing away from him, Caroline tried frantically to think, to find a way out. Bill of sale; Kleppner said he had another bill of sale that would make her black again, that would destroy all she'd worked for. It would ruin Delacroix and enslave hundreds again.

The quicksharp bite of the lash nipped at her thigh. "Not yonder way," he said. "I kin see them pistols plain as you. Gittin' mighty uppity since you been playin' like you white."

"What—" She moistened dry lips. "What do you want from me?"

"Some of this, some of that. You 'n me, we'll be seein' a heap of each other, leastways till we git our business done. Might's well be friendly, like you been learned. Ain't never forgot ol' Kleppner's pizzle, have you? Folks say no wench ever forgets the man diddled her the first time."

"There's money," Caroline said.

His free hand eased out and cupped her breast, tweaked its lax nipple. She winced, and he said, "More money than you figure—this here house and its plunder, all this good cotton land, the stock and what all you got in the bank. You kin keep right on playin' you white, that you're sure enough Miz LeCroix for a spell. Give me one speck of trouble, and ever damned one of them niggers gets his papers took back by the law."

Knees going weak, Caroline moved back and sat on the couch. How much better it would have been if Kleppner had resisted Felipe in the ballroom courtyard that fateful night. He wouldn't be here to plague her, to threaten the lives of hundreds. She leaned back and felt the slight pressure of the dirk between her shoulders. "You'll let them alone, allow them to go?"

Kleppner grunted. "They worth a peck of money, but oncet I got me a bushel of gold, I ain't about to fret over no peck. Them niggers can run off anywheres they want."

He was lying and she knew it. Once he'd sold off Delacroix and all its assets, Kleppner would make up another slave cavvy, and she would be with it. Had he come alone? She'd heard only a single horse, but some more of his ruffians might be waiting outside. Just now, he wanted more than such riches as he'd never known; he also wanted Caroline, needed to make her crawl and beg again, yearned to have her perform like a trained beast. If Kleppner owned all the treasure in Louisiana, he'd still be poor white trash, aching to prove himself not.

Running her tongue across her lips, she murmured, "You were always too strong for me, and I—I do need someone. It's been too long. I tried, but if it didn't work out, well—"

His lips curled. "You ain't foolin' me a lick. Know damned well you'd put a pistol ball in me if'n you could, but it's that fire in you makes your quim so good. That Creole son of a bitch got him a bargain when he nigh about stole you off'n me, but lookee here if ol' Kleppner ain't got you again."

477

When he leaned over her, Caroline said, "Please, not here. The house servants—"

"Don't give a hoot about no house niggers," he said and reached down for her shirt. "Let 'em get a good look and see how a white man screws."

If he broke the chain around her neck—if the dirk fell—Caroline rolled from the couch and leaped up. Serpentlike, the whip coiled about her ankles and brought her crashing to the floor. Showing yellowed teeth, Kleppner said, "Knowed you quit too easy, but that's your last try. You make to run off from me oncet more, I take about a inch off your ass with this here blacksnake, and you ain't got all that much meat to spare."

She sat up and tugged at the lash, but he snatched it from her and spread his feet, snarling, "What *you* want, you black bastard?"

Caroline spun about on her knees. "Tchaka! No, don't try to—"

But the big Mandingo was moving forward, his thick shoulders hunched and hands spread. "Netty said you was in trouble, missy."

"Back off, nigger!" Kleppner yelled. "You hear me —*back off!*"

The whip darted out and cut down across Tchaka's shoulder. Swifter almost than her eye could follow, she saw him clench the lash in one huge fist and jerk. Kleppner stumbled into her as he was yanked off balance, his knees driving her to one side.

Tchaka had the whip in both hands, its butt dragging across the floor. "Now," he said. "Now, slaver man."

She saw Kleppner spread his feet, saw the hairy hand close around the butt of the pistol in his belt. Her own hand dipped behind her head and she came up off the floor, hurled herself up and at him. The dirk slashed his wrist just as he lifted the pistol. Kleppner squalled and staggered back, but she was on him still, trying for his throat, his eyes, anything the quick little blade could reach. The pistol rattled against the floor and skidded, but Kleppner threw Caroline off and scrambled for it.

478

"Too late," Tchaka said as he kicked the weapon aside. "Too late and too little, slaver man. You don't look near so big now."

Crouching, Kleppner backed away, step by step, eyes popping and breathing heavily through his mouth.

"The sword there," Caroline said, "and pistols on the mantel."

Kleppner screamed when the whip cut into him, when it coiled snapping about his ribs and cut his shirt. He tried to run, tried to pull the lash away from Tchaka, but he wasn't strong enough. The blacksnake struck again and again, all the great strength of the Mandingo's massive arm behind it. The third stroke drove Kleppner across the room and into a wall.

"Don't cut him to pieces yet," she said, getting to her feet, "and not here, please. He has something, a paper."

"Chunk it all at her feet," Tchaka panted, "papers, purse, anything you got. Three licks ain't near what you done to me, slaver."

"Yeah," Kleppner slavered, "yeah, yeah—"

Stooping to sort through a wallet with the point of her dagger, Caroline said, "This is it."

"Make—migod—make him turn me loose," Kleppner moaned. "You g-got the bill of sale, so don't—don't let him beat on me no more."

Caroline didn't hate him now; she didn't feel anything, not revulsion or fear or rage. Memories slid cold within her, images of what this cringing man had done to her, to Solah; she saw the coffle of slaves struggling along the road, dragging the long chain; she saw black flesh that would forever wear the marks of cruel manacles.

"Tchaka," she said, "take this animal with you."

"No!" Kleppner yelped, but the treetrunk arms were around him, squeezing, holding his feet off the floor. "N-no—don't let him! He's agonna kill me—folks knowed I was comin' here—they'll come after me—no! Goddamnit, no!"

She walked to the cabinet and found the brandy, putting her back to them.

479

Kleppner tried again, desperately: "Anything you want—anything I got! Gold, missy—a heap of gold —my house and barn—horses—you can't just let him tote me out and kill me—please, *please!*"

She heard the door open and Kleppner's fingers clawing at its frame, trying to hold himself inside, trying to hold off the darkness. His voice was rasping and thin: "He'll hang for it—you all will hang for it —niggers killin' a white man—"

She didn't turn around. "No," she said, "I don't think we will. I don't think anybody will know, or care, what happened to you."

The door slammed closed, and Caroline lifted down a candle, held it to the papers crumpled in the fireplace. They made a blaze that was quickly gone.

Chapter 50

Slamming his hat upon a chair, Gilbert Rochemore snatched up a bottle and poured a glass of wine, downing it quickly. He poured two more, and turned to hand one to Caroline. "Damn them," he said. "Damn them all, and especially Henri Perritt."

"He is a banker," she said, "and so it is logical to protect his interests. If other depositors withdraw their money because of me—"

"Because of filthy lies!" Gilbert snorted.

Caroline glanced at Tchaka, standing mute in the hall with the heavy satchel of gold coins. "Hide them for us," she said to him, "so that only you know where."

Gilbert's eyes followed the Mandingo. "Ah, *ma chérie*, are you certain of that one? A fortune, after all—"

"I trust him as much as any man, no matter his color."

Gilbert hesitated, then shrugged. *"Eh bien*, but I suppose I should have hidden it in my office, instead. *Ma foi!* I was so enraged at Henri Perritt—" He drank more wine, his face flushed. "Someone, some infamous liar, is behind these rumors, these scurrilous attacks upon you. They have spread so swiftly. *Oui, oui,* the city had nothing to talk about, after it was certain the corsairs were gone and the battle has become passé. But why you, why a fine woman like you, Justina? True, none cared for the method by which you freed

481

so many slaves and yet kept them working for you, but that gives them no cause for this—this other dirt they fling."

She looked at him over her wine glass. "You do not believe I am what they say—an octoroon?"

"Of course not! I have my eyes, I have my heart. And there is no proof they can show, not a shred of evidence. If these *cochons* thrust a sheaf of so-called documents into my own hands, I would decry them as forgeries. *Sacre!* Such *absurdité*. Perhaps it is all a nefarious plot, a stratagem to force you to withdraw your money so it can be got at by thieves."

"Tchaka will take care of that," she said. "Torture could not wring the hiding place from that one."

"To think I called Henri my friend," Gilbert said. "But that is *fini;* what troubles one now is that the markets are not buying Delacroix meats and vegetables, at any price. When the cotton crop is ready, I have no doubt it will be most difficult to find a broker."

"There is money," Caroline said, "and Lucien built warehouses. We will store the bales until someone is willing to buy. Delacroix is self-sufficient, and can endure."

"Madame," the maid said from the archway.

"Oui, Toinette?"

The girl was not in uniform, but wore the casual chignon and simple dress of the *griffe libre;* even her feet were bare. She said, with an oblique glance at Gilbert, "The mission I was sent upon—"

"M'sieu Rochemore is a friend; you may speak freely."

Netty said then: "The *juju* leaders, Doctor Dambah and Madame Zozo; they whisper of a curse you carry. They call you Mam'selle *Scorpionno* and say you wear the mark of your master, the scorpion, that you will poison all of us, black and white alike."

Gilbert fisted the arm of his chair. "What nonsense!"

Caroline held up a hand to him. "Toinette, what effect is this having upon our people?"

Pausing, the girl looked down at her feet. "If it were not for the *gris-gris*—but the feather and cane dolls

482

have been left upon cabin doors, and there are some who are ever stupid."

"How many, Toinette?"

"Perhaps *trente* field hands, madame—thirty or so. They fled in the night. But no house servants have left; not one."

"Mon Dieu," Gilbert muttered, "it is a vast conspiracy. What good are house slaves—ah, servants—with no field workers?"

"We will endure," she repeated. *"Merci,* Toinette." And when the girl was gone, she said, "They are like children, some of them; unused to freedom, to making decisions, and threats baffle them—especially when backed by conjure, by voodoo."

"But what is this about the scorpion? Why should they—"

"A birthmark," Caroline answered, "upon my haunch. It was the identifying mark of Justina LeCroix, when she was taken from here by—two runaways. To the superstitious, those believers in conjure, the scorpion is enemy to their dark god Damballah, the serpent. Someone is using my people's fears, their simplicity, to ruin Delacroix plantation. But most remain loyal, because they realize that what hurts me also damages them."

Gilbert's face lost its tenseness; his brown eyes softened. "You have a—almost a saintly understanding of these people, *chérie.* Or perhaps I should say a clinical knowledge. I do not like to think of you as a saint, Justina. They are so cold and unapproachable."

He was steady, faithful, giving much and asking nothing in return. She smiled at him. "I have also been marble, Gilbert."

"But you are no statue," he protested. *"Mais non;* you are a woman so—so very much alive and warm that I—"

"You have been *très* patient, my good friend."

Passing a silken kerchief over his balding head, Gilbert said, "I had hoped to be—I have desired to be—"

He was saved from the embarrassment of putting it into words by an uproar behind the house, a rising babble of voices soon overwhelmed by the dominant bass of Tchaka. A moment later, the Mandingo dragged a squealing black into the sitting room.

" 'Scuse me, missy, but this here nigger—"

"Nigger yosef," the man spat.

Tchaka shook the man so hard that Caroline could hear his teeth pop. "Mind your manners, boy. Just 'cause missy's here, it don't save me bustin' you in two."

"What is it, Tchaka?"

"Strange niggers been creepin' around the place, hangin' up *juju* signs, talkin' trash to our folks. Rest of 'em took off, but this yeller un ain't so slick."

"You big black bastard," the captive said.

Casually, Tchaka slapped the woolly head back and forth with one great hand while he used the other to bounce the man's feet up and down against the floor. "Don't listen good, neither. Tell missy who sent you, boy."

Eyes rolling and fight gone from him, the mulatto said, "Madame Zozo."

"That's right good," Tchaka said. "Now, who she workin' for?"

"Don't know; I—wait a minute, now! Don't hit me no mo'—could be a white man, that Alcantari feller. Leastways, I hears so."

Tchaka looked at her. "Want me to snatch off a leg or arm, then turn him loose as warnin'?"

"Let him go," Caroline said, the very sound of Felipe's name chilling her. "I don't think he'll be back."

"You lucky," Tchaka said, hauling the man away. "Be sure tell the next un, he won't be."

Gilbert let out a sigh. "One sees what you mean, about your overseer; a terrifying man. Alcantari—of course; Felipe de Alcantari, the duelist. But what have you to do with him, why should he—"

"He was my—lover," she said, and watched hurt come into Gilbert's eyes. "No saint, remember?"

"I do not mean to criticize, *chérie;* a woman alone —one understands. It is just that Alcantari has such an odious reputation."

"I had no choice, Gilbert; believe that. It was before

484

there was proof of my being Justina, before I even met Lucien."

He reached to take her hand. "I will always believe you, my dear. I ask no questions, nor do I make judgments. My own life has not been faultless."

Caroline did not take away her hand. She said, "Are you very hungry, Gilbert?"

In surprise, he blinked at her. "Why do you ask?"

"It is nearly dinner time, but if you will be satisfied with wine and cheese, we can picnic in my room."

His fingers tightened over hers, this good man so hopeful that she could not tell him her true relationship with Felipe, this man to whom she owed much and was about to pay a little. There was little of the romantic about Gilbert, but he was wise and kind, and perhaps that would be enough. She had deceived herself before, in the name of love, maybe twice over, maybe not. Gilbert was dependable; he would not turn his back on her in time of need. He was a lawyer who weighed evidence, and she would not confuse him with any sort of confession.

If that is betrayal, she called silently to the shades of Jubal Blaze and Robert Gray, then I will be a traitor.

Up the stairs she led Gilbert, bearing cheese and dark wine. She thought of Felipe plotting and maneuvering out there, Felipe now with nothing to hold over her head but himself, or he would have used it already. She would ask Tchaka to bring other strong men into the big house, to sleep across thresholds and watch for Felipe, for he would surely come. He was far too impatient to wait her out; every passing day would only increase his thirst for vengeance. It was better to face Felipe here than upon ground of his own choosing.

Beside her, she could feel Gilbert tremble as they entered her bedroom, and his hands shook when he placed bottle and wedge upon the bedside table. She was beginning to know a lift of excitement herself, for it had been a long time since Robert Gray had set sail, longer still since Jubal Blaze had turned from her.

Surely there had to be more to life than struggle and fear, and if love was only a lie, then this could be a close substitute.

"Sit there." She pointed to the bed. "In a moment, I will undress you."

Gilbert swallowed. "Justina—"

Reaching to unhook the golden chain at her throat, so the hidden dirk would drop at her feet, she followed it with her dress and chemise, stepping nude from the puddle of fabric. Gilbert's eyes devoured her exposed body. "I want to undress you, Gilbert; I want to be many things to you, very good to you."

So he removed only his shoes as he lay back to pillow his head, his eyes never leaving her. Caroline sat beside him, loosening his stock, unbuttoning his ruffled shirt so she might explore the skin of his chest with her fingers. He was lightly haired and smooth of flesh, his stomach jerking softly when she leaned to kiss his nipples. Her hands turned busy at Gilbert's pantaloons when she brushed the rigid nipples of her breasts back and forth across his body. In reflex, in need, his own hands came up to caress them.

Lifting himself to help her slide down his trousers, Gilbert took the opportunity to pillow his face between her breasts, and it was her turn to quiver as his kisses fluttered upon them. Caroline found his shaft ready, and toyed with it, her hand judging length and heft and roundness, skilled at making it throb and tingle and jerk against her palm.

She moved softly upon his body, lips finding his mouth, her tongue taking the initiative, attacking his with fierce demand. She had been taken by other men, forced by some, but now she was taking; in her abandoned giving, Caroline was taking from this man the things that exiled loneliness. He was human warmth and intimate closeness, and for now, for perhaps this single, inviolable moment, she loved Gilbert Rochemore. Or she made love to him, if there was a difference.

Eagerly, he held her against him, cupping her mound as if he could never bear to release it. He caressed her hips, her buttocks, and she felt his fingertips linger at the slightly raised sign of the scorpion. Poised above him, trapping him with her hand, she eased her body gently down upon his upright manhood. Enveloping him slowly, inch by vibrant inch, she drew him into her secret places where she laved him with honey and sheathed him in wet velvets.

"Mon amour, mon amour," Gilbert groaned. *"C'est magnifique—c'est très étonnant—*amazing—"

Grinding upon him, adjusting him to suit her every need, Caroline locked his lower lip between her teeth as her nails found purchase in his shoulder, his thigh. Deliberate movements turned into harsh thrustings, into a churning, plunging frenzy whose rhythm mounted to a shuddering, straining climax. She moaned upon him, twisted upon him, so that he began to seek another cresting for them both, and in time, in sweaty and groaning coupling, it came crashing over them.

When she lifted from him and curled at his side, Gilbert said softly, "You have made me young again, Justina, strong again—if ever I was so powerful."

"And you have made me happy," she murmured. "I needed comfort, Gilbert. Lie still and rest; I will prepare the wine and cheese."

Comfortable in her nakedness, knowing that ancient Ashanti pride in her body and the wonders it could create, Caroline broke off pieces of fragrant cheese and fed him. They laughed together at silly things, at this newness that was yet an exploration between them.

And when he had eaten and drunk and smoked part of a small cigar, she dripped wine upon him, down his ribs and over his belly, into the joining of his thighs. Ever so gentle, ever so tantalizing, she began to lick off the drops, curling each into her tongue as if it were a jewel of great price.

Gilbert was of French and Spanish blood, but of a different generation, and she thought she had shocked him beyond recall. But when he stroked her hair, when he arched to her, Caroline knew she had again conquered him, that he would be completely hers in a very short time. She devoted herself to his pleasure, to teasing and withdrawing, until he gasped and writhed upon the bed and dug his hands into its sheets in spasm. At the height of his ecstasy, Gilbert cried out, went rigid, then fell back upon the pillow, rolling his head from side to side.

Rinsing her mouth with wine, she looked fondly down upon his supine form. He was a good man, a fine friend, a protector; if he did not lift her to impossibly dizzying heights, it was not for lack of trying, and she was grateful to him for making this night different and filling it with warmth.

He slept and she watched over him, sipping wine and lighting a lamp that pushed back shadows and spread false gold over the bed, over their bodies. In the cabins beyond the barns, she could hear chanting faint upon the springtime wind and wondered if some of the older blacks were not trying counter-spells, calling upon their own gods to shield them from Damballah.

She was forced to think of Felipe, and how different he was from the man in her bed. Gilbert could never be cruel, would never hurt or humiliate. Was she being fair to him, not disclosing all her past, all her doubts to him? Perhaps, but she could not hurt him either.

M'Nele, Solah, Tchaka—none of these would have let Felipe go, to cause more trouble. She had, and she was sorry; she wished her blood ties with the Ashanti were stronger. If so, he would no longer be a threat to her. Did that weakness mean she was really Justina LeCroix, white and hesitant, white and illogical? No matter; she had claimed the name, and would fight to the death to hold it.

He stirred upon the bed, and she bent to smooth his brow, to lightly kiss his cheek. Gilbert's eyes fluttered open and he said, "Never, never has there been such a woman anywhere upon the face of this earth. All my years, all my life, I have dreamed and wondered, but now I know. And I am the luckiest man in the world, *ma petite, ma chérie.*"

"You are a dear," she whispered.

He came to one elbow as she sat back, and accepted

488

the wine she poured. Again his eyes roamed her body, touching here and there with the pride of possession, the spur of memory. *"La belle Justina,* the loveliest woman man ever knew."

Smiling, she said, "Gilbert, you are beautiful in your own way. Some men are, you know." And some are not, she thought; some are hideous within themselves, some only twisted. Felipe was a horror; Jubal was malformed, and Robert Gray was—a man never to be held captive by the land or any woman. His cage was the restless sea. And her own prison—black netting, white bars? This land, a promise given?

"This should be done with formality," Gilbert said, "but I have wasted too much time as it is. Justina LeCroix, will you do me the signal honor of marrying me?"

She stopped smiling, but her eyes held to his. She said, "I do not know, Gilbert; I do not know."

Chapter 51

He had damn near ruined three horses getting here, and now that he was in New Orleans, Jubal wondered why. Morosely, he stared into his glass of brandy and eyed spiraling smoke from his cigar. Down at the livery stable his body servant Cabax was trying to put their horses back into condition, and probably trying as hard to get over the trip south, the weeks in the saddle, chilling brushes with marauding Indians and road agents. The black had lived harder and faster than ever before, and was nearly as gaunted as the stock.

Lifting his head, Jubal looked along the bar. It seemed more Americans were here now, some coming down after the battle, some of the woodsmen staying on rather than returning home. Funny how he kept expecting Tom Pickett to show his grinning face, when he knew full well the man was dead, that he'd been forced to kill him for being a British agent. Tom Pickett could have been a friend, he thought, and he damned the kind of battle that set a man like that on the wrong side.

The feel of the city had changed; it was back to its old ways, casual good living, gaming, laughing, talk of mistresses and horses and duels. The aristocrats did that; working people just kept working. Jubal found himself noticing how many light-colored blacks passed up and down the street. There was no way of telling how many were freedmen, how many slaves, and why the hell should he care one way or another. It just irritated him that so much white blood had been crossed in.

Few men approached him, although he didn't wear buckskin now, but neither did he resort to the frippery of the rich Creole, and somber clothing marked him for what he was, a Kaintuck outsider. So men who passed the time of day with him were likely to be rivermen and remnants of Jackson's army, English-speaking folks going into business here. Clannish, disdainful in their satin and silk cocoons, the Creoles tried to ignore the newcomers. But often Jubal would hear a sudden shift into English from some smoky corner table, a not too subtle remark being passed, which the speaker wanted the butt of his joke to understand.

Sometimes he would pick up a French word here and there, among the mixture of languages, and what he heard kind of washed away the effects of the brandy he kept downing. He'd listen in one bar until the conversation switched, then take himself off to another drinking place, where he'd catch the same general story, repeated and embellished and changed around some.

It seemed the name of Justina LeCroix was on damn near every tongue, and not to the good. Turned loose her niggers, they said, then *hired* back them that would stay; arming them, it was told, getting a whole goddamned black army ready out there at Delacroix plantation. Her foolishness could ruin the whole country, give niggers ideas no good for them and worse for whites.

Jubal clenched a big hand around his drinking glass as he listened, as he heard men whisper that Justina LeCroix might have herself a private nigger buck, that there could be a touch of the tarbrush to the woman herself. Nobody knew where she came from, how she suddenly appeared to lay claim to Lucien LeCroix's estate.

But the good Doctor Lejeune testified that Lucien himself acknowledged her as his sister—but was not Lucien dying and out of his head?—and had not she been involved with the notorious Baratarians, perhaps lover to Jean Lafitte himself? No matter; her actions are a thing which cannot be allowed. . . .

Jubal stamped from this cafe to that, from cool, lavish places to workingmen's bars, and always the rumors, the spite hammered at his ears until his head rang with them. He poured down brandy to still the sounds, and raw corn whiskey, too. They didn't seem to work, so he turned morose and withdrawn and wouldn't say a civil howdy to anybody.

He wasn't interested in whores, either, and spicy French food lay heavy in his belly. He found a place down by the river that catered to rivermen, where he ate honest beef and beans. But even there, they gossiped about the woman stirring up so much trouble with her niggers. It galled Jubal that nobody would allow him to forget her, that wherever he turned, her name got to him, and right behind it came the vision of her, all thundercloud hair and golden flesh. Then he'd remember the hurt look in her dark sloe eyes when he turned from her, the pain when she saw how she had sickened him.

She'd done it, damn her; it wasn't his fault, but hers, for masquerading as white, for making it so godawful easy for a man to fall in love with her. When that Creole son of a bitch faced him with the paper, all she had to do was deny it, and Jubal might have taken her word, even with the evidence staring him in the eye. But she didn't; she just stood there like a whipped hound pup and didn't scream out that she was white, that not a drop of nigger blood flowed in her veins.

Hell, even her name was a lie—Caroline Monteleone to him, Justina LeCroix to everybody else.

Stalking the city, Jubal felt a need he couldn't put word to. There was something pecking at him, driving him, and because he didn't know what in jumped-up hell it might be, that made him more ornery. Freedmen would take a quick look at his scowling face, at the size of him, and scuttle out of his way; boatmen and Kaintucks knew that look and avoided crossing his path. Even haughty Creoles were a bit more careful around him, and he silently damned them for that.

Maybe he meant to track down that goddamned Al-cantari, and concentrated on looking for him, not for a moment able to forget that sneering, uppity face with the new scar on it. But Jubal didn't know what he'd do when he found the bastard; stomp him, if it would help anything.

He was on Rue Burgundy, elbows propped on the marble counter top and drinking some bitter green stuff that left a black taste in his mouth, absinthe, they called it, when he caught sight of himself in the mirror. His eyes were bloodshot and he hadn't shaved for days, hadn't changed his clothes; he was a mess.

"Got it on good word," said a Kaintuck at the end of the bar. "This here nigger lover means to spread her pizen far's she kin reach."

And a Frenchman said, "But yes; that is understood, m'sieu. It is why the banks have cut off her credit, why no tradesman will buy goods from Delacroix plantation. Yet one hears of much gold out there, hidden by blacks preparing to use it for an uprising. Ah—it is one thing for a man to buy himself a quadroon mistress, and quite another affair for a white woman, presuming she is truly white, to bed down with sweaty black bucks."

"Reckon what she needs," the other man said, "is a good, hard *white* pizzle shoved up her. Be more'n likely to mouth it, though; white men don't grow pizzles big as a stud horse, big as a nigger."

Shoving back his glass, Jubal straightened up. He looked down the bar and said, "I figure both you bastards are right fond of runnin' off at the mouth."

The Creole paled and his hand sought his sword hilt. The Kaintuck got a good grip on a wine bottle and said, "Don't see howcome it's ary your business."

"Makin' it so," Jubal said, and moved.

The Creole never got his rapier from its scabbard. Jubal knew a thrill of joy as he snatched up the man, rattled his teeth with a good, solid butt, then flung him the length of the bar. The other man swung the bottle, but Jubal took it on the shoulder, grinned and axed

493

a fist into his face. This one broke two wooden chairs as he plunged into them and slid beneath the table.

"How about you?" Jubal asked the barkeep, the other drinkers. "Come on, how about it?" When nobody answered, Jubal said, "Oh hell."

A stiff and careful quiet hung about him as he stood chewing off the end of a cigar and thumbnailed a match to it. Outside on the street some kind of ruckus was starting up, so Jubal snorted a puff of smoke and set out to join it, when the barkeep said, "M'sieu—why is it that you protect the name of Justina LeCroix? Do you know her?"

Rolling his shoulders, Jubal said, "I ain't sure. Just seems I'm hearin' too much about her, and I figured —what if everybody's wrong?"

On Rue Burgundy, he shook himself all over and sucked in great draughts of air. He felt some better, but only a mite, like he'd gotten just a taste of cure for whatever ailed him and needed a whole lot more. Folks were hollering up the street, milling around and yapping like a pack of hounds ready to tree a coon. The crowd boiled down upon him, flinging mud and chunking rocks at a balding man who ducked and stumbled and tried to fend off men with a sweep of his walking stick.

"Hold up!" Jubal yelled as men bumped into him and swirled around him, but nobody heard or paid attention. He was pushed nearer the bald man, staggered now by a lick across the head.

"Well all right," Jubal said, and set himself good. He caught a screaming man a good one in the mouth, and teeth flew every whichaway. Then some sassy Creole made a pass at him with a sword cane, and Jubal ducked low to snatch a thin ankle. When he roared up again, he used the Frenchie like a flail, whipping him around and around and just knocking the plumb hell out of some surprised fellows.

There were yelps and curses, and Jubal threw away the Frenchman and waded in, heavy fists sledging something fierce, taking a lick now and then and laughing because it felt good, felt right. They hit at him and flung at him while he stood himself in front of the bald man and drove them back. The man was on hands and knees, shaking a bloody head, and damned if a sneaky little bastard didn't try to circle Jubal and get at him. Jubal got a good hold on that one and rammed his head into the brick wall.

Somebody nicked his arm with a knife, and somebody else busted a club across Jubal's head, but that was just fine, because he needed the sweat and blood and violent action. Kicking the feet out from under a squalling Creole, he hammered another one in the belly and mighty near took out his lights and liver. He got to stomp the Creole a time or two, but had to leave off funning when a rangy sod tried to line up a pistol at him.

Jubal hit the ground rolling, and scissored his feet around the pistolman's legs. The short gun banged when he fell, and Jubal tried to drive his face right on through the cypress blocks of the street, whooping like a crazed Indian buck. He gave that up to bellow into a knot of them, big fists pumping, giving better than he got and grinning savagely through the taste of blood in his mouth.

Then it was done. A couple of them were trying to crawl off, moaning and carrying on; more of them lay unmoving, scattered hither and yon, and a few were lighting a shuck back up the street. The bald-headed gent was up again, back braced to the wall, walking stick held ready to club. Jubal shook off blood and sweat, his whole body thrumming like a fiddle string.

"No need, mister," he said. "Looks like we run plumb out of somebody to fight."

The man's face was smeared and dirt-fouled, cuts high upon his head trickling steadily down his cheeks. His eyes cleared somewhat as Jubal approached and gave him a bandanna to soak up the bleeding. "I—I am grateful, m'sieu. That pack of dogs meant to pull me down."

"Had you by the short hairs right enough," Jubal said. "Howcome they were treein' you?"

The man swayed, and Jubal propped him on one

arm. "Here now; just hold on. There's a cafe over yonder, and time you take a swallow of brandy—"

Wiping at his head, the man said, "They will not serve me there, m'sieu—nor anywhere else."

"Hell they won't," Jubal said, and near about carried him back into the bar, where the Creole was still stiff on the floor, and the boatman crouched on the floor being sick. The barkeep's face held itself immobile and Jubal said, "Bottle of brandy."

Two glasses appeared with the bottle. Jubal propped the hurt man against the bar and poured drinks for them. The man's hand shook and liquor splashed over the rim of his glass, but he got the rest down. Jubal poured another, conscious that men were slipping past him for the street, that the cafe was emptying. He put silver atop the marble counter and reached a long arm for a solid chair, but the bald man shook his head.

"I w-will not drink where I am not welcome. My—my office is not far from here, my new friend. If you would be so kind—"

"Sure," Jubal said, "but I ain't heard anybody *say* you ain't welcome." He stared at the barkeep and the man shook his head. Jubal wrapped one arm around the bald man's waist and his other fist around the bottle. They went into the street. A constable was standing among fallen bodies there, looking helpless. When they passed him, Jubal said a polite howdy.

There had been a big window to the office, but it was smashed out, and shards of glass scattered inside. A desk was turned over and a chair kicked into matchwood; papers were flung everywhere. "Set," Jubal said, finding a whole chair and tilting it up. "Another good swallow and you'll be rarin' to go."

"Mon ami," the man said, mopping at his forehead, "I owe you my life and my honor. I had no weapon, and when they broke in upon me—ah, the *cochons,* the cowards. I am Gilbert Rochemore, attorney at law."

Jubal gave his hand. "Jubal Blaze, but you ain't beholden to me. I purely needed that little hooraw; got my juices to runnin'." He took hold of the desk and pulled it upright; some drawers fell out, but it stayed steady on its legs when he set it down. "Seems like lawyers don't get into ruckuses like that un. Leastwise, them back home don't."

Color was coming back into Rochemore's grimed face. He poured brandy on the kerchief and washed his cheeks, winced as it bit into his wounds. "I have an unpopular client; for this, they attacked me, the dogs. As if I could be frightened off."

"Might get killed off," Jubal said, with a pull at the bottle. "I don't see no constable come askin' about your window. Law against you, too? Hell; if I never tried to drink the town dry, I wouldn't be askin' what ain't none of my business."

"I am grateful for your assistance, M'sieu Blaze, and *mon Dieu!*—what a terror you were to them." Rochemore drank and blinked. "You were a—a great bear raging among yapping dogs."

"More like a mule without a lick of sense."

Rochemore put a hand to his head. "They—I was set upon because I am the only friend she has, the only champion, and a poor one at that. The city grows ever uglier, more frightened, more vicious. As soon as I recover my strength, I must ride out to warn my client." He drank again, wiped his face again. "She will be in dire need. If a mob forms—"

Jubal didn't take the bottle when it was offered. He said, "This client, she wouldn't be the one they're all gossipin' about—this Justina LeCroix?"

"Oui," Rochemore answered. "A great and beautiful lady, for all her stubborn ways. If her ways are not ours, not those of the city, still one should respect her for them, *hein?"* Leaning back in his chair, he said then: "Do you know of Justina LeCroix, m'sieu?"

"A little," Jubal said, looking at his hands and finding scratches there, a swollen knuckle. "Understand folks won't buy from her and they say she's armin niggers to revolt. They say—well, that she's beddin' down with 'em, too."

"They will not buy, and will not sell to her; the rest is a lie, a base lie. I know it to be so. The blacks, they

497

worship her, work very hard for her—and themselves. She freed them all, *oui,* but with a purpose in mind, an honorable purpose. Justina is—she is—but how can one describe Justina? There is none like her."

Jubal didn't say anything.

Rochemore roused himself. "If—I would deeply appreciate your help, m'sieu. If you would remain here until I change, until I feel strong enough to reach my horse, I will go to warn Justina to leave, to hide until this madness runs its course."

Now Jubal took the bottle; now he nodded. He said, "Don't reckon she'll listen, mister; don't expect she'll run off."

Startled, Rochemore said, "Then you *do* know her." Jubal answered: "Does anybody?"

Chapter 52

Though bathed and tended with salves and unguents, Gilbert Rochemore was still badly shaken. His ribs had been securely wrapped, and after damning the cowards who had struck him, Caroline insisted he stay in bed, propped up and sipping wine that touched his bruised cheeks with a bit of color.

"The *Américain*," he said. *"Magnifique, ma chérie;* one would not believe his awesome strength, the manner in which he flung about those curs."

Yes, she would believe; she'd known the closeness of that power, and something else—the enveloping tenderness of Jubal Blaze. When Gilbert told his rescuer's name, it had come like a blow to her heart, almost cutting off her breath. He was back in the city, but why? Surely not to see her; he'd made it plain he never wanted to lay eyes upon her again. It was a painful twist of fate that crossed his path with Gilbert Rochemore's.

"He spoke as if he might know you," Gilbert said from his pillow.

Caroline turned away. "At one time, we were acquainted," she said, then looked back. "Oh Gilbert, I am so sorry. For me, you were attacked, your office destroyed, your friends driven off."

"It is evident I had no true friend. And for you, *mon amour,* I gladly set myself against all the world."

Her smile trembled around the edges. "You are gallant, m'sieu, but the real world is not; it is filled with treachery and falseness. Rest now, *s'il vous plaît;* I must attend to plantation business. I will be with you soon."

She could not remain close to him, because the shadow of Jubal Blaze lay between them now. Caroline descended the stairs and moved through the kitchen to where Tchaka and some of the men waited her.

"We aimin' to fight?" Tchaka asked.

She put a hand upon his forearm, a pale, small hand against his muscular blackness. "We can't, Tchaka. That's the excuse they need, armed blacks facing white men. They'll swarm over us like vultures, and pick our bones clean, if the governor has to send troops to help them."

The others muttered and shifted uncomfortably. Tchaka said, "They about to do it anyhow."

"It's possible," she admitted. "News that Gilbert brought from the city isn't good, and I doubt if Toinette's spying trip will return better reports."

The Mandingo flexed his arms. "What we goin' to *do,* missy?"

"I will face them alone, when they come," she said. "*If* they come. I am a LeCroix standing upon LeCroix land. Maybe they will see and understand that, and go away."

"If'n they don't," Tchaka grunted, "it account of they see you as a mustee, or nigger lover. Won't make no never mind which; they tear you up."

Caroline searched the taut black faces—hopeful, angry, frightened, and all dependent upon her. She said, "Then it'll be only me hurt. You all have wives and children; if a bloodthirsty mob gets to them—"

"Hell," Tchaka said, "best they get moved out afore time."

Proud of their loyalty to her, Caroline nevertheless refused it. "You're free men and make your own decisions, but I ask you not to endanger your freedom and lives for me. If the mob sweeps over Delacroix, run, run far away. Tchaka knows where gold is hidden, and he'll take care of you with it, until you can care for yourselves."

"Missy—" Tchaka said, as she turned away quickly, the tears gathering in her eyes. Back in the house, she wiped at them impatiently and thought of these men, classed as animals by whites, as a lower form of life, but willing to lay down their lives for their belief in the concept of freedom. And for Justina LeCroix.

Crossing to the study, Caroline put her hands upon the mantelpiece and pressed her forehead against laced fingers, unable to think clearly. She knew only that she must somehow defend this land and its people, that she must burn from her mind the troubling image of Jubal Blaze.

"Mam'selle?"

She turned. "Toinette—back so soon?"

"One must hurry now," the girl said. "I fear there is little time. Has M'sieu Rochemore returned? What a terrible thing they did to him, such madmen they were—ahh, but not so mad as to face the Kaintuck. Now the city gossips of him, and waits for what will happen to him."

Clenching her hands, Caroline said, "What do you mean? What do you know of Jubal Blaze? Oh yes— you saw him here, but if he is in danger—"

Netty took the slave *chignon* from her head. "I think he is in the greatest danger of his life, mam'selle. Last evening, I followed him when he left M'sieu Roche- more's office. *Ma foi,* what a man! To walk the streets alone after what he did."

"Please, Toinette—"

"Mais oui; the Kaintuck traveled from cafe to cafe. It was as if he sought out trouble, and find it he did. With—with the other one, mam'selle."

Caroline lifted a hand to her breast. "The other one?"

"The *furieux* one, Alcantari; the vicious man. Of course I could not enter the cafe, but from the *ban- quette,* I could plainly hear. The Kaintuck was some- how forced to challenge Alcantari, perhaps by other men, perhaps because he was enraged and *ivre*—drunk, one understands. There was much shouting and noise, and when Alcantari stamped out, he wore a curious smile."

Oh God, thought Caroline—Felipe had trapped Jubal into issuing a challenge. Felipe therefore had the choice of weapons, and she didn't doubt for a moment that he would choose swords. Jubal knew nothing of rapiers, épées, anything like that. The fool; the great, blundering fool. He'd issued his own death warrant.

"The Dueling Oaks?" she asked. "When?"

"Dawn tomorrow. So we will not be bothered tonight; there is too much attention upon the duel, and the cafes remain open all night so that men may know which one returns from the field."

"Wolves," Caroline spat, "wolves waiting for the secondhand taste of blood. They hate Felipe, but he is one of them, and Jubal is not. They will howl when Jubal falls."

She left the girl staring and pounded upstairs. Gilbert was sitting on the edge of the bed. She said quickly, "A duel—Felipe de Alcantari and Jubal Blaze. Felipe will kill him. Gilbert, there must be seconds, *hein?* Who would assist Jubal, who would serve Felipe?"

Gilbert stood up, tucking his shirt into breeches. "I must find M'sieu Blaze and be his second. *Le docteur* —I suppose Doctor Abadie will also consent to act with us. As for Alcantari, he will find no lack of seconds, because of the city's mood."

"It is too soon," Caroline said, forcing her brain to slow. "Supper first, and the use of your carriage, not mine with the LeCroix coat-of-arms so prominent upon it. Tchaka can bring it here."

"Justina, what have you in mind? According to the code of the *duello,* no woman is allowed—"

"Foutre the code! The man is in peril because of us —yes, both of us. I will not turn my back upon him now."

After a moment, Gilbert said, "This man; there was more than an acquaintance between you? *Non*—never mind; I ask no questions about your past, *chérie.* It is enough that you include me in your present. And it is also enough that he stood between me and the pack. But rules are strict on the field, and no woman has ever—"

"Once I passed for a Baratarian," she said. "In a cloak and hat, in darkness, no one will know I am not a man."

Gilbert started to say something but changed his mind and clamped his lips together. *"Eh bien,* then. As you wish, my dear."

For all her outward calm, Caroline could only pick at the meal set before her, and excused herself while Gilbert drank coffee. Her old corsair breeches, one of Lucien's shirts and a coat, a cloak long and black, a feathered hat. And the chain about her neck, holding its dirk snug; a pistol in her belt, and she was ready for the rapier on the sitting-room mantel.

Why was she doing this? Did she actually care if Jubal was slain? Yes, damn it; at least he was a man of conviction, even if his ethics were warped, while Felipe was a deadly snake. The rumors, the whispering campaign against Delacroix—Felipe was probably behind it. If he could not have her and the land, he would destroy both. Caroline didn't have it clear in her mind what she meant to do, only that she was determined that Felipe de Alcantari would not leave the Dueling Oaks alive.

Downstairs, she paced the room like a caged tigress, clinging to a dim and fanciful hope that if Felipe was downed, perhaps the mob would not march on Delacroix. She meant to buy time, hold back sand in the hourglass, for each passing day might bring Robert Gray and his corsairs to her aid. Another faint hope, she admitted, but she must cling to something.

"Those pistols," she said to Gilbert. "Is it allowed for seconds to be armed?"

"Naturellement," he answered. "Seconds are on hand to make certain the rules of conduct are obeyed. If there is a transgression, we are to set it right, with gunfire if necessary. Justina, this wild plan of yours—"

"Take the pistols from the mantel," she said. "They are well primed. Where will you reach Jubal Blaze?"

"My office, *probablement;* he spoke of no rooms, only of a slave and horses at a stable. If we do not find him there, we will try the stable."

"The idiot," Caroline said, "the fool—allowing himself to be tricked into dueling Felipe. Upon his own terms, he would crush Felipe in his hands like a fly, but with swords—"

Tchaka had the carriage ready for them, candles burning in the glass lanterns, curtains drawn. Caroline paused and waved Gilbert inside, then motioned Tchaka down from the coachman's seat to whisper in his ear.

"Be a spell, then," he said. "Got to get hold of somethin'."

She waited beside Gilbert in the carriage, a brandy bottle at her feet. He reached for her hand. "Whatever this man means to you, *ma chérie,* I will do my duty."

Tchaka's weight made the coach creak, then the horses were moving it along. Caroline said, "I never doubted you, Gilbert, and you deserve more from me than silence. Very well; once I loved Jubal Blaze, but he did not love me in return."

"A fool," Gilbert said as the coach rocked toward the city and its dueling grounds.

"Oui," she agreed, "with the great heart of a bear, and perhaps the brain, also. But Felipe is the troublesome one, behind every filthy tale about me, directing this assault upon Delacroix. I was—" She could not tell him the truth, could not admit she'd been owned by Felipe de Alcantari. "He means to revenge himself upon me, and this is but one of his methods, this unequal duel. Felipe *enjoys* killing; it is like a warming drink of whiskey to him, like having a woman."

Silent for a while, Gilbert said, "But I do not see what help we can be. In all honor, I cannot shoot Alcantari. Besides, his seconds would then fire upon us in turn."

"I do not ask that, Gilbert. I—I do not know what I want, beyond Felipe's death. All I know is I must be there."

They rode in silence then, the horses' hooves echoing from the structures they passed in the sleeping city.

In the heart of town, there was wakefulness; Caroline could hear revelry from cafes open beyond their wont, spiteful bursts of hilarity that grated upon her nerves. It was wrong to celebrate death, whosoever it might be.

"I will wait here," she said sometime later, when the carriage stopped. "You may introduce me to him as—as M'sieu Toussaint."

"Yes," Gilbert said, getting out.

In the quiet darkness, she thought of the name she'd chosen, that of the strutting, insufferable little man Kleppner had hired to teach her manners and correct her speech, before the Quadroon Ball. She was feeling, behaving unnaturally this night, the strangeness within her guided by some dark, implacable fate. Touching the butt of the pistol, the hilt of the rapier, she told herself it was not for Jubal but for Delacroix, for what the plantation meant to so many people. Felipe alive was always a threat; yet his death might serve a cause more worthy than any in his wasted life.

They were coming. She shrank into the corner of the coach and pulled her hat lower. When Jubal climbed inside, she smelled brandy, felt the unwelcome touch of his thigh, and mumbled at the introduction.

"*Non,*" Gilbert said somewhat formally, a bit stiff, "swordplay is not a game for children, m'sieu. And Alcantari is *une bonne épée*—an excellent swordsman. If he had only chosen pistols—"

Caroline recoiled at the deep sound of Jubal's voice. "I was so goddamn mad, he just tolled me in, I reckon. Mouthin' on her thataway, and all them other bastards laughin'. Musta been a dozen of 'em atwixt us, and time I knew who he was, they had me blocked off with pistols. That's when I called him a coward and hollered for him to meet me. Expect they took that to be a challenge, because he came right back with rapiers and the Duelin' Oaks at daylight."

She could edge no farther away; the bulk of Jubal Blaze dominated the seat. Gilbert Rochemore sighed and said, "There is little directness here, beyond that which you will soon face. One can hope your strength and size will overpower skill and cunning, but this I do not believe."

She could feel Jubal shrug, the passing of his shoulder against her cloak. "Well now," he said, "reckon I had my tail in a crack afore. That son of a bitch don't skewer me slap through the heart, I mean to bust his goddamn back."

The coach rocked; Tchaka clucked to the horses. Jubal said, "Case it don't work out right, you know where my nigger is, and the horses. Boy's a good one called Cabax brought down from Carolina. He's settin' guard on our plunder, and there's a heap of it sewed in my saddle. More in the bank, come to think on it."

"A letter of credit?"

"In the Banque d'Orléans. Good thing you're a lawyer. You need a signin' from me to get it out?"

Gilbert said, "Before the duel, then. Am I to return it to your family if you are—unable?"

Caroline felt Jubal's thigh flex, heard him draw a heavy breath. "Reckon not," he answered. "Burned my bridges when I left Tarboro; turned the land over to my brother and took a share in gold. Came back down here after that, just to—to—damned if'n I know howcome, mister. So I'd consider it a favor, was you to pass the money along where it'd do some good, and you can turn Cabax loose, or whatever the hell you do when a slave gets freed. The money, well, it's a considerable amount."

Gilbert said, "And you trust me with it, m'sieu?"

"You stood up for this—Justina LeCroix against the whole damned town, and that's good enough for me. This other feller can be witness. Damned if'n you folks don't ride a long way to fight; how much more to go?"

"It is almost dawn," Gilbert said. "We are close. I will do as you ask, m'sieu, and may *le bon Dieu* be with you."

Turning on the seat, Jubal reached across Caroline to draw back a curtain. She shrank from his touch, from the grey light. " 'Scuse me," he said. "You don't talk a whole lot, do you?" Then to Gilbert: "A spell back, you called me *ami*—friend; now you keep sayin' mister. Any special cause to that?"

"I am your chief second," Gilbert said, "and will stand by you in all things."

Jealous, Caroline thought; Gilbert was furiously jealous because she'd told him she once loved Jubal Blaze. But he was a gentleman, and meant to do his duty. She wanted to reach for his hand, to say she no longer felt that passion for Jubal. The carriage drew to a stop, and she had other things to do. Opening the door on her side, she slipped to the ground, smelling fresh dew and the new morning and trampled grass; scenting death.

Tchaka swung down from his high seat, and Jubal ducked out of the coach to turn slightly and look to where lanterns glowed wan and sickly, where three cloaked men waited like so many hunched birds of prey. He stood tall and wide, shucking his coat to free his arms.

Climbing down on the other side, Gilbert was just walking around back of the carriage when Tchaka took a quick, soundless step to hit Jubal deftly behind the neck with something that made a soft and definite *thunk*. Jubal sagged and the big Mandingo caught him as he toppled, grunted him into the open door of the coach and onto the seat.

"What is this?" Gilbert said. "What manner of—"

"Do not interfere," she said. "Tchaka is binding him, and—Gilbert, forgive me."

Then Caroline was running across the damp grass, loosening her cloak as she sped, drawing the slim rapier from its sheath. Upon the waiting men before they realized what was happening, she flew at Felipe, cut viciously at him with her steel and drove him stumbling back.

They shouted at her, rushed apart to reach for weapons; one stumbled over a lantern and fell sprawling. There was Felipe, his hated face touched by the rising sun, his sword hissing free as he ducked beneath her furious charge. She turned and thrust at him, but he parried her blade.

"Ah, the bitch herself! *Bien, bien*—it is you I want, *you!*"

He was swift; cold steel nipped her upper arm as Gilbert came running, came shouting at the top of his voice: *"Non, non!* That is no duelist, but only a woman! For the love of God, stop them, stop them!"

Blade rang against blade, and Felipe smiled. "Little whore, little black whore—I shall draw your treacherous guts like a chicken."

She dropped to one knee, and it was Dominique You's voice in her head: *His crotch, his legs.*

"Chiotte—bitch!" His return sweep knocked off her hat and her hair flowed loose. But she had pinked him, blooded him.

"Alcantari!" his seconds shouted at him. "Turn away, man! You cannot fight a woman."

"This is no—no woman," he snarled, "but—a mustee wench trying to kill her master. Stay back!"

"We cannot allow—"

When Felipe wheeled to slash at them, at his own seconds in his black rage, she went for his belly again with a long, reaching stroke. The tip of her rapier tore his blouse and slid around his ribs.

Backhanding his sword, Felipe chopped at her head, and she felt the cold kiss of its passing stir her hair. He came at her in a frenzy then, his blade a play of lightning she could barely ward off. His face was terrible, lips peeled back from his teeth, deepset eyes burning with implacable hatred. Dawnlight touched the old scar she had placed upon his cheek.

The Baratarians had taught her well, and Caroline employed every ruse they'd showed her. The hilt of her rapier smashed into Felipe's chin, but he recovered his balance with remarkable agility, and got away from her following slash.

Back he drove her, and farther back as her muscles strained and sweat began to cloud her eyes. Felipe's blade was everywhere, the licking tongue of a snake, a flashing of honed steel, a constant flickering of its fatal point. She parried and struck, parried and thrust.

Her shoulder scraped the rough bark of one of the

Dueling Oaks, and she shrank from the flash of his blade, pawed left-handed for a pistol in her sash. Caroline bit back a scream when he cut her knuckles and the pistol spun away. She tried to guard against him, but his rapier darted in and out, and her sash fell away with the other weapon.

"Inch by inch," he grated, "I—will—peel your— Negro skin from—you—until you—you beg for— death!"

She slid away to put the tree between them, to recover her breath, but he was after her. Then she saw Gilbert Rochemore, his feet spread wide, the dueling pistols from Delacroix held in both hands.

"You were warned, Alcantari!" he cried, and both guns went off—high and wide, neither ball coming close to his target.

Felipe leaped after him, and Caroline stumbled behind, drawing the dirk from between her shoulders, reaching desperately with her sword, touching him with its point. Felipe turned upon her again, cursing through his teeth. In his eagerness, he almost ran onto the dirk; she tried very hard to spit him with it, but the devil's own luck rode with him and she got only his blouse.

A lock of her hair drifted past her face, and contemptuously, he slapped her cheek with the flat of his blade, enough to make her stagger. Tasting blood, gasping for breath, she retreated until her back braced against a giant oak. Caroline waited him there, sword point dropping, but the dagger tightly in her other fist.

"*Stupide!*" he panted. "Did you think yourself a match for Alcantari? Yellow wench—black whore— know your punishment now!"

Curling her body to the right, she went to both knees and stabbed upward with the dirk, missed, and flung herself down to roll. Her sword was snatched away and she closed her eyes, praying that it would be quick, that he would not torture her.

But her eyes snapped open as a roar shook the hovering leaves, and there was Jubal Blaze, cords hanging broken from his wrists, her rapier like a toothpick in his great hand.

"Alcantari! You son of a bitch, see what you can do with a *man!*"

"Gladly, Kaintuck," Felipe hissed, and lunged in a single, fluid movement.

But for all his heft, Jubal was incredibly fast, and his blade whirred down upon the stroke that should have spitted him. The very force of it whipped Felipe halfway around and threw him off balance. Coming to her knees, Caroline watched in exhausted fascination.

Recovering, Felipe feinted and thrust, but somehow Jubal made him miss, and the clang of their locked hilts rang loudly throughout the glade. Caroline heard a grunt, and saw Felipe's booted feet lifted from the earth, saw his body raised and flung kicking through the air. Catquick, he landed and came partly erect, only to meet the slam of Jubal's foot. When he rolled up again, Felipe de Alcantari was without his sword.

The bear came at him, rapier flung aside, massive arms spread. Caroline saw the white stamp of terror upon Felipe's face, his mouth open to scream. Then Jubal gathered him close, pulled him tightly to that vast and powerful body. Felipe squealed and writhed and tore at Jubal's ducked head with clawed fingers, but the crushing grip was inexorable, ever-tightening iron bands that cut off his air.

Pushing herself up, Caroline took a wavering step forward, then stopped. Felipe's head rolled back and a stain of crimson gathered at the corners of his mouth. Jubal loosened the vise then, but only to cartwheel Felipe across his hips, to lift him higher as he dropped to one knee. He brought Felipe down sharply, and she shuddered at the damp *crack!*

Jubal rolled the dying man off his knee, but the rag doll had venom left. Motionless, Caroline heard him gasp it out: "You—you think she is white because—because of that birthmark. But—it is not so. It was—it was I who reached Illinois before—before you, Kaintuck. I—bought the papers—but know the truth, for there were—*two* small girls taken to—to the North. One was—black, the other—white."

Felipe fought for breath that rattled in his throat as men edged closer, his seconds, Gilbert Rochemore, Tchaka. Weaker now, he said, "The runaway slaves had—two girls with them—and who is to know which —which one died?" He tried to laugh, and scarlet puddled his chin.

"The—the birthmark? Ah, look closely, Kaintuck. It appears to be done with—with a hot iron when she was—was very young. What black mother would not—would not wish to protect her own daughter— to have that wench pass—pass herself off someday as white? Jus-Justina Le Croix? *Mais non;* that one is—is Caroline Monteleone—mustee!"

His head lolled to one side and Felipe de Alcantari was dead, but not before his final cruelty.

Chapter 53

She looked at the hand upon hers, work-hardened and black. It was the first time Tchaka had touched her in comfort. Caroline said, "You understood; you knew I couldn't stand there and see their faces after Felipe told them. Damn them—*damn* them; I wish I were totally, truly black."

"No you don't," Tchaka said. "And you fought him good, missy; you fought him real good."

"I can't fight them all, but I have to try."

Tchaka eased away his hand. "Best you leave it to 'em, do they come. Us takes our papers, divides the money with you, and kind of fades into the city. Me and Molly, we kin stay a spell with the Choctaws. Come on with us."

Molly kneeled close, using herb poultices on Caroline's cuts and bruises. She said. "Do, missy. Easy for us to hide out, not so for you."

"And what happens to Delacroix? It's—it's so damned unfair."

"Ain't nobody promised fair," Tchaka said. "Rochemore, that big un—you figure 'em not to help none. That howcome you drove off and left 'em back yonder. Lordy—that lick I hit that big man with sand sewed up in rags, I'da thunk he wouldn't wiggle rest of the day. Tied him solid, too, but here he come bellerin'. Saved you, I reckon; them men of Alcantari's, they was watchin' me clost."

"He won't come," said Caroline. "Felipe made sure he wouldn't, and—and I don't want him to."

"Certain of that, missy?" Molly asked, taking away her medicines.

Tchaka said, "Well."

"Tell them," Caroline said. "Tell them and give them gold and send them all away. Tonight, tomorrow —sooner or later, outraged white people will march on Delacroix. I'll try to shame them, hold them off, do whatever I can to save this place, Lucien LeCroix's lands and home, even—even if I'm not his sister."

"Mast' Lucien, he dead and gone," Tchaka said. "You livin', and ain't nobody all that sure you ain't Justina."

Putting a hand to her head, she said, "They only need a hint, a suspicion, and now they have it."

He stood for a while, shifting his weight back and forth on his feet. "I be back, missy."

When he was gone, she lay upon the sofa, aching in every muscle. Not a word had Jubal Blaze said to her, not a single word. So monumental in his rage, gone blind to all but the need to smash Felipe, he'd hardly noticed her. But he'd crouched there beside the dying man, hanging upon every gasped detail that smeared the name of Justina LeCroix. Jubal *wanted* to believe.

Why had she taken his place in the duel? Because she had a much better chance of killing Felipe; if Jubal had faced him under the code the outcome might have been different. He didn't thank her for saving his hide; he resented it. Protected by a mustee—how that must have grated upon him.

Fitfully, she slept, bothered by formless dreams and rousing at every sound. Bleary-eyed, she rose at last from the sofa to bathe in cold water, but wakefulness brought only foreboding. Those other men, Felipe's seconds, had heard his final words and by now had scattered them all over the city. In the cafes, men would be gathering, buzzing, hissing along Rues Royale, Bienville, Chartres, Burgundy, knots of righteous anger tightening themselves into vengeance. That a lowly mixed blood would dare pass herself as white and lay

513

claim to an honored estate—ah, and setting free her own kind, of course—arming former slaves for insurrection. From the Quadroon Ball to mistress of Delacroix, what a leap, eh? To be sure, Alcantari had no friends, but a man's dying statement is never taken lightly.

They would drink, Caroline thought, and inflame themselves, and fan the spark until it burst into flame that would sweep them into coaches and upon horses and bring them ravening to destroy. How could she face them, and why should she? Tchaka was right—flee to safety with a share of the gold; let them burn and pillage and return to the city with blood lust unslaked.

But Lucien LeCroix had believed in her, called her sister. Oh god, she was so confused. If she was the black child taken North by M'Nele and Solah, she should run now, save herself. But if she was a LeCroix, her place was here, to the very last.

Had Felipe lied? He'd gotten to Illinois, bought off the lawyer, destroyed all documents that could possibly link her to black blood. Then he intended marrying her, and had the wedding certificate falsified. But perhaps there had been no documents up North, except those which Solah swore would prove her white.

Solah. Another lie, so that her own daughter—sired by who knows what white man—could pass and be protected?

"Mam'selle?" Netty stood in the doorway. "The cook has left, with others, so I have prepared you something. One must always eat, *hein?*"

She sat in the kitchen, forcing down a bit of this, of that, drinking much coffee. "How many are gone, Toinette?"

"Ten, a dozen—all cowards."

"Just wise. You must all go, Toinette."

"That is what Tchaka says, but he is only a *sauvage*. I was born here; Delacroix is my home. Perhaps it is also yours. If you stay, I stay, mam'selle."

Caroline said, "I am too tired to argue, but please—at least say to everyone I wish them to stay out of

514

sight, away from the house and barns, off in the fields somewhere."

She wandered into the sitting room where the only weapon remaining was a shotgun. The rapier, dueling pistols, even her dirk—out there beneath the oaks upon trampled and bloody grass. If the townsmen came, —*when* they came, there was nothing to use against them but a courage she might not be able to hold together.

Caroline had slept longer than she realized, for beyond the big window, the sun was going down, staining clouds with ominous red. Gilbert, she thought; the poor man had been stunned at Felipe's revelation, realizing he had gambled his reputation, career and life for the defense of a mustee. Now she was truly alone, but for loyal blacks even more helpless than herself. If only the Baratarians would return, if she might look up and see Robert Gray coming jaunty and confident, with a company of battle-wise and heavily armed corsairs at his back.

But Robert's love had been fleeting, and second to that he held for his true mistress, the sea. If ever he returned, it would be only for a while. He was good, he was kind, and she would never regret their dalliance; yet she could not depend upon his being here when needed. And she had no right to expect it.

She watched the sun slink lower, saw the sky go crimson, then darken to the color of blood. She couldn't look upon that any longer, and drew the drapes, wishing it were winter, that she might have the comfort of a fire in the hearth. Lighting lamps and candles didn't cheer her, and neither did a dollop of brandy.

Caroline was wearing a robe; restlessly, she climbed stairs to change into a gown, a fine dress once worn by Lucien's wife. She did up her hair and pinned it, added earrings and a necklace of no great value. If they came tonight, she must look like a woman of quality, like Justina LeCroix.

Downstairs again, she flinched at the opening of a door, but it was Tchaka. "Missy, Molly gone to Choctaws. I got horses out back, for you, me *and* that muley yeller gal, does things come to it."

"I thank you, Tchaka," she said, "for everything."

He chewed his lips. "You be makin' it, missy. It's us got to thank you."

Caroline was alone now, moving through a house gone quiet with waiting, a house without people. Its rooms were shaded with Lucien, with Gabrielle, the wife gone before him, and she felt another shadow— that of Xavier Rigaut LeCroix, the man who might have been her father. Her mother? Solah the Ashanti, or Madame LeCroix—Caroline would never know who now.

Down the road toward the city, there came a sound like the far-off rumble of thunder, a sound that expanded as it neared Delacroix. She went to the main doors and opened them to the light of torches. The mob was coming, horseback, in carriages and afoot; its noise now swelling, now falling, a many-headed, many-legged creature. As its firefly lights flowed across the lawns of Delacroix, Caroline drew a deep breath and went out onto the porch.

A grand coach rolled up, and she recognized the men who descended from it: Moreau Gaspar of Greenoaks and Valsin Fozatte, master of Maison Caresse, her neighbors. The faces gathering behind them all looked the same, pinched and vicious and hound-dog eager in dancing torchlight.

Caroline moved to the top step, chin up and head back. When they saw her, the growling subsided for a moment. Haughtily, she looked down upon them, for she was mistress of Delacroix. "Gentlemen," she called into the pool of silence, "you are trampling my flower beds."

That held them for another tick of the clock, then Fozatte said, "Manners from a yellow wench?"

And Gaspar: *"Your* flower beds? You own nothing of this land, *négresse*. You have only stolen it for a little while."

Back of them swirled rivermen, gamblers from Rue Royale, drunken Kaintucks with little idea what they were doing here, and from the window of one carriage, the smug face of a white woman watched avidly.

A man yelled: "Mustee nigger—let's draw straws to see who screws her first! Then the rest make a line."

"Burn the goddamn house first," said another. "Never cottoned to high-toned houses."

"Find *all* the blacks!" a gambler shouted. "Burn them, also—so that women may sleep in safety and no child be murdered in its bed!"

Among them, a horse jittered and men cursed at it. A flung torch arched over Caroline's head and struck the porch. She kicked it off and it struck Fozatte in the chest. His yelp of surprise touched them off, and they boiled up the steps. Rocks smashed windows and other torches flamed through to land inside the house. They had her then, bruising her arms, ripping at her bodice, bearing her back as many hands sought her breasts, her mound. Shouting men surged into the entrance hall, and pounded upstairs, pillaging, smashing what they could not carry.

Delacroix was burning.

Passing her from hand to hand, they bore her to the lawn and hurled her to earth within a circle of gloating faces. Her dress was gone, her necklace torn away. Naked, she kicked and clawed at them, but they pinned her down, spread her arms and legs wide and a cruel hand penetrated her.

Never again, she had sworn, but she was helpless, beaten. And this time, when they were done with her, they would kill her. Dirt gritted against her cheek as she rolled her head away from the drunken man who crouched between her thighs.

From the depths of her being, from the very corners of Caroline's battered soul, rose the ancient death chant of the Ashanti, brave and forlorn and without hope.

The man grunted in shock as he was lifted from her and hurled kicking into the pack. Another's face gouted red when he fell away, and yet another screeched in startled agony. Caroline's hands curled up to cover her mauled breasts, and her thighs drew together.

517

A gun went off, and another. There were clubbing noises and men dropped like felled trees, and the mob broke apart. She saw him first as blurred, then the image of him came clear. His head was thrown back and his white smile was a thing of feral joy; the fearful skinning knife whirled and glittered about him in a deadly circle. Jubal Blaze!

He stood astride her, roaring challenges, bellowing curses, huge and formidable in light from the blazing house, a mighty man in buckskins, and they scuttled back from him, cringed away from him. She felt a tugging at her arm, and there was Gilbert Rochemore, sweat beading his pate, his coat torn, a smoking pistol in his hand. Caroline crawled to him, and he braced her against Jubal's broad back as he hurriedly reloaded.

Then three wild-eyed horses came stampeding around the house, heads tossing and hooves pounding, to smash into men, into other horses tangled by harness. Inside the house, a man screamed, and another; window glass shattered as their bodies cartwheeled out and down. Tchaka, thought Caroline; the giant Mandingo was in there, fighting. And Toinette had spooked the horses into the mob.

Shivering, she went weak as Gilbert fired over a coachman's head and sent the carriage careening off. Suddenly they were gone, leaving only their broken and crippled, fading terrorized and clattering shamed into the night.

Tongues of bright flame speared forth from the house, and Jubal turned to cradle her in his arms, to walk her into a line of magnolia trees and set her gently upon her feet again. When he slipped it over her head, his buckskin shirt came to her knees, and she began to laugh, a laughter that quickly turned to hysteria.

But it did not matter, for her face was against the skin of his chest, and his strong arms were around her, a barricade against the world.

Did she faint? When the terrible tension drained from her, did she sleep? Caroline didn't know; when her eyes fluttered open, she was in the barn and Jubal was holding a glass of salvaged brandy to her lips. She drank and coughed, then looked to where only the blackened chimneys of Delacroix pointed accusing fingers at the sky.

"You—you came back," she whispered.

"Had to," he said. "You run off and left me and Gilbert."

"But—" she said, and went quiet, for she could not ask.

Then Gilbert Rochemore, standing taller and more proud, said to her, "The man Tchaka here, the wench —ah, woman—Toinette; they fought also, and I could do no less."

Caroline saw Tchaka and Toinette. "You—things have not changed, my friends. They will come back, if not as a mob, then singly and with cunning."

Gilbert said, "I have spoken with them, *chérie*. We have formed a plan, and if it is to your liking, Delacroix can be operated again, but as a company. As its legal counsel and president, I shall see to its recovery, and by *le bon Dieu,* I shall fling a challenge at any man who dares question it."

"I cannot stay," she said. "You know I cannot stay, always to remind them."

"I—I suppose not," he murmured. "Justina, I—"

"You were brave and good, Gilbert; I will remember."

Rochemore swallowed, shook his head. "And I will never forget."

They left her alone with silent Jubal then, that big, muscled and disturbingly quiet man who sat and stared at his hands.

Caroline couldn't say to him the words held in her throat. Instead, she rambled on about the freed slaves, the division of Delacroix money, her hopes that Rochemore could save the land for them, the possibility of some blacks returning to Africa. She talked herself dry and wet her mouth with brandy.

Silence hung between them again, and finally Jubal Blaze lifted his head, turned the blue of his eyes full upon her. "That man's in love with you."

"Gilbert? In his way, I suppose he is."

"Didn't ask to marry you."

"Gilbert Rochemore is white, and there will always be a question about me."

"Cared too much to have you to mistress, I reckon."

"Look," she said, a quick tide of anger rising in her, "if you want to know have I slept with him—yes. And with another man who didn't force me. No matter what you damned *men* think, a woman does sometimes have a choice. So add that to your reasons for—for turning your back on me again. I don't need you; I d-don't need anybody!"

"Hell you don't. A woman like you needs a man, much as—much as I need a woman—a bigod whole, honest and standup woman like you. I'm tryin' to be straightforward about it, Caroline. Turned it around and around in my head till I like to went crazy." Jubal stopped and rubbed his chin, glanced away from her.

"Back home," he went on, "I had me a burr under my hide I couldn't dig out. Wouldn't admit it was *you,* even when I took a share of Tarboro and gave the rest to my brother; wouldn't face howcome I beelined right for New Orleans. But when I come to after bein' pole-axed by that big nigger, and seen you fightin' *my* fight with the Creole, it struck me what a damned fool I'd been. Even a hardhead Carolina redneck don't have to be twice kicked by a mule."

Caroline felt the warmth rising, slow and gentle and pervading. She lifted from the hay they'd placed her on, a new and vital strength surging through her body. He rose and turned to her.

"It ain't goin' to be easy," he said. "We can't stay here and can't go home, so I reckon it's the western frontier—if'n you've a mind to go with me. I got plenty put by to make us a new start, and there's land out there, fine land for the takin' and the holdin'. Somewheres along the trail, there'll be a preacher, and we can get it done right."

Her smile was so wide it seemed to stretch her face, and the quickened thunder of her heart almost overwhelmed her. "But Jubal," she said, "there's still no way of knowing whether I'm all-white Justina LeCroix, or Caroline Monteleone, mustee."

He reached for her, pulled her hard to his chest where she could feel the trembling of him. "I just don't give a damn, woman. White or black, I want you for what you are."

She clung to him fiercely, possessively, and said into his manflesh: "I love you, Jubal Blaze."

"Hell," he said, "ain't that what I been tellin' you all this time? Woman, I love you so damned much I expect I'll never get over it."

When she kissed him, from a magnolia tree across the yard, its white blooms unsullied by fire and smoke and hate, a mockingbird began to sing.

The melody soared into a fresh dawn sky, sweet and pure in the heady intoxication of freedom, salute to a magnificent now, and promise of all tomorrows to come.

R. F. DELDERFIELD

Sweeping Sagas of Romance and Adventure

_____ 78777 GIVE US THIS DAY $1.95

_____ 78923 GOD IS AN ENGLISHMAN $1.95

_____ 78554 THEIRS WAS THE KINGDOM $1.50

_____ 78616 TO SERVE THEM ALL MY DAYS $1.75

_____ 80277 THE AVENUE GOES TO WAR $2.25

_____ 78862 DIANA $1.95

_____ 80278 THE DREAMING SUBURB $1.95

_____ 78981 FAREWELL THE TRANQUIL MIND $1.95

_____ 78869 THE GREEN GAUNTLET $1.95

_____ 78672 LONG SUMMER DAY $1.50

_____ 78979 MR. SERMON $1.75

_____ 78673 POST OF HONOR $1.50

_____ 78959 RETURN JOURNEY $1.95

_____ 78977 TOO FEW FOR DRUMS $1.50

Available at bookstores everywhere, or order direct from the publisher.

POCKET BOOKS
Department RK
1230 Avenue of the Americas
New York, N.Y. 10020

Please send me the books I have checked above. I am
enclosing $_____ (please add 50¢ to cover postage and
handling). Send check or money order—no cash or C.O.D.'s
please.

NAME_____

ADDRESS_____

CITY_____STATE/ZIP_____

RFD